GODLIKE MACHINES

Also Edited by Jonathan Strahan

BEST SHORT NOVELS (2004 through 2007)
FANTASY: THE VERY BEST OF 2005
SCIENCE FICTION: THE VERY BEST OF 2005
THE BEST SCIENCE FICTION AND FANTASY OF THE YEAR
(2007 - present)
ECLIPSE: NEW SCIENCE FICTION AND FANTASY
(2008 - present)
THE STARRY RIFT: TALES OF NEW TOMORROWS
LIFE ON MARS: TALES OF NEW FRONTIERS
(forthcoming)

With Lou Anders

SWORDS AND DARK MAGIC:
THE NEW SWORD AND SORCERY

With Charles N. Brown

THE LOCUS AWARDS: THIRTY YEARS OF THE BEST
IN FANTASY AND SCIENCE FICTION

With Jeremy G. Byrne

THE YEAR'S BEST AUSTRALIAN SCIENCE FICTION
AND FANTASY: VOLUME 1
THE YEAR'S BEST AUSTRALIAN SCIENCE FICTION
AND FANTASY: VOLUME 2
EIDOLON 1

With Jack Dann

LEGENDS OF AUSTRALIAN FANTASY

With Terry Dowling

THE JACK VANCE TREASURY

THE JACK VANCE READER

WILD THYME, GREEN MAGIC

HARD-LUCK DIGGINGS

With Gardner Dozois

THE NEW SPACE OPERA

THE NEW SPACE OPERA 2

With Karen Haber

SCIENCE FICTION: BEST OF 2003

SCIENCE FICTION: BEST OF 2004

FANTASY: BEST OF 2004

GODLIKE MACHINES

EDITED BY

Jonathan Strahan

SFBC SCIENCE FICTION

First Science Fiction Book Club Printing September 2010

Published by Science Fiction Book Club, 401 Franklin Avenue, Garden City, New York 11530

Visit the Science Fiction Book Club online ate www.sfbc.com

ISBN: 978-1-61664-759-9

Printed in the United States of America

In memory of the late Charles N. Brown, who read this book and loved it, with great affection and deep gratitude.

There are a handful of people who require special thanks, who went above and beyond the call to help make this book a reality. First and foremost, my sincere thanks to the book's contributors, Steve, Cory, Al, Bob, Greg, and Sean, all of whom have shown almost heroic patience and stuck with this book through some fairly long delays–I'll always be incredibly grateful to them for doing so. Second, my commissioning editor on this book, Andrew Wheeler, who bought it and believed in it. I'd also like to thank John Scalzi, Charles Stross, Gary K. Wolfe, Charles N. Brown, Howard Morhaim, Justin Ackroyd, and Jack Dann. Thanks also to the following good friends and colleagues without whom this book would have been much poorer, and much less fun to do: Lou Anders, Deborah Biancotti, Ellen Datlow, and Gardner Dozois.

As always, my biggest thanks go to Marianne, Jessica and Sophie. Every moment spent working on this book was a moment stolen from them. I only hope I can repay them.

Contents

Godlike Machines, Machinelike Gods

Jonathan Strahan

The book you are now holding was inspired by a painting. Artist Michael Whelan was commissioned to paint a cover for a reissue of the fourth novel in Isaac Asimov's Foundation series, **Foundation's Edge**. The painting, *Trantorian Dream*, depicts a small male figure standing amongst rubble, framed by enormous rusting ruins and gazing at a glowing spiral galaxy. It is an image that seems to depict, clearly and simply, much of the sense of wonder that we look to science fiction to provide.

When, back in early 2006, I approached the Science Fiction Book Club with the idea for a new book of original science fiction novellas I had that image in mind: I wanted to come up with a loose idea that would give writers enough space to create something unique, but also give them a clear idea of the *kind* of story I had in mind, and the kind of book I wanted to do.

I looked at many of the classic science fiction books and stories that I had loved, and settled on the idea of a book of stories featuring what science fiction critic Roz Kaveney dubbed 'big dumb objects'. A big dumb object is essentially an extremely large, extremely powerful structure, most likely of extraterrestrial or unknown origin. These megastructures–dyson spheres, alderson disks, matrioshka brains–and other stranger and more unusual objects drive the stories in Larry Niven's **Ringworld**, Greg Bear's **Eon**, and Frederik Pohl's **Gateway**. Even in Terry Pratchett's 'Discworld', I later realised. There is something intensely science fictional about the very notion of a big dumb object, embodying as it does both the enigmatic sense of wonder of the best SF and the urge to understand, to examine and clarify. After all, while a big dumb object may be alien and enigmatic, it's also a *made* object, and therefore is knowable and understandable.

When I suggested the book to my editor at the SF Book Club, Andrew Wheeler, he was eager, but made it clear I needed a good name for the book. I began to look around for ideas, for inspiration. I was working on another project at the time, and as research was reading Brian Aldiss's 1974 anthology, **Space Opera**. In it he explains much of the joy and wonder of space opera. The closing section of the book deals with the great machines–spacecraft and otherwise–that uniquely belong to science fiction. He titled that section of the book, 'these godlike machines'. I had my title and, at the same time, threw the first variable into the project.

I wrote to writers whose work I admired and whom I hoped would write for the book–Stephen Baxter, Cory Doctorow, Greg Egan, Robert Reed, Alastair Reynolds, and Sean Williams–and I asked if they'd write a new 'big dumb object story' for my book . Writers are funny folk and they sometimes hear what they want to hear. We don't live in the forties and fifties any more, and when they heard 'godlike machines', they began to play with the idea. Did it have to be 'godlike machines'? Couldn't it be 'machinelike gods'? How *big* did a godlike machine have to be?

Over the course of editing a number of anthologies I've realized that there are times when you need to stick to your original vision, and there are times when you need to get out of the way and let creative people do what they do best. So, I said yes. You could have an enormous enigmatic megastructure drifting in space, or buried beneath the crust of some distant world, or you could have some strange, powerful literally god-like machine. Heck, you could turn the moon into green cheese if you wanted to. All you had to do was tell an amazing science fictional tale, one that spoke to the basic idea I'd started with.

And slowly, over a period of about eight months, the stories began to drop into my mail box. In one strange powerful machines battled one another, in others something strange and mysterious happened in a distant corner of our solar system. I don't know that the book you are about to read is the most definitive addressing of the 'big dumb object' theme in science fiction, but I do know you are about to encounter a handful of stories that are made from the pure stuff of science fiction, filled with that sense of wonder many of us look for in the very best science fiction. I hope you like it as much as I do.

–Jonathan Strahan
Perth, Western Australia
June 2008/June 2010

GODLIKE MACHINES

TROIKA

Alastair Reynolds

Alastair Reynolds was born in Barry, South Wales in 1966. He has lived in Cornwall, Scotland, and the Netherlands, where he spent 12 years working as a scientist for the European Space Agency. He became a full-time writer in 2004, and recently married his long-time partner, Josette. Reynolds has been publishing short fiction since his first sale to Interzone *in 1990. Since 2000 he has published nine novels: the 'Inhibitor' trilogy, British Science Fiction Association award winner* Chasm City, Century Rain, Pushing Ice, The Prefect *and* House of Suns. *His most recent novel is* Terminal World. *His short fiction has been collected in* Zima Blue and Other Stories, Galactic North, *and* Deep Navigation. *In his spare time he rides horses.*

By the time I reach the road to Zvezdniy Gorodok acute hypothermia is beginning to set in. I recognize the symptoms from my training: stage one moving into two, as my body redirects blood away from skin to conserve heat—shivering and a general loss of coordination the result. Later I can expect a deterioration of vasomotor tone as the muscles now contracting my peripheral blood vessels become exhausted. As blood surges back to my chilled extremities, I'll start to feel hot rather than cold. Slipping ever further into disorientation, it will take an effort of will not to succumb to that familiar and distressing syndrome, paradoxical undressing. The few layers of clothes I'm wearing—the pajamas, the thin coat I stole from Doctor Kizim—will start feeling too warm. If I don't get warm soon they'll find me naked and dead in the snow.

How long have I been out? An hour, two hours? There's no way to tell. It's like being back on the *Tereshkova*, when we slept so little that a day could feel like a week. All I know is that it's still night. They'll find me when the sun is up, but until then there's still time to locate Nesha Petrova.

I touch the metal prize in my pocket, reassuring myself that it's still there.

As if invoked by the act of touching the prize, a monstrous machine comes roaring towards me out of the night. It's yellow, with an angled shovel on the front. I stumble into the path of its headlights and raise a wary hand. The snowplow sounds its horn. I jerk back, out of the way of the blade and the flurry of dirty snow it flings to one side.

I think for a moment it's going to surge on past, but it doesn't. The machine slows and stops. Maybe he thinks he's hit me. It's good—a robot snowplow wouldn't stop, so there must be someone operating this one. I hobble around to the cab, where the driver's glaring at me through an unopened window. He's got a moustache, a woolen hat jammed down over his hair and ears, the red nose of a serious drinker.

Above the snorting, impatient diesel I call: "I could use a ride to town."

The driver looks at me like I'm dirt, some piece of roadside debris he'd have been better shoveling into the verge. This far out of town, on this road, it doesn't take much guesswork to figure out where I've come from. The hospital, the facility, the madhouse, whatever you want to call it, will have been visible in the distance on a clear day—a forbidding smudge of dark, tiny-windowed buildings, tucked behind high, razor wire-topped security fencing.

He lowers the window an inch. "Do yourself a favor, friend. Go back, get warm."

"I won't make it back. Early-onset hypothermia. Please, take me to Zvezdniy Gorodok. I can't give you much, but you're welcome to these." My fingers feel like awkward tele-operated waldos, the kind we'd had on the Progress. I fumble a pack of cigarettes from my coat pocket and push the crushed and soggy rectangle up to the slit in the window.

"All you've got?"

"They're American. You know how hard these are to come by now."

The driver grunts something uninteligible, but takes the cigarettes anyway. He opens the pack to inspect the contents, sniffing at them. "How old are these?"

"You can still smoke them."

The driver leans over to the open the other door. "Get in. I'll take you as far as the first crossroad on the edge of town. You get out when we stop. You're on your own from then on."

I'll agree to any arrangement provided it gets me a few minutes in the warmth of the cab. For now I'm still lucid enough to recognize the hypothermia creeping over me. That state of clinical detachment won't last forever.

I climb in, taking deep, shivering breaths.

"Thank you."

"The edge of town, that's as far as we go," he says, in case I didn't get it the first time. His breath stinks of alcohol. "I'm caught giving you a ride, it won't be good for me."

"It won't be good for either of us."

The driver shifts the snowplow back into gear and lets her roll, the engine bellowing as the blade bites snow. "Whoever you are, whatever you're doing, it won't work. They'll find you in Zvezdniy Gorodok. It's not a big place and there's nowhere else to go. In case no one pointed it out to you, this is the arse end of nowhere. And the trains aren't running."

"I only need to get to town."

He looks at me, assessing the shabbiness of my dress, the wild state of my beard and hair. "Wild night ahead of you?"

"Something like that."

He's got the radio on, tuned to the state classical music channel. It's playing Prokofiev. I lean over and turn the volume down, until it's almost lost under the engine noise.

"I was listening to that."

"Please. Until we get there."

"Got a problem with music?"

"Some of it."

The driver shrugs–he doesn't seem to mind as much as he pretends. Panicking suddenly, imagining I might have dropped it in the snow, I pat my pocket again. But–along with Doctor Kizim's security pass–the little metal box is still there.

It takes all of my resolve not to take it out and turn the little handle that makes it play. Not because I can stand to hear it again, but because I want to be sure it still works.

The snowplow's tail lights fade into the night. The driver has kept to his word, taking us through the abandoned checkpoint, then to the first crossroad inside the old city boundary and no further. It's been good to get warm, my clothes beginning to dry, but now that I'm outside again the cold only takes a few seconds to reach my bones. The blizzard has abated while we drove, but the snow's still falling, coming down in soft flurries from a milky predawn sky.

We'd passed no other vehicles or pedestrians, and at this early hour Zvezdniy Gorodok gives every indication of being deserted. The housing blocks are mostly unlit, save for the occasional illuminated window–a pale, curtained rectangle of dim yellow against the otherwise dark edifice. The buildings, set back from the intersecting roads in long ranks, look drearily similar, as if stamped from the same machine tool–even the party images flickering on their sides are the same from building to building. The same faces, the same slogans. For a moment I have the sense of having embarked on a ludicrous and faintly delusional task. Any one of these buildings could be where she lives. They'll find me long before I have time to search each lobby, hoping to find a name.

I'd shown the driver the address I'd written down, pulled from the public telephone directory on Doctor Kizim's desk. He'd given me a rough idea of where I ought to head. The apartment complex is somewhere near the railway station–I'll have to search the surrounding streets until I find it.

"'I know where the station is," I tell the driver. "I was here when it was a sealed training facility."

"You had something to do with the space program?"

"I did my bit."

Zvezdniy Gorodok–Starry Town, or Star City. In the old days, you needed a permit just to get into it. Now that the space program is over–it has "achieved all necessary objectives," according to the official line of the Second Soviet–Zvezdniy Gorodok is just another place to live, work, and die, its utilitarian housing projects radiating far beyond the old boundary. The checkpoint is a disused ruin and the labs and training facilities have been turned into austere community buildings. More farmers and factory workers live here now than engineers, scientists, and former-cosmonauts.

I'm lucky to have got this far.

I escaped through a gap in the facility's security fence, in a neglected corner of the establishment tucked away behind one of the kitchens. I'd known about the breech for at least six months–long enough to reassure myself that no one else had noticed it, and that the break could not be seen from the administrative offices or any of the surveillance cameras. It was good fortune that the fence had that gap, but I still wouldn't have got far without the help from Doctor Kizim. I don't know if he expects me to succeed in my escape attempt, but Doctor Kizim–who had always been more sympathetic to the *Tereshkova*'s survivors than any of the other medics–had turned a conveniently blind eye. And it was his coat that I had taken. It wasn't much of a coat for blizzards, but without it I doubt that I would have made it as far as the snowplow, let alone Zvezdniy Gorodok. I just hope he doesn't get into too much trouble when they find out I took it.

I don't expect to get the chance to apologize to him.

The snow stopped falling completely, and the sun–pink and depleted of heat–is beginning to break through the gloom on the eastern horizon, when I find the railway station. I begin to explore the surrounding streets, trying to find the address. More lights have come on now and I'm noticing the beginning of daily activity. One or two citizens pass me in the snow, but they have their heads down and pay me no special attention. Few vehicles are on the roads, and since the trains aren't running, the area around the station is almost totally devoid of activity. When a large car–a Zil limousine, black and muscular as a panther– swings onto the street I'm walking down, I don't have time to hide. But the Zil sails by, tires spraying muddy slush, and as it passes I see that it's empty. The car must be on its way to collect a party official from one of the better districts.

I've been walking for an hour, trying not to glance over my shoulder too often, when I find Nesha's building. The apartment complex has an entrance lobby anyone can enter. It smells of toilets and alcohol. Some of the windows in the outer wall are covered by plywood panels, where the glass has broken. It's draughty and unlit, the tiled floor filthy with footprints and paper and smashed glass. There's a door into the rest of the building, but it can only be opened by someone inside. In my cold, sodden slippers I squelch to the buzzer panel next to the mailboxes.

I catch my breath. Everything hinges on this moment. If I'm wrong about Nesha, or if she's moved elsewhere, or died–it's been a long time, after all–then everything will have been for nothing.

But her name's still there.

N. Petrova. She lives on the ninth floor.

It may not mean anything. She may still have died or been moved on. I reach out a numb finger and press the buzzer anyway. There's no sound, no reassuring response. I wait a minute then press it again. Outside, a stray dog with mad eyes yellows the snow under a lamppost. I press the buzzer again, shivering more than when I was outside.

A woman's voice crackles through the grill above the buzzers. "Yes?"

"Nesha Petrova?" I ask, leaning to bring my lips closer to the grill.

"Who is it?"

"Dimitri Ivanov." I wait a second or two for her to respond to the name.

"From building services?"

I assume that there's no camera letting Nesha see me, if there ever was. "Dimitri Ivanov, the cosmonaut. I was on the ship, the *Tereshkova.* The one that met the Matryoshka."

Silence follows. I realize, dimly, that there's an eventuality I've never allowed for. Nesha Petrova may be too old to remember anything of importance. She may be too old to care.

I shuffle wet feet to stave off the cold.

"Nesha?"

"There were three cosmonauts."

I lean into the grill again. "I'm one of them. The other two were Galenka Makarova and Yakov Demin. They're both dead now. The VASIMIR engine malfunctioned on the way home, exposing them to too much radiation. I'm the only one left."

"Why should I believe you?"

"Because I'm standing here in pajamas and a stolen coat. Because I've come all the way from the facility just to see you, through the snow. Because there's something I want you to know."

"Then tell me."

"I'd rather show you, Nesha. Besides, I'm going to die of the cold if I stand here much longer."

I look to the outside world again, through one of the panes that hasn't been broken and covered over with plywood. Another Zil slides by. This one has bodies in it: grey-skinned men sitting upright in dark coats and hats.

"I don't want any trouble from the police."

"I won't stay long. Then I'll be on my way, and no one will have to know that I was here."

"I'll know."

"Please, let me in." I haven't bargained for this. In all the versions of this encounter that I've run through my mind before the escape, she never needed any persuasion to meet me. "Nesha, you need to understand. They tried to bury you, but you were right all along. That's what I want to tell you about. Before they silence me, and no one ever gets to find out."

After an age she says, "You think it matters now, Dimitri Ivanov?"

"It matters more than you can imagine."

The door buzzes. She's letting me in.

"It's blacker than I was expecting."

"Of course it's black," I said, pausing in my ham-fisted typing. "What other color were you expecting?"

Yakov was still staring out the porthole, at the looming Matryoshka. It was two hundred kilometers away, but still ate up more than half the sky. No stars in that direction, just a big absence like the mother of all galactic supervoids. We had the cabin lights dimmed so he could get a good view. We had already spread the relay microsats around the alien machine, ready for when the Progress penetrated one of the transient windows in Shell 3. But you couldn't see the microsats from here– they were tiny, and the machine was vast.

"What I mean is . . ." Yakov started saying.

"Is that it's black."

"I mean it's more than black. It's like–black was black, and now there's something in my head that's even darker, like a color I never imagined until now, which was always there, just waiting for this moment."

"I'm concerned about you, comrade," said Galenka, who

was riding the exercise cycle in one corner of the module. She was wearing a skin-tight load-suit, designed to preserve muscle tone even in weightlessness. Maybe I'd been in space too long, but she looked better in that load-suit every day.

"You don't feel it, then?" Yakov asked, directing his question to both of us.

"It's just dark," I said. "I guess nothing's really prepared us for this, but it's not something we should be surprised about. The last two apparitions . . ."

"Just machines, just dumb space probes. This is the first time anyone's seen it with their own eyes." Yakov turned slowly from the porthole. He was pale, with the puffy, slit-eyed look we'd all developed since leaving Earth. "Don't you think that changes things? Don't you think us being out here, us being observers, changes things? We're not just making measurements on this thing from a distance now. We're interacting, touching it, feeling it."

"And I think you need to get some sleep," Galenka said.

I folded the workstation keyboard back into its recess. I had been answering questions from schoolchildren; the selected few that had been deemed worthy of my attention by the mission schedulers.

"Tell me you don't feel a little freaked out, Dimitri."

"Maybe a bit," I allowed. "But no more than I'd feel if we were in orbit around Mars, or Venus, or creeping up on an asteroid. It's a very big thing and we're very small and a long way from home."

"This is also a very alien big thing. It was made by alien minds, for a purpose we can't grasp. It's not just some lump of rock with a gravitational field. It's a machine, a ship, that they sent to our solar system for a reason."

"It's a dead alien thing," Galenka said, huffing as she cycled harder, pushing through an uphill part of her training schedule. "Someone made it once, but it's broken now. Fucked like an old clock. If it wasn't fucked, it wouldn't be on this stupid elliptical orbit."

"Maybe this orbit is all part of the plan," Yakov said.

"He's starting to sound like Nesha Petrova," Galenka said teasingly. "Be careful, Yakov. You know what happened to her when she didn't shut up with her silly ideas."

"What plan?" I asked.

"That thing must be thousands of years old. Tens of thousand, maybe more. The fact that it's been on this orbit for 24 years proves nothing. It's an eye-blink, as far as that thing's concerned. It might just be waking up, running systems checks, rebooting itself. It came through a wormhole. Who knows what that does to something?"

"You certainly don't," Galenka said.

"She's right," I said. "It's dead. If it was going to wake up, it would have done so during the first two apparitions. We poked and prodded it enough the second time; nothing happened."

"I wish I shared your reassurance."

I shrugged. "We're just here to do a job, Yakov. Get in, get out. Then go home and get the glory, like good cosmonauts. Before I worried about the Matryoshka, I'd worry about not screwing up your part in it."

"I'm not going to screw up." He looked at me earnestly, as if I had challenged him. "Did I ever screw up in the simulations, Dimitri? Did I ever screw up once?"

"No," I admitted. "But this isn't a simulation. We're not in Star City now."

He winked at me. "Absolutely sure of that, comrade?"

I wiped the sleeve of my load-suit against the portal glass to clear the condensation. From around the curve of the ship there was a puff of silvery brightness as the pyrotechnic docking latches released their hold on the Progress. In the same instant I heard a faraway thud and felt the fabric of the ship lurch with the recoil.

"Confirm separation," Yakov reported, calling from another porthole. "Looks like a clean birth to me, boys and girls."

Galenka was webbed into a hammock at the Progress workstation, one hand on a joystick and the other tapping a keyboard. The screens before her were alive with camera views, from both the *Tereshkova* and the little robot that had just detached from it.

"Beginning thruster translation," she said, touching keys. "You should see her in a few seconds, Dimitri."

The Progress drifted over my horizon, a pea-green shuttlecock with CCCP stenciled down the side in red letters. Very slowly it pulled away from the *Tereshkova* and tipped around on two axes, pointing its nose at the forbidding darkness of the Matryoshka. "Looking good," I said, inspecting every visible inch of the spacecraft for signs of damage. "No impacts that I can see. Looks as good as the day they wheeled her out of the clean room."

"Stirring hydrazine tanks," Galenka said. "Let's see if she holds, shall we?"

"Still there," I reported, when the Progress had failed to blow itself apart. "Looks like we have a viable spacecraft. Shall I break out the vodka?"

"Let's not get ahead of ourselves–no use going in if we're blind. Beginning camera and waldo deployment–this'll be the real test."

Our little envoy looked like a cross between a spaceship and a deep-sea submersible robot, the kind they use to explore shipwrecks and pull missiles out of sunken submarines. Arms and sensors and cameras had been bolted onto the front, ruining whatever vague aerodynamics the Progress might have had. Now the equipment–stowed since launch–was slowly deploying, like a flower opening to the sun. Galenka pushed aside the joystick and tugged down a set of waldo controls, slipping her fingers into the heavy, sensor-laden gloves and sleeves. Out in space, the Progress's mechanical arms and hands echoed her gestures. It looked good to me but Galenka still frowned and made some small adjustments to the settings. Ever the perfectionist, I thought. More check-out tests followed until she signified grudging satisfaction.

"Camera assembly three is a little stiff–I wouldn't be surprised if it seizes on us mid-mission. Haptic feedback on arm two is delayed just enough to throw me off. We've lost a row of pixels on the mid infrared array–probably a bad cosmic ray strike. I'm already reading an event overflow in one of the memory buffers, and we haven't even started logging data."

"But you're happy to continue?" I asked.

"Unless we brought a second Progress no one told me about, we're stuck with this one."

"It's nothing we can repair," Yakov said. "So we may as well live with it. Even if we went out in the suits, we don't have the tools to fix those instruments."

"I don't need that spelled out," Galenka said, just barely keeping a lid on her temper.

Yakov was starting to needle both of us. The Matryoshka was getting to him in a way it wasn't yet getting to Galenka, or me for that matter. He'd started coming out with some very odd statements. The joke of his, that we were still back in Star City, that all of this was an elaborate simulation, a preparation for the mission to come–even down to the impossible-to-fake weightlessness–was beginning to wear thin.

What bothered me was that I wasn't even sure he was joking anymore.

People cracked in space. It was part of the job. I just hadn't expected it to happen to one of us, so soon in the mission. We hadn't even touched the Matryoshka yet. What was going to happen when the Progress reached the secret layers beneath Shell 3?

I tried not to think about it.

"What's your approach speed?" I asked, looming behind Galenka while she worked the controls.

"Two meters per second, on the nail."

"A little on the fast side, aren't we?"

Galenka touched a hand over the mike, so Baikonur wouldn't hear what she had to say next. "You flying this thing, or me, comrade?"

"You are, definitely." I scratched at chin stubble. "It's just that I thought we were going to keep it below one meter a second, all the way in."

"You want to sit around for thirty hours, be my guest."

"I wouldn't be the one doing the sitting."

"This is well within acceptable limits. We'll make up speed in the gaps and slow down when we hit anything knotty. Trust me on this, all right?"

"You're the pilot."

"That's the general idea."

She un-cupped the microphone. "Holding approach speed, Baikonur. Progress systems stable. One hundred meters into Shell 1. Predictive impact model still holding. No change in the status of the Matryoshka or the surrounding vacuum."

On the screen, wireframe graphics traced the vast right-angled shapes of radar-illuminated obstacles–iceberg or battle-cruiser sized slabs of inscrutably dark free-flying machinery, between which the Progress was obliged to navigate a path, avoiding not only the obstacles but the invisible threads of razor-thin force binding them together. Shell 1 was not a solid sphere, but a swarm of deadly obstacles and tripwires.

During the second apparition, the Americans had sent one of their robot probes straight through one of those field threads. It had gone instantly silent, suggesting that it had suffered a fatal or damaging collision. Years later, deep space radar had picked it up again, drifting powerless on a sun-circling orbit. A manned expedition (one of the last the Americans ever managed) was sent out to recover it and bring it back to Earth for inspection.

Yet when the astronauts got hold of part of the probe, an entire half of it drifted silently away from the other, separating along a mathematically perfect plane of bisection. The astronauts stared in mute incomprehension at the sliced-through interior of the robot, its tight-packed, labyrinthine innards gleaming back at them with the polish of chrome. The robot must have been cut in two as it passed through the Matryoshka, but so cleanly that the two parts had continued moving on exactly the same trajectory, until this moment.

Although it was only the robot we were sending in, with the *Tereshkova* parked at a safe distance, I still shuddered to think what those lines of force could do to metal and ceramic, to flesh and bone. The predictive model traced the vectors of the field lines and offered solutions for safe passage, but, try as I might, I couldn't share Galenka's unflappable faith in the power of algorithm and computer speed.

Still, like she said, she was the pilot. This was her turf and I was well advised not to trample on it. I'd have felt exactly the same way if she had dared tell me how to manage the *Tereshkova*'s data acquisition and transmission systems.

Following a plan that had been argued over for months back on Earth, it had been agreed to attempt sample collection at each stage of the Progress's journey. The predictive model gave us confidence that the robot could get close to one of the free-flying obstacles without being sliced by the field lines. Dropping the Progress's speed to less than a meter per second, Galenka brought it within contact range of a particular lump of alien machinery and extended the arms and analysis tools to their full extent. We had no idea what the obstacles were made of, but–thanks to a Chinese probe that had gone off-course during the second apparition–we did know that the outer integument was surprisingly brittle. The probe had destroyed itself utterly in its high-velocity collision, but not before chipping off vast chunks of alien material. To our delight, early surveys of the Matryoshka on its third return had shown that the impacted obstacle had not repaired itself.

The Progress anchored itself by firing sticky-tipped guy-lines onto the obstacle. Galenka used hammers, cutting devices and claws to pick away at the scabbed edge of the impact point. Pieces of integument flaked away easily–had we been out there in our EVA suits, we could have ripped them out by hand. Some of them were coal-sized, some were as large as engine blocks. Galenka loaded up a third of the Progress's cargo space before deeming the haul sufficient. She wanted room for more samples when she got further in.

"Want to bring her back, unload and return?" I asked. The plan had been to make multiple forays into the Matryoshka, until we'd exhausted our hydrazine reserves.

"Not with the systems as screwed as they are. We lose camera rotation, or blow some more memory, we're blind. Maybe we'll get three or four missions out of the robot, but right now I'm assuming this is the last one. I'd like to go deeper, at least until we have a full hold."

"You want to consult with Baikonur?"

"We have discretion here, Dimitri. Timelag's too great to go crying to mummy every time we have a decision to make." She withdrew her hands from the waldo controls and flexed her fingers. "I'm taking her further in, while we still have a ship that works."

"I'm fine with that."

"Good," she said, massively indifferent to whether I was "fine" with it or not. Then, "Where's Yakov right now, by the way?"

"Somewhere."

"One of us needs to keep an eye on him, Dimitri. Not happy with that guy. I think he's on the edge."

"We're all on the edge. It's called being in space."

"I'm just saying."

"Keep an eye on him, yes. I will."

At fifteen kilometers, the Progress cleared Shell 1 and passed into a volume of open space relatively devoid of moving obstacles or field lines. Galenka notched up the speed, until the Progress was falling inwards at a kilometer every ten seconds. There was nothing here to sample or analyse. "Normal vacuum in Gap 1," she murmured. "Or at least what the robot reads as normal. The ambient physics hasn't changed too much."

Ever since the first apparition, it had been known–or at least suspected–that the Matryoshka was not just a mysteriously layered artifact drifting through space. In some way that we didn't yet understand, the object distorted the very physics of the spacetime in which it was floating. The effects were almost too subtle to measure at the distance of the *Tereshkova*, but they became more severe the closer any probes got to the middle. Fundamental constants stopped being fundamental. The speed of light varied. Planck's constant deviated from the figure in textbooks. So did the weak mixing angle, the fine-structure constant, Newton's constant. None of this could be explained under any existing theory of physics, but it was all disturbing. It was as if the Matryoshka was dragging a chunk of another universe around with it. Perhaps it had been designed that way, or perhaps the altered spacetime was a kind of lingering contamination, a side-effect of wormhole travel.

Of course, we didn't know for sure that the Matryoshka had come through a wormhole. That was just an educated guess papered over the vast, yawning chasm of our ignorance. All we knew for sure was that it had appeared, accompanied by a flash of energy, in the middle of the solar system.

I remembered that day very well. November the sixth, 2015. My twentieth birthday, to the day. Twenty four years later–two of the Matryoshka's looping, twelve year elliptical orbits around the Sun–and here I was, staring the thing in the face, as if my whole adult life had been an arrow pointing to this moment.

Maybe it had.

I was born in 1995, in Klushino. It's a small place near Smolensk. It wouldn't have any claim to fame except Klushino is the place where Yuri Gagarin was born. I knew that name almost before I knew any other. My father told me about him; how he had been the first man in space, his unassuming modesty, how he became a deputy of the Supreme Soviet, a hero for all the world, how he had died when his training jet crashed into trees. My father told me that it was a custom for all cosmonauts to visit Gagarin's office before a mission, to see the clock on the wall stopped at the moment of his death. Years later, I paid my own respects in the office.

The thing I remember most of all about my father, though, is holding me on his shoulders when I was five, taking me out into a cold winter evening to watch our Mir space station arc across the twilight sky. I reached out to grasp it and he held me higher, as if that might make a difference.

"Do you want to go up there sometime, Dimitri?"

"Do you have to be big?"

"Yes," he said. "Big and brave and strong. But you'll do, one day."

"And if I died would they stop the clock in my office as well?"

"You won't die," my father said. Even though it was cold he had his shirt sleeves rolled up, his hair scratching against my skin.

"But if I did."

"Of course they would. Just like Comrade Gagarin. And they'd make a hero of you as well."

I take the elevator to the ninth floor of Nesha Petrova's apartment building The doors open to a chill wind, howling in from the flat farmland beyond the city. The landing is open to the elements, only a low railing along one side. When I arrive at Nesha's apartment, half way along the landing, the door is ajar. Nesha–for it can only be Nesha–is waiting in the gap, bony, long-nailed fingers curling around the edge of the door. I see half her face–her right eye, prematurely wrinkled skin, a wisp of gray hair. She looks much smaller, much older and frailer, than I ever dared to imagine.

"Whatever you have to show me, show me and go."

"I'd really like to talk to you first." I hold up my gloveless, numb-fingered hands. "Everything I told you is true. I escaped from the psychiatric facility a few hours ago, and by now they'll be looking for me."

"Then you should go now."

"I was inside the Matryoshka, Nesha. Don't you want to hear what happened to me?"

She opens the door a tiny bit more, showing me more of her face. She's old now but the younger Nesha hasn't been completely erased. I can still see the strong and determined women who stood by her beliefs, even when the state decided those beliefs were contrary to the official truth.

"I heard the rumours. They say you went insane."

I give an easy shrug. "I did, on the way home. It's the only thing that saved me. If I hadn't gone crazy, I wouldn't be standing here now."

"You said there was something I had to know."

"Give me a little of your time, then I'll be gone. That's my promise to you."

Nesha looks back over her shoulder. She's wearing a knitted shawl of indeterminate color. "It isn't much warmer in here. When you called, I hoped you'd come to fix the central heating." She pauses for a moment, mind working, then adds, "I can give you something to drink, and maybe something better to wear. I still have some of my husband's old clothes–someone may as well get some use from them."

"Thank you," I say.

"You shouldn't have come to see me. No good will come of it, for either us."

"You might say the damage is already done."

She lets me inside. Nesha might consider her apartment cold, but it's a furnace to me. After the wards and cubicles of the facility, it's bordering on the luxurious. There are a couple of items of old furniture, threadbare but otherwise serviceable. There's a low coffee table with faded plastic flowers in a vase. There are pictures on the walls, save for the part that's been painted over with television. It's beginning to flake off in the corners, so it won't be too long before someone comes along to redo it.

"I can't turn it off," Nesha says, as if I've already judged her. "You can scrape it away, but they just come and paint it on again. They take more care of that than they do the heating. And they don't like it if they think you'd done it deliberately, or tried to hide the television behind pictures."

I remember the incessant televisions in the facility; the various strategies that the patients evolved to block them out or muffle the sound. "I understand. You don't have to make allowances."

"I don't like the world we live in. I'm old enough to remember when it was different." Still standing up, she waves a hand dismissively, shooing away the memories of better times. "Anyway, I don't hear so well these days. It's a blessing, I suppose."

"Except it doesn't feel like one." I point to one of the threadbare chairs. "May I sit down?"

"Do what you like."

I ease my aching bones into the chair. My damp clothes cling to me.

Nesha looks at me with something close to pity.

"Are you really the cosmonaut?"

"Yes."

"I can make some tea."

"Please. Anything hot."

I watch her amble into the adjoining kitchen. Her clothes are still those of her early middle age, with allowance for infirmity and the cold. She wears old-looking jeans, several layers of jumpers, a scarf and the drab colored shawl. Even though we're indoors she wears big fur boots. The clothes give her an illusion of bulk, but I can tell how thin she really is. Like a bird with a lot of puffed-up plumage, hiding delicate bones. There's also something darting, nervous, and birdlike about the way she negotiates the claustrophobic angles of her apartment. I hear the clatter of a kettle, the squeak of a tap, a half-hearted dribble of water, then she returns.

"It'll take a while."

"Everything does, these days. When I was younger, old people used to complain about the world getting faster and faster, leaving them behind. That isn't how it seems to you and I. We've left the world behind–we've kept up, but it hasn't."

"How old are you?" she asks.

"Fifty one."

"Not what I'd call old. I have twenty years on you." But her eyes measure me and I know what she's thinking. I look older, beyond any doubt. The mission took its toll on me, but so did the facility. There were times when I looked in the mirror with a jolt of non-recognition, a stranger's face staring back at me. "Something bad happened to you out there, didn't it," she said.

"To all of us."

She makes the tea. "You think I envy you," she says, as I sip from my cup.

"Why would you envy me?"

"Because you went out there, because you saw it up close, because you went inside it. You cosmonauts think all astronomers are the same. You go out into space and look at the universe through a layer of armored glass, if you're lucky. Frosted with your own breath, blurring everything on the other side. Like visiting someone in a prison, not being able to touch them. You think we envy you that."

"Some might say it's better to get that close, than not go at all."

'I stayed at home. I touched the universe with my mind, through mathematics. No glass between us then–just a sea of numbers." Nesha looks at me sternly. "Numbers are truth. It doesn't get any more intimate than numbers."

"It's enough that we both reached out, wouldn't you say?" I offer her a conciliatory smile–I haven't come to pick a fight about the best way to apprehend nature. "The fact is, no one's doing much of that anymore. There's no money for science and there's certainly none for space travel. But we did something great. They can write us out of history, but it doesn't change what we did."

"And me?"

"You were part of it. I'd read all your articles, long before I was selected for the mission. That's why I came to see you, all that time ago. But long before that–I knew what I wanted to do with my life. I was a young man when the Matryoshka arrived, but not so young that I didn't have dreams and plans."

"You must be sorry about that now."

"Sometimes. Not always. No more than you regret what you did."

"It was different back then, between the Soviets. If you believed something, you said it."

"So you don't regret a word of it?"

"I had it easier than he did."

Silence. I look at a photograph on the coffee table–a young woman and a young man, holding hands in front of some grand old church or cathedral I don't recognize, in some European city I'll never see. They have bright clothes with slogans on, sunglasses, ski hats, and they're both smiling. The sky is a hard primary blue, as if it's been daubed in poster paint. "That's him," I say.

"Gennadi was a good man. But he never knew when to shut his mouth. That was his problem. The new men wanted to take us back to the old ways. Lots of people thought that was a good idea, too. The problem was, not all of us did. I was born in 1975. I'm old enough to remember what it was like before Gorbachev. It wasn't all that wonderful, believe me."

"Tell me about Gennadi. How did he got involved?"

"Gennadi was a scientist to begin with–an astronomer like me, in the same institute. That's how we met. But his heart was elsewhere. Politics took up more and more of his time."

"He was a politician?"

"An activist. A journalist and a blogger. Do you remember the internet, Dimitri?"

"Just barely." It's something from my childhood, like foreign tourists and contrails in the sky.

"It was a tool the authorities couldn't control. That made them nervous. They couldn't censor it, or take it down–not then. But they could take down the people behind it, like Gennadi. So that's what they did."

"I'm sorry."

"It's all in the past now. We had our time together; that's all that matters. Perhaps if I hadn't made such a noise about my findings, perhaps if I hadn't angered the wrong people . . ." Nesha stops speaking. All of a sudden I feel shamefully intrusive. What right have I have to barge in on this old woman, to force her to think about the way things used to be? But I can't leave, not having come this far. "His clothes," she says absent-mindedly. "I don't know why I kept them all this time, but perhaps you can use them."

I put down the tea. "Are you certain?"

"It's what Gennadi would have wanted. Always very practically-minded, Gennadi. Go into the room behind you, the cupboard on the left. Take what you can use."

"Thank you."

Even though I'm beginning to warm up, it's good to change out of the sodden old clothes. Gennadi must have been shorter than me, his trousers not quite reaching my ankles, but I'm in no mood to complain. I find a vest, a shirt and an old gray sweater that's been repaired a number of times. I find lace-up shoes that I can wear with two layers of socks. I wash my hands and face in the bedroom basin, straightening back my hair, but there's nothing I can do to tidy or trim my beard. I had plans to change my appearance so far as I was able, but all of a sudden I know how futile they'd be. They'll find me again, even if it takes a little longer. They'd only have to take one look in my eyes to know who I am.

"Do they fit?" Nesha asks, when I return to the main room.

"Like a glove. You've been very kind. I can't ever repay this."

"Start by telling me why you're here. Then–although I can't say I'm sorry for a little company–you can be on your way, before you get both of us into trouble."

I return to the same seat I used before. It's snowing again, softly. In the distance the dark threads of railway lines stretch between two anonymous buildings. I remember what the snowplow driver said. In this weather, I can forget about buses. No one's getting in or out of Zvezdniy Gorodok unless they have party clearance and a waiting Zil.

"I came to tell you that you were right," I say. "After all these years."

"About the Matryoshka?"

"Yes."

"I've known I was right for nearly thirty years. I didn't need you to come and tell me."

"Doesn't it help to know that someone else believes you now?"

"Truth is truth, no matter who else believes it."

"You constructed a hypothesis to fit the data," I said. "It was a sound hypothesis, in that it was testable. But that's all it ever was. You never got to see it tested."

She regards me with steely-eyed intensity, the earlier Nesha Petrova burning through the mask of the older one. "I did. The second apparition."

"Where they proved you wrong?"

"So they said."

"They were wrong. I know. But they used it to crush you, to mock you, to bury you. But we went inside. We penetrated Shell 3. After that–everything was different."

"Does it matter now?"

"I think it does." Now is the moment. The thing I've come all this way to give Nesha, the thing that's been in my pajama pocket, now in the trousers. I take it out, the prize folded in a white handkerchief.

I pass the bundle across the coffee table. "This is for you."

Nesha takes it warily. She unwraps the handkerchief and blinks at the little metal box it had contained. She picks it up gently, holds it before her eyes and pinches her fingers around the little handle that sticks out from one side.

"Turn it."

"What?"

"Turn the handle."

She does as I say, gently and hesitantly at first, as if fearful that the handle will snap off in her fingers. The box emits a series of tinkling notes. Because Nesha is turning the handle so slowly, it's hard to make out the melody.

"I don't understand. You came all this way to give me this?"

"I did."

"Then the rumours were right," Nesha says. "You did go mad after all."

Falling inward, the Progress began to pass through another swarm of free-flying obstacles. Like those of Shell 1, the components of Shell 2 were all but invisible to the naked eye–dark as space itself, and only a fraction of a kelvin warmer than the cosmic microwave background. The wireframe display started showing signs of fuzziness, as if the computer was having trouble decoding the radar returns. The objects were larger and had a different shape to the ones in the outer shell–these were more like rounded pebbles or all-enveloping turtle-shells, wide as cities. They were covered in scales or plaques which moved around in a weird, oozing fashion, like jostling continents on a planet with vigorous plate tectonics. Similarly lethal field lines bound them, but this far in the predictive model became a lot less trustworthy.

No runaway Chinese probe had ever collided with Shell 2, so we had no good idea how brittle the objects were. A second apparition probe operated by the European Space Agency had tried to land and sample one of the Shell 2 obstacles, but without success. That wouldn't stop Galenka from making her own attempt.

She picked a target, wove around the field lines and came in close enough to fire the sticky anchors onto one of the oozing platelets. The Progress wound itself in on electric winches until it was close enough to extend its tools and manipulators.

"Damn camera's sticking again. And I keep losing antenna lock."

"It's what they pay you for," I said.

"Trying to be helpful, Dimitri?"

"Doing my best."

She had her hands in the waldos again. Her eyes were darting from screen to screen. I couldn't make much sense of the displays myself, having never trained for Progress operations. It looked as if she was playing six or seven weirdly abstract computer games at the same time, manipulating symbols according to arcane and ever-shifting rules. I could only hope that she was just about winning.

"Cutting head can't get traction. Whatever that stuff is, it's harder than diamond. Nothing for the claws to grip, either. I'm going to try the laser."

I found myself tensing, as she swung the laser into play.

How would the Matryoshka respond to our burning a hole in it? With the same cosmic indifference that it had shown when the Chinese robot had rammed it, or when the American probe got in the way of its field lines? Nothing in our experience offered any guidance. Perhaps it had tolerated us until now, and would interpret the laser as the first genuinely hostile action. In which case losing the Progress might be the least of our worries.

I tensed.

"Picking up ablation products," Galenka said, eyeing the trembling registers of a gas chromatograph readout. "Laser's cutting into *something*, whatever it is. Lots of carbon. Some noble gases and metals: iron, vanadium, some other stuff I'm not too sure about right now. Let's see if I can cut away a sample."

The laser etched a circle into the surface of the platelet. With the beam kept at an angle to the surface, it was eventually possible to isolate a cone-shaped piece of the material. Galenka used an epoxy-tipped sucker to extract the fist-sized sample, which already seemed to be in the process of fusing back into the main structure.

"Well done."

She grinned at me. "Let's take a few more while our luck's holding, shall we?"

She pulled out of the waldo controls, disengaged the sticky anchors and applied translational thrust, shifting the Progress to a different platelet.

"You sure you don't want to take a break? We can hold here for hours if we have to, especially with the anchors."

"I'm fine, Dimitri." But I noticed that Galenka's knuckles were tight on the joystick, the effort of piloting beginning to show. There was a chisel-sharp crease in the skin on the side of her mouth that only came when she was concentrating. "Fine but a little hungry, if you must know. You want to do something useful, you can fetch me some food."

"I think that might be within my capabilities," I said.

I pushed away from the piloting position, expertly inserting myself onto a weightless trajectory that sent me careening through one of the narrow connecting throats that led from one of the *Tereshkova*'s modules to the next.

By any standards she was a large spacecraft. Nuclear power had brought us to the Matryoshka. The *Tereshkova*'s main engine was a "variable specific impulse magnetic rocket": a VASIMIR drive. It was an old design that had been dusted down and made to work when the requirements of our mission became clear. The point of the VASIMIR (it was an American acronym, but it *sounded* appropriately Russian) was that it could function in a dual mode, giving not us only the kick to escape Earth orbit, but also months of low-impulse cruise thrust, to take us all the way to the artifact and back. It would get us all the way home again, too–whereupon we'd climb into our Soyuz re-entry vehicle and detach from the mothership. The Progress would come down on autopilot, laden with alien riches–that was the plan, anyway.

Like all spacecraft, the *Tereshkova* looked like a ransacked junk shop inside. Any area of the ship that wasn't already in use as a screen or control panel or equipment hatch or analysis laboratory or food dispenser or life-support system was something to hold onto, or kick off from, or rest against, or tie things onto. Technical manuals floated in mid-air, tethered to the wall. Bits of computer drifted around the ship as if they had lives of their own, until one of us needed some cable or connector. Photos of our family, drawings made by our children, were tacked to the walls between panels and grab rails. The whole thing stank like an armpit and made so much noise that most of us kept earplugs in when we didn't need to talk.

But it was home, of a sort. A stinking, noisy shithole of a home, but still the best we had.

I hadn't seen Yakov as I moved through the ship, but that wasn't any cause for alarm. As the specialist in change of the *Tereshkova*'s flight systems, his duty load has eased now that we had arrived on station at the artifact. He had been busy during the cruise phase, so we couldn't begrudge him a little time off, especially as he was going to have to nurse the ship home again. So, while Baikonur gave him a certain number of housekeeping tasks to attend to, Yakov had more time to himself than Galenka or I. If he wasn't in his quarters, there were a dozen other places on the ship where he could find some privacy, if not peace and quiet. We all had our favorite spots, and we were careful not to intrude on each other when we needed some personal time.

So I had no reason to sense anything unusual as I selected and warmed a meal for Galenka. But as the microwave chimed readiness, a much louder alarm began shrieking throughout the ship. Red emergency lights started flashing. The general distress warning meant that the ship had detected something anomalous. Without further clarification, it could be almost anything: a fault with the VASIMIR, a hull puncture, a life-support system failure, a hundred other problems. All that the alarm told me was that the ship deemed the problem critical, demanding immediate attention.

I grabbed a handrail and propelled myself to the nearest monitor. Text was already scrolling on it.

Unscheduled activity in hatch three, said the words.

I froze for a few moments, not so much in panic as out of a need to pause and concentrate, to assess the situation and decide on the best course of action. But I didn't need much time to reflect. Since Galenka was still at her station, still guiding the Progress, it was obvious what the problem was. Yakov was trying to escape from the *Tereshkova.*

As if we were still in Star City.

There was no automatic safety mechanism to prevent that door from being opened. It was assumed that if anyone did try and open it, they must have a good reason for doing so—venting air into space, for instance, to quench a fire. The notion that one of us would do something stupid, like trying to leave the ship because we thought it was a simulation, must never have occurred to the engineers.

I pushed myself through the module, through the connecting throat, through the next module. The alarm was drilling into my head. If Yakov really did think that the ship was still in Russia, he wouldn't be concerned about decompression. He wouldn't be concerned about whether or not he was wearing a suit.

He just wanted to get out.

I reached a red locker marked with a lightning flash and threw back the heavy duty latches. I expected to see three tasers, bound with security foils.

There were no tasers–just the remains of the foil and the recessed foam shapes where the stunners had fitted.

"Fuck," I said, realizing that Yakov was ahead of me; that he had opened the locker–against all rules; it was only supposed to be touched in an emergency–and taken the weapons.

I pushed through another connecting throat, scraping my hand against sharp metal until it bled, then corkscrewed through 90 degrees to reach the secondary throat that led to the number three hatch.

I could already see Yakov at the end of it. Braced against the wall, he was turning the big yellow wheel that undid the door's massive locking mechanism. When he was done, it would only take a twist of the handle to free the hatch. The air pressure behind it would slam it open in an instant, and both of us would be sucked into space long before emergency bulkhead seals protected the rest of the ship. I tried to work out which way we were facing now. Would it be a long fall back to the Sun, or an inglorious short-cut to the Matryoshka?

"Yakov, please," I called. "Don't open the door."

He kept working the wheel, but looked back at me over his shoulder. "No good, Dimitri. I've figured this out even if you haven't. None of this is real. We're not really out here, parked next to the Matryoshka. We're just rehearsing for it, running through another simulation."

I tried to ride with his logic. "Then let's see the simulation through to the end."

"Don't you get it? This is all a test. They want to see how alert we are. They want to see that we're still capable of picking up on the details that don't fit."

The blood was spooling out of my hand, forming a scarlet chain of floating droplets. I pushed the wound to my mouth and sucked at it. "Like weightlessness? How would they ever fake that, Dimitri?"

He let go of the wheel with one hand and touched the back of his neck. "The implants. They fool with your inner ear, make you think you're floating."

"That's your GLONASS transponder. There's one on the back of my neck as well. It's so they can track and recover our bodies if the re-entry goes wrong."

"That's what they told us." He kept on turning the wheel.

"You open that door, you're a dead man. You'll kill me and put Galenka in danger."

"Listen to me," he said with fierce insistence. "This is not real. We're in Star City, my friend. The whole point of this exercise is to measure our alertness, our ability to see through delusional constructs. Escaping from the ship is the objective, the end-state."

I knew then that reasoned argument wasn't going to get me anywhere. I gave myself a hard shove in his direction, hoping to overwhelm him with sheer momentum. But Yakov was faster. His hand sprung to his pocket and came out holding one of the tasers, aimed straight at me. The barbs sprang out and contacted my chest. I'd never been shot before and I wasn't ready for the pain. It seemed to crush me into a little ball of concentrated fire, like an insect curling under the heat from a magnifying glass. I let out a brief yelp, biting my tongue, and then I didn't even have the energy to scream. The barbs were still in me. Bent double, blood dribbling from my hand and mouth, I lost all contact with the ship. Drifting, I saw Yakov leave the taser floating in mid-air while he returned his attention to the wheel and redoubled his efforts.

"You stupid fucker," I heard Galenka say, behind me.

I didn't know whether she meant Yakov–for trying to escape–or me, for trying to stop him on my own. Maybe she meant both of us.

The pain of the discharge was beginning to ebb. I could just begin to think about speaking again.

"Got a taser," I heard myself say, as if from a distance.

"Good. So have I." I felt Galenka push past me, something hard in her hand. Then I heard the strobing crackle of another taser. I kept drifting around, until the door came into view again. Through blurred and slitted eyes, I saw Yakov twitching against the metal. Galenka had fired barbs into him; now she was holding the prongs of the taser against his abdomen, the blue worm of a spark writhing between.

I reached out a hand and managed to steady myself. The pain had now all but gone, but I was enveloped in nausea and a tingling all-body version of pins and needles.

"You can stop now."

She gave the taser one last prod, then withdrew it. Yakov remained still, slumped and unconscious against the door.

"I say we kill the fucker now."

I wiped the blood from my lips. "I know how you feel. But we need him to get us home. If there's the slightest problem with the engine . . ."

"Anything happens, mission control can help us."

I worked my way down to the door. "He's not going to do this again. We can sedate him, confine him to one of the modules if necessary. Until Baikonur advise."

Galenka pushed her own taser back into her pocket, with the barbs dangling loose on their springy wires. She started turning the wheel in the opposite direction, grunting at first with the effort.

"This was a close call."

"You were right–I should have been more worried about him than I was. I didn't think he was really serious about all that Star City stuff. I mean, not *this* serious."

"He's a basket case, Dimitri. That means there are only two sane people left on this ship, and I'm being generous."

"Do you think Baikonur will be able to help?"

"They'd better. Anything goes wrong on this ship, we need him to fix it. And he's not going to be much use to us doped to his eyeballs."

We manhandled the stunned Yakov back into the main part of the *Tereshkova.* Already I could tell that he was only lightly unconscious, and that we'd have a struggle on our hands if he came around now. He was mumbling under his breath. Sweat began to bead on my forehead. Why the fuck did this have to happen to us?

"What do you reckon we should do? Confine him to his quarters?"

"And have him loose aboard the ship again, looking for a way to escape?"

"I'm not sure we have any other choice."

"We lock him in the forward module," Galenka said decisively. "He'll be safe in there. We can seal the connecting lock from our side, until Baikonur come up with a treatment regime. In the meantime we dose him on sedatives, put him under for as long as we can. I don't want that lunatic running around when I'm trying to steer the Progress through Shell 3."

I breathed in hard, trying to focus. "Where is it now?"

"Still anchored to one of the Shell 2 platelets. I'd like to take a few more samples before I detach, but from then on it's seat of the pants stuff."

She was right: it was a good plan. Better than anything I could come up with, at any rate. We took him forward to the orbiter, opened a medical kit and injected him with the sedative. I took out a tube of disinfectant and a roll of bandage for my gashed hand. Yakov stopped mumbling and became more pliant, like a big rag doll. We strapped him into a sleeping hammock and locked the door on him.

"He was pissing me off anyway," Galenka said.

I move back from the window in Nesha's apartment. Zvezdniy Gorodok is stirring to a wintery, hypothermic half-life. The snow's still coming down, though in fitful flurries rather than a steady fall. When a Zil pulls onto the street I feel a tightness in my throat. But the limousine stops, releasing its passenger, and moves on. The man strolls across the concrete concourse into one of the adjoining buildings, a briefcase swinging from his hand. He might have anything in that briefcase–a gun, a syringe, a lie detector. But he has no business here.

"You think they're looking for you."

"I know it."

"Then where are you going to go?"

Out into the cold and the snow to die, I think. But I smile and say nothing.

"Is it really so bad in the facility? Do they really treat you so badly?"

I return to my seat. Nesha's poured me another cup of tea, which–her views on my sanity notwithstanding–I take as an invitation to remain. "Most of them don't treat me badly at all–they're not monsters or sadists. I'm too precious to them for that. They don't beat me, or electrocute me, and the drugs they give me, the things they do to me, they're not to make me docile or to punish me. Doctor Kizim, he's even kind to me. He spends a lot of time talking to me, trying to get me to remember details I might have forgotten. It's pointless, though. I've already remembered all that I'm ever going to. My brain feels like a pan that's been scrubbed clean."

"Did Doctor Kizim help you to escape?"

"I've asked myself the same question. Did he mean for me to steal his coat? Did he sense that I was intending to leave? He must have known I wouldn't get far without it."

"What about the others? Were you allowed to see them?"

I shake my head. "They kept us apart the whole time Yakov and Galenka were still alive. We were questioned and examined separately. Even though we'd spent all those months in the ship, they didn't want us contaminating each other's accounts."

"So you never really got to know what happened to the others."

"I know that they both died. Galenka went first–she took the highest dosage when the VASIMIR's shielding broke down. Yakov was a little luckier, but not much. I never got to see either of them while they were still alive."

"Why didn't you get a similar dosage?"

"Yakov was mad to begin with. Then he got better, or at least decided he was better off working with us than against us. We let him out of the module where we were keeping him locked up. That was after Galenka and I got back from the Matryoshka."

"And then?"

"It was my turn to go a little mad. Inside the machine–something touched us. It got into our heads. It affected me more than it did Galenka. On the return trip, they had no choice but to confine me to the forward module."

"The thing that saved you."

"I was further from the engine when it went wrong. Inverse square laws. My dosage was negligible."

"You accept that they died, despite having no evidence."

"I believe what Doctor Kizim told me. I trusted him. He had no reason to lie. He was already putting his career at risk by giving me this information. Maybe more than his career. A good man."

"Did he know the other two?"

"No; he only ever treated me. That was part of the methodology. Strange things had happened during the early months of the debriefing. The doctors and surgeons got too close to us, too involved. After we came back from the Matryoshka, there was something different about us. It affected us all, even Yakov, who hadn't gone inside. Just being close to it was enough."

"Different in what way?" Nesha asks.

"It began in small ways, while we were still on the *Tereshkova.* Weird slips. Mistakes that didn't make sense. As if our identities, our personalities and memories, were blurring. On the way home, I sat at the computer keyboard and found myself typing Yakov's name and password into the system, as if he's sitting inside me. A few days later Galenka wakes up and tells me she dreamed she was in Klushino, a place she's never visited. It was as if something in the machine had touched us and removed some fundamental barrier in our heads, some wall or moat that keeps one person from becoming another. When the silver fluid got into us . . ."

"I don't understand. How could the doctors get too close to you? What happened to them?"

I sense her uneasiness; the realization that she may well be sharing her room with a lunatic. I have never pretended to be entirely sane, but it must only be now that the white bones of true madness are beginning to show through my skin.

"I didn't mean to alarm you, Nesha. I'll be gone shortly, I promise you. Why don't you tell me what it was like for you, back when it all began?"

"You know my story."

"I'd still like to hear it from you. From the day it arrived. How it changed you."

"You were old enough to remember it. You already told me that."

"But I wasn't an astronomer, Nesha. I was just a 20 year old kid with some ideas about being a cosmonaut. You were how old, exactly?"

"Forty years. I'd been a professional astronomer for 15 or

16 of them, by then." She becomes reflective, as if it's only now that she has given that time of her life any thought. "I'd been lucky, really. I'd made professor, which meant I didn't have to grub around for funding every two years. I had to do my share of lecturing, and fighting for my corner of the department, but I still had plenty of time for independent research. I was still in love with science, too. My little research area–stellar pulsation modes–it wasn't the most glamorous. They didn't fight to put our faces on the covers of magazine, or give us lucrative publishing deals to talk about how we were uncovering the mysteries of the universe, touching the face of god. But we knew it was solid science, important to the field as a whole." She leans forward to make a point. "Astronomy's like a cathedral, Dimitri. The ones putting the gold on the top spire get all the glory, but they'd be nothing without a solid foundation. That's where we were–down in the basement, down in the crypt, making sure it was all anchored to firm ground. Fundamental stellar physics. Not very exotic compared to mapping the large scale universe, or probing the event horizons of black holes. But vital all the same."

"I don't doubt it."

"I can remember that afternoon when the news came in. Gennadi and I were in my office. It was a bright day, with the blinds drawn. It was the end of the week and we were looking forward to a few days off. We had tickets to see a band in town that night. We just had one thing we wanted to get sorted before we finished. A paper we'd been working on had come back from the referee with a load of snotty comments, and we didn't quite agree on how to deal with them. I wanted to write back to the journal and request a different referee. The referee on our paper was anonymous, but I was sure I knew who it was–a slimy, womanising prick who'd made a pass at me at a conference in Trieste, and wasn't going to let me forget that I'd told him where to get off."

I smile. "You must have been fierce in your day."

"Well, maybe it wasn't him–but we still needed a different referee. Gennadi, meanwhile, thought we should sit back and do what the referee was telling us. Which meant running our models again, which meant a week of time on the department supercomputer. Normally, that would have meant going right back to the start of the queue. But there was a gap in the schedule–another group had just pulled out of their slot, because they couldn't get their software to compile properly. We could have their slot–but only if we got our model up and running that evening, with all the modifications the referee wanted us to make."

"You weren't going to make it to that band."

"That was when the IAU telegram came in to my inbox. I didn't even open it at first; it wasn't as if IAU telegrams were exactly unusual. It probably just meant that a supernova had gone off in a remote galaxy, or that some binary star was undergoing a nova. Nothing I needed to get excited about."

"But that wasn't what it was about."

"It was the Matryoshka, of course–the emergence event, when it came into our solar system. A sudden influx of cosmic rays, triggering half the monitoring telescopes and satellites in existence. They all turned to look at the point where the machine had come in. A flash of energy that intense, it could only be a gamma-ray burst, happening in some distant galaxy. That's what everyone thought it was at first, especially as the Matryoshka came in high above the ecliptic, and well out of the plane of the galaxy. It looked extragalactic, not some local event. Sooner or later, though, they crunched the numbers–triangulated from the slightly different pointing angles of the various spacecraft and telescopes, the slightly different detection times of the event–and they realized that, whatever this was, it had happened within one light hour of the Sun. Not so much on our doorstep, cosmically speaking, as in our house, making itself at home." Nesha smiles at the memory. "There was some wild theorizing to begin with. Everything from a piece of antimatter colliding with a comet, a quantum black hole evaporating, to the illegal test of a

Chinese super-weapon in deep space. Of course, it was none of those things. It was spacetime opening wide enough to vomit out a machine the size of Tasmania."

"It was a while before they found the Matryoshka itself."

Nesha nods. "You try finding something that dark, when you don't even know in which direction it's moving."

"Even from the *Tereshkova*, it was hard to believe it was actually out there."

"To begin with, we still didn't know what to make of it. The layered structure confused the hell out of us. We weren't used to analyzing anything like that. It was artificial, clearly, but it wasn't made of solid parts. It was like a machine caught in the instant of blowing up, but which was still working, still doing whatever it was sent to do. Without getting closer, we could only resolve the structure in the outer layer. We didn't start calling it Shell 1 until we knew there were deeper strata. The name Matryoshka didn't come until after the first fly-by probes, when we glimpsed Shell 2. The Americans called it the Easter Egg for a little while, but eventually everyone started using the Russian name."

I know that when she talks about "we", she means the astronomical community as a whole, rather than her own efforts. Nesha's involvement–the involvement that had first made her famous, then ruined her reputation, then her life–did not come until later.

The emergence event–the first apparition–caught humanity entirely unaware. The Matryoshka had come out of its wormhole mouth–if that was what it was–on an elliptical, sun-circling trajectory similar to a periodic comet. The only thing non-cometary was the very steep inclination to the ecliptic. It made reaching the Matryoshka problematic, except when it was swinging near the Sun once every 12 years. Even with a massive international effort, there was no way to send dedicated probes out to meet the artifact and match its velocity. The best anyone could do was fling smart pebbles at it, hoping to learn as much as possible in the short window while they slammed past. Probes that had been intended for Mars or Venus were hastily repurposed for the Matryoshka flyby, where time and physics made that possible. It was more like the mad scramble of some desperate, last-ditch war effort than anything seen in peacetime.

There were, of course, dissenting voices. Some people thought the prudent thing would be to wait and see what the Matryoshka had in mind for us. By and large, they were ignored. The thing had arrived here, hadn't it? The least it could expect was a welcome party.

As it was, the machine appeared completely oblivious to the attention–as it had continued to do through the second apparition. The third apparition–that was different, of course. But then again our provocation had been of an entirely different nature.

After the probes had gone by, there was data to analyze. Years of it. The Matryoshka had fallen out of each reach of our instruments and robots, but we had more than enough to keep busy until the next apparition. Plans were already being drawn up for missions to rendezvous with the object and penetrate that outer layer. Robots next time, but who knew what might be possible in the 24 years between the first and third apparitions?

"The scientists who'd had their missions redirected wanted a first look at the Matryoshka data," Nesha says. "The thinking was that they'd get exclusive access to it for six months."

"You can't blame them for that."

"There was still an outcry. It was felt that an event of this magnitude demanded the immediate release of all the data to the community. To the whole world, in fact. Anyone who wanted it was welcome to it. Of course, unless they had a lightning fast internet connection, about ten million terabytes of memory, their own Cray . . . they couldn't even begin to scratch the surface. There were collaborative efforts, millions of people downloading a fragment of the data and analyzing it using spare CPU cycles, but they still couldn't beat the resources of a single well-equipped academic department with a tame supercomputer in the basement. Above all else, we had all the analysis tools at hand, and we knew how to use them. But it was still a massive cake to eat in one bite."

"And did you?"

"No–it made much more sense to focus on what we were good at. The data hinted that the elements of the outer layer–Shell 1–were bound together by some kind of force-field. The whole thing was breathing in and out, the components moving as if tied together by a complex web of elastic filaments. The thing is, stars breathe as well. The pulsation modes in a solar-type star aren't the same as the pulsation modes in the Matryoshka. But we could still use the same methods, the same tools and tricks, to get a handle on them. And of course, there was a point to all of that. Map the pulsations in a star and you can probe the deep interior, in exactly the same way that earthquakes tell us about the structure of the Earth. There was every expectation that the Matryoshka's pulsations might tell us something about the inside of that as well."

"I guess you didn't have a clue what you'd actually find."

Nesha gives a brief, derisive laugh. "Of course not. I wasn't thinking in those terms at all. I was just thinking of frequencies, harmonics, Fourier analysis, caustic surfaces. I wasn't thinking of fucking *music*."

"Tell me how it felt."

"The first time I ran the analysis, and realized that the pulsations could be broken down into notes on the western chromatic scale? Like I was the victim of a bad practical joke, someone in the department messing with the data."

"And when you realized you weren't being hoaxed?"

"I still didn't *believe* it–not to begin with. I thought I must have screwed up in my analysis somewhere, introduced harmonics that weren't real. I stripped the tools down and put them together again. Same story: notes, chords, melody, and counterpoint. Music. That's when I started accepting the reality of it. Whatever we were dealing with–whatever had come to find us–wasn't what we had assumed. This wasn't just some dumb invention, some alien equivalent of the probes we had been sending out. The Matryoshka was a different order of machine. Something clever and complex enough to sing to itself. Or, just possibly, to us." Nesha hesitates and looks at me with an unwavering gaze. "And it was singing our music. Russian music."

"I know," I say. "It's been in my head since I came back."

No one had ever gone this deep before.

The Progress had travelled fifty kilometers into the Machine–through two layers of orbiting obstruction, each of which was ten kilometers in depth, and through two open volumes fifteen kilometers thick. Beneath lay the most difficult part of its journey so far. Though the existence of Shell 3 had been known since the second apparition, no hard data existed on conditions beneath it.

The barrier was actually a pair of tightly nested spheres, one slightly smaller than the other. The shell's material was as dark as anything already encountered, but–fortuitously for us–the spheres had holes in them, several dozen circular perforations ranging in width from one to three kilometers, spotted around the spheres in what appeared to be an entirely random arrangement. The pattern of holes was the same in both spheres, but because they were rotating at different speeds, on different, slowly precessing axes, the holes only lined up occasionally. During those windows, glimpses opened up into the heart of the Matryoshka. A blue-green glow shone through the winking gaps in Shell 3, hinting at luminous depths.

Shortly we'd know.

"How's he doing?" Galenka asked, from the pilot's position. I had just returned from the orbiter, where I had been checking on Yakov. I had fixed a medical cuff to his wrist, so that Baikonur could analyze his blood chemistry.

"Not much change since last time. He just looks at me. Doesn't say or do anything."

"We should up the medication." She tapped keys, adjusting one of the Progress's camera angles. She was holding station, hovering a few kilometers over Shell 3. Talking out of the side of her mouth she said, "Put him into a coma until we really need him."

"I talked to Baikonur. They recommend holding him at the current dosage until they've run some tests."

"Easy for them to say, half a solar system away."

"They're the experts, not us."

"If you say so."

"I think we should let them handle this one. It's not like we don't have other things to occupy our minds, is it?"

"You have a point there, comrade."

"Are you happy about taking her in? You've been in the chair for a long time now."

"It's what we came to do. Progress systems are dropping like flies, anyway–I give this ship about six hours before it dies on us. I think it's now or never."

I could only bow to her superior wisdom in this matter.

In the years since the last apparition, the complex motion of the spheres had been subjected to enormous scrutiny. It had been a triumph to map the holes in the interior sphere. Despite this, no watertight algorithm had ever been invented to predict the window events with any precision. The spheres slowed down and sped up unpredictably, making a nonsense of long-range forecasts. Unless a window was in view, the movement of the inner sphere could not be measured. Radar bounced off its flawless surface as if the thing was motionless.

All Galenka could do was wait until a window event began, then make a run for it–hoping that the aperture remained open long enough for the Progress to pass through. Analysis of all available data showed that window events occurred, on average, once in every 72-minute interval. But that was just an average. Two window events could fall within minutes of each other, or there might be a ten hour wait before the next one. The window was tight–the Progress would have to begin its run within seconds of the window opening, if it had a chance of slipping through in time. I didn't envy Galenka sitting there with her finger on the trigger, like a gunslinger waiting for her opponent to twitch.

In the event, a useful window–one that she could reach, in the allowed time–opened within 40 minutes of our conversation. Looking over her shoulder at the screens, I could hardly make out any change in Shell 3. Only when the Progress was already committed–moving too quickly to stop or change course–did a glimmer of blue-green light reassure me that the window was indeed opening. Even then, it hardly seemed possible that the Progress would have time to pass through the winking eye.

Of course, that was exactly what happened. Only a slight easing of the crease on the side of Galenka's mouth indicated that she was, for now, breathing easier. We both knew that this triumph could well be very short-lived, since the Progress would now find it even more difficult to remain in contact with the *Tereshkova.* Since no man-made signal could penetrate Shell 3, comms could only squirt through when a window was open, in whatever direction that happened to be. The swarm of relay microsats placed around the Machine were intended to intercept these burst transmissions and relay them back to the *Tereshkova.* Its puppet-strings all but severed, the robotic spacecraft would be relying more and more on the autonomous decision-making of its onboard computers.

I knew that the mission planners had subjected the Progress to every eventuality, ever scenario, they could dream up. I also knew that none of those planners seriously expected the secrets of the Matryoshka to bear the slightest resemblance to their imaginings. If it did, they'd be brutally disappointed.

The rear-looking camera showed the window sealing behind the Progress. The inside surface of Shell 3 was as pitilessly dark as its outer skin, yet all else was aglow. I shivered with an almost religious ecstasy: soon the secrets revealed here would be in the hands of the entire human species, but for now–for a delicious and precious interval–the only two souls given this privilege were Galenka and I. No other thinking creature had seen this far.

Beneath Shell 3 was another empty volume–Gap 3. Then there was another sphere. We were looking at the central 60 kilometers of the Matryoshka, three quarters of the way to whatever lay at its heart. Shell 4 looked nothing like the dark machinery we had already passed through. This was more like a prickly fruit, a nastily evolved bacterium or some fantastically complex coral formation. The surface of the sphere was barely visible, lost under a spiky, spiny accretion of spokes and barbs and twisted unicorn horns, pushing out into the otherwise empty band gap for many kilometers. There were lacy webs of matter bridging one spike to the next. There were muscular structures like the roots of enormous trees, winding and entwining around the bases of the largest outgrowths. It was all ablaze with blue-green light, like a glass sculpture lit from within. The light wavered and pulsed. Shell 3 did not look like something which had been designed and built, but rather something which had grown, wildly and unpredictably. It was wonderful and terrifying.

Then the signal ended. The Progress was on its own now, relying on its hardwired wits.

"You did well," I told Galenka.

She said nothing. She was already asleep. Her head did not loll in zero gravity, her jaw did not droop open, but her eyes were closed and her hand had slackened on the joystick. Only then did I realise how utterly exhausted she must have been. But I imagined her dreams were peaceful ones.

She had not failed the mission. She had not failed Mother Russia and the Second Soviet.

I left her sleeping, then spent two hours attending to various housekeeping tasks aboard the *Tereshkova*. Since we were only able to use the low-gain antenna–the high-gain antenna had failed shortly after departure–the data that the Progress had already sent back needed to be organized and compressed before it could be sent onwards to Earth. All the data stored aboard the *Tereshkova* would get home eventually–assuming, of course, that we did–but in the meantime I was anxious to provide Baikonur with what I regarded as the highlights. All the while I checked for updates from the Progress, but no signal had yet been detected.

Without waiting for mission control to acknowledge the data package, I warmed some food for myself, took a nip of vodka from my private supply, and then carried my meal into the part of the *Tereshkova* loosely designated as the commons/recreational area. It was the brightest part of the ship, with plastic flowers and ornaments, tinsel, photographs, postcards, and children's paintings stuck to the walls. I stationed myself against a wall and watched television, flicking through the various uplink feeds while spooning food into my mouth. I skipped soaps, quizzes, and talk shows until I hit one of the main news senders. The main state news channel showed me what the rest of the world–or the rest of the Soviet Union, at least–was getting to hear about us. The *Tereshkova* had been big news during its departure, but had fallen from the headlines during the long cruise out to the Matryoshka. Now it was a top-listed item once more, squeezing out other stories.

The channel informed its viewers that the ship had successfully launched a robotic probe through Shells 1 and 2, a triumph equal to anything achieved during the last two apparitions, and one which–it was confidently expected–would soon be surpassed. The data already returned to Earth, the channel said, offered a bounty that would keep the keenest Soviet minds engaged for many years. Nor would this data be hoarded by Russia alone, for with characteristic Soviet generosity, it would be shared with those "once-proud" nations who now lacked the means to travel into space. The brave cosmonauts who were reaping this harvest of riches were mentioned by name on several occasions. There was, of course, no word about how one of those brave cosmonauts had gone stark raving mad.

I knew with a cold certainty that they'd never tell the truth about Yakov. If he didn't recover they'd make something up–an unanticipated illness, or a debilitating accident. They'd kill the poor bastard rather than admit that we were human.

"I went to see him," Galenka said, startling me. She had drifted into the recreation area quite silently. "He's talking now–almost lucid. Want us to let him out of the module."

"Not likely."

"I agree. But we'll have to make a decision on him sooner or later."

"Well, there's no hurry right now. You all right?"

"Fine, thanks."

She had rested less than three hours, but in weightlessness–even after an exhausting task–that was enough. It was a useful physiological adaptation when there was a lot of work to be done, but it also meant that ten days in space could feel like thirty back on Earth. Or a hundred.

"Go and sleep some more, you want to. The Progress calls in, I'll wake you."

"If it calls in."

I offered a shrug. "You did everything that was expected of you. That we got this far . . ."

"I know; we should be very proud of ourselves." She stared at the screen, her eyes still sleepy.

"They're going to lie about Yakov."

"I know."

"When we get home, they'll make us stick to the story."

"Of course." She said this with total resignation, as if it was the least any of us could expect.

Soon we bored of the news and the television. While Galenka was answering letters from friends and family I went back to run my own check on Yakov. To our disappointment Baikonur still had no specific recommendations beyond maintaining the present medication. I sensed that they didn't want blood on their hands if something went wrong with him. They were happy to let us take responsibility for our ailing comrade, even if we ended up killing him.

"Let me out, Dimitri. I'm fine now."

I looked at him through armored glass of the bulkhead door. Shaking my head, I felt like a doctor delivering some dreadful diagnosis.

"You have to stay there for now. I'm sorry. But we can't run the risk of you trying to open the hatch again."

"I accept that this isn't a simulation now. I accept that we're really in space." His voice came through a speaker grille, tinny and distant. "You believe me, don't you Dimitri?"

"I'll see you later, Yakov."

"At least let me talk to Baikonur."

I placed the palm of my hand against the glass. "Later, friend. For now, get some rest."

I turned away before he could answer.

He wasn't the only one who needed sleep. Tiredness hit me unexpectedly–it always came on hard, like a wall. I slept for two hours, dreaming of being back on Earth on a warm spring day, sitting with my wife in the park, the mission happily behind me, deemed a success by all concerned. When I woke the dream's melancholic after-effects stayed with me, dogging my thoughts. I badly wanted to get home.

I found Galenka in the pilot's position.

"We have contact," she said, but I knew from her tone of voice that it wasn't all good news.

"The Progress called in?"

"She's stuck, Dimitri. Jammed in down there. Can't back out, can't go forward."

"Fuck."

What was only apparent when the Progress reached the root complex was that there was no solid surface to Shell 4; that the tangled mass of roots was, to all intents and purposes, the sphere itself. There were gaps in that tangle, too, like the interstices in a loosely bundled ball of string. Methodically and fearlessly, the Progress had set about finding a way through to whatever was underneath. On its first attempt, it had traveled no more than a third of a kilometer beneath the nominal surface before reaching a narrowing it couldn't pass through. The second attempt, picking a different entry point, had taken it a kilometer under the surface before it met a similar impasse. With fuel now running low–just enough to get it back to the *Tereshkova*, with some in reserve–the Progress had opted to make one final attempt. It was then that it had got itself stuck, lodging in a part of the thicket like a bullet in gristle.

Galenka sent commands to the Progress, to be relayed through to it when a window opened. She told it to use its manipulators to try and push itself backwards, and to wiggle its reaction thrusters in the hope that it might shake itself loose. It was the best she could do, but she wasn't optimistic. We waited three hours, by which time Baikonur were fully appraised of the situation. Then a window opened and the Progress reported that it was still jammed tight, despite executing Galenka's instructions.

"Before you say I should have listened to you," she said. "I did listen. But bringing her back in just wasn't the right decision, given what I knew at the time."

"I fully concurred, Galenka. No one's blaming you."

"Let's see what Baikonur have to say when we get back, shall we?"

"I'm sure they'll be in a forgiving mood. The amount of data we've gathered . . ."

"Doesn't begin to add up against physical samples, which we've now lost."

"Maybe."

“Maybe what? I’ve tried everything in the book. I know what that Progress can do, Dimitri. It isn’t an escape artist.”

“We do have the Soyuz,” I said.

“We need it to take us home. Anyway, the Soyuz isn’t rigged for remote control or sampling.”

“I wasn’t thinking of remote control. I was thinking, we fly the Soyuz all the way in. It’s the same size as the Progress, right? It has similar capabilities?”

“Give or take.” Her tone told me she wasn’t exactly signing up for my idea with enthusiasm. “And then what?”

“We reach the Progress, or get as close to it as we can without getting ourselves stuck. Then we EVA. It’s a microgravity environment so we should be able to move around without too much difficulty. It’ll be too risky to attempt to free the Progress, but there’s nothing to stop us transferring the artifacts. Plenty of room aboard the Soyuz, to bring them back to the *Tereshkova*.”

She breathed heavily, as if she’d just come off the exercise cycle. “This wasn’t planned for. This wasn’t in the book. No one ever mentioned going in with the Soyuz.”

“It was always an unstated option. Why do you think they sent us out here, Galenka? To operate the Progress in real-time? Part of the reason, certainly, but not all of it.”

“It’s too dangerous.”

“It was, but now we’ve got a much clearer picture of what’s inside Shell 3. We can load in the Progress’s trajectory and follow it all the way in.”

“And if we damage the Soyuz? It’s a fiery ride home without it.”

“Why should we? We’ll be taking excellent care of it.”

“Because our lives will depend on it. You’ve become very courageous all of a sudden, Dimitri. Don’t take this the wrong way, but it’s not what I expected of you.”

“I’m not trying to be anyone’s hero. My blood’s running cold at the idea of flying the Soyuz into that thing. But I happen to know the way their minds work back in Baikonur.

They'll have thought of the Soyuz option by now, realized that it's feasible."

"They won't force us to do it, though."

"No, that's not how they operate. But if we don't raise the possibility, if we don't put it on the table, they'll be very, very disappointed. More disappointed than they'll already be at us for losing the robot."

I watched her reflect on what I'd said. In this instance Galenka would have no option but to admit that my grasp of Baikonur politics was superior to hers. I had been a cosmonaut for much longer and I had seen how our superiors punished failings. The best you could hope for was incarceration. The worst was returning to your office to find a loaded revolver and a bottle of vodka.

"I hope you're right about this, Dimitri. For both our sakes."

"We have no choice," I said. "Trust me, Galenka. Nothing that happens in the Matryoshka will be as bad as what they'd do to us for failing our country."

An hour later we'd informed Baikonur of our decision. Two hours later we had their reply. I went to Yakov and told him what was going to happen.

"You can let me out now," he said, through the bulkhead window.

"Not until we're back."

"You still don't trust me?"

"It's just not a risk we can afford to take."

"Don't leave me alone on the *Tereshkova.* I'd rather go with you than stay here on my own."

"Not an option, I'm afraid. We need the extra space in the Soyuz. But I'm opening comms to your module. You'll be able to talk to Baikonur, and you'll be able to talk to us. You won't feel out of touch."

"I'm all right now," Yakov said. "Please believe me. I had a bad turn, I got confused–but everything's all right now."

"I'm sorry."

An hour after that, we were checking our suits and prepping the Soyuz for departure.

"I need bread," Nesha says. "Let's go for a walk."

"In this weather?"

"I need bread. If I don't go early, there'll be none left."

I peer through the window, at the gray-white sky. "I could fetch it for you. If you gave me some money, and told me where to go." Seeing the sceptical look on her face, I add, "I'd come back."

"We'll go together. It's good exercise for me, to get out of this place. If I didn't have errands, I'd probably never leave the building."

Nesha puts on several more layers of clothes and fetches a coat for herself. None of Gennadi's coats fit me (they're all too tight in the sleeves) so I'm forced to make do with Doctor Kizim's again. At least it's dried a bit, and I have something warm on underneath it. Nesha locks her apartment, turning keys in three separate locks, then we walk slowly to the elevator, still where I left it, on the ninth floor.

"I shouldn't have mocked you, Dimitri Ivanov. That wasn't called for."

The elevator doors close. "Mocked me?"

"About the musical box. The thing you came to give me. Now that we've spoken a little more, I see that you're not the madman I thought you might be. I should have known better."

"It's understandable."

"Did it really come from the Matryoshka?"

"All the way back."

"Why did they let you keep it?"

"Because they didn't realize its significance. By the time we got back, I knew that we weren't going to get an easy ride. The truth that we'd discovered–it wasn't going to be something our political masters wanted to hear. We were all ill–the perfect excuse for incarceration in some nameless medical facility cum prison or madhouse. Yakov and Galenka were sick with radiation exposure. I was sick with the Matryoshka inside my head. None of us were going to see daylight again."

"I read the papers and saw the television reports. They never actually lied about what happened to you."

"They didn't have to lie. As long as there was a reason not to have us out in public, they were happy."

The elevator completes its trundling, hesitant descent. We leave the building, venturing into the snow-covered street. I glance around, vigilant for prowling Zils and men in dark suits.

"I kept the musical box with me all the way home. They found it, of course, but it was always presumed to be one of my personal effects–something I'd taken aboard the ship when we left. The idea that it might be an *artifact*–a thing from the Matryoshka–that never crossed their minds."

"And you never thought to tell them?"

"They'd have destroyed it, Nesha. So I kept it close with me, all the time I was in the facility. The only person I ever showed it to was Doctor Kizim, and I don't think even he believed where it had come from."

"You must have trusted him."

"You had to trust someone in a place like that. Just like I'm trusting you now. The musical box is yours now. It's a piece of the future, in your hands."

She removes it from her coat. Until then I have no idea that she's brought it with her.

"The tune it makes . . ." She starts turning the little handle, the notes tinkling out. We're in the street, but there's no one else around to notice one old woman with a little metal box in her hands, or to question why she's turning the handle in its side. "I think I know it. It's something familiar, isn't it? Something Russian?"

"Like you always said. But please don't play it now. It makes my head hurt."

She stops turning the handle and returns the musical box to her pocket. We trudge on in silence for several more streets, until we're in sight of the shopping complex where Nesha hopes to find her bread. It looks dingy and disused, but already people are milling around outside. In their dark winter clothes, they form an amorphous, weary mass. Our premier smiles down on them from the looming side of an apartment tower, his lips moving but no sound coming out. Seagulls have pecked away at him, attracted by the flickering colors, flaking away huge pieces of his face.

"If the musical box was in the Matryoshka, then I was right about its origin," Nesha says. "It did come from the future after all."

"They never believed you. They never wanted to believe you."

She glances up at the birdshit-stained edifice, the premier's moving face. "We live in a flawless collectivized utopia. But a flawless society can't, by definition, evolve. If it proceeds from one state to another, there must have been something wrong, or sub-optimal, about it. If it gets worse, then the seeds of that worsening must have already been present. It gets better, than it has room for improvement."

"It all ends," I say, keeping my voice low. "In less than a human lifetime. That's what I learned inside the Matryoshka. That and the fact that you were right all along."

"The musical box won't make any difference."

"Except now you know."

"There was never any doubt in my mind. Not even in the darkest days, when they punished me through Gennadi." Nesha walks on a few paces. "But still. It was always only a hypothesis. To have firm proof that I was right . . . it does make a difference, to me."

"That's all I ever wanted. I felt that we owed you that much. I'm just sorry it took me so long to reach you."

"You did your best, Dimitri. You got to me in the end." Then she reaches into her pocket again and takes out the change she's saved for the bread.

"Clear," I called from the porthole, as we undocked. "Five meters. Ten meters. Fifteen." The rest of the ship came into view, silvery under its untidy-looking quilt of reflective foil. It was a bittersweet moment. I'd been looking forward to getting this view for months, but I'd always assumed it would be at mission's end, as we were about to ride the Soyuz back into Earth's atmosphere.

"Lining us up," Galenka said. She was in the command seat, wearing her EVA suit but with the helmet and gloves not yet in place.

I felt the Soyuz wheel around me as it orientated itself towards the Matryoshka. We'd be following the Progress all the way in, relying on the same collision-avoidance algorithm that had worked so well before. I kept telling myself that there was no reason for it to stop working now, just because we were aboard, but I couldn't quell my fears. My nerves had been frayed even when it had just been the robot at stake. I kept thinking of that American probe sliced in two, coming apart in two perfectly severed halves. How would it feel, I wondered, if we ran into one of those infinitely-sharp field lines? Would we even notice it at first? Would there even be pain, or just a sudden cold numbness from half our bodies?

As it was, we sailed through Shell 1 and Shell 2 without incident. All the while we remained in contact with the *Tereshkova*, and all the while the *Tereshkova* remained in contact with the microsat swarm. As windows opened and closed in Shell 3, the Progress reported on its continued existence and functionality. Nothing had happened to it since our departure. It was stuck, but otherwise operational and undamaged.

I clutched at every crumb of comfort. The Matryoshka hadn't touched the robot. It hadn't shown any sign of having noticed it. Didn't that bode well for us? If it didn't object to one foreign object, there was no reason for it to object to another, especially if we took pains not to get stuck ourselves.

Galenka brought us to a hovering standstill above Shell 3. In the microgravity environment of the Matryoshka the Soyuz only needed to exert a whisper of thrust from its attitude motors to hold station.

"You'd better get buckled in, Dimitri. When a window opens, I'm giving her the throttle. It'll feel like a booster separation, only harder."

I made sure I was tight in my seat. "I'm ready. How long do you think?"

"No idea. Just be ready for it when it comes."

The glass cockpit of the Soyuz was much more advanced than the basic frame of the ship itself, which was older than my grandmother. Before our departure, Galenka had configured the sensors and readouts to emulate the same telemetry she'd been seeing from the Progress. Now all she had to do was watch the scrolling, chattering indications for the auguries of an opening window. She'd have no more than a second or two to assess whether it was a window she could reach in time, given the Soyuz's capabilities. Deciding that there was nothing I could contribute to the matter, I closed my eyes and waited for the moment.

No matter what happened now, we had made history. We were inside the Matryoshka–the first humans to have made it this far. It had taken three apparitions to achieve this feat. Once, I would have assumed that things would only go from strength to strength with each new return. By the time of the fourth apparition, surely there'd be a permanent human presence out here, following the Matryoshka throughout its orbit. Study stations, research facilities–an entire campus, floating in vacuum.

Now I wondered if anyone would come after us. The space effort was winding down–even the *Tereshkova* was cobbled together from the bits of earlier, failed enterprises. It seemed to me–though I would never have voiced such a conviction publicly–that it was less important to my country what we found out here, than that we were seen to be doing something no one else could. The scientific returns were almost incidental. Next time, would anyone even bother sending out a ship?

"Brace," Galenka said.

The thrust came hard, like a hoof kick to the spine. It was worst than any booster separation, stage ignition or deorbit burn. I had experienced re-entry gee-loads that were enough to push me to the brink of unconsciousness, but those forces had built up slowly, over several minutes. This came instantly, and for a moment I felt as if no bone in my body could possibly have survived unbroken.

Then I realized that I was all right. The engine was still burning, but at least the gee-load was a steady pressure now, like a firm hand rather than a fist.

"We are good for insertion," Galenka said, as if that had ever been in doubt.

We sailed through the two closely-packed shells, into the luminous blue-green interstitial space above Shell 4. Once we were clear–with the window sealing above us–Galenka did a somersault roll to use the main engine to slow us down again. The thrust burst was longer and less brutal this time. She dropped our speed from hundreds of meters per second to what was only slightly faster than walking pace. The thicket lay ahead or below, depending on my mental orientation. We were making good time. There was no need to rush things now.

Maybe, just maybe, we'd get away with this.

A screen flashed red and began scrolling with error messages. "There goes the *Tereshkova*," Galenka said. "We're out of contact now." She gave me a fierce grin. "Just you and me, and an impenetrable shell of alien matter between us and the outside world. Starting to feel claustrophobic yet?"

"I'd be insane not to. Do we have a fix on the Progress?"

She jabbed a finger at another readout–target cross-hairs against a moving grid. "Dead ahead, where she said she was. Judging by the data she recorded before getting stuck, we'll be able to get within 200 meters without difficulty. I won't risk taking the Soyuz any closer, but we should be able to cover the remaining distance in suits."

"Whatever it takes." I checked my watch, strapped around the sleeve of my suit. We'd been out from the mother ship for less than three and a half hours–well ahead of schedule. We had air and fuel to spare, but I still wanted to be out of here as quickly as possible. I kept thinking of that iron ceiling overhead. "How soon until we're in position?" I asked.

"Twenty minutes, give or take."

"We spend two hours on station. Nothing changes that. If we don't succeed in unloading everything, we still leave. Are we clear on that?"

"This was your idea, Dimitri. You decide when we leave."

"I'm going to finish suiting up. We'll check comms and life-support thoroughly before we leave. And we'll make damned sure the Soyuz isn't going to drift away from us."

Galenka's estimate was on the nail. Twenty minutes later we were deep into the thicket, with blue-green structures crowding around us. Closest to us was a trunk or branch with thornlike protrusions. Galenka brought the Soyuz in against the trunk until the hull shuddered with the contact. Ordinarily I'd have been worried about a pressure rupture, but now that we were both wearing helmets that was only a distant concern. Galenka had picked her spot well, for the Soyuz was resting on one of the out-jutting thorns. Friction, and the ship's almost negligible weight, would serve to hold it in place until we were ready to leave. Galenka had even taken to pains to make sure the forward escape hatch was not blocked.

"Maybe you should stay here, while I check out the Progress," I said. I didn't feel heroic, but it seemed the right thing to say.

"If we have to unload it, it'll go quicker with two of us," Galenka responded. "We can form a supply chain, save going all the way back each time. And keep an eye on each other." She unbuckled. "You ready for this? I'm going to vent our air."

She let the air drain out through the release valve before opening the hatch. As the cabin transitioned to vacuum my suit ballooned around me, the seals and joints creaking with the pressure differential. I'd checked everything, but I was all too conscious of the thin membranes of fabric protecting me from a nasty, lung-freezing death. Every gesture, every movement, was now more awkward, more potentially hazardous than before. Tear a glove on sharp metal, and you might as well have cut your hand off.

Galenka popped the hatch. I pushed these concerns from my mind as best I could and climbed out of the Soyuz. Now that I was seeing the alien environment with my own eyes–through a thin glass visor, rather than a thick porthole or monitor–it appeared much larger, much more oppressive and strange. The all-enveloping shell was a pitiless, hope-crushing black. I told myself that a window would eventually open for us to leave, just as one had allowed us to enter. But it was hard to shake the feeling that we were little warm animals, little shivering mammals with fast heartbeats, caught in a cold dark trap that we had just sprung.

"Let's do this shit, and get back home," Galenka said, pushing past me.

We climbed down the pea-green flank of the Soyuz, using the handholds that had been bolted on for weightless operations. We left the ship with the hatch open, the last dribbles of air still venting from the hull. My feet touched the thorn. Although I had almost no weight to speak of, the surface felt solid under me. It was formed from the same translucent material as the rest of Shell 4, but it wasn't as slippery as glass or ice. I reached out a hand and steadied myself against the trunk. I felt as if I was touching bark or rock through my glove.

"I think we can do this," I said.

"The Progress should be directly under us, where this trunk constricts against the one over here. I'd rather climb than drift, if that's okay with you."

"Agreed. There are thorns all the way down, spaced every three or four meters–we should be able to use them for grabs, even if we can't get traction on the rest of it. It shouldn't be much harder coming back up."

"I'm right behind you."

If the thicket registered our presence, there was no evidence of it. The structure loomed around us, dizzying in its scale and complexity, but giving no sign of being alive or responsive to the intrusion of human technology. I began to ease, trying to imagine myself in a forest or cave system–something huge but mindless–rather than the glowing guts of an alien machine.

It took fifteen minutes of cautious progress to reach the lodged Progress. It was jammed in nose first, with the engine pointing at us. A ship like that was not normally a man-rated vehicle, but the usual variants had a hatch at the front, so that space station crews could enter the vehicle when it was docked. In the case of ours, the innards had been replaced by scientific gear, computers, additional fuel, and batteries. The docking hatch had become a kind of mouth by which the robot could feed samples into itself, using the feeler-like appendages of its sampling devices. Inside was a robotic system which sorted the samples, fed them into miniature laboratories where appropriate, and delivered whatever was left into a storage volume just ahead of the fuel tanks. We couldn't have got in through the mouth even if the Progress hadn't been jammed in nose first, but that didn't matter. A secondary hatch and docking assembly had been installed in the side, so that the sample compartment could be unloaded through the *Tereshkova*'s own docking port. Galenka, who had overtaken me in our descent from the Soyuz, was the first to reach the sample hatch. The hatch controls were designed to be opened by someone in a suit. She worked the heavy toggles until the hatch swung open, exposing the non-pressurised storage compartment. The hole in the side of the Progress was just large for a suited person to crawl through. Without hesitation she grabbed yellow handholds and levered herself inside. A few moments later the chamber lit up with the wavering light of her helmet-mounted flashlamp.

"Talk to me, Galenka."

"It's all racked and sorted, Dimitri. Must be about half a ton of stuff in here already. Some of the chunks are pretty big. Still warm, too. Going to be a bitch of a job moving all of them back to the Soyuz."

"We'll take what we can; that was always the idea. If nothing else we should make sure we've got unique samples from both Shell 1 and Shell 2."

"I'm going to try and bring out the first chunk. I'll pass it through the hatch. Be ready."

"I'm here."

But as I said that, a status panel lit up on the side of my faceplate. "Comms burst from *Tereshkova*," I said, as alphanumeric gibberish scrolled past. "A window must just have opened."

"Feeling better now?"

"Guess it's nice to know the windows are still behaving."

"I could have told you they would." Galenka grunted with the effort of dislodging the sample she had selected. "So–any news?"

"Nothing. Just a carrier signal, trying to establish contact with us. Means the ship's still out there, though."

"I could have told you that as well."

It took 20 minutes to convey one sample back to the Soyuz. Doing it as a relay didn't help–it took two of us to nurse the object between us, all the while making sure we didn't drift away from the structure. Things got a little faster after that. We returned to the jammed Progress in good time and only took 15 minutes to get the second sample back to our ship. We now had pieces of Shell 1 and Shell 2 aboard, ready to be taken back home.

A voice at the back of my head said that we should quit while we were ahead. We'd salvaged something from this mess–almost certainly enough to placate Baikonur. We had taken a risk and it had paid off. But there was still more than an hour remaining of the time I had allowed us. If we moved quickly and efficiently–and we were already beginning to settle into a rhythm–we could recover three or four additional samples before it was time to start our journey back. Who knew what difference five or six samples might make, compared to two?

"Just for the record," Galenka said, when we reached the Progress again, "I'm getting itchy feet here."

"We've still got time. Two more. Then we'll see how we're doing."

"You were a lot more jumpy until that window opened."

She was right. I couldn't deny it.

I was thinking of that when another comms burst came through. For a moment I was gladdened–just seeing the scroll of numbers and symbols, even if it meant nothing to me, made me feel closer to the *Tereshkova.* Home was just three shells and a sprint across vacuum away. Almost close enough to touch, like the space station that had sped across the sky over Klushino, when my father held me on his shoulders.

"Dimitri," crackled a voice. "Galenka. Yakov here. I hope you can hear me."

"What is it, friend?" I asked, hearing an edge in his voice I didn't like.

"You'd better listen carefully–we could get cut off at any moment. Baikonur detected a change in the Matryoshka–a big one. Shell 1 pulsations have increased in amplitude and frequency. It's like nothing anyone's seen since the first apparition. Whatever you two are doing in there–it's having an effect. The thing is waking. You need to think about getting out, while the collision-avoidance algorithm will still get you through Shell 1. Those pulsations change anymore, the algorithm won't be any use."

"He could be lying," Galenka said. "Saying whatever he needs to say that get us to go back."

"I'm not lying. I want you to come back. And I want that Soyuz back so that at least one of us can get home."

"I think we'd better move," I said.

"The remaining samples?"

"Leave them. Let's just get back to the ship as quickly as possible."

As I spoke, the comms window blipped out. Galenka pushed away from the Progress. I levered myself onto the nearest thorn and started climbing. It was quicker now that we didn't have to carry anything between us. I thought of the changing conditions in Shell 1 and hoped that we'd still be able to pick a path through the lethal, shifting maze of field-lines.

We were half way to the Soyuz–I could see it overhead, tantalising near–when Galenka halted, only just below me.

"We're in trouble," she said.

"That's why we have to keep on moving."

"Something's coming up from below. We're not going to make it, Dimitri. It's rising too quickly."

I looked down and saw what she meant. We couldn't see

the Progress anymore. It was lost under a silver tide, a sea of gleaming mercury climbing slowly through the thicket, swallowing everything as it rose.

"Climb," I said.

"We aren't going to make it. It's coming too damned fast."

I gritted my teeth: typical Galenka, pragmatic to the end. But even she had resumed her ascent, unable to stop her body from doing what her mind knew to be futile. She was right, too. The tide was going to envelope us long before we reached the Soyuz. But I couldn't stop climbing either. I risked a glance down and saw the silver fluid lapping at Galenka's heels, then surging up to swallow her lowest boot.

"It's got me."

"Keep moving."

She pulled the boot free, reached the next thorn, and for a moment it appeared that she might be capable of out-running the fluid. My mind raced ahead to the Soyuz, realizing that even if we got there in time, even if we got inside and sealed the hatch, we wouldn't be able to get the ship aloft in time.

Then the fluid took more of Galenka. It lapped to her thighs, then her waist. She slowed her climb.

"It's pulling me back," she said, grunting with the effort. "It's trying to pull me in."

"Fight it."

Maybe she did–it was hard to tell, with her movements so impeded. The tide consumed her to the chest, taking her backpack, then absorbed her helmet. She had one hand raised above her head, grasping for the next thorn. The tide took it.

"Galenka."

"I'm here." She came through indistinctly, comms crackling with static. "I'm in it now. I can't see anything. But I can still move, still breathe. It's like being in the immersion tank."

"Try and keep climbing."

"Picking up some suit faults now. Fluid must be interfering with the electronics, with the cooling system." She faded out, came back, voice crazed with pops and crackles and hisses. "Oh, God. It's inside. I can feel it. It's cold, against my skin. Rising through the suit. How the fuck did it get in?"

She faded.

"Galenka. Talk to me."

"In my helmet now. Oh, God. Oh, God. It's still rising. I'm going to drown, Dimitri. This is not right. I did not want to fucking *drown*."

"Galenka?"

I heard a choked scream, then a gurgle. Then nothing.

I kept climbing, while knowing it was useless. The tide reached me a few moments later. It swallowed me and then found a way into my suit, just as it had with Galenka.

Then it found a way into my head.

But neither of us drowned.

There was a moment of absolute terror as it forced its way down my throat, through my eye sockets, nose and ears. The drowning reflex kicked in, and then it was over. Not terror, no panic, just blissful unconsciousness.

Until I woke up on my back.

The silver tide was abating. It had left our bodies, left the inside of our suits. It was draining off them in chrome rivulets, leaving them dry and undamaged. We were lying like upended turtles, something like Earth-normal gravity pinning us to the floor. It took all my effort to lever myself into a sitting position, and then to stand up, fighting the weight of my backpack as it tried to drag me down. My suit was no longer ballooning out, suggesting that we were in some kind of pressurized environment.

I looked around, taking deep, normal breaths.

Galenka and I had arrived in a chamber, a huge iron-gray room with gill-like sluice vents in the side walls. The fluid was rushing out through the vents, exposing a floor of slightly twinkling black, like polished marble. Gray-blue light poured down through hexagonal grids in the arched ceiling. I wasn't going to take any chances on it being breathable.

I inspected the outer covering for tears or abrasions, but it looked as good as when I'd worn it.

"Galenka," I said. "Can you hear me?"

"Loud and clear, Dimitri." I heard her voice on the helmet radio, but also coming through the glass, muffled but comprehensible. "Whatever we just went through–I don't think it hurt our suits."

"Do you still have air?"

"According to the gauge, good for another six hours."

"How do you feel?"

"Like I've been scrubbed inside with caustic soda. But otherwise–I'm alright. Clear-headed, like I've just woken up after a really slong sleep. I actually feel better, more alert, than before we left the Soyuz."

"That's how I feel," I said. "Where do you think we are?"

"The heart of it. The middle of the Matryoshka. Where else could we be? It must have brought us here for a reason."

"To analyze us. To assess the foreign objects it detected, then to work out how best to recycle or dispose of them."

"Maybe. But then why keep us alive? It must recognize that we're living. It must recognize that we're thinking beings."

"Always the optimist, Dimitri."

"Something's happening. Look."

A bar of light had cut across the base of part of the wall. It was becoming taller, as if a seamless door was opening upwards. The light ramming through the widening gap was the same gray-blue that came through the ceiling. Both of us tensing, expecting to be squashed out of existence at any moment, we turned to face whatever awaited us.

Beyond was a kind of corridor, sloping down in a gently steepening arc, so that the end was not visible except as an intensification of that silvery glow. The inwardly-sloping walls of the corridor–rising to a narrow spine of a ceiling–were dense with intricately carved details, traced in the blue-gray light.

"I think we should walk," Galenka said, barely raising her voice above a whisper.

We started moving, taking stiff, slow paces in our EVA suits. We passed through the door, into the corridor. We started descending the curved ramp of the floor. Though I should have been finding it harder and harder to keep my footing, I had no sense that I was on a steepening grade. I looked at Galenka and she was still walking upright, at right angles to the surface of the floor. I paused to turn around, but already the room we had been in was angled out of view, with the door beginning to lower back down.

"Do you hear that sound?" Galenka asked.

I had been about to say the same thing. Over the huff and puff of our suit circulators it was not the easiest thing to make out. But there was a low droning noise, like the bass note of an organ. It was coming from all around us, from the very fabric of the Matryoshka. It sustained a note for many seconds before changing pitch. As we walked we heard a pattern of notes repeat, with subtle variations. I couldn't piece together the tune, if indeed there was one–it was too slow, too deep for that–but I didn't think I was hearing the random emanations of some mindless mechanical process.

"It's music," I said. "Slowed down almost to death. But it's still music."

"Look at the walls, Dimitri."

They were astonishing. The walls had been carved with a hypnotically detailed mazelike pattern, one that I could never quite get into focus. Edges and ridges of the pattern pushed out centimeters from the wall, into the corridor. I felt a strange impulse to reach out and touch, as if there was a magnetic attraction working on my fingers. Even as I acknowledged this impulse, Galenka–walking to my left–reached out her left hand and skirted the pattern on her side. She flinched and withdrew her gloved fingers with a gasp of something that could have been pain or astonishment or simple childlike delight.

"What?" I asked.

"I just got . . . I can't describe it, Dimitri. It was like–everything."

"Everything what?"

"Everything trying to get into my head. Everything at once. Like the whole universe gatecrashing my brain. It wasn't unpleasant. It was just–too much."

I reached out my hand.

"Be careful."

I touched the wall. My head began to split open with an infusion of crystalline knowledge. It was clean and brittle and virescent green, like the petal of a flower dipped in liquid nitrogen. I could feel the mental sutures straining under the pressure. I flinched back, just as Galenka had done. There could not have been more than an instant of contact, but the information that had gushed through was ringing in my skull like the after-chime of God's own church bell.

A window of comprehension had opened and slammed shut again. I was dizzy with what it had shown me. I already knew more about the Matryoshka than I had before. I already knew more than any other living person, with the possible exception of Galenka.

"It's come from the future," I said.

"I got that as well."

"They sent it here. They sent it here to carry a message to us."

I knew these things with an unimpeachable certainty, but I had no additional context for the knowledge. What future, by whom? From how far ahead, and to what purpose? What message? How had it arrived?

I couldn't stand not knowing. Now that I knew part of the truth, I needed it all.

I reached out my hand again, caressed the wall. It hit me harder this time, but the instinct to flinch away, the instinct to close my mind, was not as strong. The crystalline rush made me gasp. There couldn't be room in my head for all that was being pumped into it, and yet it continued without interruption. Layers of wisdom poured into me, cooling and stratifying like ancient rock. My head felt like a boulder perched on my shoulders. I laughed: it was the only possible response, other than screaming terror. The flow continued, increasing in pressure.

This much I understood:

The Matryoshka was a complex machine. It was layered because it had no choice but to be. Each layer was a form of armor or camouflage or passkey, evolved organically to enable it to slip through the threshing clockwork of a cosmic time machine. That time machine was older than Earth. It had been constructed by alien minds and then added to and modified by successive intelligences.

In the future, humanity found it.

At its ticking, whirling core was a necklace of neutron stars. It had been known since our own era that a sufficiently long, sufficiently dense, sufficiently fast-rotating cylinder had the property of twisting spacetime around itself until a path into the past became possible. Such a path–a mathematical trajectory in space, like an orbit–could take a signal or object to any previous point in time, provided it was no earlier than the moment of the time machine's construction.

Constructing such a machine was not child's play.

A single neutron star could be made to have the requisite density and spin, but it lacked the necessary axial elongation. To overcome this, the machine's builders had approximated a cylinder by stringing 441 neutron stars together until they were almost touching, like beads on a wire. An open-ended string would have collapsed under its own appalling self-gravity, so the ends had been bent around and joined, with the entire ensemble revolving fast enough to stabilize the neutron stars against falling inward. It still wasn't a cylinder, but locally–as far as a photon or vehicle near the necklace was concerned–it might as well have been.

The machine had catapulted the Matryoshka into the prehuman past of our galaxy. The insertion into time-reversed flight, the passage through the various filters and barriers installed to prevent illicit use of the ancient machinery, the exit back into normal timeflow, had caused eleven additional layers of shell to be sacrificed. What we saw of the Matryoshka was just the scarred kernel of what had once been a much larger entity.

But it had survived. It had come through, albeit overshooting its target era by many millions of years. Yet that had been allowed for; it was easier to leap back into the deep past and crawl forward in time than to achieve a bullseye into a relatively recent era. The emergence event was indeed the opening of a local wormhole throat, but only so that the Matryoshka (which incorporated wormhole-manipulating machinery in Shells 1 and 2) could complete the last leg of its journey.

How far downstream had it come? A hundred years? A thousand years? Five thousand?

I couldn't tell. The knowledge told me everything, but not all of that wisdom was framed in terms I could readily decode. But I could sense a thread, a sense of connectedness between the era of the Matryoshka and our own. They knew a lot about us.

Enough to know that we had made a terrible mistake.

At last I jerked my hand away from the wall. The urge to return it was almost overwhelming, but I could only take so much in one go.

"Dimitri?"

"I'm here."

"I thought you were gone for a while there."

I turned to face my comrade. Against the vastness I had been shown, the cosmic scale of the history I had almost glimpsed, Galenka appeared no more substantial than a paper cut-out. She was just a human being, translucent with her own insubstantiality, pinned in this one moving instant like dirt on a conveyor belt. It took moments for my sense of scale to normalize; to realize that, for all that the machine had shown me, I was just like her.

"They sent it back for us," I said. The words came out in a rush, and yet at the same time each syllable consumed an eternity of time and effort. "To show us how we've gone wrong. There's history here–lots of it. In these walls. Mountains, chasms, of data."

"You need to slow your breathing. That silver stuff that got into us–it's primed us in some way, hasn't it? Rewired our minds so that the Matryoshka can get into them?"

"I think–maybe. Yes."

"Get a grip, Dimitri. We still need to get home."

I made to touch the wall again. The urge was still there, the hunger–the vacuum in my head–returning. The Matryoshka still had more to tell me. It was not done with Dimitri Ivanov.

"Don't," Galenka said, with a firmness that stopped my hand. "Not now. Not until we've seen the rest of this place."

At her urging I resisted. I found that if kept to the middle of the corridor, it wasn't as bad. But the walls were still whispering to me, inviting me to stroke my hand against them.

"The Second Soviet," I said.

"What about it?"

"It falls. Fifty years from now, maybe sixty. Somewhere near the end of the century. I saw it in the history." I paused and swallowed hard. "This road we're on–this path. It's not the right one. We took a wrong turn, somewhere between the first and second apparitions. But by the time we realize it, by the time the Soviet falls, it's too late. Not just for Russia, but for Earth. For humankind."

"It came from our future. Even I felt that, and I only touched it briefly."

"There's a darkness between then and now. Like a black river we have to cross. A bad, dark time. A bottleneck. Humanity survives, but only just. It's something to do with the Second Soviet, and turning away from space. That's the mistake. When the darkness comes, it's because we've turned away from space travel. Something comes and we aren't ready for it."

We were still walking, following the arcing downslope of the corridor, towards the silver-blue radiance at its end. "The Second Soviet is the only political organization still doing space travel. If anything we're the ones holding the candle."

"It's not enough. Now that the other nations have abandoned their efforts, we have to do more than just subsist. And if we are holding the candle, it won't be for much longer."

"The Second Soviet won't like being told it's a mistake of history."

There was a fierce dryness in my throat. "It can't ignore the message in the Matryoshka. Not now."

"I wouldn't be too sure about that. But you know something, Dimitri?"

"What?"

"If this thing is from the future–from our future–then maybe it's Russian as well. Or sent back to meet Russians. Which might mean that Nesha Petrova was right after all."

"They should tell her," I said.

"I'm sure it'll be the first thing on their minds, after they've spent all these years crushing and humiliating her." Galenka fell silent for a few paces. "It's like they always knew, isn't it."

"They couldn't have."

"But they knew enough to want her to be wrong. A message from the future, intended for us? What could *we* possibly need to hear from our descendants, except their undying gratitude?"

"Everything we say is being logged on our suit recorders," I said. "Logged and compressed and stored, so that it can be sent back to the Soyuz and then back to the *Tereshkova*, and then back to Baikonur."

"Right now, comrade, there are several things I give more than a damn about than arsehole of a party official listening to what I have to say."

I smiled, because that was exactly how I felt as well.

In 60 years the Second Soviet was dust. The history I had absorbed told me that nothing could prevent that. Accelerate it, yes–and maybe the arrival of the Matryoshka would do just that–but not prevent it. They could crucify us and it wouldn't change anything.

It was a crumb of consolation.

The corridor widened, the intricate walls flanking away on either side, until we reached a domed room of cathedral proportions. The chamber was round, easily a hundred meters across, with a domed ceiling. I saw no way in or out other than the way we had come. There was a jagged design in the floor, worked in white and black marble–rapier-thin shards radiating from the middle.

The music intensified–rising in pitch, rising in speed. If there was a tune there it was almost on the point of being comprehensible. I had a mental image of a rushing winter landscape, under white skies.

"This is it, then," Galenka said. "An empty fucking room. After all this." She took a hesitant step towards the middle, then halted.

"Wait," I said.

Something was happening.

The black and white shards were pulling back from the middle, sliding invisibly into the floor's circular border, a star-shaped blackness opening up in the center. It all happened silently, with deathly slowness. Galenka stepped back, the two of us standing side by side. When the star had widened to ten or twelve meters across, the floor stopped moving. Smoothly, silently, something rose from the darkness. It was a plinth, and there was a figure on the plinth, lying down with his face to the domed ceiling. Beneath the plinth, icy with frost, was a thick tangle of pipes and coiling, intestinal machinery. We stood and watched it in silence, neither of us ready to make the first move. There was a tingle in my head that was not quite a headache just now, but which promised to become one.

The floor began to slide back into place, the jagged blades locking beneath the plinth. There was now an uninterrupted surface between the resting figure and us. Galenka and I glanced at each other through our visors then began a slow, measured walk. The slope-sided plinth rose two meters from the floor, putting the reclining figure just above our heads. It hadn't moved, or shown the least sign of life, since emerging through the floor.

We reached the plinth. There was a kind of ledge or step in the side, allowing us to bring our heads level with the figure. We stood looking at it, saying nothing, the silence only punctuated by the labored, bellows-like sound of our air circulators.

That it was human had been obvious from the moment the plinth rose. The shape of the head, the ribbed chest, the placement and articulation of the limbs–it was all too familiar to be alien. Anyway, I knew that something descended from us–something essentially human–had sent back the Matryoshka. My bright new memories told me now that I was seeing the pilot, the navigator that had steered the artifact through the vicious barbs of the booby-trapped time machine, and then up through time, skipping through a cascade of wormholes, to our present era. The pilot was ghostly pale, wraithe-thin and naked, lying on a white metallic couch or rack that at first glance appeared to be an apparatus of torture or savage restraint. But then I decided that the apparatus was merely the control and life-support interface for the pilot. It was what had kept him alive, and what had given him the reins of the vast, layered machine it was his duty to steer and safeguard.

I sensed that the journey had not been a short one. In the Matryoshka's reference frame, it had consumed centuries of subjective time. The pilot, bio-modified for longevity and uninterrupted consciousness, had experienced every howling second of his voyage. That had always been the intention.

But something had gone wrong. A miscalculation, a problem with the injection into the time machine. Or the emergence, or the wormhole skip. Something I couldn't grasp, except in the nature of its outcome. The journey wasn't supposed to have taken this long.

"The pilot went mad."

"You know this for a fact," Galenka said.

"You'd think this was a punishment–to be put inside the Matryoshka, alone, hurled back in time. But in fact it was the highest honor imaginable. They glorified him. He was entrusted with a mission of unimaginable importance."

"To change their past?"

"No. They were stuck with what they already had. You can change someone else's past, but not your own. That's how time travel works. We have a different future now–one that won't necessarily include the people who built the Matryoshka. But they did it for us, not themselves. To redeem one possible history, even if they couldn't mend their own. And he paid for that with his sanity."

Galenka was silent for long moments. I surveyed the figure, taking in more of the details. Had he been standing, he would have towered over both of us. His arms were by his sides–his hands were small and boyish, out of proportion to the rest of him. His fists were clenched. The emaciated form was partly machine. The couch extended parts of itself into his body. Glowing blue lines slipped into orifices and punctured his flesh at a dozen points. Hard, non-biological forms bulged under drum-tight flesh. His eye sockets were stuffed with faceted blue crystals, radiating a spray of glowing fibers. There was something not quite right about the shape of his skull, as if some childhood deformity had never healed in the right way. It was hairless, papered over with translucent, finely veined skin. His lips were a bloodless gash.

"The music," Galenka said, breaking the reverence. "You think it's coming from his head, don't you?"

"I think music must have comforted him during his journey. Somewhere along the way, though, it swallowed up his mind. It's locked in a loop, endlessly repeating. He's like a rat in a wheel, going round and round. By the time he came out of the wormhole, there couldn't have been enough left of him to finish the mission."

"He made the Matryoshka sing."

"It might have been the last thing he did, before the madness took over completely. The last message he could get through to us. He knew how alien the artifact would have appeared to us, with its shells of camouflage and disguise. He made it sing, thinking we'd understand. A human signal, a sign that we shouldn't fear it. That no matter how alien it appeared on the outside, there was something human at the heart. A message for the species, a last chance not to screw things up."

"Would it have killed him to use radio?"

"He had to get it through Shell 3, remember–not to mention how many shells we've come through since Shell 4. Maybe it just wasn't possible. Maybe the simplest thing really was to have the Matryoshka sing itself to us. After all, it's not as if someone didn't notice in the end."

"Or maybe he was just insane, and the music's just a side-effect."

"That's also a possibility," I said.

The impulse that had drawn my hand towards the patterned wall seemed to compel me to reach out and touch the pilot. I was moving my arm when the figure twitched, convulsing within the constraints of the couch. The blue lines strained like ropes in a squall. I jerked in my suit, nerves battling with curiosity. The figure was still again, but something about it had changed.

"Either it just died," Galenka said, "or it just came back to life. You want to take a guess, Dimitri?"

I said nothing. It was all I could do to stare at the pilot. His chest wasn't moving, and I doubted that there was a heart beating inside that ribcage. But something was different.

The pilot's head turned. The movement was glacially slow, more like a flower following the sun than the movement of an animal. It must have cost him an indescribable effort just to look at us. I could read no expression in the tight mask of his face or the blue facets of his eyes. But I knew we had his full attention.

The gash of his lips opened. He let out a long, slow sigh.

"You made it," I said. "You completed your mission."

Perhaps it was my imagination–I would never know for certain–but it seemed to me then that the head nodded a fraction, as if acknowledging what I had said. As if thanking me for bringing this news.

Then there was another gasp of air–longer, this time. It had something of death about it. The eyes were still looking at me, but all of a sudden I didn't sense any intellect behind them. I wondered if the pilot had conserved some last flicker of sanity for the time when he had visitors–just enough selfhood to die knowing whether he had succeeded or failed.

Tension exited the body. The head lolled back into the frame, looking sideways. His arm slumped to the side, dangling over the side of the plinth. The fist relaxed, letting something small and metallic drop to the floor.

I reached down and picked up the item, taking it as gingerly I could in my suit gloves. It was a tiny metal box with a handle in the side and I stared down at it as if it was the most alien thing in the universe. Which, in that moment, I think it probably was.

"A keepsake," I said, wondering aloud. "Something he was allowed to bring with him from the future. Something as ancient as the world he was aiming for. Something that must have been centuries old when he began his journey."

"Maybe," Galenka said.

I closed my own fist around the musical box. It was a simple human trinket, the most innocent of machines. I wanted to take my gloves off, to find out what it played. But I wondered if I already knew.

A little later the chrome tide came to wash us away again.

The men are waiting next to Nesha's apartment when we return with her bread. I never saw their Zil, if that was how they arrived. There are three of them. They all have heavy black coats on, with black leather gloves. The two burlier men–whose faces mean nothing to me–have hats on, the brims dusted with snow. The third man isn't wearing a hat, although he has a pale blue scarf around his throat. He's thinner than the others, with a shaven, bullet-shaped head and small round glasses that bestow a look somewhere between professorial and ascetic. Something about his face is familiar; I feel that we've known each other somewhere before. He's taking a cigarette out of a packet when our eyes lock. It's the same contraband variety I used to buy on my ride into town.

"This is my fault," I say to Nesha. "I didn't mean to bring these men here."

"We've come to take you back to the facility," the bald man says, pausing to ignite the cigarette from a miniature lighter. "Quite frankly, I didn't expect to find you alive. I can't tell you what a relief it is to find you."

"Do I know you?"

"Of course you know me. I'm Doctor Grechko. We've spent a lot of time together at the facility."

"I'm not going back. You know that by now."

"I beg to differ." He takes a long drag on the cigarette. "You're coming with us. You'll thank me for it eventually, I assure you." He nods at one of the hatted men, who reaches into his coat pocket and extracts a syringe with a plastic cap on the needle. The man pinches the cap between his gloved fingers and removes it. He holds the syringe to eye level, taps away bubbles and presses the plunger to squirt out a few drops of whatever's inside.

The railing along the balcony is very low. We're nine floors up, and although there's snow on the ground, it won't do much to cushion my fall. I've done what I came to do, so what's to prevent me from taking my own life, in preference to being taken back to the facility?

"I'm sorry I brought this on you," I tell Nesha, and make to lift myself over the railing. My resolve at that moment was total. I'm surrendered to the fall, ready for white annihilation. I want the music in my head to end. Death and silence, for eternity.

But I'm not fast enough, or my resolve isn't as total as I imagine. The other hatted man rushes to me and locks his massive hand around my arm. The other one moves closer with the syringe.

"Not just yet," Doctor Grechko–if that was his name–says. "He's safe now, but keep a good grip on him."

"What happens to Nesha?" I ask.

Grechko looks at her, then shakes his head. "There's no harm in talking to a madwoman, Georgi. Whatever you may have told her, she'll confuse it with all that rubbish she already believes. No worse than telling secrets to a dog. And even if she didn't, no one would listen to her. Really, she isn't worth our inconvenience. You, on the other hand, are extraordinarily valuable to us."

Something's wrong. I feel an icebreaker cutting through my brain.

"My name isn't Georgi."

Doctor Grechko nods solemnly. "No matter what you may currently believe, you are Doctor Georgi Kizim. You're even wearing his coat. Look in the pocket if you doubt me–there's a good chance you still have his security pass."

"No," I insist. "I am not Georgi Kizim. I know that man,

but I'm not him. I just took his coat, so that I could escape. I am the cosmonaut, Dimitri Ivanov. I was on the *Tereshkova.* I went into the Matryoshka."

"No," Doctor Grechko corrects patiently. "You are not Ivanov. You are not the cosmonaut. He was–is, to a degree–your patient. You were assigned to treat him, to learn what you could. Unfortunately, the protocol was flawed. We thought we could prevent a repeat of what happened with Yakov, but we were wrong. You began to identify too strongly with your patient, just as Doctor Malyshev began to identify with Yakov. We still don't understand the mechanism, but after the business with Malyshev we thought we'd put in enough safeguards to stop it happening twice. Clearly, we were wrong about that. Even with Ivanov in his vegetative state . . ."

"I am Ivanov," I say, but with a chink of doubt opening inside me.

"Maybe you should look in the coat," Nesha says.

My fingers numb with cold, I dig into the pocket until I touch the hard edge of his security pass. The hatted man's still keeping a good hold on my arm. I pass the white plastic rectangle to Nesha. She squints, holding it at arm's length, studying the little hologram.

"It's you," she says. "There's no doubt."

I shake my head. "There's been a mistake. Our files mixed up. I'm not Doctor Kizim. I remember being on that ship, everything that happened."

"Only because you spent so much time in his presence," Grechko says, not without compassion. "After Dimitri fell into the intermittent vegetative state, we considered the risks of contamination to be significantly reduced. We relaxed the safeguards."

"I am not Doctor Kizim."

"You are. Just as Malyshev believed he was Yakov, you believe you're Ivanov. But you'll come out of it, Georgi–trust me. We got Malyshev back in the end. It was traumatic, but eventually his old personality resurfaced. Now he remembers being Yakov, but he's in no doubt as to his core identity. We can do the same for you, I promise. Just come back with us, and all will be well."

"Look at the picture," Nesha says, handing the pass back to me.

I do. My eyes take a moment to focus–the snow and the cold are making them water–but when they do there's no doubt. I'm looking at the same face that I'd seen in the mirror in Nesha's apartment. Cleaned and tidied, but still me.

"I'm scared."

"Of course you're scared. Who wouldn't be?" Grechko stubs out the cigarette and extends a gloved hand. "Will you come with us now, Georgi? So that we can start helping you?"

"I have no choice, do I?"

"It's for the best."

Seeing that I'm going to come without a struggle, Grechko nods at the man with the syringe to put it back in his pocket. The other hatted man gives me an encouraging shove, urging me to start walking along the landing to the waiting elevator. I resist for a moment, looking back at Nesha. I crave some last moment of connection with the woman I've risked my life to visit.

She nods once.

I don't think Grechko or the other men see her do it. Then she pulls her hand from her pocket and shows me the musical box, before closing her fist on it as if it's the most secret and precious thing in the universe. As if recalling something from a dream, I remember another hand placing that musical box in mine. It's the hand of a cosmonaut, urging me to do something before he slips into coma.

I have no idea what's going to happen to either of us now. Nesha's old, but not so old that she might not have decades of life ahead of her. If she's ever doubted that she was right, she now has concrete proof. A life redeemed, if it needed redeeming. They'll still humiliate her at every turn, given the chance. But she'll know with an iron certainty they're wrong, and she'll also know that everything they stand for will one day turn to dust.

"Am I really Doctor Kizim?" I ask Grechko, as the elevator takes us down.

"You know it in your heart."

I stroke my face, comparing what I touch with the memories I feel to be real. "I was so sure."

"That's the way it happens. But it's a good sign that you're already questioning these fundamental certainties."

"The cosmonaut?" I ask, suddenly unable to mention him by name.

"Yes?"

"You mentioned him being in an intermittent vegetative state."

"He's been like that for a while. I'm surprised you don't remember. He just lies there and watches us. Watches us and hums, making the same tune over and over again. One of us recognized it eventually." With only mild interest Grechko adds, "That piece by Prokofiev, the famous one?"

"Troika," I say, as the door opens. "Yes, I know it well."

They take me out into the snow, to the Zil that must have been waiting out of sight. The man with the syringe walks ahead and opens the rear passenger door, beckoning me into it as if I'm some high-ranking party official. I get in without causing a scene. The Zil's warm and plush and silent.

As we speed away from Star City, I press my face against the glass and watch the white world rush by as if in a sleigh-ride.

RETURN TO TITAN

Stephen Baxter

Stephen Baxter is one of the most important science fiction writers to emerge from Britain in the past 30 years. His "Xeelee" sequence of novels and short stories is arguably the most significant work of future history in modern science fiction. Baxter is the author of more than 40 books and over 100 short stories. His most recent book is Stone Spring, *first in the 'Northland' trilogy.*

Members of the Poole family have shown up in Baxter's Xeelee series, most recently in Transcendant, *the story collection that closed the "Destiny's Children" sequence. In "Return to Titan" Baxter sends Harry Poole, his son Michael, and an unlikely crew into the outer reaches of our solar system to do a little business and explore something very strange indeed.*

PROLOGUE

Probe

The spacecraft from Earth sailed through rings of ice.

In its first week in orbit around Saturn it passed within a third of a million kilometers of Titan, Saturn's largest moon. Its sensors peered curiously down at unbroken haze.

The craft had been too heavy to launch direct with the technology of the time, so its flight path, extending across seven years, had taken it on swingbys past Venus, Earth, and Jupiter. Primitive it was, but it was prepared for Titan. An independent lander, a fat pie-dish shape three meters across, clung to the side of the main body. Dormant for most of the interplanetary cruise, the probe was at last woken and released.

And, two weeks later, it dropped into the thick atmosphere of Titan itself.

Much of the probe's interplanetary velocity was shed in ferocious heat, and the main parachute was released. Portals opened and booms unfolded, and more than a billion kilometers from the nearest human engineer, instruments peered out at Titan. Some 50 kilometers up the surface slowly became visible. This first tantalizing glimpse was like a high-altitude view of Earth, though rendered in somber reds and browns.

The landing in gritty water-ice sand was slow, at less than 20 kilometers per hour.

After a journey of so many years the surface mission lasted mere minutes before the probe's internal batteries were exhausted, and the chatter of telemetry fell silent. It would take two more hours for news of the adventure to crawl at lightspeed to Earth, by which time a thin organic rain was already settling on the probe's upper casing, as the last of its internal heat leaked away.

And then, all unknown to the probe's human controlers back on Earth, a manipulator not unlike a lobster's claw closed around *Huygens*'s pie-dish hull and dragged the crushed probe down beneath the water-ice sand.

I

Earthport

"There's always been something wrong with Titan." These were the first words I ever heard Harry Poole speak–though I didn't know the man at the time–words that cut through my hangover like a drill. "It's been obvious since the first primitive probes got there 1600 years ago." He had the voice of an older man, 70, 80 maybe, a scratchy texture. "A moon with a blanket of air, a moon that cradles a whole menagerie of life under its thick atmosphere. But that atmosphere's not sustainable."

"Well, the mechanism is clear enough. Heating effects from the methane component keep the air from cooling and freezing out." This was another man's voice, gravely, a bit somber, the voice of a man who took himself too seriously. The voice sounded familiar. "Sunlight drives methane reactions that dump complex hydrocarbons in the stratosphere–"

"But, son, where does the methane come from?" Harry Poole pressed. "It's destroyed by the very reactions that manufacture all those stratospheric hydrocarbons. Should all be gone in a few million years, ten million tops. So what replenishes it?"

At that moment I could not have cared less about the problem of methane on Saturn's largest moon, even though, I suppose, it was a central facet of my career. The fog in my head, thicker than Titan's tholin haze, was lifting slowly, and I became aware of my body, aching in unfamiliar ways, stretched out on some kind of couch.

"Maybe some geological process." This was a woman's voice, a bit brisk. "That or an ecology, a Gaia process that keeps the methane levels up. Those are the obvious options."

"Surely, Miriam," Harry Poole said. "One or the other. That's been obvious since the methane on Titan was first spotted from Earth. But *nobody knows.* Oh, there have been a handful of probes over the centuries, but nobody's taken Titan seriously enough to nail it down. Always too many other easy targets for exploration and colonization–Mars, the ice moons. Nobody's even walked on Titan!"

Another man, a third, said, "But the practical problems–the heat loss in that cold air–it was always too expensive to bother, Harry. And too risky . . ."

"No. Nobody had the vision to see the potential of the place. That's the real problem. And now we're hamstrung by these damn sentience laws."

"And you think we need to know." That gravel voice.

"We need Titan, son," Harry Poole said. "It's the only hope I see of making our wormhole link pay for itself. Titan is, ought to be, the key to opening up Saturn and the whole outer System. We need to prove the sentience laws don't apply there, and move in and start opening it up. That's what this is all about."

The woman spoke again. "And you think this wretched creature is the key."

"Given he's a sentience curator, and a crooked one at that, yes . . ."

When words like "wretched" or "crooked" are bandied about in my company it's generally Jovik Emry that's being discussed. I took this as a cue to open my eyes. Some kind of glassy dome stretched over my head, and beyond that a slice of sky-blue. I recognized the Earth seen from space. And there was something else, a sculpture of electric blue thread that drifted over a rumpled cloud layer.

"Oh, look," said the woman. "It's alive."

I stretched, swivelled and sat up. I was stiff and sore, and had a peculiar ache at the back of my neck, just beneath my skull. I looked around at my captors. There were four of them, three men and a woman, all watching me with expressions of amused contempt. Well, it wasn't the first time I'd woken with a steaming hangover in an unknown place surrounded by strangers. I would recover quickly. I was as young and healthy as I could afford to be: I was around 40, but AS-preserved at my peak of 23.

We sat on couches at the center of a cluttered circular deck, domed over by a scuffed carapace. I was in a GUTship, then, a standard interplanetary transport, if an elderly one; I had traveled in such vessels many times, to Saturn and back. Through the clear dome I could see more of those electric-blue frames drifting before the face of the Earth. They were tetrahedral, and their faces were briefly visible, like soap films that glistened gold before disappearing. These were the mouths of wormholes, flaws in spacetime, and the golden shivers were glimpses of other worlds.

I knew where I was. "This is Earthport." My throat was dry as moondust, but I tried to speak confidently.

"Well, you're right about that." This was the man who had led the conversation earlier. That 70-year-old voice, comically, came out of the face of a boy of maybe 25, with blond hair, blue eyes, a smooth AntiSenescence marvel. The other two men looked around 60, but with AS so prevalent it was hard to tell. The woman was tall, her hair cut short, and she wore a functional jumpsuit; she might have been 45. The old-young man spoke again. "My name is Harry Poole. Welcome to the *Hermit Crab*, which is my son's ship–"

"Welcome? You've drugged me and brought me here–"

One of the 60-year-olds laughed, the gruff one. "Oh, you didn't need drugging; you did that to yourself."

"You evidently know me–and I think I know you." I studied him. He was heavy set, dark, not tall, with a face that wasn't built for smiling. "You're Michael Poole, aren't you? Poole the wormhole engineer."

Poole just looked back at me. Then he turned to the blond man. "Harry, I have a feeling we're making a huge mistake trying to work with this guy."

Harry grinned, studying me. "Give it time, son. You've always been an idealist. You're not used to working with people like this. I am. We'll get what we want out of him."

I turned to him. "Harry Poole. You're Michael's father, aren't you?" I laughed at them. "A father who AS-restores himself to an age younger than your son. How crass. And, Harry, you really ought to get something done about that voice."

The third man spoke. "I agree with Michael, Harry. We can't work with this clown." He was on the point of being overweight, and had a crumpled, careworn face. I labeled him as a corporate man who had grown old laboring to make somebody else rich–probably Michael Poole and his father.

I smiled easily, unfazed. "And you are?"

"Bill Dzik. And I'll be working with you if we go through with this planned jaunt to Titan. Can't say it's an idea I like."

This was the first I had heard of a trip to Titan. Well, whatever they wanted of me, I had had quite enough of the dismal hell-hole of the Saturn system, and had no intention of going back now. I had been in worse predicaments before; it was just a question of playing for time and looking for openings. I rubbed my temples. "Bill–can I call you Bill?–I don't suppose you could fetch me a coffee."

"Don't push your luck," he growled.

"Just tell me why you kidnapped me."

"That's simple," Harry said. "We want you to take us down to Titan."

Harry snapped his fingers, and a Virtual image coalesced before us, a bruised orange spinning in the dark: Titan. Saturn itself was a pale yellow crescent with those tremendous rings spanning space, and moons hanging like lanterns. And there, glimmering in orbit just above the plane of the rings, was a baby-blue tetrahedral frame, the mouth of Michael Poole's wormhole, a hyper-dimensional road offering access to Saturn and all its wonders–a road, it seemed, rarely traveled.

"That would be illegal," I pointed out.

"I know. And that's why we need you." And he grinned, a cold expression on that absurdly young face.

II

Finance

"If it's an expert on Titan you want," I said, "keep looking."

"You're a curator," Miriam said, disbelief and disgust

thick in her voice. "You work for the intraSystem oversight panel on sentience law compliance. Titan is in your charge!"

"Not by choice," I murmured. "Look–as you evidently targeted me, you must know something of my background. I haven't had an easy career . . ." My life at school, supported by my family's money, had been a series of drunken jaunts, sexual escapades, petty thieving, and vandalism. As a young man I never lasted long at any of the jobs my family found for me, largely because I was usually on the run from some wronged party or other.

Harry said, "In the end you got yourself sentenced to an editing, didn't you?"

If the authorities had had their way I would have had the contents of my much-abused brain downloaded into an external store, my memories edited, my unhealthy impulses "re-programmed", and the lot loaded back again–my whole self rebooted. "It represented death to me," I said. "I wouldn't have been the same man as I was before. My father took pity on me–"

"And bought you out of your sentence," Bill Dzik said. "And got you a job on sentience compliance. A sinecure."

I looked at Titan's dismal colors. "It is a miserable posting. But it pays a bit, and nobody cares much what you get up to, within reason. I've only been out a few times to Saturn itself, and the orbit of Titan; the work's mostly admin, run from Earth. I've held down the job. Well, I really don't have much choice."

Michael Poole studied me as if I were a vermin infesting one of his marvelous interplanetary installations. "This is the problem I've got with agencies like the sentience-oversight curacy. I might even agree with its goals. But it's populated by time-wasters like you, it doesn't do what it's supposed to achieve, and all it does is get in the way of enterprise."

I found myself taking a profound dislike to the man. And I've never been able to stomach being preached at. "I did nobody any harm," I snapped back at him. "Not much, anyhow. Not like you with your grand schemes, Poole, reordering the whole System for your own profit."

Michael would have responded, but Harry held up his hand. "Let's not get into that. And after all he's right. Profit, or the lack of it, is the issue here. As for you, Jovik, even in this billion-kilometers-remote "sinecure" you're still up to your old tricks, aren't you?"

I said nothing, cautious until I worked out how much he knew.

Harry waved his hand at his Virtual projection. "Look–Titan is infested with life. That's the basic conclusion of the gaggle of probes that, over the centuries, have orbited Titan or penetrated its thick air and crawled over its surface or dug into its icy sand. But life isn't the point. The whole *System* is full of life–life that blows everywhere, in impact-detached rocks and lumps of ice. Life is commonplace. The question is sentience. And sentience holds up progress."

"It's happened to us before," Michael Poole said to me. "The development consortium I lead, that is. We were establishing a wormhole Interface at a Kuiper object called Baked Alaska, out on the rim of the System. Our purpose was to use the ice as reaction mass to fuel GUTdrive starships. Well, we discovered life there, life of a sort, and it wasn't long before we identified sentience. The xenobiologists called it a Forest of Ancestors. The project ground to a halt; we had to evacuate the place–"

"Given the circumstances in which you've brought me here," I said, "I'm not even going to feign interest in your war stories."

"All right," Harry said. "But you can see the issue with Titan. Look, we want to open it up for development. It's a factory of hydrocarbons and organics, and exotic life forms some of which at least are related to our own. We can make breathable air from the nitrogen atmosphere and oxygen extracted from water ice. We can use all that methane and organic chemistry to make plastics or fuel or even food. Titan *should* be the launch pad for the opening-up of the outer System, indeed the stars. But we're not going to be allowed to develop Titan if there's sentience there. And our problem is that nobody has established that there isn't."

I started to see it. "So you want to mount a quick and dirty expedition, violating the planetary-protection aspects of the sentience laws, prove there's no significant mind down there, and get the clearance to move in the digging machines. Right?" And I saw how Bill Dzik, Miriam, and Michael Poole exchanged unhappy glances. There was dissension in the team over the morality of all this, a crack I might be able to exploit. "Why do you need this so badly?" I asked.

So they told me. It was a saga of interplanetary ambition. But at the root of it, as is always the case, was money–or the lack of it.

III

Negotiation

Harry Poole said, "You know our business, Jovik. Our wormhole engineering is laying down rapid-transit routes through the System, which will open up a whole family of worlds to colonization and development. But we have grander ambitions than that."

I asked, "What ambitions? Starships?"

"That and more," Michael Poole said. "For the last few decades we've been working on an experimental ship being built in the orbit of Jupiter . . ."

And he told me about his precious *Cauchy*. By dragging a wormhole portal around a circuit light-years across, the GUTship *Cauchy* would establish a wormhole bridge–not across space–but across fifteen centuries, to the future. So, having already connected the worlds of humanity with his wormhole subway System, Michael Poole now hoped to short-circuit past and future themselves. I looked at him with new respect, and some fear. The man was a genius, or mad.

"But," I said, "to fund such dreams you need money."

Harry said, "Jovik, you need to understand that a mega-engineering business like ours is a ferocious devourer of cash. It's been this way since the days of the pioneering railway builders back in the nineteenth century. We fund each new project with the profit of our previous ventures and with fresh investment–but that investment is closely related to the success of the earlier schemes."

"Ah. And you're stumbling. Yes? And this is all to do with Saturn."

Harry sighed. "The Saturn transit was a logical development. The trouble is, nobody needs to go there. Saturn pales beside Jupiter! Saturn has ice moons; well, there are plenty in orbit around Jupiter. Saturn's atmosphere could be mined, but so can Jupiter's, at half the distance from Earth."

Miriam said, "Saturn also lacks Jupiter's ferociously energetic external environment, which we're tapping ourselves in the manufacture of the *Cauchy.*"

"Fascinating," I lied. "You're an engineer too, then?"

"A physicist," she replied, awkward. She sat next to Michael Poole but apart from him. I wondered if there was anything deeper between them.

"The point," said Harry, "is that there's nothing at Saturn you'd want to go there for–no reason for our expensive wormhole link to be used. Nothing except–"

"Titan," I said.

"If we can't get down there legally, we need somebody to break us through the security protocols and get us down there."

"So you turned to me."

"The last resort," said Bill Dzik with disgust in his voice.

"We tried your colleagues," Miriam said. "They all said no."

"Well, that's typical of that bunch of prigs."

Harry, always a diplomat, smiled at me. "So we're having to bend a few pettifogging rules, but you have to see the vision, man, you have to see the greater good. And it's a chance for you to return to Titan, Jovik. Think of it as an opportunity."

"The question is, what's in it for me? You know I've come close to the editing suites before. Why should I take the risk of helping you now?"

"Because," Harry said, "if you don't you'll *certainly* face a reboot." So now we came to the dirty stuff. Harry took over; he was clearly the key operator in this little cabal, with the other engineer types uncomfortably out of their depth. "We know about your sideline."

With a sinking feeling I asked, "What sideline?"

And he used his Virtual display to show me. There went one of my doctored probes arrowing into Titan's thick air, a silver needle that stood out against the murky organic backdrop, supposedly on a routine monitoring mission but in fact with a quite different objective.

There are pockets of liquid water to be found just under Titan's surface, frozen-over crater lakes, kept warm for a few thousand years by the residual heat of the impacts that created them. My probe now shot straight through the icy carapace of one of those crater lakes, and into the liquid water beneath. Harry fast-forwarded, and we watched the probe's ascent module push its way out of the lake and up into the air, on its way to my colleagues' base on Enceladus.

"You're sampling the subsurface life from the lakes," Harry said sternly. "And selling the results."

I shrugged; there was no point denying it. "I guess you know the background. The creatures down there are related to Earth life, but very distantly. Different numbers of amino acids, or something–*I* don't know. The tiniest samples are gold dust to the biochemists, a whole new toolkit for designer drugs and genetic manipulation . . ." I had one get-out. "You'll have trouble proving this. By now there won't be a trace of our probes left on the surface." Which was true; one of the many ill-understood aspects of Titan was that probes sent down to its surface quickly failed and disappeared, perhaps as a result of some kind of geological resurfacing.

Harry treated that with the contempt it deserved. "We have full records. Images. Samples of the material you stole from Titan. Even a sworn statement by one of your partners."

I flared at that, "Who?" But, of course, it didn't matter.

Harry said sweetly. "The point is the sheer illegality–and committed by you, a curator, whose job is precisely to guard against such things. If this gets to your bosses, it will be the editing suite for you, my friend."

"So that's it. Blackmail." I did my best to inject some moralistic contempt into my voice. And it worked; Michael, Miriam, Bill wouldn't meet my eyes.

But it didn't wash with Harry. "Not the word I'd use. But that's pretty much it, yes. So what's it to be? Are you with us? Will you lead us to Titan?"

I wasn't about to give in yet. I got to my feet suddenly; to my gratification they all flinched back. "At least let me think about it. You haven't even offered me that coffee."

Michael glanced at Harry, who pointed at a dispenser on a stand near my couch. "Use that one."

There were other dispensers in the cabin; why that particular one? I filed away the question and walked over to the dispenser. At a command it produced a mug of what smelled like coffee. I sipped it gratefully and took a step across the floor towards the transparent dome.

"Hold it," Michael snapped.

"I just want to take in the view."

Miriam said, "OK, but don't touch anything. Follow that yellow path."

I grinned at her. "Don't *touch* anything? What am I, contagious?" I wasn't sure what was going on, but probing away at these little mysteries had to help. “Please. Walk with me. Show me what you mean.”

Miriam hesitated for a heartbeat. Then, with an expression of deep distaste, she got to her feet. She was taller than I was, and lithe, strong-looking.

We walked together across the lifedome, a half-sphere 100 meters wide. Couches, control panels and data entry and retrieval ports were clustered around the geometric centre of the dome; the rest of the transparent floor area was divided up by shoulder-high partitions into lab areas, a galley, a gym, a sleeping area and shower. The layout looked obsessively plain and functional to me. This was the vessel of a man who lived for work, and only that; if this was Michael Poole’s ship it was a bleak portrait.

We reached the curving hull. Glancing down I could see the ship’s spine, a complex column a couple of kilometers long leading to the lode of asteroid ice used for reaction mass by GUTdrive module within. And all around us wormhole Interfaces drifted like snowflakes, while intraSystem traffic passed endlessly through the great gateways.

“All this is a manifestation of your lover’s vision,” I said to Miriam, who stood by me.

“Michael’s not my lover,” she shot back, irritated. The electric-blue light of the exotic matter frames shone on her cheekbones.

“I don’t even know your name,” I said.

“Berg,” she said reluctantly. “Miriam Berg.”

“Believe it or not, I’m not a criminal. I’m no hero, and I don’t pretend to be. I just want to get through my life, and have a little fun on the way. I shouldn’t be here, and nor should you.” Deliberately I reached for her shoulder. A bit of physical contact might break through that reserve.

But my fingers *passed through* her shoulder, breaking up into a mist of pixels until they were clear of her flesh, and then reformed. I felt only a distant ache in my head.

I stared at Miriam Berg. "What have you done to me?"

"I'm sorry," she said gravely.

I sat on my couch once more—*my* couch, a Virtual projection like me, the only one in the dome I wouldn't have fallen through, and sipped a coffee from my Virtual dispenser, the only one that I could touch.

It was, predictably, Harry Poole's scheme. "Just in case the arm-twisting over the sample-stealing from Titan wasn't enough."

"I'm a Virtual copy," I said.

"Strictly speaking, an identity backup . . ."

I had heard of identity backups, but could never afford one myself, nor indeed fancied it much. Before undertaking some hazardous jaunt you could download a copy of yourself into a secure memory store. If you were severely injured or even killed, the backup could be loaded into a restored body, or a vat-grown cloned copy, or allowed to live on in some Virtual environment. You would lose the memories you had acquired after the backup was made, but that was better than non-existence . . . That was the theory. In my opinion it was an indulgence of the rich; you saw backup Virtuals appearing like ghosts at the funerals of their originals, distastefully lapping up the sentiment.

And besides the backup could never be *you*, the you who had died; only a copy could live on. That was the idea that started to terrify me now. I am no fool, and imaginative to a fault.

Harry watched me taking this in.

I could barely ask the question: "What about me? The original. Did I die?"

"No," Harry said. "The real you is in the hold, suspended. We took the backup after you were already unconscious."

So that explained the ache at the back of my neck: that

was where they had jacked into my nervous system. I got up and paced around. "And if I refuse to help? You're a pack of crooks and hypocrites, but I can't believe you're deliberate killers."

Michael would have answered, but Harry held up his hand, unperturbed. "Look, it needn't be that way. If you agree to work with us, *you*, the Virtual you, will be loaded back into the prime version. You'll have full memories of the whole episode."

"But I won't be *me*." I felt rage building. "I mean, the copy sitting here. *I* won't exist anymore–anymore than I existed a couple of hours ago, when you activated me." That was another strange and terrifying thought. "*I* will have to die! And that's even if I cooperate. Great deal you're offering. Well, into Lethe with you. If you're going to kill *me* anyway I'll find a way to hurt you. I'll get into your systems like a virus. *You can't control me.*"

"But I can." Harry clicked his fingers.

And in an instant everything changed. The four of them had gathered by Harry's couch, the furthest from me. I had been standing; now I was sitting. And beyond the curved wall of the transparent dome, I saw that we had drifted into Earth's night.

"How long?" I whispered.

"Twenty minutes," Harry said carelessly. "Of course I can control you. You have an off switch. So which is it to be? Permanent extinction for all your copies, or survival as a trace memory in your host?" His grin hardened, and his young-old face was cold.

So the *Hermit Crab* wheeled in space, seeking out the wormhole Interface that led to Saturn. And I, or rather *he* who had briefly believed he was me, submitted to a downloading back into his primary, myself.

He, the identity copy, died to save my life. I salute him.

IV

Wormhole

Released from my cell of suspended animation, embittered, angry, I chose to be alone. I walked to the very rim of the lifedome, where the transparent carapace met the solid floor. Looking down I could see the flaring of superheated, ionised steam pouring from the GUTdrive nozzles. The engine, as you would expect, was one of Poole's own designs. "GUT" stands for "Grand Unified Theory," the system which describes the fundamental forces of nature as aspects of a single superforce. This is creation physics. Thus men like Michael Poole use the energies which once drove the expansion of the universe itself for the triviality of pushing forward their steam rockets.

Soon the *Hermit Crab* drove us into the mouth of the wormhole that led to the Saturn system. We flew lifedome first at the wormhole Interface, so it was as if the electric-blue tetrahedral frame came down on us from the zenith. It was quite beautiful, a sculpture of light. Those electric blue struts were beams of exotic matter, a manifestation of a kind of antigravity field that kept this throat in space and time from collapsing. Every so often you would see the glimmer of a triangular face, a sheen of golden light filtering through from Saturn's dim halls.

The frame bore down, widening in my view, and fell around us, obscuring the view of Earth and Earthport. Now I was looking up into a kind of tunnel, picked out by the flaring of sheets of light. This was a flaw in spacetime itself; the flashing I saw was the resolution of that tremendous strain into exotic particles and radiations. The ship thrust deeper into the wormhole. Fragments of blue-white light swam from a vanishing point directly above my head and swarmed down the spacetime walls. There was a genuine sensation of speed, of limitless, uncontrollable velocity. The ship shuddered and banged, the lifedome creaked like a tin shack, and I thought I could hear that elderly GUTdrive screaming with the strain. I gripped a rail and tried not to cower.

The passage was at least mercifully short. Amid a shower of exotic particles we ascended out of another electric-blue Interface–and I found myself back in the Saturn system, for the first time in years.

I could see immediately that we were close to the orbit of Titan about its primary, for the planet itself, suspended in the scuffed sky of the lifedome, was about the size I remembered it: a flattened globe a good bit larger than the Moon seen from Earth. Other moons hung around their primary points of light. The sun was off to the right, with its close cluster of inner planets, so Saturn was half-full. Saturn's only attractive feature, the rings, were invisible, for Titan's orbit is in the same equatorial plane as the ring system and the rings are edge-on. But the shadow of the rings cast by the sun lay across the planet's face, sharp and unexpected.

There was nothing romantic in the view, nothing beautiful about it, not to me. The light was flat and pale. Saturn is about ten times as far from the sun as Earth is, and the sun is reduced to an eerie pinpoint, its radiance only a hundredth that at Earth. Saturn is misty and murky, an autumnal place. And you never forgot that you were so far from home that a human hand, held out at arm's length towards the sun, could have covered all of the orbit of Earth.

The *Crab* swung about and Titan itself was revealed, a globe choked by murky brown cloud from pole to pole, even more dismal and uninviting than its primary. Evidently Michael Poole had placed his wormhole interface close to the moon in anticipation that Titan would someday serve his purposes.

Titan was looming larger, swelling visibly. Our destination was obvious.

Harry Poole took charge. He had us put on heavy, thick-layered exosuits of a kind I'd never seen before. We sat on our couches like fat pupae; my suit was so thick my legs wouldn't bend properly.

"Here's the deal," Harry said, evidently for my benefit. "The *Crab* came out of the wormhole barreling straight for Titan. That way we hope to get you down there before any of the automated surveillance systems up here can spot us, or anyhow do anything about it. In a while the *Crab* will brake into orbit around Titan. But before then you four in the gondola will be thrown straight into an entry." He snapped his fingers, and a hatch opened up in the floor beneath us to reveal the interior of another craft, mated to the base of the lifedome. It was like a cave, brightly lit and with its walls crusted with data displays.

I said, "Thrown straight in, Harry? And what about you?"

He smiled with that young-old face. "I will be waiting for you in orbit. Somebody has to stay behind to bail you out, in case."

"This *gondola* looks small for the four of us."

Harry said, "Well, weight has been a consideration. You'll mass no more than a tonne, all up." He handed me a data slate. "Now this is where you come in, Jovik. I want you to send a covering message to the control base on Enceladus."

I stared at the slate. "Saying what, exactly?"

Harry said, "The entry profile is designed to mimic an unmanned mission. For instance you're going in hard–high deceleration. I want you to make yourselves look that way in the telemetry–like just another unmanned probe, going in for a bit of science, or a curacy inspection, or whatever it is you bureaucrat types do. Attach the appropriate permissions. I'm quite sure you're capable of that."

I was sure of it too. I opened the slate with a wave of my hand, quickly mocked up a suitable profile, let Harry's systems check I hadn't smuggled in any cries for help, and squirted it over to Enceladus. Then I handed the slate back. "There. Done. You're masked from the curacy. I've done what you want." I waved at the looming face of Titan. "So you can spare me from *that*, can't you?"

"We discussed that," said Michael Poole, with just a hint of regret in his voice. "We decided to take you along as a fall-back, Jovik, in case of a challenge. Having you aboard will make the mission look more plausible; you can give us a bit more cover."

I snorted. "They'll see through that."

Miriam shrugged. "It's worth it if it buys us a bit more time."

Bill Dzik stared at me, hard. "Just don't get any ideas, desk jockey. I'll have my eye on you all the way down and all the way back."

"And listen," Harry said, leaning forward. "If this works out, Jovik, you'll be rewarded. We'll see to that. We'll be able to afford it, after all." He grinned that youthful grin. "And just think. You will be one of the first humans to walk on Titan. So you see, you've every incentive to cooperate, haven't you?" He checked a clock on his data slate. "We're close to the release checkpoint. Down you go, team."

They all sneered at that word, and at the cheerful tone of the man who was staying behind. But we filed dutifully enough through the hatch and down into that cave of instrumentation, Miriam first, then me, with Bill Dzik at my back. Michael Poole was last in; I saw him embrace his father, stiffly, evidently not a gesture they were used to. In the gondola, our four couches sat in a row, so close that my knees touched Miriam's and Dzik's when we were all crammed in there in our suits. The hull was all around us, close enough for me to have reached out and touched it in every direction, a close-fitting shell. Poole pulled the hatch closed, and I heard a hum and whir as the independent systems of this gondola came on line. There was a rattle of latches, and then a kind of sideways shove that made my stomach churn. We were already cut loose of the *Crab*, and were falling free, and rotating.

Poole touched a panel above his head, and the hull turned transparent. It was as if we four in our couches were suspended in space, surrounded by glowing instrument panels, and blocky masses that must be the GUT engine, life support, supplies. Above me the *Crab* slid across the face of Saturn, GUTdrive flaring, and below me the orange face of Titan loomed large.

I whimpered. I have never pretended to be brave.

Miriam Berg handed me a transparent bubble-helmet. "Lethe, put this on before you puke."

I pulled the helmet over my head; it snuggled into the suit neck and made its own lock.

Bill Dzik was evidently enjoying my discomfort. "You feel safer in the suit, right? Well, the entry is the most dangerous time. But you'd better hope we get through the atmosphere's outer layers before the hull breaches, Emry. These outfits aren't designed to work as pressure suits."

"Then what?"

"Heat control," Michael Poole said, a bit more sympathetic. "Titan's air pressure is fifty percent higher than Earth's, at the surface. But that cold thick air just sucks away your heat. Listen up, Emry. The gondola's small, but it has a pretty robust power supply–a GUT engine, in fact. You're going to need that power to keep warm. Away from the gondola your suit will protect you, there are power cells built into the fabric. But you won't last more than a few hours away from the gondola. Got that?"

I was hardly reassured. "What about the entry itself? Your father said we'll follow an unmanned profile. That sounds a bit vigorous."

Bill Dzik barked a laugh.

"We should be fine," Poole said. "We don't have full inertial control, we don't have the power, but in the couches we'll be shielded from the worst of the deceleration. Just sit tight."

And then Poole fell silent as he and the others began to work through pre-entry system checks. Harry murmured in my ear, telling me that fresh identity backups had just been taken of each of us and stored in the gondola's systems. I was not reassured. I lay helpless, trussed up and strapped in, as we plummeted into the center of the sunlit face of Titan.

V

Titan

Fifteen minutes after cutting loose of the *Crab*, the gondola encountered the first wisps of Titan's upper atmosphere, thin and cold, faintly blue all around us. Still a thousand kilometers above the ground I could feel the first faltering in the gondola's headlong speed. Titan's air is massive and deep, and I was falling backside first straight into it.

The first three minutes of the entry were the worst. We plunged into the air with an interplanetary velocity, but our speed was reduced violently. Three hundred kilometers above the surface, the deceleration peaked at sixteen gravities. Cushioned by Poole's inertial field I felt no more than the faintest shaking, but the gondola creaked and banged, every joint and structure stressed to its limits. Meanwhile a shock wave preceded us, a cap of gas that glowed brilliantly: Titan air battered to a plasma by the dissipating kinetic energy of the gondola.

This fiery entry phase was mercifully brief. But still we fell helplessly. After three minutes we were within 150 kilometers of the surface, and immersed in a thickening orange haze, the organic-chemistry products of the destruction of Titan's methane by sunlight. Poole tapped a panel. A mortar banged above us, hauling out a pilot parachute a couple of meters across. This stabilized us in the thickening air, our backs to the moon, our faces to the sky. Then a main parachute unfolded sluggishly, spreading reassuringly above me.

For fifteen minutes we drifted, sinking slowly into a deep ocean of cold, sluggish air. Poole and his colleagues worked at their slates, gathering data from sensors that measured the physical and chemical properties of the atmosphere. I lay silent, curious but frightened for my life.

As we fell deeper into the hydrocarbon smog the temperature fell steadily. Greenhouse effects from methane products keep Titan's stratosphere warmer than it should be. Sixty kilometers above the surface we fell through a layer of hydrocarbon cloud into clearer air beneath, and then, at 40 kilometers, through a thin layer of methane clouds. The temperature was close to its minimum here, at only 70 degrees or so above absolute zero. Soon it would rise again, for hydrogen liberated from more methane reactions contribute to another greenhouse effect that warms up the troposphere. The mysterious methane that shouldn't have been there warms Titan's air all the way to the ground.

Fifteen minutes after its unpackaging the main parachute was cut away, and a smaller stabilizer canopy opened. *Much* smaller. We began to fall faster, into the deep ocean of air. "Lethe," I said. "We're still 40 kilometers high!"

Bill Dzik laughed at me. "Don't you know anything about the world you're supposed to be guarding, curator? The air's thick here, and the gravity's low, only a seventh of Earth normal. Under that big parachute we'd be hanging in the air all day . . ."

The gondola lurched sideways, shoved by the winds. At least it shut Dzik up. But the winds eased as we fell further, until the air was as still and turgid as deep water. We were immersed now in orange petrochemical haze. But the sun was plainly visible as a brilliant point source of light, surrounded by a yellow-brown halo. The crew gathered data on the spectra of the solar halo, seeking information on aerosols, solid or liquid particles suspended in the air.

Gradually, beneath our backs, Titan's surface became visible. I twisted to see. Cumulus clouds of ethane vapor lay draped over continents of water ice. Of the ground itself I saw a mottling of dark and white patches, areas huge in extent, pocked by what looked like impact craters, and incised by threading valleys cut by flowing liquid, ethane or methane. The crew continued to collect their science data. An acoustic sounder sent out complex pulses of sound. Miriam Berg showed me how some echoes came back double, with reflections from the surfaces and bottoms of crater lakes, like the one my sampling probe had entered.

The gondola rocked beneath its parachute. Poole had suspended his inertial shielding, and under not much less than Titan's one-seventh gravity I was comfortable in my thick, softly layered exosuit. The crew's murmuring as they worked was professional and quiet. I think I actually slept, briefly.

Then there was a jolt. I woke with a snap. The parachute had been cut loose, and was drifting away with its strings dangling like some jellyfish. Our fall was slow in that thick air and gentle gravity, but fall we did!

And then, as Bill Dzik laughed at me, a new canopy unfurled into the form of a globe, spreading out above us. It was a balloon, perhaps 40, 50 meters across; we were suspended from it by a series of fine ropes. As I watched a kind of hose snaked up from beneath the gondola's hull, and pushed up into the mouth of the balloon, and it began to inflate.

"So that's the plan," I said. "To float around Titan in a balloon! Not very energetic for a man who builds interplanetary wormholes, Poole."

"But that's the point," Poole said testily, as if I had challenged his manhood. "We're here under the noses of your curators' sensors, Emry. The less of a splash we make the better."

Miriam Berg said, "I designed this part of the mission profile. We're going to float around at this altitude, about eight kilometers up—well above any problems with the topography but under most of the cloud decks. We ought to be able to gather the science data we need from here. A couple of weeks should be sufficient."

"A couple of weeks in this suit!"

Poole thumped the walls of the gondola. "This thing expands. You'll be able to get out of your suit. It's not going to be luxury, Emry, but you'll be comfortable enough."

Miriam said, "When the time comes we'll depart from this altitude. The *Crab* doesn't carry an orbit-to-surface flitter, but Harry will send down a booster unit to rendezvous with us and lift the gondola to orbit."

I stared at her. "We don't carry the means of getting off this moon?"

"Not on board, no," Miriam said evenly. "Mass issues. The need to stay under the curacy sensors' awareness threshold. We're supposed to look like an unmanned probe, remember. Look, it's not a problem."

"Umm." Call me a coward, many have. But I didn't like the idea that my only way off this wretched moon was thousands of kilometers away, and depended on a complicated series of rendezvous and coupling manoeuvres. "So what's keeping us aloft? Hydrogen, helium?"

Poole pointed at that inlet pipe. "Neither. This is a hot air balloon, Emry, a Montgolfier." And he gave me a lecture on how hot-air technology is optimal if you must go ballooning on Titan. The thick air and low gravity make the moon hospitable for balloons, and at such low temperatures you get a large expansion in response to a comparatively small amount of heat energy. Add all these factors into the kind of trade-off equation men like Poole enjoy so much, and out pops hot-air ballooning as the low-energy transport of choice on Titan.

Miriam said, "We're a balloon, not a dirigible; we can't steer. But for a mission like this we can pretty much go where the wind takes us; all we're doing is sampling a global ecosphere. And we can choose our course to some extent. The prevailing winds on Titan are easterly, but below about two kilometers there's a strong westerly component. That's a tide, raised by Saturn in the thick air down there. So we can select which way we get blown, just by ascending and descending."

"More stealth, I suppose. No need for engines."

"That's the idea. We've arrived in the local morning. Titan's day is 15 Earth days long, and we can achieve a lot before nightfall–in fact I'm intending that we should chase the daylight. Right now we're heading for the south pole, where it's summer." And there, as even I knew, methane and ethane pooled in open lakes–the only stable such liquid bodies in the System, save only for those on Earth and Triton.

"Summer on Titan," Poole said, and he grinned. "And we're riding the oldest flying machine of all over a moon of Saturn!" Evidently he was starting to enjoy himself.

Miriam smiled back, and their gloved hands locked together.

The envelope snapped and billowed above us as the warm air filled it up.

VI

Landfall

So we drifted over Titan's frozen landscape, heading for the south pole. For now Michael Poole kept us stuck in that unexpanded hull, and indeed inside our suits, though we removed our helmets, while the crew put the gondola through a fresh series of post-entry checks. I had nothing to do but stare out of the transparent hull, at the very Earthlike clouds that littered the murky sky, or over my shoulder at the landscape that unfolded beneath me.

Now we were low enough to make out detail, I saw that those darker areas were extensive stretches of dunes, lined up in parallel rows by the prevailing wind. The ground looked raked, like a tremendous zen garden. And the lighter areas were outcroppings of a paler rock, plateaus scarred by ravines and valleys. At this latitude there were no open bodies of liquid, but you could clearly see its presence in the recent past, in braided valleys and the shores of dried-out lakes. This landscape of dunes and ravines was punctuated by circular scars that were probably the relics of meteorite impacts, and by odder, dome-like features with irregular calderas–volcanoes. All these features had names, I learned, assigned to them by Earth astronomers centuries dead, who had eagerly examined the first robot-returned images of this landscape. But as nobody had ever come here those names, borrowed from vanished paradises and dead gods, had never come alive.

I listened absently as Poole and the others talked through their science program. The atmosphere was mostly nitrogen, just as on Earth, but it contained five percent methane, and that methane was the key to Titan's wonders, and mysteries. Even aside from its puzzling central role in the greenhouse effects which stabilized the atmosphere, methane was also key to the complicated organic chemistry that went on there. In the lower atmosphere methane reacted with nitrogen to create complex compounds called tholins, a kind of plastic, which fell to the ground in a sludgy rain. When those tholins landed in liquid water, such as in impact-warmed crater lakes, amino acids were produced–the building blocks of our kind of life . . .

As I listened to them debate these issues it struck me than none of them had begun his or her career as a biologist or climatologist: Poole and Berg had both been physicists, Dzik an engineer and more lately a project manager. Both Berg and Dzik had had specialist training to a decent academic standard to prepare for this mission. They all expected to live a long time; periodically they would re-educate themselves and adopt entirely different professions, as needs must.

I have never had any such ambition. But then, somehow, despite AS technology, I do not imagine myself reaching any great age.

Their talk had an edge, however, even in those first hours. They were all ethically troubled by what they were doing, and those doubts surfaced now that they were away from Harry Poole's goading.

"At some point," Miriam Berg said, "we'll have to face the question of how we'll react if we *do* find sentience here."

Bill Dzik shook his head. "Sometimes I can't believe we're even here, that we're having this conversation at all. I remember exactly what you said on Baked Alaska, Michael. 'The whole System is going to beat a path to our door to see this–as long as we can work out a way to protect the ecology . . . And if we can't, we'll implode the damn wormhole. We'll get funds for the *Cauchy* some other way.' That's what you said."

Poole said harshly, clearly needled, "That was 13 years ago, damn it, Bill. Situations change. People change. And the choices we have to make change too."

As they argued, I was the only one looking ahead, the way we were drifting under our balloon. Through the murk I thought I could see the first sign of the ethane lakes of the polar regions, sheets of liquid black as coal surrounded by fractal landscapes, like a false-color mock-up of Earth's own Arctic. And I thought I could see movement, something rising up off those lakes. Mist, perhaps? But there was too much solidity about those rising forms for that.

And then the forms emerged from the mist, solid and looming.

I pulled my helmet on my head and gripped my couch. I said, "Unless one of you does something fast, we may soon have no choices left at all."

They looked at me, the three of them in a row around me, puzzled. Then they looked ahead, to see what I saw.

They were like birds, black-winged, with white lenticular

bodies. Those wings actually flapped in the thick air as they flew up from the polar seas, a convincing simulacrum of the way birds fly in the air of Earth. Oddly they seemed to have no heads.

And they were coming straight towards us.

Michael Poole snapped, "Lethe. Vent the buoyancy!" He stabbed at a panel, and the others went to work, pulling on their helmets as they did so.

I felt the balloon settle as the hot air was released from the envelope above us. We were sinking–but we seemed to move in dreamy slow motion, while those birds loomed larger in our view with every heartbeat.

Then they were on us. They swept over the gondola, filling the sky above, black wings flapping in an oily way that, now they were so close, seemed entirely unnatural, not like terrestrial birds at all. They were huge, each 10, 15 meters across. I thought I could *hear* them, a rustling, snapping sound carried to me through Titan's thick air.

And they tore into the envelope. The fabric was designed to withstand Titan's methane rain, not an attack like this; it exploded into shreds, and the severed threads waved in the air. Some of the birds suffered; they tangled with our threads or collided with each other and fell away, rustling. One flew into the gondola itself and crumpled like tissue paper, and then fell, wadded up, far below us.

And we fell too, following our victim-assassin to the ground. Our descent from the best part of eight kilometers high took long minutes; we soon reached terminal velocity in Titan's thick air and weak gravity. We had time to strap ourselves in, and Poole and his team worked frantically to secure the gondola's systems. In the last moment Poole flooded the gondola with a foam that filled the internal space and held us rigid in our seats, like dolls in packaging, sightless and unable to move.

I felt the slam as we hit the ground.

VII

Surface

The foam drained away, leaving the four of us sitting there in a row like swaddled babies. We had landed on Titan the way we entered its atmosphere, backside first, and now we lay on our backs with the gondola tilted over, so that I was falling against Miriam Berg, and the cladded mass of Bill Dzik was weighing on me. The gondola's hull had reverted to opacity so we lay in a close-packed pearly shell, but there was internal light and the various data slates were working, though they were filled with alarming banks of red.

The three of them went quickly into a routine of checks. I ignored them. *I was alive.* I was breathing, the air wasn't foul, and I was in no greater discomfort than having Dzik's unpleasant bulk pressed against my side. Nothing broken, then. But I felt a pang of fear as sharp as that felt by that Virtual copy of me when he had learned he was doomed. I wondered if his ghost stirred in me now, still terrified.

And my bowels loosened into the suit's systems. Never a pleasant experience, no matter how good the suit technology. But I wasn't sorry to be reminded that I was nothing but a fragile animal, lost in the cosmos. That may be the root of my cowardice, but give me humility and realism over the hubristic arrogance of a Michael Poole any day.

Their technical chatter died away.

"The lights are on," I said. "So I deduce we've got power."

Michael Poole said, gruffly reassuring, "It would take more than a jolt like that to knock out one of my GUT engines."

Dzik said spitefully, "If we'd lost power you'd be an icicle already, Emry."

"Shut up, Bill," Miriam murmured. "Yes, Emry, we're not in bad shape. The pressure hull's intact, we have power, heating, air, water, food. We're not going to die any time soon."

But I thought of the flapping birds of Titan and wondered how she could be so sure.

Poole started unbuckling. "We need to make an external inspection. Figure out our options."

Miriam followed suit, and laughed. She said to me, "Romantic, isn't he? The first human footfalls on Titan, and he calls it an external inspection."

Bill Dzik dug an elbow in my ribs hard enough to hurt through the layers of my suit. "Move, Emry."

"Leave me alone."

"We're packed in here like spoons. It's one out, all out."

Well, he was right; I had no choice.

Poole made us go through checks of our exosuits, their power cells, the integrity of their seals. Then he drained the air and popped open the hatch in the roof before our faces. I saw a sky somber and brown, dark by comparison with the brightness of our internal lights, and flecks of black snow drifted by. The hatch was a door from this womb of metal and ceramics out into the unknown.

We climbed up through the hatch in reverse order from how we had come in: Poole, Dzik, myself, then Miriam. The gravity, a seventh of Earth's, was close enough to the Moon's to make that part of the experience familiar, and I moved my weight easily enough. Once outside the hull, lamps on my suit lit up in response to the dark.

I dropped down a meter or so, and drifted to my first footfall on Titan. The sandy surface crunched under my feet. I knew it was water ice, hard as glass. The sand at my feet was ridged into ripples, as if by a receding tide. Pebbles lay scattered, worn and eroded. A wind buffeted me, slow and massive, and I heard a low bass moan. A black rain smeared my faceplate.

The four of us stood together, chubby in our suits, the only humans on a world larger than Mercury. Beyond the puddle of light cast by our suit lamps an entirely unknown landscape stretched off into the infinite dark.

Miriam Berg was watching me. "What are you thinking, Jovik?" As far as I know these were the first words spoken by any human standing on Titan.

"Why ask me?"

"You're the only one of us who's looking at Titan and not at the gondola."

I grunted. "I'm thinking how like Earth this is. Like a beach somewhere, or a high desert, the sand, the pebbles. Like Mars, too, outside Kahra."

"Convergent processes," Dzik said dismissively. "But *you* are an entirely alien presence. Here, your blood is as hot as molten lava. Look, you're leaking heat."

And, looking down, I saw wisps of vapor rising up from my booted feet.

The others checked over the gondola. Its inner pressure cage had been sturdy enough to protect us, but the external hull was crumpled and damaged, various attachments had been ripped off, and it had dug itself into the ice.

Poole called us together for a council of war. "Here's the deal. There's no sign of the envelope; it was shredded, we lost it. The gondola's essential systems are sound, most importantly the power." He banged it with a gloved fist; in the dense air I heard a muffled thump. "The hull's taken a beating, though. We've lost the extensibility. I'm afraid we're stuck in these suits."

"Until what?" I said. "Until we get the spare balloon envelope inflated, right?"

"We don't carry a spare," Bill Dzik said, and he had the grace to sound embarrassed. "It was a cost-benefit analysis–"

"Well, you got that wrong," I snapped back. "How are we supposed to get off this damn moon now? You said we had to make some crackpot mid-air rendezvous."

Poole tapped his chest, and a Virtual image of Harry's head popped into existence in mid-air. "Good question. I'm working on options. I'm fabricating another envelope, and I'll get it down to you. Once we have that gondola aloft again I'll have no trouble picking you up. In the meantime," he said more sternly, "you have work to do down there. Time is short."

"When we get back to the *Crab*," Bill Dzik said to Poole, "you hold him down and I'll kill him."

"He's my father," said Michael Poole. "*I'll* kill him."

Harry dissolved into a spray of pixels.

Poole said, "Look, here's the deal. We'll need to travel if we're to achieve our science goals; we can't do it all from this south pole site. We do have some mobility. The gondola has wheels; it will work as a truck down here. But we're going to have to dig the wreck out of the sand first, and modify it. And meanwhile Harry's right about the limited time. I suggest that Bill and I get on with the engineering. Miriam, you take Emry and go see what science you can do at the lake. It's only a couple of kilometers," he checked a wrist map patch and pointed, "that way."

"OK." With low-gravity grace Miriam jumped back up to the hatch, and retrieved a pack from the gondola's interior.

I felt deeply reluctant to move away from the shelter of the wrecked gondola. "What about those birds?"

Miriam jumped back down and approached me. "We've seen no sign of the birds since we landed. Come on, curator. It will take your mind off how scared you are." And she tramped away into the dark, away from the pool of light by the gondola.

Poole and Dzik turned away from me. I had no choice but to follow her.

VIII

Lake

Walking any distance was surprisingly difficult.

The layered heat-retaining suit was bulky and awkward,

but it was flexible, and that was unlike the vacuum of the Moon, where the internal pressure forces even the best skinsuits to rigidity. But on Titan you are always aware of the resistance of the heavy air. At the surface the pressure is half as much again as on Earth, and the density of the air four times that at Earth's surface. It is almost like moving underwater. And yet the gravity is so low that when you dig your feet into the sand for traction you have a tendency to go floating off the ground. Miriam showed me how to extend deep, sharp treads from the soles of my boots to dig into the loose sand.

It is the thickness of the air that is the challenge on Titan; you are bathed in an intensely cold fluid, less than 100 degrees above absolute zero, that conducts away your heat enthusiastically, and I was always aware of the silent company of my suit's heating system, and the power cells that would sustain it for no more than a few hours.

"Turn your suit lights off," Miriam said to me after a few hundred meters. "Save your power."

"I prefer not to walk into what I can't see."

"Your eyes will adapt. And your faceplate has image enhancers set to the spectrum of ambient light here . . . Come on, Jovik. If you don't I'll do it for you; your glare is stopping me seeing too."

"All right, damn it."

With the lights off, I was suspended in brown murk, as if under an autumn sky obscured by the smoke of forest fires. But my eyes did adapt, and the faceplate subtly enhanced my vision. Titan opened up around me, a plain of sand and wind-eroded rubble under an orange-brown sky– again not unlike Mars, if you know it. Clouds of ethane or methane floated above me, and beyond them the haze towered up, a column of organic muck tens of kilometers deep. Yet I could see the sun in that haze, a spark low on the horizon, and facing it a half-full Saturn, much bigger than the Moon in Earth's sky. Of the other moons or the stars, indeed of the *Crab*, I could see nothing. All the colors were drawn from a palette of crimson, orange, and brown. Soon my eyes longed for a bit of green.

When I looked back I could see no sign of the gondola, its lights already lost in the haze. I saw we had left a clear line of footsteps behind us. It made me quail to think that this was the only footstep trail on all this little world.

We began to descend a shallow slope. I saw lines in the sand, like tide marks. "I think we're coming to the lake."

"Yes. It's summer here, at the south pole. The lakes evaporate, and the ethane rains out at the north pole. In 15 years' time, half a Saturnian year, it will be winter here and summer there, and the cycle will reverse. Small worlds have simple climate systems, Jovik. As I'm sure a curator would know . . ."

We came to the edge of the ethane lake. In that dim light it looked black like tar, and sluggish ripples crossed its surface. In patches something more solid lay on the liquid, circular sheets almost like lilies, repellently oily. The lake stretched off black and flat to the horizon, which curved visibly, though it was blurred in the murky air. It was an extraordinary experience to stand there in an exosuit and to face a body of liquid on such an alien world, the ocean black, the sky and the shore brown. And yet there was again convergence with the Earth. This was a kind of beach. Looking around I saw we were in a sort of bay, and to my right, a few kilometers away, a river of black liquid had cut a broad valley, braided like a delta, as it ran into the sea.

And, looking that way, I saw something lying on the shore, crumpled black around a grain of paleness.

Miriam wanted samples from the lake, especially of the discs of gunk that floated on the surface. She opened up her pack and extracted a sampling arm, a remote manipulator with a claw-like grabber. She hoisted this onto her shoulder and extended the arm, and I heard a whir of exoskeletal multipliers. As the arm plucked at the lily-like features some of them broke up into strands, almost like jet-black seaweed, but the arm lifted large contiguous sheets of a kind of film that reminded me of the eerie wings of the Titan birds that had attacked us.

Miriam quickly grew excited at what she was finding.

"Life," I guessed.

"You got it. Well, we knew it was here. We even have samples taken by automated probes. Though we never spotted those birds before." She hefted the stuff, films of it draped over her gloved hand, and looked at me. "I wonder if you understand how exotic this stuff is. I'm pretty sure this is silane life. That is, based on a silicon chemistry, rather than carbon . . ."

The things on the lake did indeed look like jet black lilies. But they were not lilies, or anything remotely related to life like my own.

Life of our chemical sort is based on long molecules, with a solute to bring components of those molecules together. Our specific sort of terrestrial life, which Miriam called "CHON life," after its essential elements carbon, hydrogen, oxygen, and nitrogen, uses water as its solute, and carbon-based molecules as its building blocks: carbon can form chains and rings, and long stable molecules like DNA.

"But carbon's not the only choice, and nor is water," Miriam said. "At terrestrial temperatures silicon bonds with oxygen to form very stable molecules."

"Silicates. Rock."

"Exactly. But at *very* low temperatures, silicon can form silanols, analogous to alcohols, which are capable of dissolving in very cold solutes–say, in this ethane lake here. When they dissolve they fill up the lake with long molecules analogous to our organic molecules. These can then link up into polymers using silicon-silicon bonds, silanes. They have weaker bonds than carbon molecules at terrestrial temperatures, but it's just what you need in a low-energy, low-temperature environment like this. With silanes as the basis you can dream up all sorts of complex molecules analogous to nucleic acids and proteins–"

"Just what we have here."

"Exactly. Nice complicated biomolecules for evolution to play with. They are more commonly found on the cooler, outer worlds–Neptune's moon Triton for example. But this lake is cold enough. The energy flow will be so low that it must take a *lo-ong* time for anything much to grow or evolve. But on Titan there is plenty of time." She let the filmy stuff glide off her manipulator scoop and back into the lake. "There's so much we don't know. There has to be an ecology in there, a food chain. Maybe the films are the primary producers–an equivalent of the plankton in our oceans, for instance. But where do they get their energy from? And how do they survive the annual drying-out of their lakes?"

"Good questions," I said. "I wish I cared."

She stowed her sample bottles in her pack. "I think you care more than you're prepared to admit. Nobody as intelligent as you is without curiosity. It goes with the territory. Anyhow we should get back to the gondola."

I hesitated. I hated to prove her right, that there was indeed a grain of curiosity lodged in my soul. But I pointed at the enigmatic black form lying further along the beach. "Maybe we should take a look at that first."

She glanced at it, and at me, and headed that way without another word.

It turned out, as I had suspected, that the crumpled form was a bird. I recalled one hitting our gondola during their assault and falling away; perhaps this was that very casualty.

It was a block of ice, about the size of my head, wrapped up in a torn sheet of black film. With great care Miriam used her manipulator arm to pick apart the film, as if she was unwrapping a Christmas present. The ice mass wasn't a simple lump but a mesh of spindly struts and bars surrounding a hollow core. It had been badly damaged by the fall. Miriam took samples of this and of the film.

"That ice lump looks light for its size," I said. "Like the bones of a bird."

"Which makes sense if it's a flying creature." Miriam was growing excited. "Jovik, look at this. The filmy stuff, the wings, look identical to the samples I took from the surface of the lake. It has to be silane. But the ice structure is different." She broke a bit of it open, and turned on a suit lamp so we could see a mass of very thin icicles, like fibers. It was almost sponge-like. Inside the fine ice straws were threads of what looked like discolored water. "Rich in organics," Miriam said, glancing at a data panel on her manipulator arm. "I mean, our sort of organics, CHON life, carbon-water–amino acids, a kind of DNA. There are puzzles here. Not least the fact that we find it *here*, by this lake. CHON life has been sampled on Titan before. But it's thought carbon-water life can only subsist here in impact-melt crater lakes, and we're a long way from anything like that . . ."

Her passion grew, a trait I have always found attractive.

"I think this is a bird, one of those we saw flying at us. But it seems to be a composite creature, a symbiosis of these hydrocarbon wings and the ice lump–saline life cooperating with CHON life. Just remarkable. You wonder how it came about in the first place . . . but I guess there are examples of just as intricate survival strategies in our own biosphere. Give evolution enough time and anything is possible. I wonder what it is they both *want*, though, what the two sides in this symbiosis get out of the relationship . . .

"It's a genuine discovery, Jovik. Nobody's seen this before–life from two entirely different domains working together. And I wouldn't have noticed it if not for you." She held out the ice lump to me. "They'll probably name it after you."

Her enthusiasm was fetching, but not that much. "Sure. But my concern right now is how much power we have left in these suit heaters. Let's get back to the gondola."

So she stowed away the remaining fragments of the Titan

bird, Jovik Emry's contribution to System science, and we retraced our path back to the gondola.

IX

Gondola

The days are very long on Titan, and by the time we got back to the gondola nothing seemed to have changed about the landscape or the sky, not a diffuse shadow had shifted. We found Poole and Dzik happily fixing big balloon wheels to axles slung beneath the crumpled hull.

When they were done, we all climbed back aboard. Poole had reset some of the interior lamps so they glowed green, yellow and blue; it was a relief to be immersed once more in bright Earth light.

We set off in our gondola-truck for the next part of our expedition. We were making, I was told, for an impact crater believed to hold liquid water, which itself was not far from a cryovolcano, another feature of interest for the science types. This site was only perhaps 100 kilometers from where we had come down.

Miriam transferred her samples to cold stores, and ran some of them through a small onboard science package. She jabbered about what she had discovered. Poole encouraged her more than Dzik did, but even that wasn't much.

Dzik and Poole were more interested in that moment with playing with the gondola. Like overgrown boys they sat at an improvised driver's console and fussed over gear ratios and the performance of the big tires. Poole even insisted on driving the bus himself, though Titan was so flat and dull for the most part he could easily have left the chore to the onboard systems. That proved to me the fallacy of not bringing along specialist biologists on a jaunt like this. It was only Miriam who seemed to have a genuine passion for the life systems we were supposed to be here to study; Dzik and Poole were too easily distracted by the technology, which was, after all, only a means to an end.

They had however rearranged the interior to make it feel a little less cramped. The couches had been separated and set up around the cabin, so you could sit upright with a bit of elbow room. The cabin was pressurized, so we could remove our helmets, and though the expandable walls didn't work any more there was room for one at a time to shuck off his or her exosuit. Poole ordered us to do so; we had already been inside the suits for a few hours, and the suits, and ourselves, needed some maintenance. Poole had set up a curtained-off area where we could let our discarded suits perform their self-maintenance functions while we had showers–of water recycled from our urine and sweat, which was deemed a lot safer than melt from the ice moon. Poole himself used the shower first, and then Miriam. She was hasty, eager to get back to her work, and kept talking even while she cleaned up.

After Miriam was out of the shower I took my turn. It was a miserable drizzle and lukewarm at that, but it was a relief to let my skin drink in the water. I was quick, though; with the unknown dangers of Titan only centimeters away beyond the gondola's fragile metal walls, I didn't want to spend long outside the security of the suit.

After me, Bill Dzik followed, and it was an unlovely stink his suit released. I was spitefully glad that for all his bluster his reaction to the terrors of our landing must have been just as ignoble as mine.

After a couple of hours we reached our destination. Safely suited up, I sat in my couch and peered over Miriam's and Poole's shoulders at the landscape outside. That cryovolcano was a mound that pushed out of the landscape some kilometers to the west of us. It had the look of a shield volcano, like Hawaii or Mons Olympus, a flat-profiled dome with a caldera on the top. It wasn't erupting while we sat there, but I could see how successive sheets of 'lava' had plated its sides.

That lava was water ice, heavily laced with ammonia, which had come gushing up from this world's strange mantle, a sea of ammonia and water kilometers down beneath our tires.

As for the crater lake I saw nothing but a plain, flatter and even more featureless than the average, covered with a thin scattering of ice sand. But the lake was there, hidden. Poole extracted radar images which showed the unmistakeable profile of an impact crater, right ahead of us, kilometers wide. Such is the vast energy pulse delivered by an infalling asteroid or comet–or, in Saturn's system, perhaps a ring fragment or a bit of a tide-shattered moon–the water locally can retain enough heat to remain liquid for a long time, thousands of years. Such a lake had formed here, and then frozen over with a thin crust, on top of which that skim of sand had been wind-blown. But the briny lake remained, hoarding its heat.

And, studded around the lake's circular rim, were more sponge-like masses like the one we had discovered wrapped up in silane film at the shore of the polar lake. These masses were positioned quite regularly around the lake, and many were placed close by crevasses which seemed to offer a route down into the deep structure of the ice rock beneath us. Miriam started gathering data eagerly.

Meanwhile Poole was puzzling over some images returned from the very bottom of the crater lake. He had found motion, obscure forms laboring. They looked to me like machines quarrying a rock deposit. But I could not read the images well enough, and as Poole did not ask my opinions I kept my mouth shut.

Miriam Berg was soon getting very agitated by what she was finding. Even as she gathered the data and squirted it up to Harry Poole in the *Crab*, she eagerly hypothesised. "Look–I think it's obvious that Titan is a junction between at least two kinds of life, the silanes of the ethane lakes and the CHON sponges. I've done some hasty analysis on the CHON tissues.

They're like us, but not identical. They use a subtly different subset of amino acids to build their proteins; and they have a variant of DNA in there–a different set of bases, a different coding system. The silanes, meanwhile, are like the life systems we've discovered in the nitrogen pools on Triton, but again not identical, based on a different subset of silicon-oxygen molecular strings.

"It's possible both forms of life were brought here through panspermia–the natural wafting of life between the worlds in the form of something like spores, blasted off their parent world by impacts and driven here by sunlight and gravity. If the System's CHON life arose first on Earth or Mars, it might easily have drifted here and seeded in a crater lake, and followed a different evolutionary strategy. Similarly the silanes at the poles found a place to live, and followed their own path, independently of their cousins . . ."

The transfer of materials from the oily ethane lakes to the water crater ponds might actually have facilitated such creations. You need membranes to make life, something to separate the inside of a cell from the outside. As water and oil don't mix, adding one to the other gives you a natural way to create such membranes.

She shook her head. "It seems remarkable that here we have a place, this moon, a junction where families of life from different ends of Sol System can coexist."

"But there's a problem," Bill Dzik called from his shower. "Both your silanes and your sponges live in transient environments. The ethane lakes pretty much dry up every Titan year. And each crater lake will freeze solid after a few thousand years."

"Yes," Miriam said. "Both forms need to migrate. And that's how, I think, they came to cooperate . . ."

She sketched a hasty narrative of the CHON sponges emerging from the crater lakes, and finding their way to the summer pole. Maybe they got there by following deep crevasses, smashed into Titan's ice crust by the impacts that dug out crater lakes like this one in the first place. Down there they would find liquid water, kilometers deep and close to the ammonia ocean. It would be cold, briny, not to terrestrial tastes, but it would be liquid, and survivable. And at the pole they would find the silane lilies floating on their ethane seas. The lilies in turn needed to migrate to the winter pole, where their precious life-stuff ethane was raining out.

Miriam mimed, her fist touching her flattened palm. "So they come together, the sponges and the lilies–"

"To make the Titan birds," I said.

"That's the idea. They come flapping up out of the lake, just as we saw, heading for the winter pole. And meanwhile, maybe the sponges get dropped off at fresh crater lakes along the way. It's a true symbiosis, with two entirely different spheres of life intersecting–and cooperating, for without the migration neither form could survive alone." She looked at us, suddenly doubtful. "We're all amateurs here. I guess any competent biologist could pick holes in this the size of the center of Saturn's rings."

Dzik said, "No competent biologist would even be hypothesising this way, not with so few facts."

"No," Virtual Harry said tinnily. "But at least you've come up with a plausible model, Miriam. And all without the need to evoke even a scrap of sentience. Good job."

"There are still questions," Miriam said. "Maybe the sponges provide the birds'intelligence, or at least some kind of directionality. But what about power? The lilies especially are a pretty low-energy kind of life form . . ."

Michael Poole said, "Maybe I can answer that. I've been doing some analysis of my own. I can tell you a bit more about the silane lilies' energy source. Believe it or not–even on a world as murky as this–I think they're photosynthesising." And he ran through the chemistry he thought he had identified, using entirely different compounds and molecular processing pathways from the chlorophyll-based green-plant photosynthesis of Earth life.

"Of course," Miriam said. "I should have seen it. I never even asked myself what the lilies were *doing* while they were lying around on the lake's surface . . . Trapping sunlight!"

Harry was growing excited too. "Hey, if you're right, son, you may already have paid for the trip. Silane-based low-temp photosynthesisers would be hugely commercially valuable. Think of it, you could grow them out of those nitrogen lakes on Triton and go scudding around the outer System on living sails." His grin was wide, even in the reduced Virtual image.

Poole and Miriam were smiling too, staring at each other with a glow of connection. Theirs was a strange kind of symbiosis, like silane lily and CHON sponge; they seemed to need the excitement of external discovery and achievement to bring them together.

Well, there was a happy mood in that grounded gondola, the happiest since we had crashed. Even Bill Dzik as he showered was making grunting, hog-like noises of contentment.

And just at that moment there was a crunching sound, like great jaws closing over metal, and the whole bus tipped to one side.

Poole and Miriam staggered and started shouting instructions to each other. I had my helmet over my head in a heartbeat.

Then there was another crunch, a ripping sound–and a scream, gurgling and suddenly cut off, and an inward rush of cold air that I felt even through my exosuit. I turned and saw that near the shower partition, a hole had been ripped in the side of the gondola's flimsy hull, revealing Titan's crimson murk. Something like a claw, or a huge version of Miriam's manipulator arm, was working at the hull, widening the breach.

And Bill Dzik, naked, not meters from the exosuit that could have saved him, was already frozen to death.

That was enough for me. I flung open the hatch in the gondola roof and lunged out, not waiting for Miriam or Poole. I hit the Titan sand and ran as best I could, the exosuit laboring to help me. I could hear crunching and chewing behind me. I did not look back.

When I had gone 100 meters I stopped, winded, and turned. Poole and Miriam were following me. I was relieved that at least I was not stranded on Titan alone.

And I saw what was becoming of our gondola. The machines that had assailed it–and they were machines, I had no doubt of it–were like spiders of ice, with lenticular bodies perhaps ten meters long, and each equipped with three grabber claws attached to delicate low-gravity limbs. Four or five of these things were laboring at the wreck of our gondola. I saw that they had gone for the wheels first, which was why we had tipped over, and now were making a fast job of ripping the structure apart. Not only that, beyond them I saw a line of similar-looking beasts carrying silvery fragments that could only be pieces of the gondola off up the rising ground towards the summit of the cryovolcano. Some of the larger components of the wreck they left intact, such as the GUT engine module, but they carried them away just as determinedly.

In minutes, I saw, there would be little left of our gondola on the ice surface–not much aside from Bill Dzik, who, naked, sprawled and staring with frozen eyeballs, made an ugly corpse, but did not deserve the fate that had befallen him.

Harry Poole's head popped into Virtual existence before us. "Well," he said, "that complicates things."

Michael swatted at him, dispersing pixels like flies.

X

Spiders

"Dzik is dead," I said. "And so are we." I turned on Michael Poole, fists bunched in the thick gloves. "You and your absurd ambition–it was always going to kill you one day, and now it's killed us all."

Michael Poole snorted his contempt. "And I wish I'd just thrown you into a jail back on Earth and left you to rot."

"Oh, Lethe," Miriam said with disgust. She was sifting through the scattered debris the spiders had left behind. "Do you two have any idea how ridiculous you look in those suits? Like two soft toys facing off. Anyhow you aren't dead yet, Jovik." She picked up bits of rubbish, rope, a few instruments, some of her precious sample flasks, enigmatic egg-shaped devices small enough to fit in her fist–and food packs.

Michael Poole's curiosity snagged him. "They didn't take everything."

"Evidently not. In fact, as you'd have noticed if you weren't too busy trading insults with your passenger, they didn't take *us.* Or Bill."

"What, then?"

"Metal. I think. Anything that has a significant metal component is being hauled away."

"Ah." Poole watched the spiders toiling up their volcano, bits of our ship clutched in their huge claws. "That makes a sort of sense. One thing this moon is short of is metal. Has been since its formation. Even the core is mostly light silicate rock, more like Earth's mantle than its iron core. Which maybe explains why every surface probe to Titan across 1600 years has disappeared without a trace–even the traces of your illegal sample-collectors, Emry. They were taken for the metal."And," he said, chasing the new idea, "maybe that's what we saw in the radar images of the deeps of the crater lake. Something toiling on the floor, you remember, as if quarrying? Maybe it was more of those spider things after the metallic content of the meteorite that dug out the crater in the first place."

"Well, in any event they left useful stuff behind," said Miriam, picking through the debris. "Anything ceramic, glass fiber, plastic. And the food packs. We won't starve, at least."

Poole had homed in on theory, while she focused on the essentials that might keep us alive. That tells you everything about the man's lofty nature.

"But they took the GUT engine, didn't they?" I put in sharply. "Our power source. Without which we'll eventually freeze to death, no matter how well fed we are."

"And, incidentally," Miriam said, "the identity-backup deck. We cached the backups in the GUT engine's own control and processing unit, the most reliable store on the gondola. If we lose that, we lose the last trace of poor Bill too."

I couldn't help but glance at Dzik's corpse, fast-frozen on the ice of Titan.

Not Poole, though. He was watching those receding spiders. "They're heading down into the volcano. Which is a vent that leads down into the mantle, the ammonia sea, right? Why? What the hell are those things?"

Miriam said, "One way to find out." She hefted one of those ceramic eggs in her right hand, pressed a stud that made it glow red, and hurled it towards the nearest spider. It followed a low-gravity arc, heavily damped in the thick air, and it seemed to take an age to fall. But her aim was good, and it landed not a meter from the spider.

And exploded. Evidently it had been a grenade. The spider shattered satisfactorily, those ugly claws going wheeling through the air.

Miriam had already started to run towards the spider. You couldn't fault her directness. "Come on."

Poole followed, and I too, unwilling to be left alone with Bill's frozen remains. Poole called, "What did you do that for?"

"We want to know what we're dealing with, don't we?"

"And why are we running?"

"So we can get there before the other spiders get rid of it."

And sure enough the other spiders, still laden with bits of the gondola, had already turned, and were closing on their shattered fellow. They didn't seem perturbed by the sudden destruction of one of their kind, or of our approaching presence. They seemed to perceive only what was essential to them–only what was metallic.

We got there first, and we squatted around the downed spider in a splash of suit light. The spider hadn't broken open; it was not enclosed by a hull or external carapace. Instead it had shattered into pieces, like a smashed sculpture. We pawed at the debris chunks, Miriam and Poole talking fast, analyzing, speculating. The chunks appeared to be mostly water ice, though Poole speculated it was a particular high-pressure form. The internal structure was not simple; it reminded me of a honeycomb, sharp-edged chambers whose walls enclosed smaller clusters of chambers and voids, on down through the length scales like a fractal. Poole pointed out threads of silver and a coppery color–the shades were uncertain in Titan's light. They were clearly metallic.

"So the spiders at least need metal," Miriam said. "I wonder what the power source is."

But we weren't to find out, for the other spiders had closed in and we didn't want to get chomped by accident. We backed off, dimming our suit lights.

Miriam asked, "So, biological or artificial? What do you think?"

Poole shrugged. "They seem dedicated to a single purpose, and have these metallic components. That suggests artificial. But that body interior looks organic. Grown."

I felt like putting Poole in his place. "Maybe these creatures transcend your simple-minded categories. Perhaps they are the result of a million years of machine evolution. Or the result of a long symbiosis between animal and technology."

Poole shook his head. "My money's on biology. Given enough time, necessity and selection can achieve some remarkable things."

Miriam said, "But why would their systems incorporate metal if it's so rare here?"

"Maybe they're not native to Titan," I said. "Maybe they didn't evolve here." But neither of them were listening to me. "The real question is," I said more urgently, "what do we do now?"

The head of Harry Poole, projected somehow by our suit's comms systems, popped into existence, the size of an orange, floating in the air. The small scale made his skin look even more unnaturally smooth. "And that," he said, "is the first intelligent question you've asked since we pressganged you, Jovik. You ready to talk to me now?"

Michael Poole glared at his father, then turned and sucked water from the spigot inside his helmet. "Tell us how bad it is, Harry."

"I can't retrieve you for seven days," Harry said.

I felt colder than Titan. "But the suits–"

"Without recharge our suits will expire in three days," Poole said. "Four at the most."

I could think of nothing to say.

Harry looked around at us, his disembodied head spinning eerily. "There are options."

"Go on," Poole said.

"You could immerse yourselves in the crater lake. The suits could withstand that. It's cold in there, the briny stuff is well below freezing, but it's not as cold as the open air. Kept warm by the residual heat of impact, remember. Even so you would only stretch out your time by a day or two."

"Not enough," Miriam said. "And we wouldn't get any work done, floating around in the dark in a lake."

I laughed at her. "Work? Who cares about work now?"

Poole said, "What else, Harry?"

"I considered options where two people might survive, rather than three. Or one. By sharing suits."

The tension between us rose immediately.

Harry said, "Of course those spiders also left you Bill's suit. The trouble is the power store is built into the fabric of each suit. To benefit you'd have to swap suits. I can't think of any way you could do that without the shelter of the gondola; you'd freeze to death in a second."

"So it's not an option," Poole said.

Miriam looked at us both steadily. "It never was."

I wasn't sure if I was relieved or not, for I had been determined, in those few moments when it seemed a possibility, that the last survivor in the last suit would be myself.

"So," Poole said to Harry, "what else?"

"You need the gondola's GUT engine to recharge your suits," Harry said. "There's just no alternative."

I pointed at the toiling spiders on the cryovolcano. "Those beasts have already thrown it into that caldera."

"Then you'll have to go after it," Harry said, and, comfortably tucked up in the *Crab*, he grinned at me. "Won't you?"

"How?" I was genuinely bewildered. "Are we going to build a submarine?"

"You won't need one," Harry said. "You have your suits. Just jump in . . ."

"Are you insane? You want us to jump into the caldera of a volcano, after a bunch of metal-chewing monster spiders?"

But Miriam and Poole, as was their way, had pounced on the new idea. Miriam said, "Jovik, you keep forgetting you're not on Earth. That 'volcano' is just spewing water, lava that's colder than your own bloodstream." She glanced at Harry. "The water's very ammonia-rich, however. I take it our suits can stand it?"

"They're designed for contact with the mantle material," Harry said. "We always knew that was likely. The pressure shouldn't be a problem either."

Poole said, "As for the spiders, they will surely leave us alone if we keep away from them. We know that. We might even use them in the descent. Follow the spiders, find the engine. Right?"

Harry said, "And there's science to be done." He displayed data in gleaming Virtual displays–cold summaries only meters away from Bill Dzik's corpse. Harry said that his preliminary analysis of our results showed that the primary source of the atmosphere's crucial methane was nothing in the air or the surface features, but a venting from the cryovolcanoes. "And therefore the ultimate source is somewhere in the ammonia sea," Harry said. "Biological, geological, whatever–it's down there."

"OK," Poole said. "So we're not going to complete the picture unless we go take a look."

"You won't be out of touch. I'll be able to track you, and talk to you all the way in. Our comms link has a neutrino-transmission basis; a few kilometers of ice or water isn't going to make any difference to that."

A few *kilometers*? I didn't like the sound of that.

"So that's that," Miriam said. "We have a plan."

"You have a shared delusion," I said.

They ignored me. Poole said, "I suggest we take an hour out. We can afford that. We should try to rest; we've been through a lot. And we need to sort through these supplies, figure out what we can use."

"Yeah," said Miriam. "For instance, how about nets of ice as ballast?"

So he and Miriam got down to work, sorting through the junk discarded by the spiders, knotting together cable to make nets. They were never happier than when busy on some task together.

And there was Bill Dzik, lying on his back, stark naked, frozen eyes staring into the murky sky. I think it tells you a lot about Michael Poole and even Miriam that they were so focussed on their latest goal that they had no time to consider the remains of this man whom they had worked with, apparently, for decades.

Well, I had despised the man, and he despised me, but something in me cringed at the thought of leaving him like that. I looked around for something I could use as a shovel. I found a strut and a ceramic panel from some internal partition in the gondola, and used cable to join them together.

Then I dug into the soil of Titan. The blade went in easily; the icy sand grains didn't cling together. As a native of Earth's higher gravity I was over-powered for Titan, and lifted great shovelfuls easily. But a half-meter or so down I found the sand was tighter packed and harder to penetrate, no doubt some artefact of Titan's complicated geology. I couldn't dig a grave deep enough for Bill Dzik. So I contented myself with laying him in my shallow ditch, and building a mound over him. Before I covered his face I tried to close his eyes, but of course the lids were frozen in place.

All the time I was working I clung to my anger at Michael Poole, for it was better than the fear.

XI

Volcano

So we climbed the flank of the cryovolcano, paralleling the trail followed by the ice spiders, who continued to toil up there hauling the last useful fragments of our gondola. We were laden too with our improvised gear—rope cradles, bags of ice-rock chunks for ballast, food packs. Miriam even wore a pack containing the pick of her precious science samples.

It wasn't a difficult hike. When we had risen above the sand drifts we walked on bare rock-ice, a rough surface that gave good footing under the ridges of our boots. I had imagined we'd slip walking up a bare ice slope, but at such temperatures the ice under your feet won't melt through the pressure of your weight, as on Earth, and it's that slick of meltwater that eliminates the friction.

But despite the easy climb, as we neared the caldera my legs felt heavy. I had no choice but to go on, to plunge into ever greater danger, as I'd had no real choice since being pressganged in the first place.

At last we stood at the lip of the caldera. We looked down over a crudely carved bowl perhaps half a kilometer across, water-ice rock laced with some brownish organic muck. Most of the bowl's floor was solid, evidently the cryovolcano was all but dormant, but there was a wide crevasse down which the spiders toiled into darkness. The spiders, laden as they were, clambered nimbly down the sides of this crevasse, and Poole pointed out how they climbed back up the far side, unladen. If you listened carefully you could hear a crunching sound, from deep within the crevasse.

This was what we were going to descend into.

"Don't even think about it," Miriam murmured to me. "Just do it."

But first we needed a tame spider.

We climbed a few paces down the flank, and stood alongside the toiling line. Miriam actually tried to lasso a spider as it crawled past us. This was a bit over-ambitious, as the thick air and low gravity gave her length of cable a life of its own. So she and Poole worked out another way. With a bit of dexterity they managed to snag cable loops around a few of the spider's limbs, and Poole threw cable back and forth under the beast's belly and over its back and tied it off, to make a kind of loose net around the spider's body. The spider didn't even notice these activities, it seemed, but continued its steady plod.

"That will do," Poole said. "All aboard!" Grasping his own burden of pack and ballast nets he made a slow-motion leap, grabbed the improvised netting, and set himself on the back of the spider. Miriam and I hurried to follow him.

So there we were, the three of us sitting on the back of

the beast with our hands wrapped in lengths of cable. The first few minutes of the ride weren't so bad, though the spider's motion was jolting and ungainly, and you always had the unpleasant awareness that there was no conscious mind directing this thing.

But then the lip of the caldera came on us, remarkably quickly. I wrapped my hands and arms tighter in the netting.

"Here we go!" Michael Poole cried, and he actually whooped as the spider tipped head first over the lip of the crevasse, and began to climb down its dead vertical wall. I could not see how it was clinging to the sheer wall–perhaps with suckers, or perhaps its delicate limbs found footholds. But my concern was for myself, for as the spider tipped forward we three fell head over heels, clinging to the net, until we were hanging upside down.

"Climb up!" Poole called. "It will be easier if we can settle near the back end."

It was good advice, but easier said than done, for to climb I had to loosen my grip on the cable to which I was clinging. I was the last to reach the arse end of the descending spider, and find a bit of respite in a surface I could lie on.

And all the while the dark of the chasm closed around us, and that dreadful crunching, chewing noise from below grew louder. I looked up to see the opening of this chimney as a ragged gash of crimson-brown, the only natural light; it barely cast a glow on the toiling body of the spider. Impulsively I ordered my suit to turn on its lights, and we were flooded with glare.

Poole asked, "Everybody OK?"

"Winded," Miriam said. "And I'm glad I took my claustrophobia pills before getting into the gondola. Look. What's that ahead?"

We all peered down. It was a slab of ice that appeared to span the crevasse. For an instant I wondered if this was as deep as we would have to go to find our GUT engine. But there was no sign of toiling spiders here, or of the pieces of our gondola, and I feared I knew what was coming next. That sound of crunching grew louder and louder, with a rhythm of its own.

"Brace yourselves," Poole said–pointless advice.

Our spider hit the ice floor. It turned out to be a thin crust, easily broken–that was the crunching we had heard, as spider after spider smashed through this interface. Beyond the broken crust I caught one glimpse of black, frothy water before I was dragged down into it, head first.

Immersed, I was no colder, but I could feel a sticky thickness all around me, as if I had been dropped into a vat of syrup. My suit lamps picked out enigmatic flecks and threads that filled the fluid around me. When I looked back, I saw the roof of this vent already freezing over, before it was broken by the plunging form of another spider, following ours.

Michael Poole was laughing. "Dunked in molten lava, Titan style. What a ride!"

I moaned, "How much longer? How deep will we go?"

"As deep as we need to. Have patience. But you should cut your lights, Emry. Save your power for heating."

"No, wait." Miriam was pointing at the ice wall that swept past us. "Look there. And there!"

And I made out tubular forms, maybe half a meter long or less, that clung to the walls, or, it seemed, made their purposeful way across it. It was difficult to see any detail, for they quickly shot up and out of our field of view.

"Life?" Poole said, boyishly excited once more.

Miriam said, "It looks like it, doesn't it?" Without warning us she loosened one hand from the net, and grabbed at one of the tubes and dragged it away from its hold on the wall. It wriggled in her hand, pale and sightless, a fat worm; its front end, open like a mouth, was torn.

"Ugh," I said. "Throw it back!"

But Miriam was cradling the thing. "Oh, I'm sorry. I hurt you, didn't I?"

Poole bent over it. "Alive, then."

"Oh, yes. And if it's surviving in this ammonia lava, I wouldn't mind betting it's a cousin of whatever's down below in the sea. More life, Michael!"

"Look, I think it's been browsing on the ice. They are clustered pretty thickly over the walls." And when I looked, I saw he was right; there the tube-fish were, browsing away, working their way slowly up the vent. "Maybe they actively keep the vent open, you think?"

Poole took a small science box from Miriam's pack, and there, together, even as we rode that alien back down into the throat of the volcano, they briskly analyzed the beast's metabolism, and the contents of the water we were immersed in, and sent the results back to the *Hermit Crab*. Harry's Virtual head popped up before us, grinning inanely, even in that extreme situation.

I had seen enough. With a snap, I made my suit turn its lights off. I had no desire to sit shivering in the dark as invisible ice walls plummeted past me. But I was gambling that curiosity would get the better of Poole and Miriam, and I was right; soon it was Poole whose suit glowed, spending his own precious power to light me up, as they labored over their pointless science.

"So I was right," Miriam breathed at last. "This vent, and the mantle ocean, host a whole other life domain—*a third* on Titan, in addition to the silanes and the CHON sponges. Ammono life . . ."

Titan's liquid mantle is thought to be a relic of its formation, in a part of the solar nebula where ammonia was common. Titan was born with a rocky core and a deep open ocean, of water laced with ammonia. The ocean might have persisted for a billion years, warmed by greenhouse effects under a thick primordial atmosphere. A billion years is plenty of time for life to evolve. With time the ocean surface froze over to form an icy crust, and at the ocean's base complex high-pressure forms of ice formed a deep solid layer enclosing the silicate core. Ice above and below, but still the liquid ocean persisted between, ammonia-rich water, very alkaline, very viscous. And in that deep ocean a unique kind of life adapted to its strange environment, based on chemical bonds between carbon and nitrogen-hydrogen chemical groups rather than carbon-oxygen, using ammonia as its solute rather than water: "ammono life," the specialists call it.

"Yes, a third domain," Miriam said. "One unknown elsewhere in Sol System so far as I know. So here on Titan you have a junction of three entirely different domains of life: native ammono life in the mantle ocean, CHON life in the crater lakes blown in from the inner system, and the silane lilies wafting in from Triton and the outer cold. Incredible."

"More than that," Harry said tinnily. "Michael, that tube-fish of yours is not a methanogen–it doesn't create methane–but it's full of it. Methane is integral to its metabolism, as far as I can see from the results you sent me. It even has methane in its flotation bladders."

Miriam looked at the tube-fish blindly chewing at the ice walls. "Right. They collect it somehow, from some source deep in the ocean. They use it to float up here. They even nibble the cryovolcano vent walls, to keep them open. They have to be integral to delivering the methane from the deep ocean sources to the atmosphere. So you have the three domains not just sharing this moon but cooperating in sustaining its ecology."

Harry said, "Quite a vision. And as long as they're all stupid enough, we might make some money out of this damn system yet."

Miriam let go of her tube-fish, like freeing a bird; it wriggled off into the dark. "You always were a realist, Harry."

I thought I saw blackness below us, in the outer glimmer of Poole's suit lamps. "Harry. How deep is this ice crust, before we get to the mantle ocean?"

"Around 35 kilometers."

"And how deep are we now? Can you tell?"

"Oh, around 35 kilometers."

Michael Poole gasped. "Lethe. Grab hold, everybody."

It was on us almost at once: the base of the vent we had followed all the way down from the cryovolcano mouth at the surface, a passage right through the ice crust of Titan. I gripped the net and shut my eyes.

As we passed out of the vent, through the roof of ice and into the mantle beneath, I felt the walls recede from me, a wash of pressure, a vast opening-out.

And we fell into the dark and cold.

XII

Ocean

Now that the walls were gone from under its limbs I could feel that the spider was swimming, or perhaps somehow jetting, ever deeper into that gloopy sea, while the three of us held on for our lives. Looking up I saw the base of Titan's solid crust, an ice roof that covered the whole world, glowing in the light of Poole's lamps but already receding. And I thought I saw the vent from which we had emerged, a much eroded funnel around which tube-fish swam languidly. Away from the walls I could more easily see the mechanics of how they swam; lacking fins or tails, they seemed to twist through the water, a motion maybe suited to the viscosity of the medium. They looked more like vast bacteria than fish.

Soon we were so far beneath the ice roof that it was invisible, and we three and the crab that dragged us down were a single point of light falling into the dark. And Poole turned off his suit lamps!

I whimpered, "Lethe, Poole, spare us."

"Oh, have a heart," Miriam said, and her own suit lit up. "Just for a time. Let him get used to it."

I said, "Get used to what? Falling into this endless dark?"

"Not endless," Poole said. "The ocean is no more than–how much, Harry?"

"250 kilometers deep," Harry said, mercifully not presenting a Virtual to us. "Give or take."

"250 . . . How deep are you intending to take us, Poole?"

"I told you," Michael Poole said grimly. "As deep as it takes. We have to retrieve that GUT engine, Emry. We don't have a choice–simple as that."

"And I have a feeling," Miriam said bleakly, "now we're out of that vent, that we may be heading all the way down to the bottom. It's kind of the next logical choice."

"We'll be crushed," I said dismally.

"No," Harry Poole piped up. "Look, Jovik, just remember Titan isn't a large world. The pressure down there is only about four times what you'd find in Earth's deepest oceans. Five, tops. Your suit is over-engineered. Whatever it is that kills you, it won't be crushing."

"How long to the bottom, then?"

Harry said, "You're falling faster than you'd think, given the viscosity of the medium. That spider is a strong swimmer. A day, say."

"A day!"

Miriam said, "There may be sights to see on the way down."

"What sights?"

"Well, the tube-fish can't exist in isolation. There has to be a whole ammono ecology in the greater deeps."

My imagination worked overtime. "Ammono sharks. Ammono whales."

Miriam laughed. "Sluggish as hell, in this cold soup. And besides, they couldn't eat you, Jovik."

"They might spit me out after trying." I tried to think beyond my immediate panic. "But even if we survive–even if we find our damn GUT engine down there on the ice–how are we supposed to get back?"

Poole said easily, "All we need to do is dump our ballast and we'll float up. We don't need to bring up the GUT engine, remember, just use it to recharge the suits."

Miriam said, "A better option might be to hitch a ride with another spider."

"Right. Which would solve another problem," Poole said. "Which is to find a cryovolcano vent to the surface. The spiders know the way, evidently."

Harry said, "And even if the spiders let you down, I could guide you. I can see you, the vent mouths, even the GUT engine. This neutrino technology was worth the money it cost. There's no problem, in principle."

At times I felt less afraid of the situation than of my companions, precisely because of their lack of fear.

Miriam fetched something from a pack at her waist, I couldn't see what, and glanced at Poole. "Novak's not going to survive a descent lasting a day. Not in the dark."

Poole looked at me, and at her. "Do it."

"Do what?"

But I had no time to flinch as she reached across, and with expert skill pressed a vial into a valve in the chest of my exosuit. I felt a sharp coldness as the drug pumped into my bloodstream, and after that only a dreamless sleep, cradled in the warmth of my cushioned suit.

So I missed the events of the next hours, the quiet times when Poole and Miriam tried to catch some sleep themselves, the flurries of excitement when strange denizens of Titan's ammono deep approached them out of the dark.

And I missed the next great shock suffered by our strange little crew, when the base of Titan's underground ocean, an ice floor 300 kilometers beneath the surface, at last hove into view. The strange landscape of this abyssal deep, made of folded high-pressure ices littered by bits of meteorite rock, was punctured by vents and chasms, like an inverted mirror image of the crust far above us. *And the spider we rode did not slow down.* It hurled itself into one of those vents, and once more its limbs began to clatter down a wall of smooth rock-ice.

Harry warned Miriam and Poole that this latest vent looked as if it penetrated the whole of this inner layer of core-cladding ice–Ice VI, laced by ammonia dihydrate–a layer another 500 kilometers deep. At the base of this vent there was only Titan's core of silicate rocks, and there, surely, the spiders' final destination must lie.

There was nothing to be done but to endure the ride. It would take perhaps a further day. So Poole and Miriam allowed the spider to drag us down. More tube-fish, of an exotic high-pressure variety, grazed endlessly at the icy walls. Miriam popped me another vial to keep me asleep, and fed me intravenous fluids. Harry fretted about the exhaustion of our power, and the gradual increase of pressure; beneath a column of water and ice hundreds of kilometers deep, we were approaching our suits' manufactured tolerance. But they had no choice to continue, and I, unconscious, had no say in the matter.

When the ride was over, when the spider had at last come to rest, Miriam woke me up.

I was lying on my back on a lumpy floor. The gravity felt even weaker than on the surface. Miriam's face hovered over me, illuminated by suit lamps. She said, "Look what we found."

I sat up. I felt weak, dizzy–hungry. Beside me, in their suits, Miriam and Poole sat watching my reaction. Then I remembered where I was and the fear cut in.

I looked around quickly. Even by the glow of the suit lamps I could not see far. The murkiness and floating particles told me I must be still immersed in the water of Titan's deep ocean. I saw a roof of ice above me–not far, 100 meters or so. Below me was a surface of what looked like rock, dark and purple-streaked. I was in a sort of ice cavern, then, whose walls were off in the dark beyond our bubble of light. I learned later that I was in a cavern dug out beneath the lower icy mantle of Titan, between it and the rocky core, 800 kilometers below the icy plains where I had crash-landed days before. Around us I saw ice spiders, toiling away at their own enigmatic tasks, and bits of equipment from the gondola, chopped up, carried here and deposited. There was the GUT engine! My heart leapt; perhaps I would yet live through this.

But even the engine wasn't what Miriam had meant. She repeated, "Look what we found."

I looked. Set in the floor, in the rocky core of the world, was a hatch.

XIII

Hatch

They allowed me to eat and drink, and void my bladder. Moving around was difficult, the cold water dense and syrupy; every movement I made was accompanied by the whir of servomotors, as the suit labored to assist me.

I was reassured to know that the GUT engine was still functioning, and that my suit cells had been recharged. In principle I could stay alive long enough to get back to the *Hermit Crab.* All I had to do was find my way out of the core of this world, up through 800 kilometers of ice and ocean . . . I clung to the relief of the moment, and put off my fears over what was to come next.

Now that I was awake, Michael Poole, Miriam Berg, and Virtual Harry rehearsed what they had figured out about methane processing on Titan. Under that roof of ice, immersed in that chill high-pressure ocean, they talked about comets and chemistry, while all the while the huge mystery of the hatch in the ground lay between us, unaddressed.

Harry said, "On Earth 95 percent of the methane in the air is of biological origin. The farts of animals, decaying vegetation. So could the source be biological here? You guys have surveyed enough of the environment to rule that out. There could in principle be methanogen bugs living in those ethane lakes, for instance, feeding off reactions between acetylene and hydrogen, but you found nothing significant. What about a delivery of the methane by infalling comets? It's possible, but then you'd have detected other trace cometary gases, which are absent from the air. One plausible possibility remains . . ."

When Titan was young its ammonia-water ocean extended all the way to the rocky core. There, chemical processes could have produced plentiful methane: the alkaline water reacting with the rock would liberate hydrogen, which in turn would react with sources of carbon, monoxide or dioxide or carbon grains, to manufacture methane. But that process would have been stopped as soon as the ice layers plated over the rock core, insulating it from liquid water. What was needed, then, was some way for chambers to be kept open at the base of the ice, where liquid water and rock could still react at their interface. And a way for the methane produced to reach the ocean, and then the surface.

"The methane could be stored in clathrates, ice layers," Harry said. "That would work its way to the surface eventually. Simpler to build vents up through the ice, and encourage a chemoautotrophic ecosystem to feed off the methane, and deliver it to higher levels."

"The tube-fish," I said.

"And their relatives, yes."

Looking up at the ice ceiling above me, I saw how it had been shaped and scraped, as if by lobster claws. "So the spiders keep these chambers open, to allow the methane-creating reactions to continue."

"That's it," Michael Poole said, wonder in his voice. "They do it to keep a supply of methane pumping up into the atmosphere. And they've been doing it for billions of years. Have to have been, for the ecologies up there to have evolved as they have–the tube-fish, the CHON sponges, the silanes. *This whole world is an engine*, a very old engine. It's an engine for creating methane, for turning what would otherwise be just another nondescript ice moon into a haven, whose purpose is to foster the life forms that inhabit it."

"And where there is an engine, there are engineers," Miriam said.

"Yes. But why did they build all this?"

None of them could answer that.

"Ha!" I barked laughter. "Well, the why of it is irrelevant. The spiders are clearly sentient–or their makers are. You have found precisely what you were afraid of, haven't you, Michael Poole? Sentience at the heart of Titan. You will never be allowed to open it up for exploitation now. So much for your commercial ambitions!"

"Which you were going to share in," Harry reminded me, scowling.

I sneered. "Oh, I'd only have wasted the money on drugs and sex. To see you world-builders crestfallen is worth that loss. So what's under the hatch?"

They glanced at each other. "The final answers, we hope," Michael Poole said.

Miriam said, "We've put off looking under there until we brought you round, Jovik."

Poole said, "We've no idea what's under there. We need everybody awake, ready to react. We might even need your help, Emry." He looked at me with faint disgust. "And," he said more practically, "it's probably going to take three of us to open it. Come see."

We all floated through the gloopy murk.

The hatch was a disc of some silvery metal, perhaps three meters across, set flush into the roughly flat rocky ground.

Spaced around its circumference were three identical grooves, each maybe ten centimeters deep. In the middle of each groove was a mechanism like a pair of levers, hinged at the top.

Michael said, "We think you operate it like this." He knelt and put his gloved hands to either side of the levers, and mimed pressing them together. "We don't know how heavy the mechanism will be. Hopefully each of us can handle one set of levers, with the help of our suits."

"Three mechanisms," I said. "This is a door meant to be operated by a spider, isn't it? One handle for each of those three big claws."

"We think so," Miriam said. "The handles look about the right size. We think the handles must have to be worked simultaneously–one spider, or three humans."

"I can't believe that after a billion years all they have is a clunky mechanical door."

Poole said, "It's hard to imagine a technology however advanced that won't have manual backups. We've seen that the spiders themselves aren't perfect; they're not immune to breakdown and damage."

"As inflicted by us." I gazed reluctantly at the hatch. "Must we do this? You've found what you wanted–or didn't want. Why expose us to more risk? Can't we just go home?"

Miriam and Michael just stared at me, bewildered. Miriam said, "You could walk away, without *knowing*?"

Poole said, "Well, we're not leaving here until we've done this, Emry, so you may as well get it done." He crouched down by his handle, and Miriam did the same.

I had no choice but to join them.

Poole counted us down: "Three, two, one."

I closed my gloved hands over the levers and pushed them together. It was awkward to reach down, and the mechanism felt heavy; my muscles worked, and I felt the reaction push me up from the floor. But the levers closed together.

The whole hatch began to vibrate.

I let go and moved back quickly. The others did the

same. We stood in a circle, wafted by the currents of the ammonia sea, and watched that hatch slide up out of the ground.

It was like a piston, rising up one meter, two. Its sides were perfectly smooth, perfectly reflective, without a scuff or scratch. I wondered at how old it must be. Michael Poole, fool that he was, reached up a gloved monkey-curious hand to touch it, but Miriam restrained him. "I'd like to measure the tolerances on that thing," he murmured.

Then the great slab, around three meters wide and two tall, slid sideways. Poole had to step out of the way. The scrape across the rough rock ground was audible, dimly. The shift revealed a hole in the ground, a circle—and at first I thought it was perfectly black. But then I saw elusive golden glimmers, sheets of light like soap bubbles; if I turned my head a little I lost it again.

"Woah," Harry Poole said. "There's some exotic radiation coming out of that hole. You should all back off. The suits have heavy shielding, but a few meters of water won't hurt."

I didn't need telling twice. We moved away towards the GUT engine, taking the light with us. The hole in the ground, still just visible in the glow of our suit lamps, looked a little like one of the ethane lakes on the surface, with that metallic monolith beside it. But every so often I could make out that elusive golden-brown glimmer. I said, "It looks like a facet of one of your wormhole Interfaces, Poole."

"Not a bad observation," Poole said. "And I have a feeling that's exactly what we're looking at. Harry?"

"Yeah." Harry was hesitating. "I wish you had a better sensor suite down there. I'm relying on instruments woven into your suits, internal diagnostic tools in the GUT engine, some stray neutrino leakage up here . . . Yes, I think we're seeing products of stressed spacetime. There are some interesting optical effects too–light lensed by a distorted gravity field."

"So it's a wormhole interface?" Miriam asked.

"If it is," Poole said, "it's far beyond the clumsy monstrosities we construct in Jovian orbit. And whatever is on the other side of that barrier, my guess is it's not on Titan . . ."

"Watch out," Miriam said.

A spider came scuttling past us towards the hole. It paused at the lip, as if puzzled that the hole was open. Then it tipped forward, just as the spider we rode into the volcano had dipped into the caldera, and slid head first through that sheet of darkness. It was as if it had fallen into a pool of oil that closed over the spider without a ripple.

"I wouldn't recommend following," Harry said. "The radiations in there are deadly, suit or no suit; you couldn't survive the passage."

"Lethe," Michael Poole said. He was actually disappointed.

"So are we done here?" I asked.

Poole snapped, "I'll tell you something, Emry, I'm glad you're here. Every time we come to an obstacle and you just want to give up, it just goads me into trying to find a way forward."

"There *is* no way forward," I said. "It's lethal. Harry said so."

"We can't go on," Miriam agreed. "But how about a probe? Something radiation-hardened, a controlling AI–with luck we could just drop it in there and let it report back."

"That would work," Poole said. Without hesitation the two of them walked over to the GUT engine, and began prying at it.

For redundancy the engine had two control units. Miriam and Poole detached one of these. Containing a sensor suite, processing capabilities, a memory store, it was a white-walled box the size of a suitcase. Within this unit and its twin sibling were stored the identity backups that had been taken of us before our ride into Titan's atmosphere. The little box was even capable of projecting Virtuals; Harry's sharp image was being projected right now by the GUT engine hardware, rather than through a pooling of our suits' systems as before.

The box was small enough just to be dropped through the interface, and hardened against radiation. It would survive a passage through the wormhole–though none of us could say if it would survive what lay on the other side. And it had transmitting and receiving capabilities. Harry believed its signals would make it back through the interface, though probably scrambled by gravitational distortion and other effects, but he was confident he could construct decoding algorithms from a few test signals. The unit was perfectly equipped to serve as a probe through the hatch, save for one thing. What the control box didn't have was intelligence.

Michael Poole stroked its surface with a gloved hand. "We're sending it into an entirely unknown situation. It's going to have to work autonomously, to figure out its environment, work out some kind of sensor sweep, before it can even figure out how to talk to us and ask us for direction. Running a GUT engine is a pretty simple and predictable job; the AI in there isn't capable of handling an exploration like these."

"But," I said, "it carries in its store backups of four human intellects–mine, dead Bill, and you two geniuses. What a shame we can't all ride along with it!"

My sarcasm failed to evoke the expected reaction. Poole and Miriam looked at each other, electrified. Miriam shook her head. "Jovik, you're like some idiot savant. You keep on coming up with such ideas. I think you're actually far smarter than you allow yourself to be."

I said honestly, "I have no idea what you're talking about."

"The idea you've suggested to them," Harry said gently,

"is to revive one of the dormant identity-backup copies in the unit's store, and use *that* as the controlling intelligence."

As always when they hit on some new idea Poole and Miriam were like two eager kids. Poole said, "It's going to be a shock to wake up, to move straight from Titan entry to this point. It would be least disconcerting if we projected a full human animus."

"You're telling me," said the head of Harry Poole.

"And some enclosing environment," Miriam said. "Just a suit? No, to be adrift in space brings in problems with vertigo. I'd have trouble with that."

"The lifedome of the *Crab*," Poole said. "That would be straightforward enough to simulate to an adequate degree. And a good platform for observation. The power would be sufficient to sustain that for a few hours at least . . ."

"Yes." Miriam grinned. "Our observer will feel safe. I'll get to work on it . . ."

I asked, "So you're planning to project a Virtual copy of one of us through the wormhole. And how will you get him or her back?"

They looked at me. "That won't be possible," Poole said. "The unit will be lost. It's possible we could transmit back a copy of the memories the Virtual accrues on the other side—integrate them somehow with the backup in the GUT engine's other store—"

"No," Harry said regretfully. "The data rate through that interface would never allow even that. For the copy in there it's a one way trip."

"Well, that's entirely against the sentience laws," I put in. They ignored me.

Poole said, "That's settled, then. The question is, *who*? Which of the four of us are you going to wake up from cyber-sleep and send into the unknown?"

I noticed that Harry's disembodied floating head looked away, as if he were avoiding the question.

Poole and Miriam looked at each other. Miriam said, "Either of us would go. Right?"

"Of course."

"But we should give it to Bill," Miriam said firmly.

"Yeah. There's no other choice. Bill's gone, and we can't bring his stored backup home with us . . . We should let his backup have the privilege of doing this. It will make the sacrifice worthwhile."

I stared at them. "This is the way you treat your friend? By killing him, then reviving a backup and sending it to another certain death?"

Poole glared at me. "Bill won't see it that way, believe me. You and a man like Bill Dzik have nothing in common, Emry. Don't judge him by your standards."

"Fine. Just don't send me."

"Oh, I won't. You don't deserve it."

It took them only a few more minutes to prepare for the experiment. The control pack didn't need any physical modifications, and it didn't take Miriam long to program instructions into its limited onboard intelligence. She provided it with a short orientation message, in the hope that Virtual Bill wouldn't be left entirely bewildered at the sudden transition he would experience.

Poole picked up the pack with his gloved hands, and walked towards the interface, or as close as Harry advised him to get. Then Poole hefted the pack over his head. "Good luck, Bill." He threw the pack towards the interface, or rather pushed it; its weight was low but its inertia was just as it would have been on Earth, and besides Poole had to fight against the resistance of the syrupy sea. For a while it looked as if the pack might fall short. "I should have practiced a couple of times," Poole said ruefully. "Never was any use at physical sports."

But he got it about right. The pack clipped the rim of the hole, then tumbled forward and fell slowly, dreamlike, through that black surface. As it disappeared autumn gold glimmered around it.

Then we had to wait, the three of us plus Harry. I began to wish that we had agreed some time limit; obsessives like Poole and Miriam were capable of standing there for hours before admitting failure.

In the event it was only minutes before a scratchy voice sounded in our suit helmets. "Harry? Can you hear me?"

"Yes!" Harry called, grinning. "Yes, I hear you. The reception ought to get better, the clean-up algorithms are still working. Are you all right?"

"Well, I'm sitting in the *Crab* lifedome. It's kind of a shock to find myself here, after bracing my butt to enter Titan. Your little orientation show helped, Miriam."

Poole asked, "What do you see?"

"The sky is . . . strange."

Miriam was looking puzzled. She turned and looked at Harry. "That's not all that's strange. That's not Bill!"

"Indeed not," came the voice from the other side of the hole. "I am Michael Poole."

XIV

Virtual

So, while a suddenly revived Michael Poole floated around in other-space, the original Poole and his not-lover Miriam Berg engaged in a furious row with Harry.

Poole stormed over to the GUT engine's remaining control pack, and checked the memory's contents. It didn't contain backup copies of the four of us; it contained only one ultra-high-fidelity copy of Michael Poole himself. I could not decide which scared me more: the idea that no copies of myself existed in that glistening white box, or the belief I had entertained previously that there had. I am prone to existential doubt, and am uncomfortable with such notions.

But such subtleties were beyond Michael Poole in his anger. "Miriam, I swear I knew nothing about this."

"Oh, I believe you."

They both turned on the older Poole. "Harry?" Michael snapped. "What in Lethe is this?"

Disembodied-head Harry looked shifty, but he was going to brazen it out. "As far as I'm concerned there's nothing to apologize for. The storage available on the *Crab* was always limited, and it was worse in the gondola. Michael's my son. Of course I'm going to protect him above others. What would you do? I'm sorry, Miriam, but–"

"You aren't sorry at all," Miriam snapped. "And you're a cold-hearted bastard. You knowingly sent a backup of your son, who you say you're trying to protect, through that wormhole to die!"

Harry looked uncomfortable. "It's just a copy. There are other backups, earlier copies–"

"Lethe, Dad," Michael Poole said, and he walked away, bunching his fists. I wondered how many similar collisions with his father the man had had to suffer in the course of his life.

"What's done is done," came a whisper. And they all quit their bickering, because it was Michael Poole who had spoken–the backup Poole, the one recently revived, the one beyond the spacetime barrier. "I know I don't have much time. I'll try to project some imagery back . . ."

Harry, probably gratefully, popped out of existence, thus vacating the available processing capacity, though I was sure his original would be monitoring us from the *Crab*.

Poole murmured to Miriam, "You speak to him. Might be easier for him than me."

She clearly found this idea distressing. But she said, "All right."

Gradually images built up in the air before us, limited views, grainy with pixels, flickering.

And we saw Virtual Poole's strange sky.

The Virtual *Crab* floated over a small object–like an ice moon, like one of Titan's Saturnian siblings, pale and peppered with worn impact craters. I saw how its surface was punctured with holes, perfectly round and black. These looked like our hatch; the probe we had despatched must have emerged from one of them. Things that looked like our spiders toiled to and fro between the holes, travelling between mounds of some kind of supplies. They were too distant to see clearly. All this was bathed in a pale yellow light, diffuse and without shadows.

The original Poole said, "You think those other interfaces connect up to the rest of Titan?"

"I'd think so," Miriam said. "This can't be the only deep-sea methane-generation chamber. Passing through the wormholes and back again would be a way for the spiders to unify their operations across the moon."

"So the interface we found, set in the outer curved surface of Titan's core, is one of a set that matches another set on the outer curved surface of that ice moon. The curvature would seem to flip over when you passed through."

This struck me as remarkable, a paradox difficult to grasp, but Poole was a wormhole engineer, and used to the subtleties of spacetime manipulated and twisted through higher dimensions; slapping two convex surfaces together was evidently child's play to him, conceptually.

Miriam asked Virtual Poole, "But where are you? That's an ice moon, a common object. Could be anywhere in the universe. Could even be in some corner of our own System."

Poole's Virtual copy said, his voice a whispery, channel-distorted rasp, "Don't jump to conclusions, Miriam. Look up."

The viewpoint swivelled, and we saw Virtual Poole's sky.

A huge, distorted sun hung above us. Planetoids hung

sprinkled before its face, showing phases from crescents to half-moons, and some were entirely black, fly-speck eclipses against the face of the monster. Beyond the limb of the sun more stars hung, but they were also swollen, pale beasts, their misshapen discs visible. And the space between the stars did not look entirely black to me, but a faint, deep crimson with a pattern, a network of threads and knots. It reminded me of what I saw when I closed my eyes.

"What a sky," Poole murmured.

"Michael, you're far from home," Miriam called.

Virtual Poole replied, "Yes. Those stars don't fit our main sequence. And their spectra are simple–few heavy elements. They're more like the protostars of our own early universe, I think: the first generation, formed of not much more than the hydrogen and helium that came out of the Big Bang."

"No metals," observed Miriam Berg.

"I'll send through the data I'm collecting–"

"Getting it, son," came Harry Poole's voice.

The others let Virtual Poole speak. His words, the careful observations delivered by a man so far from home, or at least by a construct that felt as if it were a man, were impressive in their courage.

"This is not our universe," he whispered. "I think that's clear. This one is young, and small–according to the curvature of spacetime, only a few million light years across. Probably not big enough to accommodate our Local Group of galaxies."

"A pocket universe, maybe," Miriam said. "An appendix from our own."

"I can't believe the things you have been calling 'spiders' originated here," the Virtual said. "You said it, Miriam. No metals here, not in this entire cosmos. That's why they were scavenging metals from probes, meteorites."

"They came from somewhere else, then," Poole said. "There was nothing strange in the elemental abundance we recorded in the spider samples we studied. So they come from elsewhere in our own universe. The pocket universe is just a transit interchange. Like Earthport."

The Virtual said, "Yes. And maybe behind these other moons in my sky lie gateways to other Titans–other sustained ecologies, maybe with different biological bases. Other experiments."

Miriam said, "So if metals are so essential for the spiders, why not have supplies brought to them through the interchange?"

"Maybe they did, once," the Virtual said. "Maybe things broke down. There's a sense of age here, Miriam. This is a young cosmos maybe, but I think this is an old place . . ."

The real Poole murmured, "It makes sense. The time axis in the baby universe needn't be isomorphic with ours. A million years over there, a billion years here."

The Virtual whispered, "Those spiders have been toiling at their task on Titan a long, long time. Whoever manufactured them, or bred them, left them behind a long time ago, and they've been alone ever since. Just doing their best to keep going. Looking at them, I get the impression they aren't too bright. Just functional."

"But they did a good job," Miriam said.

"That they did."

"But why?" I blurted out. "What's the purpose of all this, the nurturing of an ecology on Titan for billions of years–and perhaps similar on a thousand other worlds?"

"I think I have an idea," Virtual Poole whispered. "I never even landed on Titan, remember. Perhaps, coming at all this so suddenly, while the rest of you have worked through stages of discovery, I see it different . . .

"Just as this pocket universe is a junction, so maybe Titan is a junction, a haven where different domains of life can coexist. You've found the native ammono fish, the CHON sponges that may originate in the inner system, perhaps even coming from Earth, and the silanes from Triton and beyond. Maybe there are other families to find if you had time to look.

All these kinds of life, arising from different environments–but all with one thing in common. All born of planets, and of skies and seas, in worlds warmed by stars.

"But the stars won't last forever. In the future the universe will change, until it resembles our own time even less than our universe resembles this young dwarf cosmos. What then? Look, if you were concerned about preserving life, all forms of life, into the very furthest future, then perhaps you would promote–"

"Cooperation," said Miriam Berg.

"You got it. Maybe Titan is a kind of prototype of an ecology where life forms of such different origins can mix, find ways of using each other to survive–"

"And ultimately merge, somehow," Miriam said. "Well, it's happened before. Each of us is a community with once-disparate and very different life forms toiling away in each of our cells. It's a lovely vision, Michael."

"And plausible," his original self said gruffly. "Anyhow it's a hypothesis that will do until something better comes along."

I sneered at that. This dream of cosmic cooperation struck me as the romantic fantasy of a man alone and doomed to die, and soon. We all project our petty lives upon the universe. But I had no better suggestions to make. And, who knows? Perhaps Virtual Poole was right. None of us will live to find out.

"Anyhow," I said, "charming as this is–are we done *now*?"

Miriam snapped, "We can't abandon Michael."

"Go," whispered Virtual Poole. "There's nothing you can do for me. I'll keep observing, reporting, as long as I can."

I gagged on his nobility.

Now Harry intruded, grabbing a little of the available Virtual projection capacity. "But we've still got business to conclude before you leave here."

XV

Resolution

Poole frowned. "What business?"

"We came here to prove that Titan is without sentience," Harry said. "Well, we got that wrong. Now what?"

Miriam Berg was apparently puzzled we were even having the conversation. "We report what we've found to the sentience oversight councils and elsewhere. It's a major discovery. We'll be rapped for making an unauthorised landing on Titan, but–"

"Is that the sum of your ambition?" I snapped. "To hope the authorities will be lenient if you reveal the discovery that is going to ruin you?"

She glared at me. "What's the choice?"

"Isn't it obvious?" I looked at her, and Poole, who I think was guessing what I was going to say, and Harry, who looked away as he usually did at moments of crisis. Suddenly, after days of pointless wonders, I was in my element, the murky world of human relationships, and I could see a way forward where they could not. "*Destroy this*," I said. I waved a hand. "All of it. You have your grenades, Miriam. You could bring this cavern down."

"Or," Harry said, "there is the GUTdrive. If that were detonated, if unified-field energies were loosed in here, the wormhole interface too would surely be disrupted. I'd imagine that the connection between Titan and the pocket universe would be broken altogether."

I nodded. "I hadn't thought of that, but I like your style, Harry. Do it. Let this place be covered up by hundreds of kilometers of ice and water. Destroy your records. It will make no difference to the surface, what's going on in the atmosphere, not immediately. Nobody will ever know all this was here."

Harry Poole said, "That's true. Even if methane generation stops immediately the residual would persist in the atmosphere for maybe ten million years. I venture to suggest that if the various multi-domain critters haven't learned to cooperate in that time, they never will. Ten megayears is surely enough."

Miriam looked at him, horrified by his words. "You're suggesting a monstrous crime," she breathed. "To think of destroying such a wonder as this, the product of a billion years–to destroy it for personal gain! Michael, Lethe, leave aside the morality, surely you're too much of a scientist to countenance this."

But Poole sounded anguished. "I'm not a scientist anymore, Miriam. I'm an engineer. I build things. I think I sympathize with the goals of the spider makers. What I'm building is a better future for the whole of mankind–that's what I believe. And if I have to make compromises to achieve that future–well. Maybe the spider makers had to make the same kind of choices. Who knows what they found here on Titan before they went to work on it . . ."

And in that little speech, I believe, you have encapsulated both the magnificence and the grandiose folly of Michael Poole. I wondered then how much damage this man might do to us all in the future, with his wormholes and his time-hopping starships–what horrors he, blinded by his vision, might unleash.

Harry said unexpectedly, "Let's vote on it. If you're in favor of destroying the chamber, say yes."

"No!" snapped Miriam.

"Yes," said Harry and Poole together.

"Yes," said I, but they all turned on me and told me I didn't have a vote.

It made no difference. The vote was carried. They stood looking at each other, as if horrified by what they had done.

"Welcome to my world," I said cynically.

Poole went off to prepare the GUT engine for its last task. Miriam, furious and upset, gathered together our equipment, such as it was, her pack with her science samples, our tangles of rope.

And Harry popped into the air in front of me. "Thanks," he said.

"You wanted me to make that suggestion, didn't you?"

"Well, I hoped you would. If I'd made it they'd have refused. And Michael would never have forgiven me." He grinned. "I knew there was a reason I wanted to have you along, Jovik Emry. Well done. You've served your purpose."

Virtual Poole, still in his baby universe, spoke again. "Miriam."

She straightened up. "I'm here, Michael."

"I'm not sure how long I have left. What will happen when the power goes?"

"I programmed the simulation to seem authentic, internally consistent. It will be as if the power in the *Crab* lifedome is failing." She took a breath, and said, "Of course you have other options to end it before then."

"I know. Thank you. Who were they, do you think? Whoever made the spiders. Did they build this pocket universe too? Or was it built *for* them? Like a haven?"

"I don't suppose we'll ever know. Michael, I'm sorry. I–"

"Don't be. You know I would have chosen this. But I'm sorry to leave you behind. Miriam–look after him. Michael. I, we, need you."

She looked at the original Poole, who was working at the GUT engine. "We'll see," she said.

"And tell Harry–well. You know."

She held a hand up to the empty air. "Michael, please–"

"It's enough." The Virtuals he had been projecting broke up into blocks of pixels, and a faint hiss, the carrier of his voice, disappeared from my hearing. Alone in his universe, he had cut himself off.

The original Poole approached her, uncertain of her

reaction. "It's done. The GUT engine has been programmed. We're ready to go, Miriam. Soon as we're out of here–"

She turned away from him, her face showing something close to hatred.

XVI

Ascension

So, harnessed to a spider oblivious of the impending fate of its vast and ancient project, we rose into the dark. It had taken us days to descend to this place, and would take us days to return to the surface, where, Harry promised, he would have a fresh balloon waiting to pick us up.

This time, though I was offered escape into unconsciousness, I stayed awake. I had a feeling that the last act of this little drama had yet to play itself out. I wanted to be around to see it.

We were beyond the lower ice layers and rising through 250 kilometers of sea when Miriam's timer informed us that the GUT engine had detonated, far beneath us. Insulated by the ice layer, we felt nothing. But I imagined that the spider that carried us up towards the light hesitated, just fractionally.

"It's done," Poole said firmly. "No going back."

Miriam had barely spoken to him since the cavern. She had said more words to *me.* Now she said, "I've been thinking. I won't accept it, Michael. I don't care about you and Harry and your damn vote. As soon as we get home I'm going to report what we found."

"You've no evidence–"

"I'll be taken seriously enough. And someday somebody will mount another expedition, and confirm the truth."

"All right." That was all he said. But I knew the matter was not over. He would not meet my mocking eyes.

I wasn't surprised when, twelve hours later, as Miriam slept cradled in the net draped from the spider's back, Poole took vials from her pack and pressed them into her flesh, one by a valve on her leg, another at the base of her spine.

I watched him. "You're going to edit her. Plan this with Dad, did you?"

"Shut up," he snarled, edgy, angry.

"You're taking her out of her own head, and you'll mess with her memories, with her very personality, and then you'll load her back. What will you make her believe–that she stayed up on the *Crab* with Harry the whole time, while you went exploring and found nothing? That would work, I guess."

"I've got nothing to say to you."

But I had plenty to say to him. I am no saint myself, and Poole disgusted me as only a man without morality himself can be disgusted. "I think you love her. I even think she loves you. Yet you are prepared to mess with her head and her heart, to serve your grandiose ambitions. Let me tell you something. The Poole she left behind in that pocket universe, the one she said goodbye to, he was a better man than you will ever be again. Because he was not tainted by the great crime you committed when you destroyed the cavern. And because he was not tainted by *this.*

"And let me make some predictions. No matter what you achieve in the future, Michael Poole, this crime will always be at the root of you, gnawing away. *And Miriam will never love you.* Even though you wipe out her memory of these events, there will always be something between you; she will sense the lie. She will leave you, and then you will leave her. And you have killed Titan. One day, millions of years into the future, the very air will freeze and rain out, and everything alive here will die. All because of what you have done today. And, Poole, maybe those whose work you have wrecked will some day force you to a reckoning."

He was open, defenceless, and I was flaying him. He had no answer. He cradled the unconscious Miriam, even as his machines drained her memory.

We did not speak again until we emerged into the murky daylight of Titan.

EPILOGUE

Probe

It didn't take Michael long to check out the status of his fragile craft.

The power in the lifetime's internal cells might last–what, a few hours? As far as he could tell there was no functional link between the dome and the rest of the *Hermit Crab*; none of his controls worked. Maybe that was beyond the scope of Miriam's simulation. So he had no motive power.

He didn't grouse about this, nor did he fear his future. Such as it was.

The universe beyond the lifedome was strange, alien. The toiling spiders down on the ice moon seemed like machines, not alive, not sentient. He tired of observing them. He turned on lights, green, blue. The lifedome was a little bubble of Earth, isolated.

Michael was alone, in this whole universe. He could feel it.

He got a meal together. Miriam's simulation was good, here in his personal space; he didn't find any limits or glitches. Lovingly constructed, he thought. The mundane chore, performed in a bright island of light around the lifetime's small galley, was oddly cheering.

He carried the food to his couch, lay back with the plate balancing on one hand, and dimmed the dome lights. He finished his food and set the plate carefully on the floor. He drank a glass of clean water.

Then he went to the freefall shower and washed in a spray of hot water. He tried to open up his senses, to relish every particle of sensation. There was a last time for everything, for even the most mundane experiences. He considered finding some music to play, a book to read. Somehow that might have seemed fitting.

The lights failed. Even the instrument slates winked out.

Well, so much for music. He made his way back to his couch. Though the sky was bright, illuminated by the protosun, the air grew colder; he imagined the heat of the lifedome leaking out. What would get him first, the cold, or the failing air?

He wasn't afraid. And he felt no regret that he had lost so much potential life, all those AS-extended years. Oddly, he felt renewed: young, for the first time in decades, the pressure of time no longer seemed to weigh on him.

He was sorry he would never know how his relationship with Miriam might have worked out. That could have been something. But he found, in the end, he was glad that he had lived long enough to see all he had.

He was beginning to shiver, the air sharp in his nostrils. He lay back in his couch and crossed his hands on his chest. He closed his eyes.

A shadow crossed his face.

He opened his eyes, looked up. There was a ship hanging over the lifedome.

Michael, dying, stared in wonder.

It was something like a sycamore seed wrought in jet black. Night-dark wings which must have spanned hundreds of kilometers loomed over the *Crab*, softly rippling.

The cold sank claws into his chest; the muscles of his throat abruptly spasmed, and dark clouds ringed his vision.

Not now, he found himself pleading silently, his failing vision locked onto the ship, all his elegiac acceptance gone in a flash. *Just a little longer. I have to know what this means. Please–*

Poole's consciousness was like a guttering candle flame. Now it was as if that flame was plucked from its wick. That flame, with its tiny fear, its wonder, its helpless longing to survive, was spun out into a web of quantum functions, acausal and nonlocal.

The last heat fled from the craft; the air in the translucent dome began to frost over the comms panels, the couches, the galley, the prone body. And the ship and all it contained, no longer needed, broke up into a cloud of pixels.

THERE'S A GREAT BIG BEAUTIFUL TOMORROW/NOW IS THE BEST TIME OF YOUR LIFE

Cory Doctorow

Cory Doctorow was born in Toronto, Canada in 1971. A self-described "renaissance geek," he was raised by Trotskyist schoolteachers in the wilds of Canada, attended alternative schools in Toronto, worked at a SF specialty bookstore, dropped out of high school, and briefly moved to Mexico to write. He has worked as a programmer, web designer, volunteer in Central America, CIO, founder of a software company, and as an advocate, before becoming a full-time writer last year. Doctorow began selling fiction when he was 17, and published a small handful of stories through the early and mid 1990s. His story "Craphound" appeared in 1998, and he won the John W. Campbell Award for Best New Writer in 2000. His best known short fiction is a series of stories that use the titles of famous SF short stories, revisiting the assumptions underpinning their narratives. So far "Anda's Game" has been selected for the prestigious Best American Short Stories and "I, Robot" was nominated for the Hugo Award. His first novel, Down and Out in the Magic Kingdom *was followed by collections* A Place So Foreign and Eight More *and* Overclocked, *and novels* Eastern Standard Tribe, Someone Comes to Town, Someone Leaves Town, Little Brother, *and* Makers. *His latest novel is* For the Win, *a young adult science fiction novel about greenfarming.*

In the story that follows Doctorow turns the idea of godlike machines on its head, and shows us instead some very different machines.

PART 1: A SPARKLING JEWEL

I piloted the mecha through the streets of Detroit, hunting wumpuses. The mecha was a relic of the Mecha Wars, when the nation tore itself to shreds with lethal robots, and it had the weird, swirling lines of all evolutionary tech, channelled and chopped and counterweighted like some freak dinosaur or a race-car.

I loved the mecha. It wasn't fast, but it had a fantastic ride, a kind of wobbly strut that was surprisingly comfortable and let me keep the big fore and aft guns on any target I chose, the sights gliding along on a perfect level even as the neck rocked from side to side.

The pack loved the mecha too. All six of them, three aerial bots shaped like bats, two ground-cover streaks that nipped around my heels, and a flea that bounded over buildings, bouncing off the walls and leaping from monorail track to rusting hover-bus to balcony and back. The pack's brains were back in dad's house, in the old Comerica Park site. When I found them, they'd been a pack of sick dogs, dragging themselves through the ruined city, poisoned by some old materiel. I had done them the mercy of extracting their brains and connecting them up to the house network. Now they were immortal, just like me, and they knew that I was their alpha dog. They loved to go for walks with me.

I spotted the wumpus by the plume of dust it kicked up. It was well inside the perimeter, gnawing at the corner of an old satellite Ford factory, a building gone to magnificent ruin, all crumbled walls and crazy, unsprung machines. The structural pillars stuck up all around it, like columns around a Greek temple.

The wumpus had the classic look. It stood about eight feet tall, with a hundred mouths on the ends of whipping tentacles. Its metallic finish was smeared with oily rainbows that wobbled as the dust swirled around it. The mouths whipped back and forth against the corner of the factory, taking chunks out of it. The chunks went into the hopper on its back and were broken up into their constituent atoms, reassembled into handy, safe, rich soil, and then ejected in a vertical plume that was visible even from several blocks away.

Wumpuses don't put up much fight. They're reclamation drones, not hunter-killer bots, and their main mode of attack was to assemble copies of themselves out of dead buildings faster than I could squash them. They weren't much sport, but that was OK: there's no *way* Dad would let me put his precious mecha at risk against any kind of big game. The pack loved hunting wumpus, anyway.

The air-drones swooped around it in tight arcs. They were usually piloted by Pepe, the hysterical Chihuahua, who loved to have three points-of-view, it fit right in with his distracted, hyperactive approach to life. The wumpus didn't even notice the drones until one of them came in so low that it tore through the tentacles, taking three clean off and disordering the remainder. The other air-drones did victory loops in the sky overhead and the flea bounded so high that it practically disappeared from sight, then touched down right next to the wumpus.

This attack was characteristic of Gretl, the Irish Setter mix who thought she was a kangaroo. The whole pack liked the flea, but Gretl was born to it. She bounced the wumpus six times, knocking it back and forth like an air-hockey puck, leaping free before it could bring its tentacles to bear on her.

The ground effect bots reached the wumpus at the same time as I did. Technically, I was supposed to hang back out of range and get it with the mecha's big guns, to make sure that it didn't get a bite or two in on the mecha's skin, scratching the finish. But that was *no fun at all.* I liked to dance with the wumpus, especially when the pack was in on it, all of us dodging in and out, snatching the wumpus's tentacles, kicking it back and forth. The ground effect bots were clearly piloted by Ike and Mike, two dogs that had been so badly mutilated when I found them that I couldn't even guess at their breed. They must have been big beasts at one point. They were born to ground effect bots, anyway, bulling the wumpus around.

The wumpus was down to just a few tentacles now, and I could see into its hopper, normally obscured by the forest of waving arms and mouths. The hopper itself was lined with tentacles, but thin ones, whiplike, each one fringed with hairy cilia. The cilia branched and branched again, down to single-molecule pincers, each one optimized to break apart a different kind of material. I knew better than to reach inside that hopper with the mecha's fists–even after I'd killed the wumpus, the hopper would digest anything I fed it, including me.

Its foot-spoked wheels spun madly as we batted it around like a cat playing with a mouse. They could get traction on anything, given enough time to get their balance, but we weren't going to give it the chance. The air-drones snipped the last of the tentacles and I touched the control that whistled the pack back. They obediently came to my heels and I put the wumpus in my sights. The wumpus seemed to sense what was coming. It stopped struggling and settled down on the feet of its wheels. I methodically blew apart its hopper with my depleted uranium guns, chipping away at it, blowing it open, cilia waving and spasming. Now the wumpus was just a coil of metallic skin and logic with a hundred wheels, naked and stripped. I used the rocket-launcher on it and savored the debris-fountain that rose from it. Sweet!

"Jimmy Yensid, you are cruel and vile!" The voice bounced off the walls of the ruined buildings around me, strident and shrill. I rotated the mecha's cowl and scanned the ground. There she was, standing on top of a dead hover-bus, a spider-goat behind her on a tether. I popped the cowl and shinned down the mecha, using the grippy hand-and-toe-holds that tried to conform to my grasp.

"Hello, Lacey!" I called. "You're looking very pretty today." Dad had always taught me to talk to girls this way, though there weren't many meat girls in my world, just the ones I saw online and, of course, the intriguing women of the Carousel of Progress, back in the center of Comerica Park. And it was true. Lacey Treehugger was ever so pretty–with a face as round as a pie-plate and lips like a drawn-up bow. Talking to Lacey was as forbidden as destroying the mecha, maybe more so, but Dad could tell if the mecha got scratched and he had no way of finding out if I had been passing the time of day with pretty Lacey.

She was taller than me now, which was only to be expected, because she was not immortal and so she was growing at regular speed while I was going to stick to my present, neat little size for a good while yet. I didn't mind that she was taller, either–I liked the view.

"Hello, hello," I said as I scaled the hover, coming up to stand next to her. "Hello!" I said to the spider-goat, holding out the flat of my hand for it to sniff. It brayed at me and menaced me with its horns. "Come on, Louisa, play nice."

She tugged on the goat's lead, a zizzing spool of something that felt as soft as felt but which could selectively tighten at the loop-end when the goat got a little too edgy. "This *isn't* Louisa, Jimmy. This is Moldavia. Louisa died last week." She glared at me.

"I'm sorry to hear it," I said. "She was a good goat."

"She died from eating bad sludge," Lacey said. Ah. Well, that explained it. Lacey's people hated Dad's preserve here in the old city of Detroit. They hadn't made the wumpuses, but they fully supported their work. The Treehuggers wanted all of the old industrial world converted back to the kind of thing you could let a goat eat without worrying about it dropping dead, turning to plastic, or everting its digestive tract.

"You should keep a closer eye on your goats, Lacey," I said. "It's not safe for them to wander around here."

"It *would be* if you'd leave off hunting those innocent wumpuses. The way you took that poor thing apart, it was sickening."

"Lacey, it's a *machine.* It doesn't have feelings. I was just having a little fun."

"Sickening," she repeated. She had her short hair in tiny braids today, which is one of the many ways I loved to see it. Each braid was tipped with a tiny, glittering bead of fused soil, stuff that her people collected as a reminder of the bad old days.

"How's your parents?"

She didn't manage to hide her smile. "Their weirdness is terminal. This week they decided that we were going to try to sell spider-goat silk to India. I'm all like, India? Are you crazy? What does India want with our textiles? They don't even *need* clothes there anymore, not since desidotis came out." Desidotis were self-cleaning, self-replicating, and could reconfigure themselves. No one who made dollars could afford them–they were denominated in rupees only. "And they went, have you *seen* how the Rupee is trading today? So they're all over iBay, posting auction listings in broken Hindi. I'm all like, you *know* that India is the world's largest English-speaking nation, right?"

I shook my head. "You're right. Terminally weird."

She gave me a playful shove. "You're one to talk. At least mine are human!"

So technically it was true. Dad refused to call himself a human anymore. Ever since he attained immortality, decades before I was born, he'd called himself a transhuman. But when he said he wasn't human, it was a boast. When Lacey said it, it sounded like an insult. It bugged me. Dad didn't want me "deracinating" myself with Lacey. Lacey didn't trust me because I wasn't a "real" human. It wasn't like I wanted to be a mayfly, like the Treehuggers were, but I still hated it when Lacey looked down her nose at me.

"I really do hate the way you take those wumpuses apart," she said. "It gives me the creeps. I know they're not alive, but you really seem to be enjoying it."

"The pack enjoys it," I said, gesturing at my robots, who

were wrestling each other around my feet. "It's in their nature to hunt."

She looked away. "I don't like them, either," she said, barely above a whisper.

"Come on," I said. "They're better off now than they were when I found them. At least I haven't screwed around with their germ plasm. I'm just using technology to let them be better dogs. Not like Louisa there." I pointed to the spider-goat.

"Moldavia," she said.

I knew I had her there. I pressed my advantage. "You think she enjoys giving silk? Somewhere in her head, she knows she's supposed to be full of milk."

Lacey looked out over the ruins of Detroit. "Pretty around here," she said.

"Yeah," I said. It was. The ruins were glorious. They were all I'd ever known, except for fly-overs in the zepp. Michigan countryside was pastoral and picturesque, but it wasn't anything so magnificent as Detroit's ruins. So much ambition. Made me proud to be (trans)human. "I wish you guys would stop trying to take it away from us."

This is how conversation with Lacey always went, each of us picking fights with the other. It was all we knew, the best way we had to relate. Neither of us really meant it. It was just an excuse to stand close enough to her to count the hairs on her arms, to watch the sun through her eyelashes.

She looked at me. "It's not like you let anyone else come by and see it anyway. You just hoard it all to yourself."

"You come by whenever you want. What's the problem?"

"You treat it like your own private playground. You know how many people could live here?"

"None," I said. "It would kill them within a week." I was immune, thanks to my transhuman liver. Dad's liver wasn't quite so trick, but he made do by eating cultured yogurt filled with microbes that kept him detoxed. He said it was a small price to pay for continued residence in his museum.

"You *know* what I mean," she said, socking me again. "Let the wumpuses do their thing, turn this whole place back into forests, grow some treehouses . . . How many? A million? Two million?"

"Sure," I said. "Provided you didn't care about destroying all this history."

"There are billions of blown-out steel-belted radials!" she said. "All over the world. What the hell makes yours so special?"

"What if this was ancient Rome?" I said. "What if we were all sitting around, thinking about pounding down all those potsherds, and you were all like, Jimmius Yensidus, what are you saving all those potsherds for? Rome is full of them. They're a health hazard! The centurions keep cutting their feet on them!"

"You are a total idiot," she said.

We got to this point in every discussion. Half the time, I called her an idiot. Half the time it was the other way around. We sat down on the bus and she put her arm around me. I leaned in for my kiss. Dad would totally splode if he knew. Deracination!

Sorry, Dad. She kissed me slowly, with a lazy bit of tongue that made the hair on my neck stand up. She was probably getting a little old for me, but I found that I quite liked older women.

She broke it off and sighed. "You're so young," she said. "We can't keep doing this."

"I'm two months older than you," I said, baiting her. I knew what she meant.

"You used to be. These days, it's like you're ten. I'm almost 14, Jimmy."

"So go kiss some Treehugger boys on the spider-goat farm," I said.

She sighed again. "Are you really happy here?"

"Are you happy where you are?"

"I'm happy enough. It's peaceful."

"Boring."

"Yeah," she said.

"It's not boring around here. Going out with Dad is *awesome.*" Dad collected pieces for his museum from all over the world. We'd gone to France together the year before to get the Girl and the Sultan's Elephant from Marseilles. The semi-robotic puppets were 11 meters tall and we'd stashed them in a high-school gym near the bus-station. We couldn't work them on our own, they needed a crew of 20 or more, but I was working on training the pack to help out. Trying, anyway. Pepe kept trying to eat the Elephant.

"But you're all *alone.* And your Dad is so *weird.*"

"He's weird, but he's a lot of fun. I won't live here forever, anyway. Once I'm post-pube, I'm going on a vision-quest. It's part of the package. Then I'll find somewhere to settle down."

"You've got it all figured out, huh?"

Pepe had been circling high overhead as we chatted, occasionally dipping down to play with the ground effect critters. Now all three of his drones lofted high, making wide circles. That was the signal that he was seriously freaking out.

I stood up to get a better look at him, Lacey grabbing at my hand. I followed the wide, swooping curves of the drones, turning to watch, and saw two of them get shot out of the sky, one-two, just like that, disappearing in a hail of debris.

Lacey squeezed my hand.

"Kurzweil on a crutch," I breathed. I headed for the mecha, but Lacey wouldn't let go of my hand. "Come on," I said, looking into her scared face. "You ride shotgun, I'll get you home safe." She shook her head. Her eyes were white. The pack was going crazy around us, nipping at our heels, racing in circles. The flea was springing high, high, higher. The crack of artillery. A flight of rockets screamed overhead, then touched down somewhere. The sound was incredible, like nothing I'd ever heard, and the earth shook so hard that I slipped and went down on one knee.

"Come ON," I said to Lacey, "get in!"

I grabbed for the bottom rung of the mecha's handholds and felt it grip me back. I looked over my shoulder. Lacey was hugging the goat. Dammit. The goat.

"We'll take her too!" I said. I reached for the goat, but she butted at me and shied back. "Lacey, you can't stay here," I said. There was the rattle of small arms, another volley of rockets. A cloud of dust boiled down the street. I barely managed to yank my shirt over my head before it overtook us, blotting out the sky, filling every pore with grey, shattered concrete. It was like a wumpus plume gone metastatic, filling the entire world.

I tugged my shirt back into place and looked around.

Lacey was gone.

I jumped down from the hover and ran around the bus. The pack were everywhere around me. I tried to whistle them up and send them in a search pattern for Lacey and the goat, but I needed the mecha for that.

I wasn't thinking straight.

I turned and crouched down and put my face in my hands and breathed deeply. Then I stood up, thumped the ground-effect critters behind the ears, and climbed into the mecha and sealed the cowl, turning on air, radiation, and flash-bang filters at max. The screens were all going bonkers. I took another deep breath. First things first. Pepe was still up there. I dropped his sensorium on the side-screens, dialed back to when he first started to circle, absently watching the attacks unfold.

On the main screens, I put up the view from the ground effects and the flea, and told them to fan out and look for Lacey. Pepe had been watching the attack when Lacey went missing, so his rewind wasn't any help there, but at least I could watch the attack that had unfolded.

There were eight mechas in formation, coming across the river from where Windsor used to be. It was our least guarded flank–we counted on the river as the first line of defense. If I was planning an invasion, that's where I'd strike, too.

The mechas were smaller than mine. They were barely bigger than their pilots, more powered armor than vehicles. I recognized them as coming from the earliest years of the Mecha Wars, whereas my mecha was the last generation produced, a juggernaut that stood four times larger than them. The pack hadn't found Lacey. I looked at the screens and decided that Lacey had gone to ground somewhere, hiding in a ruined building. Fine. She'd be as safe there as she was anywhere. I began to run for Windsor.

Dad wouldn't answer his phone. I dropped mine into the mecha's hopper and told it to keep on redialing him. It kept getting the voicemail: "You have reached Robin Yensid and the Detroit Conservation Zone. We are delighted to hear from another telephone user. Your choice of communications technology is appreciated. Help keep the telephone alive! That said, I can't come to my phone right now. Leave me a message and I'll phone you back."

My mecha ran full tilt, bent almost double. The cockpit remained level on the end of the mecha's flexible stalk of a neck, rolling silently from side to side to keep from upsetting me. It didn't even spill my coffee.

Who'd be attacking Detroit? Dad believed that the wumpuses were made by some kind of co-op in San Diego, deep greens who'd made the viral bots and released them into the wild more than ten years ago. I'd checked out the co-op's presence a couple times and it was mostly arguments about who was supposed to be tucking the oxen into bed each night, and what kinds of stories were appropriate to read to the calves. Apparently, the co-op had changed focus after their wumpus phase and had gone into farming. In any event,

I didn't think that they were the kind of gang that could send eight members across the continent in mechas to make sure that the last real city got ploughed under by wumpuses.

The mecha told me that it had the eight enemy craft in range of its missiles. I stopped and dropped the third leg for stability and sighted on the flank closest to me. I thought I'd pick them off in order, closest to furthest, and hope that the far ones wouldn't even notice what I was up to until I'd already done it.

I told the missile which mecha to attack–it was purple, and Pepe's imaging showed a driver behind the cowl that was about Dad's size, though I couldn't tell sex or age. I put my finger over the button and got ready to press it. But I didn't push the button.

I had killed a million wumpuses. I'd put some dogs out of their misery, beasts too far gone to join the pack. I'd swatted flies and sploded mosquitos with lasers. But I'd never killed a human being. Technically, I was a transhuman, so was that still murder? My thumb thought so.

Dad's voicemail came up again. The mecha closest to me was swiveling towards me. I could hear its radar scattering off my armor. I hit the button and my mecha rocked as the rocket screamed away from the frame on my mecha's chest. The missile corkscrewed through a tracker-confounding set of spirals, shaking off radar chaff as it went. The chaff was propelled as well, and it, too, moved through corkscrews, so that even *I* couldn't figure out which was the real missile and which were the drones.

Then, the moment of contact.

The real missile hit the mecha dead center. I watched its nose-cam as it kissed the chest-plate, seeing the mouth of the man (woman?) inside, shot up through the clear shield. The mouth made a perfect O. Then the chest-cam stopped working. I looked out with my naked eyes in time to see the mecha come apart in an expanding cloud of debris. Not all the debris was made of metal. There was a red mist in the air.

Something wet hit the ground. It must have been part of a person, once, but now it looked like roadkill. Like the dogs that couldn't make it into the pack.

I was a murderer. The person in that mecha might have been an immortal like me. Or she might have been made into an immortal, like Dad. Might have lived forever.

The other mechas were targeting me now, three moving to flank me, two grasping forearms and locking at the ankles to make a single unit, which rose into the air on rotors over their shoulders.

I had already armed the remaining missiles and targeted the four closest to me without even thinking of it. I played a lot of mecha sims on slow days, sometimes using the console in front of the huge, chunky TV in the living room of the fourth scene of the Carousel of Progress. Dad did not approve of this, so I didn't tell him.

I launched the battery and used the recoil time to bring the evaders up to nominal. This was the mecha's gymnastics program, a set of heavily randomized backsprings and twirls and such, supposedly impossible for a targeting system to get a lock on, but nevertheless calculated to keep the enemy in range at all times. Theoretically, the brave pilot (ahem, me) could continue to harass and kill the enemy while pulling four gees through a set of acrobat maneuvers. The evaders were better than the carny rides Dad kept refurbished and running, but truth be told, they'd never failed to make me puke.

But as the missiles screamed toward the enemy mechas and the airborne unit bore down on me, big guns blazing, puking seemed like a sensible alternative to dying. I hit the evaders and dug in.

I'd ridden the evaders dozens of times, but this was the first time I kept my eyes open. The nausea didn't rush up and overtake me. Instead, I remained utterly focused on the enemy craft, my gaze locked on them as my body rocked and flipped. My missiles had taken down two more, the other missiles had disappeared, either foiled by anti-targeting system or knocked out of the sky.

I threw more bad stuff in their direction, using the conventional depleted uranium rounds as the flips and turns brought me into range. The evaders were hard on the mecha's power-cells, so the maneuvers only ran for a few minutes, but it felt like hours. When we ground to a halt, my mecha and I, we were much closer to the enemy craft than before. There had been eight of them. Now there were three. The two that had taken to the sky were lying in a twisted wreckage near me.

The pack were barking like crazy, filling the cockpit with alerts. The flea was bouncing up and down on the downed aerial unit, savaging the pilots through their cowls. It kept replaying its video of the kill, the flea leaping up to land on the rotors' mast, biting down on the drive-shaft and hanging on as the rotors bent, collided, spun away, the flea bounding free of the dying craft as it spun out and spiraled down.

The remaining mecha were moving with more discipline and purpose than their brethren had. I no longer had the advantage of surprise. These three were taking cover behind Dad's favorite office tower, a big white marble thing done in a style Dad called "deco." They lobbed missiles over the building, apparently using orbitals or something stratospheric for targeting.

Two could play at that game. I whistled up the flea and Pepe and sent them around the back of the tower, giving me some guidance for my own targeting systems. My mecha knew well enough to automatically interface with the lads, tying them straight into its guidance systems. I fired some grenades at the parking structure opposite their covering building, letting the mecha calculate the bank shot so that they bounced off and landed amid the enemies.

Two more down, and the other two were on the move, streaking out from behind the building. Holy crap, they were *fast.* They fired in unison at me, letting me have it with guided missiles, grenades, conventional ammo. I tried evasive maneuvers but it was no good. They shot the mecha's left leg out from under it and I tumbled . . .

. . . and kept rolling. The Mecha Wars were vicious, and once a ronin mecha was in the field, it might go months without a resupply or maintenance. These bastards kept coming at you no matter what, pulling themselves along on whatever limbs were left, until there was nothing left to fight with.

My mecha came up in a three-pointed stance, like one of the ground effect vehicles, like it was doing yoga, coming into a downward dog. The cowl swung around and I was upright again, atop the thorax of my newly bug-like fighting machine.

The ground effect puppies nipped at my heels as I scuttled toward the enemy, closing. I was down to nothing but conventional ammo now, so it was close fighting. In a pinch, my mecha could uproot a building and clobber them with it. Two minutes before, I'd been agonizing about becoming a murderer. Now I wanted to tear their legs off and beat them to death with them.

The dogs wanted to do their thing and I gave them the nod over my command channel. The entire pack converged on one of the two mechas–the closer one–grabbing its limbs and tumbling it to the ground, rending the metal away from the cowl. I actually heard the pilot scream. It made me grin.

That left one more. He–it was a he, I was close enough to see that now–he had planted himself in a fencer's stance, presenting the side of his body to me as he raised his near hand straight out toward me, the maws of his guns yawning towards me. His other arm was curled across his chest, fanning up and down, trying to keep me in his sights at all times.

I scuttled my mecha forward, taking cover when I could, using trucks and houses, even a beautiful neon sign that Dad always stopped to admire when we were out for walks. It sploded and came down with a series of crystal tinkling noises.

I got as many shots off at it as I could, but it was fresh,

with a seemingly endless supply of ammo to harry me with whenever I tried to target it.

Then it got me, bouncing a grenade off the ground ten yards ahead of me, sending it sailing right into the mecha's midsection, so that I flipped and rolled and rolled and rolled. *Now* I felt nauseated.

When I finally stopped rolling, I knew I was about to die. The mecha's lights were all dark, all systems down. Dad was going to *kill* me. I chuckled and groaned. My ribs, pressed into the crash harness, felt like a handful of dried twigs rattling against one another.

I struggled to release the webbing as I punched the trigger for the charges that blew out the cowl. I would die on my feet.

I got out of the mecha just in time to see the ground effect puppies streaking toward the enemy mecha, who was raising his guns for the triumphant kill. I saw in an instant what they intended, and turned my face away just as they collided with him, exploding in a shower of hot metal. I dived back into the cowl, heedless of my ribs, and curled into a ball as the debris rained down around me.

When I straightened up, the remaining mecha was a twisted, blackened wreck, streaked with red. The two doggies had gone into suicide-bomber mode when they saw that my life was endangered, blowing themselves up and taking the remaining enemy with them. Good doggies. When I got back home, I'd give their brains some extra endorphins. They'd earned it. Of course, finding them some more bots to pilot wasn't going to be easy. Dad's museum-city was cratered with the aftermath of my battle, buildings razed, fires blazing.

I took a tentative step away from the wreckage of my mecha and stumbled, gasping at the pain in my ribs. Then I remembered that I'd left my phone in the cockpit and had to crawl back in to get it. It was still redialing Dad, still getting his voicemail.

A part of my brain knew that this meant that he was in

deep trouble, somewhere in Detroit. That part seemed to be locked in a padded room, judging by its muffled cries. The part in charge didn't worry about Dad at all–Dad was fine, he was back at Comerica, waiting for me. He was going to be so *pissed* about the mecha. It was the last of its kind, as Dad never tired of reminding me. And several of his favorite buildings were in ruin. This was going to be ugly.

I pocketed the phone and whistled up the pack. It was just the flea and Pepe now. Pepe perched on the flea's shoulder and let me pet his carapace. I tested my legs. Wobbly, but serviceable. Without the mecha, it'd be harder to talk to the pack, but they'd be OK on their own. They had good instincts, my pups.

Normally, it was a ten-minute walk from the Ambassador Bridge to Comerica. Hell, the People Mover monorail went most of the way. But I could see a People Mover from where I stood, and it was stock still, motionless on the track. Someone had cut its power. I took some tentative steps. My ribs grated and I gasped and nearly fell over. The flea bounced to me and nuzzled at me. I leaned on it and it trundled forward slowly. This was going to take a lot more than ten minutes. If only Dad would pick up the phone, he could come and get me.

We were halfway to Comerica when my phone rang.

"Dad?"

"Jimmy, thank God. Are you OK?"

I had been very brave all the way from the wreckage, biting back my whimpers of pain and soldiering on. But now I couldn't stop my tears. "I broke my ribs, Dad," I said, around the sobs. "It hurts."

"Where are you?"

"I'm almost home," I said. "Can you come get me?"

"Jimmy, listen carefully. I–" there was a crash on the other end of the phone. It continued rumbling, and I realized I was hearing it with my other ear as well. I looked out over the city and saw Dad's harrier screaming around in a tight arc that must have pulled eight gees. The last time he'd taken the harrier out, I'd been a little kid, only five or six, and he'd flown it like it was made of eggshell. Now it was zipping around like an overclocked Pepe.

The harrier was circling something I couldn't see, and it had all its guns blazing. Dad was knocking the holy hell out of his city, and somehow that made things scarier than ever. He *never* would have–

"Listen carefully, Jimmy! Go home. Get in the zepp. Go away from here. I'll find you. Do you–" the harrier made another tight turn. Something huge was over it, in the sky. A flying battle-platform? I'd seen pictures of those. They'd been big in Europe, during the Mecha Wars. I'd never seen one in person. I didn't think they'd made it to this continent.

"Dad?"

The harrier zigged and zagged like a dragonfly, then rocketed straight up, guns still blazing, rolling from side to side as it laid down a line of fire over the batteries slung under the platform's belly. The platform returned fire, and Dad's voice rang out of the phone: "GO!"

I went. My ribs had stiffened up as I watched the air-battle, but I pushed on. I didn't worry about crying out when they hurt. I screamed the whole way. I couldn't hear myself over the noise of the guns. The flea kept me upright. Somehow, I made it home.

Comerica's doors were shut up tight, the security scanners live and swiveling to follow me. They were wide-angle and could follow me without moving an inch, but the swiveling let you know they were live. Each one had a pain-ray beneath it, aperture as wide as the muzzle of a blunderbuss. I once came home without my transponder–left in the mecha, in the old car-barn–and got a faceful of pain-ray. Felt like my face was *melting*. I never forgot my transponder again.

For a second, though, I couldn't find it and I had a vision

of it sitting in the wrecked cockpit of my mecha, a ten-minute walk away that might as well have been in one of the moon colonies. Then I found it, transferred absently to one of the many pockets that ran down the sleeves of my sweater.

I let myself in and collapsed in the vestibule, on one of Dad's live divans. It purred and cuddled me, which set my ribs afire again. On the other side of the dome there was a model room for a robot hotel that Dad had rescued from Atlantic City. It had a robutler that could do rudimentary first aid. I'd grown up playing hospital with it. Now I limped over and let myself in, summoning the bot. It had a queer gait, a half-falling roll that was like a controlled stagger. It clucked over my ribs, applied a salve, waited for the numbness to set it, then taped me up, getting my ribs into alignment.

I stood up, numb from chin to hip, and dismissed the robutler. Its blank face bowed to me as it slid back into its receptacle. Dad let me stay in the hotel room on my birthday sometimes. As I left it, I realized that I'd never see it again.

In the middle of the field, the tethered zepp strained at its mooring lines. The Spirit of the People's Will was a Chinese mini-freighter, the kind of thing you could still find in the sky, but Dad collected it anyway. The first time he saw its stubby lines, playful like a kid's toy, he rushed out and got one for the museum. "An instant classic," he called it, "like the Mac, or the Mini. Perfection."

The zepp's cargo hoist was already loaded. Dad must have done that, before getting in the harrier and setting out to defend our turf. The hoist was groaning under a prodigious weight, and I groaned too, once I saw what it was. Dad had put the Carousel onto the hoist.

The Carousel of Progress debuted in 1964, at the New York World's Fair. Walt Disney built it for General Electric—a six-scene robotic stage-play about the role of technology in making our lives better. It was Dad's most treasured possession in the entire world. I seriously believe that if it was a choice between me and it, he might pick it.

In fact, he had sort of done that.

Ten minutes had gone by since I'd made it home, and the sounds of the air battle still raged outside. The zepp was going to have a hard time attaining lift-off with all that weight, and I still hadn't grabbed my own stuff.

Yes, Dad had said to go right away, no delay. Yes, there was a war raging outside the walls. But I wasn't going to leave my friends behind.

The pack's den was in the back of my room, four overgrown canisters that I kept under my desk. The canisters were standard issue brain-storage–drop as much of the nervous system as you can scrape together into one, and it would grow silicon into the ganglia until it had an interface, keeping the whole thing awash in nutrients and wicking waste products out to an evaporator. I had to remember to add a little sugar every now and again, and to whisk away the residue in the evaporator, but apart from that, they did their thing all on their lonesome. Dad had been worried that I wouldn't be able to take care of a pet, let alone four pets, but the pack were the happiest doggies in the state. I'd find them somewhere to live when I got to wherever I was going. I certainly wasn't going to leave them behind.

The Carousel stood so high on the cargo hoist that I was able to simply climb its service ladder to the roof and then reach up and catch the boarding ramp for the gondola. I yanked it down, hearing–but no longer feeling–the pain in my ribs.

The zepp had already warm-booted, all systems nominal. The radars reported a clear lift-off path through Comerica's retracted dome–Dad had added it early on, before I was born, with Mom's help. I had flown the zepp before, but always with Dad at my elbow. It wasn't rocket science, of course. The thing rose until you told it to stop, then moved in whichever direction you steered it. It was a zepp–easier to pilot than a mecha.

The zepp lumbered into the sky, dragged down by the

Carousel. We cleared the lip of Comerica and picked up speed, rising a little more cleanly as the Carousel and the zepp made their peace with each other. The lights on the pack's cylinders blinked nervously. I looked around the gondola's open windows, trying to spot the harrier and the battle-platform, half not wanting to see, in case what I saw was Dad being blasted out of the sky.

But there they were, Dad still flying circles around the giant thing, its many rotors and gasbags all straining to keep it aloft and stationary. Smaller drones and even a couple manned planes took off after Dad as I watched and he blasted them out of the sky with contemptuous ease. Dad liked to practice in sims a lot. He might be the world's greatest organic fighter-pilot at this point. Not that that meant much–who cared about being a fighter pilot anymore?

The platform's big guns followed Dad through the sky, seemingly always a little behind him. He anticipated their curve, dodging the twisting, seeking fingers of lightning, the hails of ammo, the guided missiles. He was good–I found myself grinning hard and pumping my fist as Dad took out another battery–but I could see that he wasn't good enough. He had to be good a million times. They had to get lucky once. They would.

As I came up level with the platform, it seemed to notice me, turning a battery toward me. The shells it lofted at me hung in the sky nearby, then sploded in a deadly hail of millions of microscale daisy-cutters. I yanked hard at the yoke and floored it and the zepp turned away, but not enough. I heard a scritching noise as the deadly little bots skittered on the zepp's armored balloon and gondola, scrabbling for purchase. They rained down past the gondola's windows, like dandruff being shrugged off the zepp's scalp.

Dad's harrier screamed over to the battery that had attacked me, flipping and rolling as he opened up on it, pouring fire down until the side of the platform nearest me literally began to melt, liquefying under withering fire and dripping molten metal in rivulets down the side of the platform. I could see men and mechas running to the affected area, moving up replacement guns, firing on Dad, and then the harrier screamed past me. I caught a glimpse of Dad, in his augmented reflex helmet and crash-suit. He seemed to be saluting me, though he went past so fast I couldn't say for sure. I saluted back and engaged the zepp's props, setting a course east.

I put the zepp on autopilot and turned all the sensor arrays up to maximum paranoia and then went back to watch the dogfight between the harrier and the platform from the rear of the gondola.

Something had hit Dad. There was smoke rising from the mid-section of the harrier, just behind the cockpit. Those things could soak up a lot of damage and still keep turning over, but it was clear, even from this distance, that Dad wouldn't last forever. I found some binox in an overhead compartment and watched Dad dodge and weave. I wanted to call him before I got out of range of our towers, but I didn't want to distract him.

It didn't matter. One of the questing, bent fingers of lightning seized the harrier and followed it as it tried to circle away. Smoke poured from the harrier's engines. The lighting stopped and the harrier began a lazy, wobbly glide toward the platform, Dad's last charge, a suicide trajectory. Two missiles lifted off from the platform, arcing for the harrier, and they caught it before it could crash.

My heart thudded in my ears, audible over the growl of the zepp's turbines. I dialed the binox up higher, letting them auto-track, then switching back over to manual because they kept focusing on the damned *shrapnel* and I want to find Dad.

Maybe I saw him. It looked like a man in a crash-suit, there amid the rolling smoke and the expanding cloud of metal and ceramic. Looked like a man, maybe, for an instant, lost amid the smoke. Maybe he landed on the platform and fought his way free—or was taken prisoner.

Maybe Dad was still immortal.

In any event, I still was.

PART 2: NO PRIVACY AT ALL AROUND THIS PLACE!

The cultists didn't mind that I keep the Carousel up and running. Twenty years before, I set it down before the old administrative building of the college where they had their headquarters, and they'd never once asked me to shut it down.

Oh, sure, they put a wire in my head, did it on the first day. That wasn't optional: if you stayed with the cultists, you needed to have the wire in your head. It was for the good of the colony.

But being immortal has its advantages (besides the obvious ones). My brain just kind of *ate* that wire–denatured it, anyway. It took a couple weeks, so for the first little while, I was just like all the other cultists, a transceiver for human emotion. I remember that period hazily, but it wasn't altogether terrible. Once you were attuned to the emotions of everyone else in town, everything was kind of . . . It's hard to describe. Huge. Mellow. The emotional state of three million people has a certain inertia, and it's hard to shift in one direction or another. It dampens all the extremes. Sometimes you'd get a *little* happy, or a *little* miserable, but never those raging, spectacular blisses and rages.

It was probably good therapy for me, just then. It probably helped me get by without Dad.

But like I say, it only took a couple weeks for the wire to lose its efficacy. I could still feel a little tickle that let me know, more or less, what the groupmind was thinking, but it never loomed up large. And I could get as angry or happy as I wanted and my neighbors never seemed to notice, so I guess I wasn't transmitting much.

Here's what happened as I steamed east, away from

Detroit and the ruins of my father's city/museum. It was smooth sailing for the first couple hours, then I started to hear ominous *clunks* and thuds. I knew it must be the little daisy cutters. Some of them must have found soft spots in the bag's armor–that was the point of a billion little daisy cutters instead of just one big one–a brute-force attack on the entire defensive perimeter of the target. An attacker only has to find one hole–a defender needs to be seamless.

The Zepp's idiot lights got redder and redder as time went by, one critical system after another failing. By the time I thought to bring her down–I was in shock, I guess, plus I was young then–it was too late. Altitude controls were locked.

I watched, helpless, clutching the pack's canisters, as we drifted in the winds, sometimes going higher, sometimes dipping down. The Carousel was a destabilizing force: every time the wind gusted, it rocked like a pendulum, and as the zepp's gyros wound down, we rocked with it.

The zepp set itself down in North Carolina, amid the leftovers of the old UNC campus, settling gently. I slid/stumbled down the ramp with the pack in hand. The zepp was still losing altitude, inching lower and lower. Soon enough, the gondola would come down on the top of the Carousel, doing who-knew-what damage. I did a little executive planning and decided that I had a way better chance of bringing the Carousel up to nominal than I did the daisy-cutter wormed zepp, and I blew the cargo hoist loose, cutting the zepp free so that it lofted away, to ply its idiot way through the skies, unmanned and dying.

The thing about immortality is, it's complicated. A mixed blessing. Dad's immortality was a much simpler thing, really: a collection of hacks and tricks to wind back his body's clock, to repair the damage of the ages, to make him young again. Like his yogurt, for his liver.

With me, it was all about the germ plasm. I'd been modded down in my nuclei, a transhuman by birth, a native of the transhuman condition. And no one knew what that meant, really. Including me.

So while it was apparent early on that I was aging slowly—retaining maximal brain plasticity by keeping my physical age as young as possible—no one seemed to suspect just how slowly I was going to age. I was chronologically 13 when I landed in North Carolina, but I was physically more like 10. At the time, I assumed that meant that I'd just go on, aging slowly, but aging.

Not so, as it turned out.

Twenty years later, I was still 11. Maybe 13. Let me put it this way: no pubes. This was not what I had in mind when I pictured immortality. I had . . . stirrings. But they were like phantom limbs, there but not there, elusive, an itch I couldn't scratch.

The cultists were mildly curious about this, in the same way that they were mildly curious about most things. They weren't worked up about it or anything. They didn't get worked up about anything. That was the point. But they liked having kids and they wanted to know when I'd be ready to help out in that department. So they asked, every now and again, frankly. And I told them the truth. Why not? They weren't going to throw me out—not as long as they thought I was a wirehead.

The only person who had a problem with my perpetual adolescence was me. There were moods that came on me, now and again, sudden and ferocious. Terrors, too. It came with the brain plasticity—I could adapt to anything, but nothing ever stuck. I could never approximate the incredible conviction of the cultists—not even the lesser conviction of the normals who traded with them every now and again. I'd believe something for a day or two—like wanting to overthrow the cult and rescue the wireheads from their surgical bondage—and then it would seem like a stupid idea, and then a distant memory. Only my journals showed me how changeable my weather was. When I got them down off the seat I kept them on in the Carousel and thumbed through them, it wrenched something in my chest. Sometimes I cried. Sometimes I cried for a long time.

Mostly I tried to distract myself from all of this. One good way to do that was to keep the Carousel tuned up. The cultists liked it–it was a relaxing place to sit and watch a show, something they didn't get much of in Raleigh Durham since the wires went in.

The Carousel was a four-part show with an intro and afterword, "the longest-running stage show in the history of the world," in which primitive robots told the story of how General Electric and Thomas Edison had rescued them from the dark ages. The robots rotated in and out, appearing behind scrims and delivering corny jokes, singing and tapping their toes, while their electrical appliances clattered, clanked, and showed themselves off.

Dad had loved the Carousel. Not in the "I love chocolate" sense of love. In the "I love you, darling, and I want to marry you and spend the rest of my life with you," sense. Disney World–where the Carousel ended up some time after the '64 World's Fair–had not fared well in the Mecha Wars. All of the Animal Kingdom and Epcot were fused-glass ruins, and most of the Magic Kingdom had burned down. But the Carousel had been only a little scuffed, its control systems fused from EMP weapons.

Dad and I spent a week separating the Carousel from its foundations. It was like digging an old tree out of a forest–digging a wide circle around it, taking the whole root ball with it. In the Carousel's case, it was the control apparatus for the show, spanning two basement levels beneath it. The entire Magic Kingdom was built two storeys off the ground, specifically to leave room for the control systems. Over the years, these systems had sprawled sideways and downwards, retrofitted solid-state controllers replacing the original mechanicals. We took lots of pictures–visual and millimeter-wave radar–of the whole setup and emailed them to a little cluster Dad had that could evolve itself to solve complex vision problems. Overnight, they mailed us back clean architectural as-built diagrams that helped a lot.

Dad had a lot of older, less collectable mechas he kept around for duty like this. We'd driven down to Florida on the path of the old I-75 in a platoon of these things, each of us driving at the head of a column of lumbering beasts that were slaved to our control units. They weren't much to look at, they weren't all that smart, but those big boys were *strong.* Twenty-two of them lifted and carried the Carousel all the way home to Detroit. The Pack were in a frenzy once we got back, delighted to have me around again. They'd patrolled the museum-city while we were away, emailing me with anything urgent that they didn't know how to cope with. That was before the wumpuses, so there wasn't much by way of risk to our humble home.

Once we got the Carousel home, we set to work restoring it. Dad was insistent that we not fix it *too* well. In a couple of the scenes, the Dad robot was really weird around the neck, its cervical controllers bulging at the flesh like it had swallowed a wheel-rim, sideways. I was pretty sure we could do better than that, but Dad insisted that that was part of the charm, and so I printed a new controller that was an exact match. I even resisted the temptation to replace the glassy, weird eyeballs with something vat-grown from one of my kits.

"It's not supposed to be realistic, Jimmy," he said. "You need to understand that."

I didn't understand it at the time, but I came to understand it eventually. It was the show. It had a dream-like quality, a kind of ethereal logic that seemed perfectly sensible in the show, but which evaporated when the show ended like the secret technique for levitating evaporating as you wake from sleep.

Each of the four sequences showed the progress that technology made, generation to generation. A wood stove turns into an electric range, then a self-cleaning range, then a voice-controlled microwave oven. At every turn, the world *progressed*, got *better*. The problems posed by each stove got solved. We had lots of different sound-tracks we could run for the ride–it had been redesigned several times–but the original one held the key for me: "At every turn in our history there was always someone saying 'Turn back. Turn back.' But there is no turning back. Not for us. Not for our carousel. The challenge always lies ahead. And as long as man dreams and works and builds together, these years too can be the best time of your life."

I lived in the future that they were talking about in the ride, but we didn't have "progress" anymore. We'd outgrown progress. What we had was *change*. Things changed whenever anyone wanted to change them: design and launch a fleet of wumpuses, or figure out a way to put an emotional antenna in your head, or create a fleet of killer robots, or invent immortality, or gengineer your goats to give silk. Just do it. It'll catch on, or it won't. Maybe it'll catch itself on. Then the world is . . . different. Then someone else changes it.

The status quo doesn't protect itself, it needs defending if it's going to stay put. The problem is that technology gives more of an advantage to an attacker than to a defender. A defender needs to mount a perfect defense. An attacker needs to find one hole in the defense. So once technology gets going, anything can be knocked down–evil doesn't stand–but nothing much can be erected in its place. Look at Dad's museum.

I've thought about leaving North Carolina and heading back to Detroit, believe me I have. But the cult isn't so bad. They're all nice and friendly and they come as close to stability as anything I've ever experienced. Plus they're pretty good with medical technology, and their biologists don't mind if I ask them nosy, ignorant questions about curing my immortality–at least enough to get my testicles to descend.

Twenty years have gone by and I have two–count 'em,

two–pubic hairs. I call them Yeti and Sasquatch. I am as flexible as a ten-year-old–I can get my forehead down on my knee or clasp my arms over my shoulder–and I can run around all day. But like I said, I can't stay interested in much for longer than a few days. My brain and body are so plastic that I can't manage to do anything that requires any kind of stability. I'm like the perfect metaphor for the whole world.

No one knows how to de-immortalize me yet. All I want is a little bit of it, a little bit of aging. A couple more years. Life's pretty good at 18, it seems to me. 18 would be a good age.

I didn't recognize Lacey when I saw her. It had been twenty years, and the years had changed her.

I was out in the bush, looking for wild mushrooms. Mostly you got kombucha, big ones, and they made delicious tea. Supposedly they were a little hallucinogenic, but it appeared that my marvelous immortal liver didn't much care to have me enter a state of elevated reality, so all I got out of it was tea. It was good tea, though.

I had the pack with me. I'd built them new bodies, better suited to the quiet life among the cultists. The bodies resembled furry mechanical squirrels. They could crawl all over you without freaking you out or making you feel threatened, which was exactly what I wanted from them. They were still frisky–even though they had aged a little and become a little less experimental, a little more prone to hanging around the Carousel and its immediate grounds. The canisters containing their nervous systems and brains could keep them alive for some time yet, I was sure, but they wouldn't live forever. Lucky little bastards.

It was crisp autumn and the leaves were ten million flaming colors, crunching underfoot as we sought out the kombuchas. I was bending to inspect something that Pepe had found–Pepe still loved to have more than one PoV, so I'd given him four squirrels to drive at once–and when I looked up, I was staring into her boots, lace-up numbers, old fashioned with thick waffle-soles.

I kept looking up. She was a woman, in her mid-thirties. Her hair had grown out into an irregular mob of curls, her round face rosy-cheeked from the chilly weather. Fine lines radiated out from her drawn-up bow lips, and her eyes had small lines to match at their corners.

"Hello," I said. She wasn't a wirehead, I could tell that just by looking at the hair. They liked to wear it short so as not to interfere with the antenna.

"Jimmy?" she said, putting her hand to her chest. She was wearing a smart cowl that breathed gently around her, keeping her warm and dry.

I cocked my head, trying to place her. She looked so familiar, but I couldn't place her, not exactly–

"Jimmy!" she said, and grabbed me in a hard hug. There was a woman under that cowl, boobs and hips. She was a whole head taller than me. But the smell was the same. Or maybe it was the hug.

"Lacey!" I said, and squeezed back, barely getting my arms around her.

She practically lifted me off my feet, and she squeezed so hard that all the breath went out of me.

"Lacey!" I croaked, "easy there!"

She set me down, a little reluctantly, and took a step back. "Jesus Christ, Jimmy, you haven't changed *at all.*"

I shrugged. "Immortal," I said.

She put her hand to her chest and looked at me, her mouth open. "Yeah, of course," she said. "Immortal."

"I'm trying to cure it," I said. "Not all the way. But I thought if I could age up to, you know, 18 or so . . ."

"Jimmy," she said, "please stop talking about this for now. I'm out of weirdness quotient for the day."

I had some snacks in my bag–the tortillas and tomatoes that the cult favored for staple crops–so I sat down and spread out my picnic tarp and offered her a seat, then something to eat.

She sat down and we ate together. We used to do this, back in Detroit, sneak picnics together out in the boonies, in an abandoned building or, in a pinch, cupped in one of my mecha's hands. We fell into the easy rhythm of it as though no time at all had passed since then. For me, none had–at least not physically.

I told her about the zepp ride and the daisy cutters, about the slow landing and my settling in here, bound to the Carousel, not wanting to abandon it.

She got a little misty when she remembered the attack on Detroit. "I remember the zeppelin lifting off, and all the explosions in the sky. I was hiding under something– a truck, I think–and trying to keep the goat from going crazy. What was her name? Louisa?"

"Moldavia," I said. I couldn't believe she didn't remember that. It was like yesterday to me.

"Moldavia! We ate her, you know. I remember that now. Mom and Dad couldn't get their silk into India and the farm took a turn for the worse and–"

She broke off and rolled up another chopped tomato salad in another tortilla, sprinkled some basil and cilantro on it from the little herb bag I kept.

"What happened afterward?" I asked. "What happened to Detroit?"

"Oh," she said. "Oh, well. The wumpuses came, of course. Took about two weeks for them to get through it all, and when they were done, there were so many of them that they mostly ate each other for another week, which was really gross, but when that was done, there was just good land. We farmed it for a while. Mostly redwoods. Big ones–400 footers. Anything for a carbon-credit. They were cheap and easy."

I closed my eyes and rocked back on my tailbone. I'd stood by the Carousel for 20 years because, somewhere in my mind, I expected that Dad would be getting the museum back together and that wherever the Carousel was, he would come. He wouldn't abandon it.

Somewhere in the back of my mind, I expected that Dad was alive, immortal, coming for me. That we'd have our immortality together. It was lonely, being the only one.

"Redwoods," I finally said. It came out in a croak.

"Big mutant ones," she said, eating her burrito, apparently oblivious to me. "Didn't last, of course. What does? They all got some kind of blight that petrified them where they stood. We think it was some kind of exotic mesoite that traded their carbon for calcium, harvesting the good stuff for who-knows-what. It went top down, so it took a while for us to notice. For a while, they all stayed upright, white and chalky. Then they crumbled until they were nothing but powder, which blew away."

"What doesn't?" I said. I was still thinking of Dad. I knew I'd get over it though. Brain plasticity.

"Yeah," she said. "Mom and Dad hung in there with the rest of the Treehuggers for a while, but I wasn't going to stay there forever, I knew that much. I went west on my sixteenth, got as far as the Oregon coast. Kept it touch with the parents for a while, but they moved to Bangalore when I was about 25 and so that was it for them and me. I dated this guy who found me a job maintaining these weird brain-scanners at a research facility and I did that for a while too, which would have given my parents seizures if they knew. I probably stayed in that job for longer than I would have, just for that reason.

"But the people who ran the research station got bored or went broke–they didn't ever tell us peons–and one day they didn't show up for work. We all kept coming in and cleaning the floors and keeping the machines running and signing for deliveries for a week, but then we figured that they weren't coming back. So I hit the road again (the boyfriend didn't last as long as the job) and now I'm here. And so are you!"

She ate another burrito. She could really put them away.

She told me more minutiae from the road, places she'd

been and people she'd met, talking for a long, long time. So long that I started to shiver as the sun dipped low. The pack whined around me, climbing up on my lap and my shoulders and head. Lacey was oblivious to the passage of time, her cowl keeping her warm. I had one like it that I'd bought from a traveller a couple years before, but I didn't wear it much–it was too big for me and it tripped me up a little.

"We got to get going," I said. "I'm freezing."

She stopped talking and looked around. There was something hunted in her look. She stood up and slapped at her cowl to knock the crumbs off it and then she looked around again.

"So," she said. "So. Nice to see you again, Jimmy. Really nice! You can send me email or something sometime if you want to. Good luck with everything."

I stopped folding up the tarp and putting away the leftovers. "Why? Where are you going?"

She looked around for a third time, then pointed south. "That direction looks promising. Do you know what's there?"

I followed her finger through the woods. "About half a day's walk will get you down to Jordan Lake. Nice places around there. Holiday cottages. Keep on going and you'll hit Myrtle Beach, eventually. Might take you a week or two. Where are you headed, anyway?"

"It was really great to see you." She grabbed me in another one of those hugs, so fierce that I couldn't breathe for a moment.

"Where are you going?" I said again, once she'd released me.

She felt in her cowl and found a hanky, blew her face on it and wiped away all the stuff she'd started leaking all of a sudden.

"I just go," she said, finally. "That's all I've done for the past two years, Jimmy. I just go, and keep going. All the places are different, but they're all the same, too. Nothing's like what I'm looking for."

“What are you looking for?”

“I don’t know, but I’ll know it when I see it. I just hope that I find it soon.”

“If you go off that way, you’re going to end up walking all night before you get to a hotel.”

She laughed. “I don’t really . . . use . . . hotels,” she said. “I stay out here, with all the nature. Product of my upbringing. Once a Treehugger . . .”

I hadn’t had a real conversation in ten years. It was a million to one chance, running into Lacey in the woods. Also: maybe she knew a little more about Detroit?

“Why don’t you come over to my place?” I said at last. “I’ve got plenty of room. I promise you, my place isn’t the same.”

She crouched down and looked in my eyes. “I don’t think that’s such a good idea, Jimmy,” she said. “But thank you.”

We didn’t really argue. We hardly discussed it. But somehow, she ended up taking my hand and letting me lead her back home, ducking the occasional wirehead on the way.

Back in Detroit, my dad had reconstructed the Carousel’s elaborate concrete ramp and queue area, but I didn’t have the resources to do that here, so to get up on my Carousel’s apron, you had to scramble up a chest-high wall that shielded the machinery beneath the stage and seats. I got myself up—the pack skittered up around me, scaling the wall as though it were horizontal—and then I helped Lacey up. Her hands were strong and her palms were dry, her fingertips calloused and raspy on my wrists.

“This way,” I said, and led her inside.

Of course, I wasn’t running the show at the time. I don’t, usually. Not that I have power woes—the cell that Dad fitted it with won’t run out of isotopes for a couple centuries yet, but it saves wear-and-tear on the parts, and those can be a bitch to replace.

The Carousel is designed to seat six audiences at once, rotating continuously around the stage in 60-degree wedges.

Between each stage is a little baffle that soaks up the noise from the adjoining set and provides a little space for the operators to hide out from the customers. At least, that's how I used it. I suppose I could have set my bed up on one of the stages, or on the sloping auditorium aisles. I could have even removed some of the painstakingly restored seats. But all that felt wrong, after all the work that Dad put into getting it all so cherry and pristine.

So I kept my bedroll in the gap between the first two scenes, and my clothes and things between the remaining gaps. The pack's canisters were stashed under the stage in the third scene, which held a little maintenance hollow that we'd always kept tools and such in.

Lacey laughed when I let her in. "You live here?"

"I forget, did you ever get to ride this?"

"No, but I remember when you brought it back. We all came out to watch the mechas carry it through our forest. You knocked down a bunch of trees to make way."

I shrugged. "It's a wide load."

"So what's it do?"

I showed her, turning it on and then rushing to sit down next to her. The lights went down and the curtains parted, and a spotlight played over the old "General Electric" logo. I loved that logo. Imagine a time when there were companies that made their fortune being generally electrical! These days, electrical stuff was very specific indeed.

The narration started. Dad told me that the actor's name was Jean Shepherd, and I'd heard his spiel a billion times, so often that I sometimes mixed up his calm, warm baritone with my memory of my father's voice, the two all blended in my infinitely plastic mind. The narrator welcomed us to Walt Disney's Carousel of Progress and told us some of its history, then started with the real heavy philosophy: "The challenge always lies ahead. And as long as man dreams and works and builds together, these years too can be the best time of your life."

I looked at Lacey to see if she'd noticed the way that the voice over had just dropped that on us. The challenge always lies ahead. Progress! She was looking heavy-lidded, but attentive.

The curtains parted and we got to the first scene. Dad—not my dad, the dad on stage—was wearing a cravat and fanning himself with a newspaper. The dog lay at his feet, doing comedy barks. Dad told us all about the miracle of his icebox ("holds 50 pounds of ice!") and his gas lamps. Then the lights came up on the scrim scenes on the wings of the stage and we got to meet Mom, who was ironing. Mom complained that even though it only takes five hours to do the laundry with her new "wash day marvel," her spare time is taken up with canning and cleaning the oven. This is supposed to be funny.

Then the other side lit up and we got to meet Jimmy. Not me—the son. His name is also Jimmy. I'm sure it's just a coincidence. After all, I'd been around for years before Dad got the Carousel. And Mom probably wouldn't have let him name me after an old robot. Probably.

Jimmy was looking through a stereoscope at pornography—well, pictures of hoochie-coochie girls—and Dad gave him a good-natured ribbing. I'd seen this scene hundreds of times, but this time, sitting next to Lacey, remembering our necking sessions, it made me a little uncomfortable.

The remaining scenes introduced Sister (in a corset, worrying that she is "indecent") and Grandma and Grandpa, listening to a "talking machine" with their pet parrot.

Then it was over and the singing started, "There's a great big beautiful tomorrow/Shining at the end of every day!" and the stage rotated. We came around to the next scene—the 1920s and electricity—and I heard a sound from Lacey, beside me. She was snoring. Her head was down on her chest and she was sleeping soundly. Her lips were parted a little and her face looked worried in sleep. I realized that she'd looked worried since I'd met her.

I got up and stopped the ride, resetting all the shows and powering them down. From the six slices of the Carousel, I heard the robots ceasing their spiels and going to sleep. The pack–who didn't much care for the show–came out of hiding and began to race around the aisles, nipping at each others' heels.

Lacey was going to have to sleep somewhere. I hadn't really thought about that. I went and checked out my narrow bed. I'd filled the space between two stages with a pile of pillows. It was comfortable enough. Did it smell bad? Maybe it did. The shower was outside, in a little prefab building I'd bought off a traveller, and I didn't always remember to use it.

Lacey probably had some kind of bed, anyway. I got up and grabbed her pack. It felt like it was full of rocks. Man, she had to be *strong.* Another perk of adulthood–of mortality.

I gave her shoulder a little shake, and her head lolled and she snored. I gave her another shake, a little harder this time. Her eyes opened a crack, then she straightened up slowly and opened and closed her mouth a few times.

"It's been a long day," she said. "Sorry, Jimmy."

I showed her my bed and she laughed. "It's like the den of some burrowing animal."

I felt obscurely ashamed. Twenty years here and I had practically nothing to show for it. The pack's new bodies. The maintenance I'd done on the Carousel. My pathetic pile of pillows.

She put her arm around my shoulders and gave me a squeeze. "It's great," she said. "It's just the kind of thing I would have loved, 20 years ago." That made me feel even worse. I slumped.

"Poor Jimmy," she said. "You're very generous to offer me a place to sleep, you know."

"Do you have a bed in your pack?"

She nodded. "I do, indeed. But screw it. It's a pain to set up. I don't need it here. Besides, I'm so tired I could drop where I stand. Where's the bathroom?"

I told her, warning her to keep a low profile–I wasn't sure how I was going to explain her to the cultists, who'd want her to get a wire in her head if she wasn't just passing through–and started to dig through my clothes, looking for enough stuff to make another bed out of between two of the other theater-sections.

She came back, shivering a little, clapping her hands together. "Cold around here at night," she said, before casually pulling her cowl over her head, then stripping off her sweater–spidergoat silk, it looked like–and then her tights. Just as quick as that, she was naked.

I'd never seen a naked woman before. I know that sounds silly, but physiologically, I was still a little kid. I didn't have a girlfriend. Every now and again, I'd get a little curious about it, feel something that might be horniness, like an itch somewhere in my lower belly, but most of the time I didn't think about sex. The cultists had plenty of sex, but behind closed doors. Once I'd seen some pornography that a traveller had brought through, but she'd snatched it away as soon as she noticed me eyeballing it, warning me that this wasn't the kind of thing a kid like me should be looking at. I didn't bother to explain my unique chronological circumstances.

My eyes were flicking from one part of her to another. Her breasts. Her thighs. The curls at her pubis. I'd seen Dad naked every now and again, but not for decades. I'd seen pubic hair before, but it had never been this interesting. She had little tufts of hair in her armpits, too. So much hair!

She seemed not to notice me staring, but she eventually turned away and bent to rummage in her pack. Her genitals winked at me as she did. I realized that I had an erection, a strange little boner in my pants. I got them now and again, and they were usually just a nuisance, something that got in the way.

She straightened up, holding a long shirt that she slipped into. It hung down to her thighs.

"All right," she said. "Me to bed. You sleep left or right?"

It took me a minute to get that she was asking me a question. I blinked a couple times. "What?"

"Left or right side of the bed? I can do either."

I fumbled for words. "I'm going to sleep over there." I pointed at the pile of clothes I'd been assembling.

She clucked her tongue and crossed her eyes. "Don't be stupid. There's room for both of us there. I'm not going to put you out of your bed. Get in."

I hesitated.

"Get in!" she said, clapping her hands.

I turned away and awkwardly stripped down to my underpants and shirt. I worried again that I might smell. I didn't wash my clothes all that often. They were wicking and dirt-shedding and had impregnated antibacterials, so I didn't see why I should. But maybe I smelled. The cultists wouldn't say anything. Wireheads didn't notice that kind of thing.

She clapped her hands again and pointed at the pillow. "March, young man!"

Then I was whirling back in time. That was what Dad used to say when I was dragging my ass around. Had I told her that? Did she know it anyway? Had she guessed? Was it a coincidence?

She repeated herself and pointed. I crawled into the bed. The pack bounded in after me, assuming their usual positions all around me, snuggling and burrowing among the pillows. She laughed.

A moment later, the pillows shifted around me as she climbed in next to me. I tried to press myself up against my wall, giving her as much space as possible, but she gathered me in her arms and squeezed me like a teddy bear.

"Good night, Jimmy," she said. Her face smelled of soap and her hair smelled of woodsmoke. It tickled my cheeks. She kissed the top of my head.

A weird thing happened then. I stopped thinking about her being naked. I stopped thinking about her being my old friend Lacey. Suddenly, all I could think about was how good this felt, being held to a soft bosom, enfolded in strong arms. Dad hugged me plenty. But I didn't remember my mother. She'd died not long after I was born. Poisoned by Detroit. She hadn't eaten her yogurt, didn't get her microbes, and so her liver gave out. Dad barely talked about her, and the photos of her had vanished with Detroit itself, consumed by some wumpus and turned into arable land.

Lacey squeezed me again, and I found that I was crying. Silently at first, then I must have let out a whimper because she went "Shhh, shhh," and squeezed me harder. "It's OK," she murmured into my hair, and words like that, and rocked me back and forth, and then I was crying harder.

I cried myself out there in the pillows, in Lacey's arms. I don't know what I wept for, but I remember the feeling as not altogether sad. There was some joy there, a feeling of homecoming in the arms of my old friend. The pack snuggled in among us, and they were ticklish, so soon we were both laughing and rocking back and forth.

"Good night, Lacey," I said.

"Good night, Jimmy," she said. She kissed the top of my head again and squeezed me harder and I let myself relax in her arms.

The wireheads don't mind the occasional houseguest, but anyone who's going to actually *live* in the settlement needs to join the cult. They don't want any violent, emotional, unpredictable people running around, making things difficult for them. The deal is a simple one: get the wire in your head, get free food, shelter, and community forever. Don't get the wire in your head and you have to get out of town.

You'd be surprised at how many people don't want to play along with this system (I guess I count as one of those people). The cult's gotten pretty good at spotting freeloaders who want to live in the peace and prosperity of the cult but don't want to join up. These people seem to think that so long as they're doing their share of the work, they should be able to stick around. What they don't understand is that the *work* isn't the important part: robots can do the heavy lifting, as much as we let them do of it.

The important thing is the *stability*. Here in wirehead country, nothing important ever changes. New people come in. Old people die. Babies are born. Kids go to school–I went with them for a little while, in my wirehead days, but I decided I didn't need to keep going to classes after three or four years and no one seemed to mind. No one minds what anyone else does, once you're a wirehead. Since we can all feel each others' emotions, it's impossible to resent someone without him knowing about it, and it's impossible to feel guilty without letting others know it. Your whole attitude towards your neighbors is on permanent display, visible from a mile off (my own antenna seems to radiate a calm acceptance no matter what I'm feeling, and lets me know what others are feeling without swamping me with their emotions).

The work gets done. "Progress" never happens. We've banished progress, here in the wirehead cult. That's OK by me, I suppose. Who needs it?

"So I had been living in Florida, up near Jacksonville, in wiki country," Lacey said, over our breakfast. I kept a larder of fresh fruit in the maintenance space under the stage, and Lacey had been glad to help me slice up a couple of delicious fruit salads. I'd put up some yogurt a few days before and it was mature enough to pour overtop, with some sunflower seeds left over from the last autumn.

"The city was good, but it got to me, all that change, all the time. I tried to garden a little patch of it, just a little spot where I could put up a house, but there were so many trolls who kept overwriting my planning permission with this idea for a motorcycle racing track. I'd revert their changes, they'd revert back. Then one of the Old Ones would come by and freeze my spot for a month and lecture us. Then they'd be back at Day 31. I only met them face to face once. I'd pictured them as old Florida bikers, leathery and worn, but they were teenagers! Just kids."

I looked away, at the blue sky overhead, visible through the riotous colors of the leaves.

"Sorry," she said. "You know what I mean, though. They were like, eight 16 year olds, and they'd built their bikes to burn actual hydrocarbons. These things made so much goddamned noise! Your old mecha was quieter! They rode them up to my house one day, left all six in my garden, among my flowers, growling, and rang my doorbell.

"I had built a little gypsy caravan with flower-boxes and bright paint, all prefab vat-grown woodite, impervious to weather and bugs, watertight at the seams, breathing through a semi-permeable roof and floor. It was a really nice piece of engineering–my parents would have liked it!

"I answered the door and they pointed to their motorcycles and explained that they'd spent an entire year building and tuning them and that my little house was the only thing stopping them from building a racetrack. They wanted me to move the house to somewhere else. They were extra pissed because my house had *wheels*, so how hard could it be to relocate? They even offered to find me somewhere else, get me a tow. I told them no, I liked it there, liked my garden (what was left of it), liked the creek down the hill from me, liked my view of the big city down the other side of the hill, all its lights.

"They told me that their parents had lots of money and they could get me a real big place somewhere up high in the city, maybe even put my caravan on a roof there." She stopped talking while we picked our way down a hillside. We were headed for my own creek, which was cold and brisk, but still swimmable, for a week or two. I'd brought a bar of soap.

"I told them to get off my land. I also recorded them from my front window as they shouted things at me and threw stuff at my door. It turned out to be dead animals. They left a dead rabbit or squirrel on my doormat every day for a week.

I added pictures to the Discuss page for the zoning, and the Old Ones were properly affronted and froze their editing privileges.

"But they didn't let up. They had a whole army of sock-puppets they were paying in Missouri, a boiler-room outfit where they'd do actual work on the wiki, improve it a lot, build up credibility and make themselves very welcome, then come and edit my zoning. It got so I was doing nothing but staying home all day and reverting and arguing with these guys.

"Then I went away for a couple days–there was a barbecue festival in a big field outside of town and I got invited to compete, so I was working over a smoker there, and when I got back, guess what?"

"Your caravan was gone and they were racing motorcycles where it used to be."

"Exactly," she said. "Exactly. They'd knocked down the trees, dammed the stream, paved everything, put in half-pipes. Even if I changed the zoning back, I wouldn't want to live there again."

"I woulda been pissed," I said, getting down to my skin and jumping into the stream, sputtering and blowing. Normally I'd have waded in a few millimeters at a time, but I was still uncomfortable being nude in front of her, so I just plunged. She followed suit.

"You'd think, huh," she said. "But I was just resigned at that point. I moved to the city, which had its own charms. Remember that they said they could get me a rooftop? Well, it turns out that roofs were easy to get. Not many people want to sleep on the 90th floor of a tower, but I found it as peaceful as anything. I strung up my hammock and put up my tents and settled in to love my view."

Sometimes it was hard to remember that this was *Lacey Treehugger*, the girl who'd thought that all concrete was a sin. 90 floors up! Damn.

There were more people coming down to the creek.

Double damn. Lacey had been there three days and we had managed to avoid my neighbors the whole time, but my luck had run out.

They had the typical wirehead look: one-piece, short-sleeved garments that shed dirt, so they glowed faintly. Stripes and piping were the main decoration. Someone had designed this outfit in the early days of the cult and no one had ever redesigned it. Of course not. Why change anything around here?

There were three of them. I recognized them at once: Sebastien, a guy in his twenties whom I'd known since he was a baby; Tina, an older woman with teak-colored skin; and Brent, her son, who was 11, the same as me, sort of.

"Hello there," Sebastien said. I felt the tickle of their emotions from the vestiges of my antenna, a kind of oatmeal-bland wash of calm nullity. "Haven't seen you in a few days." He noticed Lacey and squinted at her. She had sunk down so that only her round face stuck up out of the sluggish water. "Hello to you, too," he said. "I'm Sebastien, this is Tina and Brent." They all waved, except for Brent, who was bending down and examining a frog he'd found on a flat rock.

"This is my friend Lacey," I said. Sebastien drove me crazy. He was born and bred to the cult and always wanted to talk to me about how much better life was now that I was living with the wireheads. He was the kind of zealot who made me worry that if I didn't match his enthusiasm that he'd try to figure out if my antenna was working properly. Talking to him always put me on my guard.

Lacey waved.

"We're here for a swim," he said, like it wasn't obvious. He didn't ask if we minded–no wirehead would–but instead just started stripping down to the bathing trunks he wore under his jumpsuit, giving me an accidental glimpse of his bony ass. Tina did the same, taking his hand and squeezing it, then Brent struggled out of his. Tina and her ex-husband had Brent and then split when he was still a baby, one of those weird, calm wirehead divorces, so mellow they might as well be happening underwater.

They slipped into the water with us and I knew I was going to have to say something. "I'm sorry," I said, "but we're not wearing anything in here. Do you mind looking away while we get out?"

Sebastien and Tina had made it in to their shins, their bodies broken out in gooseflesh from the icy, bracing water. "Oh, Jimmy," Tina said. "We're sorry." All three of them caught her sadness and looked downcast. Reflexively, I looked sad too. Gradually, they caught the larger emotion of the group, still perceptible at this distance, and got happier again.

"Don't worry about it," I said once the sun had risen on their moods again. "It was inconsiderate of us. I didn't think anyone else would be down by the river on a day like this."

"We like it cold," Sebastien said. "Wakes up the body." Then Brent took a few toddling steps into the water, slipped, and splashed them. They laughed and splashed him back. There was a moment of frenzy as they caught each others' surprise and glee, and then it, too, dampened down.

"Well, we're just about done here," I said.

"Nice to meet you," Lacey said. They'd turned their backs, but I caught Brent sneaking a peek before he looked away, too.

"Nice to meet you, too," Tina said. "You be sure and come by the general meeting tonight, all right?"

I grunted as noncommittally as I could, while pulling on my jumpsuit over my wet legs. It wicked away the wet as I struggled into it. I just wanted to get away from there–they were curious about Lacey, I could tell that even without a fully functional antenna.

Lacey just pulled her smartcloak over her head and let her boots conform themselves to her feet. We had walked idly and slowly to the river, but we hurried away.

"I'm not supposed to be here, am I?" Lacey said.

"No," I said. "Yes." I helped her up onto the side-trail

that I used when I didn't want to talk to anyone. "It's complicated. They're going to want you to get wired, or leave."

"And getting wired–you wouldn't recommend it?"

I shrugged. "They're nice people. If you had to choose a group of people to share your state of mind with, they'd be a pretty good choice."

"But you don't think it's a good idea."

I shrugged again. "I let them put a wire in my head," I said.

"Your brain ate it, though."

I looked around, suddenly paranoid. There was no one. "Shhh. Yes. But I didn't know that my brain would eat it when I let them install it."

"So why'd you do it?"

I thought back. "I was a kid," I said at last. "I'd just lost my Dad and my home. They were nice to me. They said that they'd leave me alone once I had the wire fitted. That was all I wanted."

"Did you like it?"

"Having a wire? Well, not the worst thing in the world, having a wire. I never felt lonely. And when I was sad, it passed quickly. I think it would have been a lot harder without it."

"So you think it's therapeutic, then? Maybe I should get one after all."

I turned around and took her hands. "Don't, OK? Please. I like you this way."

We got home and sat down in the theater seats. I thought we'd talk about it, but we seemed to have run out of words. I wished for a moment that we had matching antennae so I could know what she was feeling. That was pretty weird.

"Show me this play," she said. "I fell asleep the other night."

So I started it up. I'd done a major, three-year-long maintenance project on it that had just wrapped up, so it was running as good as new. I was proud of the work I'd done. I wished that Dad could see it. Lacey was nearly as good.

We sat through the opening scene and rotated around the arc of the circle by 60 degrees and went through the change to the roaring 20s, and the family's kitchen was now filled with yarn-like wires coming off the ceiling light and leading to all the appliances. Dad was wearing a bow-tie now, and fanning himself with Souvenir of Niagara Falls fan. Dad wants to show us all his new modern appliances, and so they all switch on and start flapping and clacking while frenetic music plays in the background. Then a "fuse" blows–I looked this up, it means that he overloaded a crude breaker in the power-supply–and the whole street goes dark. A neighbor threatens to beat him, but then "Jimmy"–yes, Jimmy again–changes the fuse and the lights come back.

Mom and sister are getting into costume–there's a Fourth of July party that night–and Dad has to join them, but he gets us to sing his song. I noted that Lacey tapped her toe as we went around the arc, and it made me feel very good.

After the show, I made us diner and Lacey told me more funny stories from the road. Then we crawled into bed and she enfolded me in her arms. We'd done that every night. I didn't cry anymore, and it felt so good. Like something I'd always missed.

"They're going to come for you," I said, lying with my eyes open, feeling her arms around me.

"They are, huh?"

"Put a wire in your head."

"And you don't think I should do that."

"I'll go with you." I swallowed. "If you want."

She squeezed me harder. "I don't think you'll be able to carry this thing, do you?"

"I don't mind."

"Liar. You've been taking care of this thing for 20 years, Jimmy!"

"That was when I thought that Dad would come back for it. Doesn't sound like he'll come back now. Stupid terrorists."

"Who?"

"The assholes who attacked Detroit. Whoever they were." I noticed that she'd stiffened a little. "I thought they were thieves at first, after our stuff. But from what you say, it sounds like they were terrorists–they just wanted to destroy it all. We probably had the last mountain of steel-belted radials in the world, you know?"

She didn't say anything for a bit. "I can go in the morning. We can stay in touch."

"I want to go with you." I surprised myself with the vehemence of it. "I need to get away from here. I need to get away from this *thing*." I punched out at the wall at the edge of the bed, giving it a hard thump and sending the pack scurrying around in circles. "Fuck this thing. It's a prison. It's stuck me down here. Just another one of Dad's stupid ideas."

"You shouldn't talk about your Dad that way. He was–"

"What? He was an asshole! Look at me! Do you think I want to be like *this* forever?"

"You told me that you thought you'd found a cure for it–"

I laughed. "Sure, sure. But I've thought that for 20 years. Nothing's worked."

She hugged me tighter. "It's not all bad, is it? It could be worse. You could be getting old, like me. I get what I can out of the neutriceuticals, but you know, it gets harder every day. I can't walk as far as I used to. Can't see as well. Can't hear as well. I'm getting wrinkled, I keep finding grey hairs–"

"Come on," I said. "You're a beautiful woman. You got to grow up. I'm just a little kid! I'm going to stay a little kid forever. You got to change. Not just change, either–*progress*! You got to progress, to get better and smarter and wiser and, you know, *more*!"

"I'm just saying it's not as good as you think it is."

"You get to have sex!" I blurted. "You get to know what it's like."

"You've never?"

"Never," I said. "Physiologically, I'm 11 or 12. No adult would have sex with me. And it's not right for me to make out with little kids. The last girl I kissed was you, Lacey."

"Oh, Jimmy," she said. She stroked my hair. "I'm sorry. It's hard to know how to think of you. Sometimes I think you're just a little kid, but you're actually a little older than me, aren't you?"

"Yeah," I said. "But my brain doesn't age much either. It's too plastic. I don't get to build up layers of experience one on top of another–it slips out underneath. I really have to concentrate to think properly. The local scientists would be freaked out about this if they could be freaked out about anything. This is probably the only place in the world where never changing is considered to be a signal virtue."

I realized that I was balling up my fists and so I relaxed them and took some deep breaths. Lacey was snuggled up against me and it was warm and good. I tried to focus on that, and not the yawning pit in my gut.

"You're not going to take me with you, are you?"

She swallowed. "We'll see."

I knew what that meant.

I tried not to let her hear me cry, but it shook my ribs, and she hugged me harder. She didn't say "I'll take you with," though. Of course not. She didn't want to have a kid, an instant son.

I woke from a strange dream of kissing and sliding skin. I had a rock hard erection, like nothing I'd ever felt before. There was that itch again, in my belly, that I supposed meant "horny," though I'd never felt it like this. Lacey had drooped away from me in her sleep and was lying on her back beside me. In the dim light of the pack's glowing power-indicators, I could see her chest rising and falling, her nipples visible through the thin fabric of her night-shirt. I remembered what she'd looked like naked the other night. She must have noticed my reaction, because she'd changed in private every night since. I realized that that was what I'd been dreaming of.

I reached out with a tentative hand and let it barely graze over her breast. She didn't stir. It felt soft, giving under my finger. My mouth was bone dry. I pulled back the coverlet. Her long t-shirt had ridden up, and I could see her legs all the way up to the curve of her hip. I touched her hip, stroking it with the same hesitancy. Warm. Jouncy–firm but giving. I touched her thigh. She muttered something and stirred.

I froze. She put one hand on her tummy, and her shirt rucked up higher. Now I could see all her hair down there. It was too dark to see anything more. I put my hand on her thigh again, halfway up. Her breathing didn't change. I slid my hand higher. Higher still.

My smallest finger brushed up against something very soft and a little moist, something that felt like a warm mushroom.

"Jimmy?"

I knew that she was awake, fully awake. I snatched my hand away.

"God, I'm sorry Lacey."

"What are you doing, Jimmy?"

"I –" I couldn't find the words. It was too embarrassing, too weird. Too creepy.

"It was the sex talk, huh?"

I swallowed. I calmed myself down. I decided I could talk about this like a man of science. "I'm not quite physiologically there, when it comes to sex. I'm sort of stuck between the first stage of sexual maturity and childhood. Normally, it's not a problem, but . . ." I ran out of science.

"Yeah," she said. "I wondered about that. Come here, Jimmy."

Awkwardly, I snuggled up to her, letting her spoon behind me.

"No," she said. "Turn around."

I turned around. I had my little boner again, and I was conscious of how it must be pressing against her thigh, the way her breasts were pressed against my chest. Her face was inches from mine, her breath warm on my lips.

She kissed me.

She kissed *exactly* like I remembered it, 20 years before. Slowly, with a lazy bit of tongue. Her teeth were warm in her mouth as I tentatively reciprocated. She took my hand and put it on her breast. Her nipple was a little bump in the center of my palm, the flesh of her breast yielding under my hand. I squeezed it and rubbed it and touched it, almost forgetting the kiss. She laughed a little and pulled her shirt up and pulled my face down to her breasts. I kissed them, kissed the nipples, unsure of what to do, but hearing her breath catch when I did something right. I tried to do more of that. It was fascinating. The pack roused itself and squirmed over us. I pushed them away.

She gave a soft little moan. Her hands roamed over my back, squeezed my butt. Her hand found my little boner. I gave a jolt, then another as she started to move her hand. Then I felt something like a sneeze, that started in my stomach and went *down.* There was sticky stuff on her hand.

"Wow," I said. "I didn't know I could do that."

"Let's find out what else you can do," she said.

The next day was my scheduled day at the research station, but I didn't want to leave Lacey alone in the Carousel, not now that Sebastien and Tina knew about her. They might come by to ask her some questions about her intentions.

Besides, there was the matter of what we'd done the night before. It had lasted for a long time. There was a lot I didn't know. When we were done, I knew a *lot* more. And it was all I could think of, from the moment I woke up with the smells on me and the small aches here and there; while I was in the bathroom and pissing through a dick that felt *different*, gummy and sticky; while I was washing up and digging some grapefruits out of my storehouse for breakfast, slicing them open and grabbing water from the osmotic filter for the day.

Lacey was sitting up in bed, the pack arrayed around her, the sheet not covering her beautiful breasts. Her hair was in great disarray and her mouth was a little puffy and swollen from kissing.

"Good morning," she said, and smiled at me, her little bow mouth widening into a giant grin.

I smiled back and handed her a grapefruit. I cuddled up to her as we ate and she laughed when I got a squirt of grapefruit in the eye. We didn't say much, but then the Flea, who is also in charge of my calendar reminders, began to chitter at me to tell me it was time to go to the lab.

"What's he want?"

"I'm supposed to see the researchers here. About my immortality. I go every couple of weeks and they do more tests, measure me. Whatever Dad did to my germline wasn't documented anywhere public. He had all these buddies around the world who had treated themselves to make them immortal, and they were all refining the process. None of them seem to be anywhere that we can find them, so we're trying to reverse-engineer them."

"What kind of researchers would a place like this have? I'd have thought that they would be pretty hostile to R&D in a place that isn't supposed to change."

"Well, when the whole world is changing all the time, it takes a lot of R&D to respond to it so that you don't change along with it. Some of them are pretty good. I looked up their bios. They were highly respected before they became wireheads. Mellowing out your emotions shouldn't interfere with your science anyway."

"Are they trying to cure your immortality or replicate it?"

I turned to look at her. "What do you mean? Cure it, of course."

"Really? If they don't want any change, wouldn't it make sense to infect everyone with it?"

"It makes a perverse kind of sense, I suppose. If you were into conspiracy theories, it would be believable. But I know these guys–they don't have it in them to lie to me, or to make me sad on purpose. That's the good thing about living here: you can always be sure that the people around you are every bit as nice as they seem. Sincere."

"If you say so," she said. Even though she didn't have an antenna, I could feel her skepticism. Fine, be skeptical. Wireheads didn't scheme, they just *did stuff*, that was what it meant to be a wirehead. She nuzzled my neck. I turned my head and we kissed. It was weird with the lights on.

I broke it off and said, "I've got to get to the lab." The Flea was running in little circles and chiding me, making the point. I pulled on my jumpsuit and zipped it up.

"Will you be long?"

I shrugged. "Couple hours," I said. "Don't answer the door, OK? I mean, just lay low. Stay here. My neighbors–"

"I get it," she said. "Don't want to get kidnapped and wired up, right?"

"They won't kidnap you. Just put the question to you and kick you out if you give the wrong answer."

She opened her arms. "Come give me a kiss goodbye, my brave protector," she said. I leaned in and let her give me a hard hug and a harder kiss. The hug felt like that first night, when it was just the chance to have a human being holding me; the kiss felt like the night before, when we'd done things I'd never given much thought to.

"Love you, Jimmy," she whispered fiercely in my ear.

Dad used to say that a lot. "You too," I said, because it was what I always said to him.

The sun was high and the day was crisp, the kind of weather that made you forget just how hot it could be in the summer. Drifts of colored leaves rustled around me as the bare trees sighed in the wind. The sun was bright and harsh. I'd been through many of these autumns, but I'd never had a day that felt this *autumnal*, this crisp and real and vivid.

There were plenty of wireheads out and about. Some of them were driving transports filled with staple crops grown in our fields. Some were chatting with traders, who blew through town every day. Some were just sitting on a bench and smiling and nodding at the passers-by, which might as well be the cult's national sport.

They greeted me, one and all. Everyone knew me and no one asked me nosy questions about my . . . condition. Everyone knew enough to know that I was just the kid who wouldn't grow up, and that I could give them a fine show if they came and knocked on my door.

Normally that felt good. Today, it loomed over me, oppressing me. They'd all have heard about Lacey by now. They were seeing me walk down the street, so they knew that Lacey must be alone in the Carousel. They'd be thinking together, wondering about her, thinking about going over there to find out when she'd be signing up for her wire. And that was the one thing I *didn't* want. Lacey had managed to change over the past 20 years, becoming an adult, leaving behind Treehuggerism, having adventures. Turning into a woman. I didn't want her frozen in time the way we all were. *I* didn't want to be frozen in time anymore. Besides, she knew my secret now, that my antenna didn't work the way everyone else's did. If she became a wirehead, she'd tell them about it. She'd have to.

The labs had been in the old University bioscience

building, but a trader had sold the researchers a self-assembling lab-template a couple years before. The wireheads had held a long congress about putting up a major building, but in the end, the researchers were made so clearly miserable by the prospect of not being able to put up a new building that they'd prevailed; the wireheads had caved in just to get them to cheer the hell up.

The new building looked like a giant heap of gelatinous frogspawn: huge, irregular bubbles in a jumble that spread wide and high. The template had taken in the disciplinary needs of the researchers and analyzed their communications patterns to come up with an optimal geometry for clustering research across disciplines and collaborative groupings. The researchers loved it–you could feel that just by getting close to the building–but no one else could make any sense of it, especially since the bubbles moved themselves around all the time as they sought new, higher levels of optimal configuration.

I could usually find my research group without much trouble. I climbed up a few short staircases, navigated around some larger labs filled with equipment that Dad would have loved, and eventually arrived at their door. There were three of them today: Randy, the geneticist; Inga, the endocrinologist; and Wen, the oncologist.

"You think it's cancer again, huh?"

Randy and Inga nodded gravely at Wen. "That's our best guess, Jimmy. It's the cheapest and easiest way to get cells to keep on copying themselves. We thought we'd try you out on some new anti-cancer from India." Inga was in her thirties; I'd played with her when she was my age. Now she seemed to see me as nothing more than a research subject.

Wen nodded and spread his hands out on the table. "We infiltrate your marrow with computational agents that do continuous realtime evaluation of your transcription activity, looking for anomalies, comparing the data-set to baseline subjects. Once we have a good statistical picture of what's happening, we intervene in anomalous transcriptions, correcting them. It's a simple approach, just brute force computation, but there's a new IIT nanoscale petaflop agent that raises the bar on what 'brute force' really means."

"And this works?"

They all looked at each other. I felt their discomfort distantly in my antenna. "It's had very successful animal trials."

"How about human trials?" I already knew the answer.

"Dr Chandrasekhar at IIT has asked us to serve as a test site for his human trials research. He was very impressed with your germ plasm. He's been culturing it for months." Randy was getting his geek back, a pure joy I could feel even through my muffled receiver. "You should see the stuff he's done with it. Your father–"

"A genius, I know." I didn't usually mind talking about Dad, but that day it felt wrong. I'd pictured him once, briefly, as Lacey and I had been together, and had zigged wrong and ended up bending myself at an awkward angle. It was the thought of what Dad would say if he caught me "deracinating."

"He didn't keep notes?"

"Not where I could get at them. He had a lot of friends around the world–they all worked on it. There's probably lots more like me, somewhere or other. He told me he'd let me in once I was old enough."

"Probably worried about being generation-gapped," Randy said sagely.

"I don't get it," I said.

"You know. Whatever he'd done to himself, you were decades further down the line. If he'd kept up what he was doing, and if you'd joined him, you'd have been able to do it again, make a kid who was way more advanced than you. You'd end up living forever like a caveman among your genius superman descendants. So he wanted to keep the information from you." He shrugged. "That's what Chandrasekhar says, anyway. He's done a lot of research on immortality cabals. He didn't know about your Dad's, though. He was very impressed."

"So you said." I hadn't really thought about this before. Dad was–Dad. He was all-seeing, all-knowing, all-powerful. He hadn't just fathered me, he'd *designed* me. Of course, he'd designed me to patch all the bugs in his own genome, but–

"So as I said, we've cultured a lot of your plasm and run this on it. What we get looks like normal aging. Mitochondrial shortening. Maturity."

"How big a culture?" I was raised by a gifted bioscientist. I knew which questions to ask.

"Several billion cells," Inga said, with a toss of her hair. I could feel their discomfort again, worse than before.

"Right . . ." I did some mental arithmetic. "So, like, a ten-centimeter square of skin?"

The three of them grinned identical, sheepish grins. "It scales," Inga said. "There's a 400 kilo gorilla running it right now. Stable for a year. Rock solid."

I shook my head. "I don't think so," I said. "I mean, it's very exciting and all, but I've already been a guinea pig once, when I was born. Let someone else go first this time."

They all looked at each other. I felt the dull throb of their anxiety. They looked at me.

"We've been looking for someone else to trial this on, but there's no one else with your special–" Wen groped for the word.

"There has to be," I said. "Dad didn't invent me on his own. There was a whole team of them. They all wanted to make their contributions. There's probably whole cities full of immortal adolescents out there somewhere."

"If we could find them, we'd ask them. But no one we know has heard of them. Chandrasekhar has put the word out everywhere. He swings a big stick. He said to ask if you know where your Dad's friends lived?"

"Dad had a huge fight with those people when I was born, some kind of schism. I never saw him communicating with them."

"And your mother?"

"Dead. I told you. When I was an infant. Don't remember her, either." I swallowed and got my temper under control. Someday, someone was going to notice that even when I looked all pissed off, my antenna wasn't broadcasting anything and I'd be in for it. They'd probably split me open and stick five more in me. Or tie me naked to a tree and leave me there as punishment for deceiving them. It's amazing how cruel you can be when there's a whole city full of people who'll soak up your conscience and smooth it out for you.

"Chandrasekhar says–"

"I'm getting a little tired of hearing about him. What is it? Is it ego? You want to impress this bigshot doctor from the civilized east, prove to him that we're not just a bunch of bumpkins here? We *are* a bunch of bumpkins here, guys. We live in the woods! That's the *point.* What do you think *they'd* all say if they knew you were trying this?" I waved my arm in an expansive gesture, taking in the whole town. I knew what it was like to have a dirty little secret around there, and I knew I'd get them with that.

Inga's face clouded over. "Listen to me, Jimmy. You started this. You came to us and asked us to investigate this. To cure you. It's not our fault that answering your question took us to places you never anticipated. We're busy people. There are plenty of other things we could be doing. We all have to do our part."

The other two were flinching away from the sear of her emotion. I did what any wirehead would do when confronted with such a blast: I left.

There was a small crowd hanging around the Carousel as I got back to it. They weren't exactly blocking the way, more like milling about, chatting, being pastoral, but always in the vicinity of my home. Someone came out of my outhouse: Brent. A moment later, I spotted Sebastien.

"We were hoping for a ride," he said. "Brent was asking about it again."

Uh-huh. "And these other people?"

My antenna wasn't radiating sarcasm or anger, though my voice was full of both. He believed the evidence of his antenna and continued to treat me as though I was calm and quiet.

"Other riders, I suppose."

"Well, I'm not giving any rides today," I said. "You can all go home."

"Is it broken again?"

"No," I said.

"Oh," he said.

Brent and Tina wandered up. Brent looked at me with his head cocked to one side. "Hi Jimmy," he said. "We want to go inside and ride around."

"Not today. Try me again in a week."

Tina put a hand on my arm. It was warm and maternal. It made me feel weird. "Jimmy, you know you have to bring her around to council if she's going to stay here. It's the way we do things."

"She's not staying," I said.

"She's stayed long enough. We can't ignore it, you know. It's not fair for you to ask us to pretend we didn't see her. We all have a duty. Your friend can get the operation, or she can go."

"She's not staying," I said. *Neither am I* is what I didn't say.

"Jimmy," she said, but I didn't want to hear what she had to say. I shook off her arm and climbed the ramp up to my door, sliding it aside, stepping in quickly and sliding it shut behind me.

"Look, I'm a nest!" The entire pack had swarmed Lacey, perching on her arms, head, shoulders and chest. She was sitting in the front row of the theater, balancing. "These are some fun little critters. I can't believe they lived this long!"

I shrugged. "Far as I can tell, they're immortal." I shrugged again. "Poor little fuckers."

She shook off the pack. They raced around under the seats. They were starting to get squirrelly. I really should have been taking them out for walks more often. She came and gathered me in her arms. It felt good, and weird.

"What's going on?"

"Let's go, OK? The two of us."

"You don't mean out for a walk, do you?"

"No."

She let go of me and sat on the stage. We were in the "future" set, which Dad said was about 1989, but not very accurate for all that. The lights on the Christmas tree twinkled. I'd wiki-tagged everything in the room, and the entry on Christmas trees had been deeply disturbing to me. All that *family* stuff. So . . . treehugger. Some of the wireheads did Christmas, but no one ever invited me along, thankfully.

"I don't think that's a good idea, Jimmy. It's dangerous out there."

"I can handle danger." I swallowed. "I've killed people, you know. That last day I saw you, when they came for Detroit. I killed eight of them. I'm not a kid."

"No, you're not a kid. But you are, too. I don't know, Jimmy." She sighed and looked away. "I'm sorry about last night. I never should have–"

"*I'm not a kid!* I'm older than you are–just because I look like this doesn't mean I'm not 32, you know. It doesn't mean I'm not capable of love." I realized what I'd just said.

"Jimmy, I didn't mean it like that. But whatever you are, we can't be, you know, a couple. You can see that, right? For God's sake, Jimmy, we're not even the same species!"

It felt like she'd punched me in the chest. The air went out of my lungs and I stared at her, pop-eyed, for a long moment.

I felt tears prick at my eyes and I realized how childish

they'd make me seem, and I held them back, letting only one choked snuffle escape. Then I nodded, calmly.

"Of course. I didn't want to be part of any kind of couple with you. Just a traveling companion. But I can take care of myself. It's fine."

She shook her head. I could see that *she* had tears in *her* eyes, but it didn't seem childish when she did it. "That's not what I meant, Jimmy. Please understand me–"

"I understand. Last night was a mistake. We're not the same species. You don't want to travel with me. It's not hard to understand."

"It's not like that–"

"Sure. It's much nicer than that. There are a million nice things you can say about me and about this that will show me that it's really not about me, it's just a kind of emergent property of the universe with no one to blame. I understand perfectly."

She bit her lip.

"That's it, huh?"

She didn't say anything. She shook her head.

"So? What did I get wrong, then?"

Without saying another word, she fled.

I went outside a minute later. My neighbors were radiated curiosity. No one asked me anything about the woman who'd run out of the Carousel and taken off. Her stuff was still in my little sleeping-space and leaned up against the stage. I packed it as neatly as I could and set it by the door. She could come and get it whenever she wanted.

The fourth scene in the Carousel of Progress is that late eighties sequence. We had other versions of it in the archives, but the eighties one always appealed to Dad, so that was the one that I kept running most of the time.

Like I said, it's Christmas time, and there's a bunch of

primitive “new” technology on display–a terrible video-game, an inept automatic cooker, a laughable console. The whole family sits around and jokes and plays. Grandpa and grandma are vigorous, independent. Sister and brother are handsome young adults. Mom and Dad are a little older, wearing optical prostheses. Dad accidentally misprograms the oven and the turkey is scorched. Everyone laughs and they send out for pizza.

I always found that scene calming. It was supposed to be set a little in the future, to inspire the audience to see the great big beautiful tomorrow, shining at the end of every day (for a while, the theme of the ride had been, “Now is the best time of your life,” which seemed to me to be a little more realistic–who knew what tomorrow would be like?).

Dad believed in progress, I’ve come to realize. He made me because he thought that the human race would be supplanted by something transhuman, beyond human. Like it would go, squirrel, monkey, ape, caveman, human, me. He was the missing link between the last two steps, the human who’d been modded into transhumanism.

But if Dad were alive today, he’d probably be learning from his mistakes with me and making a 2.0 version. Someone who made me look as primitive as I made Dad look. And 20 years after 2.0, there’d be a 3.0, a whole generation more advanced. Maybe 20 feet tall and able to grow extra limbs at will.

And in a thousand years, we’d still be alive, weird, immortal cavemen surrounded by our telepathic, shapeshifting, hyperintelligent descendants.

Progress.

I heard Lacey let herself in on the second night. I’d lain awake all night the first night, waiting for her to come back for her bedroll and her cowl. When she didn’t, I figured she’d found somewhere warm to stay. There had been a lot of treehouse seed in the air for the past four or five years, and the saplings were coming up now, huge, hollow root-balls protruding from the ground. They grew very fast, like all good carbon-sinking projects, but they had a tendency to out-compete the local species, so the wireheads chopped them down and mulched them when they took root. Still, you didn't have to go very far into our woods to find one.

I spent the next day paying social calls on wireheads, letting their talk about crops and trade while away the hours, just spending the time away from home so I wouldn't have to see Lacey if she came back for her things that day. But when I came home and said hello to the pack and made dinner, her pack was still by the door. At that point, I decided she wouldn't come back for it for a while. Maybe she'd found a nice traveller to go caravanning with.

She let herself in quietly, but the pack was roused, and a second later I was roused too. My bedding still smelled like her. I was going to have to wash it. Or maybe burn it.

I sat up and padded through the gloom into the fourth scene. She was sitting in a middle row aisle seat with her pack between her knees, watching the silent silhouettes of the robots in their Christmas living room.

I shrugged and turned it on. We watched them burn the turkey. They ordered out for pizza. They sang: "There's a great big beautiful tomorrow/shining at the end of every day." The Carousel rotated another 60 degrees and back to the beginning. The show ended.

"Safe travels," I said to her.

She rocked in her seat as if I'd slapped her. "Jimmy, I have something I need to tell you. About that day in Detroit. Something I couldn't tell you before." She took a shuddering breath.

"You have to understand. I didn't know what my parents were planning. They didn't like you any more than your dad liked me, so I was a little suspicious when they told me to take my spidergoat and go and play with you over in the city.

But things had been really tense around the house and we'd just had another blazing fight and I figured they wanted to have a discussion without me around and so they told me to do the thing that would be sure to distract me.

"I didn't realize that they wanted me to distract you, too.

"They told me later that someone else had gone into town to lure your father away, too. The idea was the get both of you away from your defenses, to demolish your capacity to attack, and then to turn the wumpuses loose on the city until there was nothing left, then to let you go. But your dad got away, figured out what was going on, got into his plane and–"

She shut her mouth. I looked at her, letting this sink in, waiting for some words to come.

"They told me this later, you understand. Weeks later. Long after you were gone. I had no idea. They had friends in Buffalo who had the mechas and the flying platform, friends who were ideologically committed to getting rid of the old cities. They hated your dad. He had lots of enemies. They didn't tell me until afterward, though. I was just . . . bait."

I remembered how fast she had disappeared when the bombs started falling. And not into the mecha, which should have been the safest place of all. No, she'd gone out of the city.

"You knew," I said.

She wiped her eyes. "What?"

"You *knew*. That's why you scarpered so quickly. That's why you didn't get into the mecha. You knew that they were coming for us. You knew you had to get out of the city."

"Jimmy, no–"

"Lacey, yes." The calm I felt was frightening. The pack twined around my feet, nervously. "You knew. You knew, you knew, you knew. Have you convinced yourself that you didn't know?"

"No," she said, putting her hands in front of her. "Jimmy, you don't understand. If I knew, why would I have come back here to confess?"

"Guilt," I said. "Regret. Anger with your parents. You were just a kid, right? Even if you knew, they still tricked you. They were still supposed to be protecting you, not using you to lure me away. Maybe you have a crush on me. Maybe you just want to screw with my head. Maybe you've just been distracting me while someone comes in to attack the wireheads."

She gave a shiver when I said that, a little violent shake like the one I did at the end of a piss. I saw, very clearly in the footlights from the stage, her pupils contracting.

"Wait," I said. "Wait, you're here to attack the *wireheads*? Jesus Christ, Lacey, what the hell is wrong with you? They're the most harmless, helpless bunch of farmers in the world. Christ, they're practically Treehuggers, but without the stupid politics."

She got up and grabbed her pack. "I understand why you'd be paranoid, Jimmy, but this isn't fair. I'm just here to make things right between us–"

"Well, forgive me," I said. "What could I possibly have been thinking? After all, you were only just skulking around here, gathering intelligence, slipping off into the night. After all, you only have a history of doing this. After all, it's only the kind of thing you've been doing since you were a little girl–"

"Goodbye, Jimmy," she said. "You have a nice life, all right?"

She went out into the night. My chest went up and down like a bellows. My hands were balled into fists so tight it made my arms shake. The pack didn't like it. "Follow her," I whispered to Ike and Mike, the best trackers in the pack. "Follow her"–a command they knew well enough. I'd used them to spy on my neighbors after arriving here, getting the lay of the land. "Follow her," I said again, and they disappeared out the door, silent and swift.

I could watch and record their sensorium from my console. I packed a bag, keeping one eye on it as I went. I grabbed the pack's canisters. They were too heavy to carry, but I had a little wagon for them. I piled them on the wagon, watching its suspension sag under the weight.

Ike and Mike had her trail. She headed into the woods with the uneasy gait of a weeping woman, but gradually she straightened out. She kept on walking, picking up speed, clipping on an infra-red pince-nez when she came under the canopy into the real dark. I noted it and messaged Ike and Mike about their thermal signatures. They fell back and upped the zoom on their imaging, the picture going a little shaky as they struggled to stabilize the camera at that magnification.

She emerged from the woods into a clearing heaped high with rubble. I watched her sit down with her feet under her, facing it. She was saying something. I moved Ike up into mic range. She didn't say much, though, and by the time he was in range, she fell silent.

The rubble stirred. Some rocks skittered down the side of the pile. Then a tentacle whipped out of the pile, a still-familiar mouth at the end of it. The mouth twisted around and grabbed up one of the larger rocks and began to digest it. More tentacles appeared, five, then fifty, then hundreds. The rubble shifted and revealed the wumpus beneath it.

It was the biggest one I'd ever seen. It had been twenty years since I'd last seen one of those bastards, and maybe my memories were faulty, but this one seemed different. Meaner. Smarter. Wumpuses were usually bumblers, randomwalking and following concentration gradients for toxins, looking for cities to eat, mostly blind. This one unfolded itself and moved purposefully around the clearing, its wheels spinning and grinding. As it rolled, smaller wumpuses fell out of its hopper. It was . . . spawning!

It seemed to sense Ike and Mike's presence, turning between one and the other. They were deep in the woods, running as cold as possible, camouflaged, perfectly still, communicating via narrow, phased-array signals. They should be undetectable. Nevertheless, I gave them the order to shut down comms and pull back slowly to me.

I stood out on the porch, waiting for them to rejoin me in the dark, hearing the sounds of the night woods, the wind soughing through the remaining leaves, the sounds of small animals scampering in the leaves and the distant, frying bacon sound of the wumpus and its litter digesting.

There was no chance that Lacey was doing something good with that wumpus. She had lied from the minute she met me in the woods. She had scouted out the wirehead city. She had gone back and reported to some kind of highly evolved descendant of the wumpuses that ate every city on the continent.

I had already been ready to go. I could just follow through on my plan, hit the road and never look back. The wireheads weren't my people, just people I'd lived with.

If I was a better person, my instinct would be to stay and warn them. Maybe to stay and fight. The wumpus would need fighting, I knew that much.

I'm not a good person. I just wanted to go.

I didn't go–and not because I'm a good person. I didn't go because I needed to see Inga and find out if she really had the cure for my immortality.

Inga lived in the same house she'd grown up in. I'd gone over to play there, 20 years ago. Her parents had just grown new rooms as their kids had grown up, married, and needed more space. Now their place had ramified in all directions, with outbuildings and half-submerged cellars. I took a chance that Inga's room would be where it had been the last time.

I knocked on the door, softly at first. Then louder.

The man who answered the door was old and grey. His pajamas flapped around him in the wind that whipped through the autumn night. He scrubbed at his eyes and looked at me.

“Can I help you?” His antenna radiated his peevish sleepiness.

“Inga,” I said. My heart was hammering in my chest and the sweat of my exertions, lugging the pack’s canisters across town, was drying in the icy wind, making me shiver. “I need to see Inga.”

“You know what time it is?”

“Please,” I said. “I’m one of her research subjects. It’s urgent.”

He shook his head. The irritation intensified. With all the other wireheads asleep, there was no one to damp his emotion. I wondered if he was souring their dreams with his bad vibes.

“She’s in there,” he said, pointing to another outbuilding, smaller and farther away from the main house. I thanked him and pulled my wagon over to Inga’s door.

She answered the door in a night-shirt and a pair of heavy boots. Her hair was in a wild halo around her head and limned by the light behind her and I had a moment where I realized that she was very beautiful, something that had escaped me until then.

“Jimmy?” she said, peering at me. “Christ, Jimmy–”

“Can I come in?”

“What’s this about?”

“Can I come in?”

She stood aside. I felt her irritation, too.

Her room was small and crowded with elaborate sculpture made from fallen branches wound with twine. Some of them were very good. It was a side of her I’d never suspected. Weirdly enough, being a wirehead didn’t seem to diminish artistic capacity–there were some very good painters and even a couple of epic poets in the cult that I quite liked.

“You know that there’s been a woman staying with me?”

She made a face. “It’s not any of my business, and I don’t really have any romantic advice–”

I cut her off. I told her everything. Even the sex parts.

Even the antenna parts. Especially the wumpus parts. For such a big load of secrets, it didn't take long to impart.

"So you think she'll attack the city?"

I suppressed my own irritation–maybe it was the dull reflection of hers. "I know she will." I took out my console and showed her the pictures of the wumpus.

"So you're telling me this. Why? Why not wake up someone important? Someone who can help us?"

"I don't think there's any helping us. You saw it. You saw its babies. It's coming for us, soon. This place is all over. I don't know if it eats people, but it's going to eat everything man-made here. That's what they do."

I felt her draw strength and calm from the sleeping people around us, from the whole city, dissipating her fear through the network.

"So why *are* you here?"

"I want you to give me the Chandrasekhar treatment before I go."

"You're leaving?"

I gestured at my wagon.

"And you want the cure? Yesterday you didn't want to be a guinea pig."

"Yesterday I thought there'd be a tomorrow. Now I'm not so sure. I want the cure."

She folded her arms and stared at me.

"Your antenna isn't totally dead, you know," she said at last. "I can sort of feel a little of what you're feeling. It's too bad it doesn't work better. That's not a good way to feel."

"You'll do it?"

"Why not? It's the end of the world, apparently."

The sound of frying bacon filled the night as we worked in her lab. We dilated the windows at first, so we could track the progress of the wumpuses through town. There were a lot of angry shouts and sobs, but nothing that sounded like screams of pain. The wumpuses were apparently eating the buildings and leaving the people, just as they had two decades before.

The procedure was surprisingly simple–mostly it was just installing some code on my console and then a couple of shots from a long, thin bone-needle. That hurt, but less than I expected. I made sure I had the source-code as well as the object code in case I needed to debug anything: the last thing I wanted was to be unable to manage my system.

We watched in fascination as statistical data about my transcriptions began to fill the screens around us. The app came with some statistically normal data-sets that overlaid the visualizations of my own internal functionality. It was clear even to my eye that I was pretty goddamned weird down there at the cellular level.

"What happens now?"

"The thing wants a full two month's worth of data before it starts doing anything. So basically, you run that for a couple of months, and then it should prompt you for permission to intervene in your transcriptions to make them more normal."

"Two months? That must suck if you've got cancer."

"Cancer might kill you in two months and it might not. Bad nanites messing with your cellular activity is a lot scarier."

"I've been trying not to think of that," I said.

The frying bacon noises were growing louder.

"No more shouts," Inga said. Her eyes were big and round. "What do you think is going on out there?"

I shook my head. "I'm an idiot, give me a second."

I gathered the pack in my arms and gave them their instructions, then tossed them out the window. They scampered down the building side and I fired up the console.

"There," I said, pointing. The wumpuses were moving in a long curved line now, a line as wide as the town, curving up like a pincer at the edges. They moved slowly and deliberately through the night. Pepe found a spot where they were working their way through a block of flats, tentacles whipping back and forth, great plumes of soil arcing out behind them. People ran out of the house, carrying their belongings, shouting at the wumpuses, throwing rocks at them. The wumpuses took no notice, save to snatch the thrown rocks out of the air and drop them into their hoppers.

An older man–I recognized him as Emmanuel, one of the real village elders around here–moved around to confront the wumpus that was eating his house. He shouted more words at it, then took another step toward it.

One of the tentacles moved faster than I'd ever seen a wumpus go. It whipped forward and snatched Emmanuel up by the torso and lifted him high in the air. Before he could make a sound, it had plunged him headfirst into its hopper. One of his legs kicked out, just once, before he disappeared.

The other wireheads around him were catching the fear, spread by the wires, too intense to damp down. They screamed and ran and the wumpuses picked them up, one after another, seeming to blindly triangulate on the sounds of their voices. Each one went headfirst into the hopper. Each one vanished.

I stood up and whistled the pack back to me.

I moved for the door. Inga blocked my way.

"Where are you going?"

"Away," I said. I thought for a moment. "You can come if you want."

She looked at me and I realized that what I'd always mistaken for pity was really a kind of disgust. Why not? I was the neighbor kid who'd never grown up. It *was* disgusting.

"You brought her here," she said, quietly. I wondered from the tone of her voice if she meant to kill me, even though she'd just treated me.

"She came here," I said. "I had nothing to do with it. Just a coincidence. Sit in one place for 20 years and everyone you've ever known will cross your path. Whatever she's doing, it's nothing to do with me. I explained that."

Inga slumped into a lab-chair.

"Are you coming?" I asked.

She cried. I'd never heard a wirehead cry. Either there wasn't enough mass in the wirehead network to absorb her emotion or the prevailing mood was complete despair. I stood on the threshold, holding my wagon filled with the pack's canisters. I reached out and grabbed her hand and tugged at it. She jerked it away. I tried again and she got off her stool and stalked deeper into labs.

That settled it.

I left, pulling my wagon behind me.

The sound of frying bacon was everywhere. I had the pack running surveillance patterns around me, scouting in all directions, their little squirrel cases eminently suited to this kind of thing. We were a team, my pack and me. We could keep it up for days before their batteries needed recharging. I'd topped up the nutrients in their canisters before leaving the Carousel.

The frying bacon sound had to include the destruction of the Carousel. Every carefully turned replacement part, all those lines of code. The mom and the dad and the son and the sister and the grandparents and their doggies. Dad's most precious prize, gone to wumpusdust.

The sound of frying bacon was all around us. The sound of screams. Lacey had arrived from the west. To the east was the ocean. I would go south, where it was warm and where, if the world was coming to an end, I would at least not freeze to death.

There was a column of refugees on the southbound roadway, the old Route 40. I steered clear of them and crashed through the woods instead, the wagon's big tires and suspension no match for the uneven ground, so that I hardly moved at all.

The pack raced ahead and behind me, playing lookout.

They were excited, scared. I could still hear the screams. Sometimes a wirehead would plunge past me in the night, charging through the woods.

The wumpus came on me without warning. It was small, small enough to have muzzled through the trees without knocking them aside. Maybe as tall as me, not counting those whiplike tentacles, not counting the mouths on the end of them, mouths that opened and shut against the moonlight sky in silhouette.

I remembered all those wumpuses I'd killed one tentacle at a time. These wumpuses seemed a lot smarter than the ones I'd known in Detroit. Someone must have kludged them up. I wondered if they knew how I'd played with their ancestors. I wondered if Lacey had told them.

Wumpuses only have rudimentary vision. Their keenest sense is chemical, an ability to follow concentration gradients of inorganic matter, mindlessly groping their way to food sources. They have excellent hearing, as well. I stood still and concentrated on not smelling inorganic.

The wumpus's tentacles danced in the sky over me. Then moving as one, the pack leapt for them.

The pack's squirrel bodies looked harmless and cute, but they had retractable claws that could go through concrete, and teeth that could tear your throat out. The basic model was used for antipersonnel military defense.

The wumpus recoiled from the attack and its tentacles flailed at the angry little doggies that were mixed among its roots, trying to pick the off even as they uprooted tentacle after tentacle.

I cheered silently and pulled the wagon away as fast as I could. I looked over my shoulder in time to see one of my doggies get caught up in a mouth and tossed into the hopper, vanishing into a plume of dust. That was OK–I could get them new bodies, provided that I could just get their canisters away with me.

I tugged the wagon, feeling like my arm would come off,

feeling like my heart would burst my chest. I had superhuman strength and endurance, but it wasn't infinite.

In the end, I was running blind, sweat soaking my clothes, eyes down on the trail ahead of me, moving in any direction that took me away from the frying bacon sound.

Then, in an instant, the wagon was wrenched out of my hand. I grabbed for it with my stiff arm, turning around, stumbling. There was another wumpus there, holding the wagon aloft in two of its mouths. The canisters tumbled free, bouncing on the forest floor. The wumpus caught three of them on the first bounce, triangulating on the sound. I watched helplessly as it tossed my brave, immortal, friends into its hopper, digesting them.

Then the fourth canister rolled away and I chased after it, snatching at it, but my fingertips missed it. A hand reached out of the dark and snatched it up. I followed the hand back into the shadows.

"Oh, Jimmy," Lacey said.

I leapt for her, fingers outstretched, going for the throat.

She sidestepped, tripped me with one neat outstretched foot, then lifted me to my feet by my collar. I grabbed for the canister, the last of my friends, and she casually flipped it into the wumpus's hopper.

A spray of dust coated us. The plume. My friend.

I began to cry.

"Jimmy," she said, barely loud enough to be heard over the frying bacon. "You don't understand, Jimmy. They're safe now. It's copying them. Copying everything. That's what we never understood about the wumpuses. They're making copies of the things that they eat."

She set me down and grabbed me by the shoulders. "It's OK, Jimmy. Your friends are safe now, forever. They can never die now. The wireheads, too."

I stared into her eyes. I'd loved her. She was quite mad.

"What do you get out of it?"

"What did your father get out of what he did? He made

one child immortal. We'll save the world. The whole world." She smiled at me, like she expected me to smile back. I smiled back and she relaxed her grip on my arms. That's when I clapped her ears, cupping my hands like I'd been taught to do if I wanted to rupture her eardrums. Dad liked to work through self-defense videos with me.

She went down with a shout and I stepped on her stomach as I clambered over her and ran, ran, ran.

PART 3: THERE'LL ALWAYS BE THE GOOD GUYS SHOOTIN' IT OUT WITH THE BAD GUYS

I used to drive mechas for joyriding. Now it's a medical necessity.

I piloted my suit down the Keys, going amphibious and sinking to the ocean-bottom rather than risk the bridges. The bridges were where the youth gangs hung out, eyes luminous and hard. You never knew when they'd swarm you and mindrape you.

I hated the little bastards.

The Second Wumpus Devastation had destroyed–or preserved, if you preferred–every hominid in the Keys, and taken down every human-made structure. Today, we survivors lived in treehouses and ate breadberries.

Looking at old maps, I can see that my treehouse is right in the middle of the site of the old KOA Campground on Sugarloaf Key. I like it for the proximity to Haiti, where an aggressive military culture kept the island wumpus-free and hence in possession of several generations of functional mechas. There were a few years there, after I escaped from the wireheads and the wumpuses, when I grew into a strapping buck and was able to earn one of these lethal little bastards by serving in an anti-wumpus militia.

"Earn" is probably the wrong word. The youth gangs wiped out the militias a few years into my stint. You'd be out on patrol and then a group of these kids would glide out of the bush so silent it was like they were on rails. They'd surround you, hypnotizing you with those eyes of theirs, with those *antennas* of theirs, and you'd be frozen like a mouse pinned by a cobra's gaze. They'd squid you right through your armor, dropping the superconducting quantum field around your head, ripping through your life, your deep structures, your secrets and habits, making a record for the cloud, or wherever it was all the data went to.

After a thorough mindraping, hard militiamen would be reduced to shell-shocked existential whiners, useless for combat. They'd abandon their powered suits and wander off into the bush, end up in some taproom, drinking to forget the void they faced as their brains were spooled out like an archival tape being transferred to modern media.

I'd been caught out one day, the air-conditioner wheezing to keep my naked flesh cool in the form-fitting cradle of the mecha. The mecha was only twice as tall as me, practically child-sized compared to the big ones we'd had in Detroit, and it was cranky and balky. I could pick up an egg with Dad's mecha and not break the shell. The force-feedback manipulators in this actually *clicked* through a series of defined settings, click-click-click, the mecha's hands opening and closing in a clittery clatter like a puppet's.

I waded through the swampy bush, navigating by the wumpusplume on the horizon. Somewhere, a couple clicks away, something was converting one of Florida's precious remaining human-made structures into soil–and taking the humans along with it. No one knew if the wumpuses and the youth gangs were on the same side. No one knew if there were "sides." The first gen of wumpuses had been made by a half-dozen agrarian cultists on the west coast. They'd been modded and hacked by any number of tinkerers who'd captured them, decompiled them, and improved them. I hear that the first generations actually came with source-code and a makefile, which must have been handy.

They stepped out of the brush in unison. It took an eyeblink. They were utterly silent.

And a little familiar.

They were me. Me, during that long, long pre-adolescence, when I was ageless and lived among the wireheads.

Oh, not exactly. There were minor variations in their facial features. Some wore their hair long and shaggy. Others kept it short. One had freckles. One was black. Two might have been latino.

But they were also *me.* They looked like brothers to one another, and they looked like my own brothers. I can't explain it better than that: I knew they were me the same way I knew that the guy I saw in my shaving mirror was me.

They surrounded my mecha in a rough circle and closed in on me. They looked at me and I looked at them, rotating my mecha's cockpit through a full 360. I'd always assumed that they came out of a lab somewhere, like the wumpuses. But up close, you could see that they'd been dressed at some point: some had been dressed in precious designer kidsclothes, others in hand-me-down rags. Some bore the vestiges of early allegiance to one subculture or another: implanted fashion-lumps that ridged their faces and arms, glittering bits of metal and glass sunk into their flesh and bones. These young men hadn't been hatched: they'd been born, raised, and *infected.*

They made eye contact without flinching. I fought a bizarre urge to wave at them, to get out of the mecha and talk to them. It was that recognition.

Then they raised their hands in unison and I knew that the mindrape was coming. I braced against it. The fields apparently came from implanted generators. They had the stubs of directional antennas visible behind their left ears, just as the stories said. I felt a buzzing, angry feeling, emanating from the vestiges of my wirehead antenna, like a toothache throughout my whole head.

I waited for it to intensify. I didn't think I could move.

I tried. My hand twitched a little, but not enough to reach my triggers. I don't know if I could have killed them anyway.

The rape would come, I knew it. And I was helpless against it. I struggled with my own body, but all I could accomplish was the barest flick of an eye, the tiniest movement of a fingertip.

Then they broke off. My arm shot forward to my controls, my knuckles mashing painfully into the metal over the buttons. An inch lower and I would have mown them down where they stood. Maybe it would have killed them.

They backed away slowly, moving back into the woods. If I had been mindraped, it had been painless and nearly instantaneous, nothing like the descriptions I'd heard.

I watched the gang member directly ahead of me melt back into the brush, and I put the mecha's tracers on him, stuck it on autopilot and braced myself. These mechas used millimeter-wave radar and satellite photos to map their surroundings and they'd chase anything you told them to, climbing trees, leaping obstacles. They weren't gentle about it, either: the phrase "stealthy mecha" doesn't exist in any human language. It thundered through the marshy woods, splashing and crashing and leaping as I jostled in my cocoon and focused on keeping my lunch down.

The kid was fast and seemed to have an intuitive grasp of how to fake out the mecha's algorithms. He used the water to his great advantage, stepping on slippery logs over bog-holes that my mecha stepped into a second later, mired in stinky, sticky mud. Once I got close enough to him to see the grime on the back of his neck and count the mosquito bites on his cheek, but then he slipped away, darting into a burrow hole as my mecha's fingers clicked behind him.

That night, I returned to camp and found that only three other militiamen had made it back, out of 18. I climbed out of my mecha and we did a little of the weird yoga they'd taught us in basic to get our bodies back after being trapped immobile in a rubber, form-fitting suit for eight hours in the mecha. None of us spoke of the day. We knew what had happened to our comrades. Some of them had been my friends. One, a pretty Haitian girl named Monique, had been my lover. She'd been teaching me French. We knew we could find them by canvassing the nearby bars. They'd be spending the last of their money, drinking and crying until the money ran out. We'd next see them begging on a street, tears slipping down their cheeks.

I didn't tell them about being caught by the youth gang, nor about the unsuccessful mind-rape. I certainly didn't tell them about seeing myself in the faces of the youth gang.

By the morning, there were only two of us left. Grad, a taciturn older man, had left his mecha but taken his pack. I wished him good luck.

I looked into the eyes of the remaining militiaman. Technically, he was my superior, having the pip that made him into a nominal corporal. But Marcus wasn't really noncom material, didn't like making eye contact. Didn't like conflict. He'd been promoted for valor in the field after losing it on a bunch of wumpuses and taking down like thirty in an afternoon, while they flailed at him. When we'd pried him, shaking, out of his mecha, his eyes had still been lit up like glowbugs, and he had a huge, throbbing boner.

Marcus ticked a salute off his forehead at me, then grabbed his own pack and walked off. That left me alone. The sounds of the forest were loud around me. Mosquitos bit at my neck and whined in my ears. I climbed into my mecha and clomped off, but not on my patrol route: I headed south, down to the Keys, making an executive decision to take an extended scouting trip into unknown territory. Without any particular plan to return.

OK, so I stole the mecha. I also never got my last three pay-packets. Let's call it even.

Good thing I did, too. I found a gray hair in my eyebrow within a week. Within a month, the hair on my chest had gone white and the wrinkles had spread from the corners of my eyes to the tops of my arms. Six months later, I needed a cane. Within a year, it was two canes.

It was the stuff in my marrow, of course. All those borrowed years, undone with a single injection. I tried to shut them down using the console, but they weren't responding. I presumed that somewhere–Chennai, maybe–some colleague of Chandrasekhar would be fascinated to hear about this. Someone who'd love to know about the long-term outcomes in his experiment.

Being the long-term outcome was less fun.

I piloted my mecha up the walls of the treehouse on Sugarloaf Key. The bottom floors have something wrong with them, some mutant gene that caused their furnishings to extrude from the ceiling and walls. The upper floors were all right, though, and I have very simple needs.

Climbing out of the mecha gets harder every day. Just looking at my body gets harder, to tell the truth. The wrinkles, the liverspots, the swollen joints. My physical age is impossible to guess, but I feel like I'm 120, a skeleton wrapped in papery skin. Every vein stands out, every bone, every joint.

I inched down the limb of the treehouse and into my room. I had a little air-breathing radio-oven and a narrow bed padded with dried boughs from the tree. There was a comfortable sofa that I'd improved with a couple big pillows. It was more than I needed. By the time I got home from a day's foraging, there wasn't anything to do except choke down a little food and rest my bones until my bladder got me up, which it did, like clockwork, every two hours, all night long. There are lots of things I try not to dwell upon. The fact that this is all my fault is one of those things.

It was later that night, the third or fourth time I stumbled to the oubliette for yet another piss, that some sound caught me and brought me to the door. I'm not sure what it was:

nighttimes are a riot of ocean noises, animal sounds, insect sounds, wind soughing through the boughs. Something was different that night. I took up my canes and tottered to the door, leaning on the jamb.

My mecha stood before me, cheap and nasty and lethal, a silhouette in the moonlight. I looked out into the woods, I looked down at the floor, and finally I looked up.

He was sitting on one of the high, thin branches of my treehouse. He was wearing loose pantaloons that hung in folds around his legs, a tight zippered jacket, and a confusion of rings and necklaces. It was dark and he was all in shades of gray, except for his luminous white face, peering at me from his hood and his halo of elaborately braided hair.

"Hello there," he said. He seemed to be on the verge of laughing at some private joke, and somehow I knew that I wasn't the butt of it. "Sorry to wake you. We have business to discuss. Can I come in?"

I looked up at him, squinting. I thought about toggling the floodlights on my mecha, but decided that whatever he wanted, I wasn't in a position to deny it to him. Out of my mecha, I was helpless. He could knock me over with a puff of air.

I backed away from the door, leaning on my canes, and jerked my chin at the insides of my place. "Guess so," I said.

I struggled into a pair of shorts before hitting the lights. His pupils dilated with the telltale snap of night-vision enhancements, so the shorts were redundant. He'd already seen everything. What did I have to be modest about anyway?

He was tall and thin, his hair a mad ash-blond dandelion clock around his face. He had a foxlike chin and nose, and a wide mouth that curled up at the corners in a profusion of dimples, making his smile look like a caricature.

"Would you like tea?" I asked. It helped me sleep sometimes, so I was in the habit of making tea in the middle of the night.

"You make it with those chanterelles you pick?"

I narrowed my eyes at him. "You know a lot about me."

"It's not really tea at that point. More like consomme. But I'll try some."

I put the dried mushrooms in my tea egg and dropped it into a jar of water from the treehouse's condenser, then stuck it in the cooker, letting it figure out the timing and all.

"You know a lot about me," I said again.

"I know a lot about you," he agreed. He sat down on the edge of my bed. "I helped design you, if you want to know the truth. I knew your parents."

I looked more closely at him. He barely seemed a day over thirty. So he was telling me that he was an immortal, then. About time I met another one.

"That's an interesting story. On the other hand, you could be a thirty year old jerk who likes to snoop."

"You remember the time you came to Florida to get the Carousel of Progress? Your father slipped away one evening after dinner, told you to stay in your mecha, told you he had an appointment with someone?" He smiled and smiled, the corners of his mouth curling in on themselves. "We talked all night long. He was very happy with how you were working out, but there were some improvements we agreed we would make in the next generation.

"He loved the Carousel of Progress. It was almost impossible to get him to talk about anything else.

"Your mother–he said you didn't remember her. I do. A great beauty, smart too. Acid tongue. She could flay the skin off you at a thousand miles' distance over a mailing list.

"I've followed your career very closely ever since. I felt I owed it to your father. Lost you for a while, but you turned up again in an Indian gentleman's research notes, a gentleman from the IIT. Chandrasekhar.

"He had certain novel theories about transcription. As this is my area of specialty, I paid close attention. Given what I knew of your design, I could tell that his ideas wouldn't apply. On the other hand, I also knew something that you never suspected.

"Chandrasekhar's little friends in your bloodstream were also gathering a copy of your genome for someone else's use. Don't know if old Race Car was in on it or not, but I wouldn't put it past him. Dude's always been jealous of my mad genomic skills.

"But it's no coincidence that the Midwich plague came along within a few years of you taking the cure. Those little bastards are spreading around the world like a pandemic."

I forgot about the tea. The cooker shrilled at me a few times, but I couldn't do anything about it. I was transfixed. This guy clearly knew things that I'd wondered about all my life, like my operating parameters, like my parents' life histories, like what happened to Detroit, like who made the youth gangs. The cooker shut itself off.

He laughed. His laugh was the oldest thing about him. It was positively ancient and there wasn't a single nice thing about it. It snapped me back to myself.

"Why?" I said.

"Why what?" The corners of his mouth curled another notch.

"Why are you here now? Why have you been watching me? Why haven't you come before? Just–*why*?"

"How about that tea?" He stood up and helped himself. He took a sip. "Delicious. More like consomme than tea, though." He took another sip, looked out into the night. "I was pretty bummed when you took the cure. I could see where it was going to go. You were our little group's proudest moment, you know, the pinnacle of our achievement. I could tell from looking at Chandrasekhar's publications that it wasn't going to work out–and I could also read the writing on the wall: someone was going to get hold of our work and set to work improving it.

"You're the only one, you know. As you might imagine,

experimental verification of immortality is a long-term process, not the kind of thing you can do in a hurry. The plan was to let you run for a half century or so before the rest of us had our own kids." He laughed again, that old laugh. "Pretty silly to think that there'd be anything recognizable left after 50 years. It's easy to believe you understand the future just because you've got a reasonable handle on the present, I guess.

"The raid on Detroit was about getting you, you know—your genome, anyway. Originally the plan had been to seduce you, but that wouldn't have gotten your whole genome, just the zygotic half you left behind. Anyway, it was made irrelevant by the fact that the Treehuggers weren't about to let their daughter be deflowered by an inhuman monster. So instead, they raided you. Your father died to keep you safe.

"Then what do you do with that legacy? Piss it away because you don't like your protracted adolescence. You would have aged eventually, you know. If all had gone according to plan. You were impatient, and now, well, look at you. You're certainly paying the price for it, aren't you?"

"Leave." I hadn't known that that was what I was going to say until I said it. Once I said it, I said it again. "Leave. Now." I was seeing red. How dare he blame me for what happened to me?

He laughed and that didn't endear him to me at all. "Oh, Jimmy. You're letting your ego get ahead of your good sense again. You needn't be condemned to repeat the mistakes of the past, you know. You can choose otherwise.

"I haven't answered one of your questions yet. Why now? Because I can reverse it. I can undo what Chandrasekhar did. It's my area of speciality, after all. I can make you young again."

"Leave," I said. I didn't believe him for a moment.

He laughed. "I'll come back later, once you've had a chance to think it over."

The next day, climbing into my mecha hurt more than usual. The heat arrived early that day, so I woke up in a sweat. The tree's sap-tap yielded sweet water that was already sickly warm, but I drank cup after cup of it before suiting up. It could keep me going all day. I barely looked at my room as I left it, not wanting to see the two cups by the sink, the evidence that I hadn't dreamt my visitor in the night.

The mecha's cargo pouch bulged with my week's foraging: irregular lumps of concrete that still betrayed a few human-made, razor-sharp edges, angles you just couldn't find anymore in a post-wumpus world; half a steel-belted radial that had rested under a rock where the wumpuses had missed it; and the great prize, a whole bag of tampon applicators, what the locals called "beach whistles," discovered in a dried-out septic tank up on Little Duck Island.

This was my living: collecting the junk of our erased civilization. I knew an assemblage sculptor who'd pay handsomely for it in processed cereals, refined sugars, and the other old evils that were nearly impossible to derive from the utopian plants that sprouted all around us. There were sweet edible flowers you could put in your tea, there were mushroom loaves that tasted like whole-grain bread, but there weren't any Twinkie bushes or cigarette trees.

The thing about the main road is that you can see down it for a long, long way, so theoretically it should be hard for the youth gangs to stage an ambush. And the old roadbed was kept smooth by the passage of feet, yielding a less bumpy ride in the mecha, which was a comfort to my old bones.

I stayed away from the road from a little before dusk to a little after dawn. The youth gangs grew more fearless then—or so it seemed to me—and they owned all the high-traffic routes after dark.

But it's not a hard-and-fast rule. That day, they surrounded me on the road, moving like they were on casters, that same eerie precision. It had been five years since I last met a youth gang in the woods at the eve of the militia's dissolution, but I still recognized these kids. They were the same kids—not just similar looking, the same kids, I'd never forget their faces.

They hadn't aged a day.

Again, I rotated my mecha at the waist, looking at each in turn. They met my gaze calmly.

They were filthy now, so grimed that they were all the same mottled brown and green. One appeared to have fungus growing on his shirt. Two were barefoot. They looked like they needed a parent to sit them down and bathe them and put them in a new suit of clothes. And administer a spanking.

I found the one I'd chased to his hidey hole, the one who'd moved with so much preternatural grace and agility. I gave the mecha his scent, told it to track him, only him, to grab him, no matter what. Then I spun a little around, looking a different one in the eyes, hoping to trick them all about the focus of my attention.

They each raised an arm in unison, and tried to mind-rape me. The headache returned, the same headache, bookmarked and reloaded five years later, and I slapped at the activator control as it descended. *Fetch*, mecha, *fetch*!

The mecha lurched and spun and grabbed, in a series of clicks and thuds. I'd told it to put itself into relentless pursuit mode, without any consideration for me. I heard one of my ribs snap and gasped. That old rib was the same one that had snapped all those years ago.

The headache disappeared, swallowed by the pain in my chest. I heard/felt the rib-ends grating, had a momentary vision of the sharp rib-end punching through my lung. The mecha would be my grave. It would chase the boy and catch him or not, and I would bubble out my last bloody breaths, immortal no longer.

But we were lurching too hard for me to spend time on these visions. The boy was running and dodging through the jungle, again choosing his route based on the mecha's limitations, the places it couldn't leap or smash through. I took over the controls and added my smarts to the mecha, trying to model the boy's behavior and guess where he would go next.

There, he was going to jump into that swampy patch and pull himself out along that old rotting log. So, coil the legs and spring, aiming for the log, doubling over in the air and grabbing for him. Little fucker wasn't going to generation gap me again.

I did it, roared into the air and roared at the pain in my ribs. Caught him on the first bounce. Wrapped my hands around his skinny chest and turned him right side up and held him in front of my faceplate.

He was eerily calm. I could feel him trying to work his way into my head, his SQUID battering my mind. I flipped on my PA.

"Cut it out," I said. I was breathing hard, each inhale agony from my ribs. "Why can't you little creeps just leave me alone?"

"Jimmy," he said. "What have you done to yourself?"

He spoke in my father's voice.

I think I blacked out for a while. I don't know how long I was out, but then I was back and he was just disappearing into another hidey hole, his scrap of a shirt still caught in my mecha's fist. I grabbed for him, but the pain in my ribs nearly made me black out again.

I switched on the mecha's medical stuff and let the needles and probes sink into me while I set the inertial tracker to backtrack–gently–to home. I could see my artist friend some other time and do my trade.

The man with the rings and necklaces and the dandelion clock of hair was waiting for me when I got back.

"That was some chase-scene," he said, as I pried myself out of my tin can.

"Hand me my canes," I gasped, stepping onto the wide limb that led into my treehouse.

He shook his head as he did so. "You don't look so good."

"You want to tape up my ribs?"

"Not especially," he said. He rummaged in his pack and then tossed me something. "Compression shirt. Just put it on and let it do its thing."

In the end, he had to help me into the t-shirt, which was snug and electric blue. It gradually tightened itself around me, like a full-body hug. He showed me how to get it to loosen up for later when I wanted to take it off. I slumped onto my bed.

"What have you done to yourself?" he said.

"You're the second person to ask me that today."

"Yeah, I heard."

"You've been following me, huh."

He pointed to the sky. "Midges," he said. "My familiars. I have millions of them, all around these parts. They keep me filled in on all the doings on my territory."

"Your territory."

"I'm the shaman of the southland, son. You should be honored. Most people don't even know I exist. I've come to you twice."

"You said you could reverse this," I said, gesturing with my skeletal, liver-spotted arm.

"I said that. It's not hard, really. Just need to send a kill signal to Chandrasekhar's bots and your cells' natural robustness will kick in, lengthening your mitochondria. Once it reaches critical length, bam, you'll just grow back into the boy we programmed you to be."

"I want to stop at 18," I said. "That was a good age."

He nodded sagely. "Might take the last couple thousand years off your life, you know."

"How many will that leave me with, though?"

"Oh, *lots*," he said. "I mean, not into the stelliferrous period when the stars grow cold, but put it this way: plate tectonics will have rendered the Earth's continents unrecognizable."

"I thought you said that it took a long time to judge the success of immortality?"

"I've got really good models. Lots of compute power these days, if you know where to look."

"All right then, do it. Make me young."

"Ah, there's a little matter of payment, see? Always pay for what you get. There's no other way to run a world." His smile curled in and in, the dimples multiplying.

"I have half an old tire I could let you have," I said, shrugging and slumping back into my bed. "I guess you could have the mecha, once I'd recovered."

He nodded. "Mighty generous of you. But I had something else in mind: a favor."

I closed my eyes, knowing that this was going to be bad.

"It's those kids. You heard what the one you caught said to you. He's not himself anymore. The Midwich virus turns kids into harvesters for a vast upload-space where models of the consciousness of billions of humans exist in a hive-mind."

"They do what now?"

"They steal your mind and put it in a big computer."

"Why?"

"Because they're programmed to. Whoever designed the Midwich virus wants them to. The second wumpus war was the same thing. Those human-attacking wumpuses were scanning and copying the humans they ate. I think that the Midwich hive-mind has assimilated the wumpus-mind, but I don't know for sure. Maybe they're rivals."

"But *why*?"

He shrugged. "You know the answer. We both do. They do it because someone thought it would be cool. The line between thought and deed is pretty fine these days."

"And why me?"

"Jimmy," he said, sounding disappointed. "You know the answer. You're not stupid. You're our superhuman. Start acting like one. Why you?"

"Because the youth gangs have no effect on me?"

"Yes. And?"

"Because they're derived from me, somehow?"

"Yes. And?"

"Because my father is in there, somehow?"

"Yes. That's a weird one, isn't it? We all assumed he was dead. Maybe he was in cold storage, awaiting scanning. Maybe they scanned him right away."

"What do you want of me?"

"That part's easy," he said.

I'd spent so much time ducking youth gangs, but now I was actively seeking them out. Perversely, I couldn't find them. I stuck to the main roads, ranging up and down the keys, letting the mecha drive itself while I kept my eye out for them.

It was one of those perfect days on the keys, when the sky was a cloudless blue to forever, the air scented with delicious, wet jungle smells. I took a break and did a little fishing, using the mecha's radar to spot and plot the fish, then diving forward and snapping up a big grouper and cupping it in the mecha's hands while it thrashed. I put it in a refrigerated compartment on one thigh for later. I loved to pack them in mud, build a fire and put them among the coals. It had been a long time since I'd had fish. But I'd have something to celebrate tonight.

I jogged up and down the keys some more. I came to the place where I'd run into the youth gang the day before and checked to see if the mecha had still buffered the route it took chasing down my little friend. It had. I set the inertial tracker to re-run it, letting the shaman's brace do the work.

I came to it, an unimpressive hill covered in scrub, the entrance to the cave hidden by branches. I dug at the hill with the mecha's huge hands. It was slow going.

An hour later, I had barely made a dent in the hill, and I

still hadn't found any of the kids. The tunnel twisted and dipped around the tree roots.

Fuck it. Once upon a time, my mecha had an enormous supply of short-range missiles, not nearly so smart as the ones on my original beast, back in Detroit, but still able to get the job done. When I walked out of the militia, I had the good sense to fill up my frame, the dozen-by-dozen grid that held a gross of explosives.

Over the years, they'd been depleted. The last couple I'd fired hadn't detonated on contact, but had gone up a few minutes later–luckily I'd had the good sense to keep back of the unexploded munitions.

I backed off from the hill and sighted down the tunnel. The flavors of missile I had left were really antipersonnel, low on heat, high on concussion. I figured that if I could get the missile deep enough into the hillside, the concussion wave would crack it open like an egg.

I fired. And missed. The missile tried valiantly to steer itself into the hole that I'd told it to aim for, but it just wasn't up to it. It screamed into the top of the hill and blew, most of the concussion going up and out into the sky, making an incredible roar that the mecha's cowling did little to dampen. I waited for my head to stop ringing and fired another missile, correcting a little.

This one went true, right down into the tunnel, down and down. I counted one hippo, two hippo, and *whoom*, there was a deep *crump* from down below the mecha and the hill disintegrated into the sky.

It sploded like an anthill in a hurricane, turning into gobs of mud that arced in all directions in a rapidly expanding sphere. Caught in it were flinders of tree-root that stuck to my cowl and slid down slowly. For a moment, I caught a glimpse of the crater I'd made, then two huge trees–something derived from cypruses–topped into it, followed by a great inrush of water from the surrounding water table.

I waded in as the water rushed and swirled and scooped my arms through the soup, looking for evidence of the youth gang that had burrowed there, but whatever evidence there had been was now gone. I'd had visions of the hill opening like a stone, splitting dryly and revealing a neat cross-section of the tunnels inside. I hadn't really thought about the water table.

The mud was sucking dangerously at the mecha's legs. If I got it stuck here and had to abandon it, I'd never be able to walk out of the swamp on my own. I levered myself out of the sinkhole and stepped out into the world. I was covered in mud. The skin of the mecha would shed the dirt eventually, but for now, my shiny metal carapace was covered in disgusting, reeking glop.

I was clearly not going about this right.

I moved back out onto the road and headed for the Sugarloaf Key bridge. The wumpuses had left the bridges intact–otherwise how would they make their way up and down the keys?–and they were the most conspicuous remaining example of human life in the good old days. It was the bridges that the youth gangs staked out most avidly.

It was there I'd find them.

Being covered in mud had its advantages. I crouched under the bridge amid the rocks and made myself invisible. I set the mecha to estivate and recharge its batteries, leaving only its various ears and eyes open.

Before shutting down, I primed my whole remaining missile battery, getting them aimed for fast launch, and recorded a macro for getting myself out of there when the time came, before the bridge could come down around my ears. It would be quite a bounce, but I was prepared to give up a rib or two if that's what it took.

Now it was just a matter of staying alert. I kept thinking about my mouth-watering fish and the feast I'd cook that night, drifting off into mouth-watering reverie. Then I'd snap back to my surroundings, looking back at my screens.

Nothing. Nothing. Nothing.

Then: something.

Gliding out of the wilderness at both ends of the bridge like they were on casters. Silent. Eerie. I waited for them to converge on the center of the bridge before I hit it and quit it.

Ker-BLAM! I barely had time to take satisfaction in the incredible, synchronized splosion of the struts at both ends of the bridge giving way, tossing lumps of reinforced concrete high into the sky. I was in the belly of the mecha as it sprang away, leaping nearly as high, landing with coiled legs, pushing off, somersaulting in mid-air, coming down blam-blam, one foot, two foot, on the remaining section of bridge, snatching out with both hands, seizing a wriggling child in each hand, knocking their heads together and leaping away.

I let the mecha pilot itself for a while while I kept an eye out for pursuit. They'd all scattered when I'd chased them before, but that didn't mean they'd do the same when I *caught* a couple of them.

There they were, giving chase, leaping over obstacles, skittering through the dirt. And ahead–more of them, a dozen of them, gliding out of the bush. A couple hours ago, I hadn't been able to find any of them, now they were boiling out of the underbrush.

I wasn't sure what they could do to my mecha, but I didn't want to find out.

The mecha's arms pumped for balance, flailing the kids' bodies back and forth like rag-dolls. I tried to get a look at them. I'd snatched up my little friend and one of his buddies, darker skinned, with longer hair. Both had blood on their faces. Either the missile concussion had done that, or I had, when I'd banged their heads together. Like I said, there's not a lot of fine motor control in those mecha suits.

I was breathing hard and it hurt like hell. Felt like another rib had cracked. Aging was coming on pretty quick.

Here's the thing: the mecha has some pretty heavy guns, regular, old-fashioned projectile weapons. I hadn't fired them much in the line of duty, because wumpuses are missile jobs unless you want to chip away at them all day on full auto. So my clips were full.

I could have sprayed those kids as they came out of the jungle, short, auto-targeted bursts. I'm pretty sure that however immortal the little bastards were, they weren't immortal enough to survive ten or twenty explosive slugs in the chest and head.

Why didn't I shoot the kids? Maybe it's because I knew they were my brothers. Maybe I just couldn't shoot kids, even if they weren't kids. Maybe I could plan a neat little explosion and kidnapping, but not gun down my enemies face to face.

The shaman said he needed the kids brought to him at old Finds Bight in the Saddlebunch Keys. That was pretty rough terrain, jungle and swamp the whole way. But the mecha knew how to get there.

One of the kids was thrashing now, trying to get free. The mecha's gyros groaned and creaked as it tried to compensate for the thrashing and the weird terrain.

I dropped the kid. I only needed one.

I watched him fall in the rear-view as the mecha leapt a hillock and went over double, using its free hand as a stabilizing leg, running like a three-legged dog.

That was when one of the kids came down on my mecha's back, clinging to it. I could see the kid through the cowl, its face completely expressionless as its eyes bored into me.

The youth gang's squid needs more than one node to be fully effective–they can't own your mind on their own. But that doesn't mean that one kid is helpless. Far from it.

It felt like my head was slowly filling with blood, crushing my brain and making my eyes bug out. Red mist crept around the edges of my vision and blood roared in my ears like the ocean. I couldn't move anything.

I almost smiled. Idiot child. If I couldn't move, I couldn't divert the mecha, and it knew where it was going.

"You're the only one that can run this mission," the shaman had said, sitting in my treehouse. "You're the only one they can't just think to death. You might have spoiled your immortality, but that's still intact. You and them, you're all on the same footing. Bring one to me. I'm going to get a login to their little hobby-world. I'm going to blow it wide open. We'll be able to go there–without having our minds raped by those little pin-dicks."

I didn't exactly black out. My vision contracted to a hazy disc ringed by red-black pulses timed to my heartbeat, and I could barely hear, but I hadn't blacked out. I was still conscious.

So I saw more kids drop onto the mecha's canopy as we galloped toward Saddlebunch. Some slid off when we leapt and jumped, but most stayed on. They had ropes. They lashed themselves down. They did something under the mecha too. Lassoing the legs, it seemed, from the little I could see. Working without any facial expression. Again. Again.

Leaping free, holding onto the ropes. I felt the mecha jerk as the ropes went taut, skidding and tumbling. Then it was up again, running again, on its feet again. Ropes! Inside, I smiled. Idiot kids.

Over the surf-roar of blood in my ears, I heard something else, new sounds. Clattering. The ropes. Something tied to the ends of the ropes.

The mecha jerked again, caught up short.

Anchors, that's what it was. The mecha twisted from side to side, incidentally dislodging the child who stared at me through the carapace. The red haze receded, my muscles came back to me and I leapt to my controls.

I swung the mecha back upright to give me more maneuverability and put my fingers on the triggers of all four guns.

I rotated around to target the anchors behind me. A couple rounds severed the tight ropes. The kid who'd ridden my carapace was just getting to his feet beside the mecha. Another rattle of the guns took care of him, and he burst open.

This is weird, but I'd never shot any person before. I'd blown up wumpuses and taken out the mechas and their drivers in Detroit, but I'd never done *this* before. There was an immediacy to the way he twisted and fell, the way his lungs opened out like wings from the hole the slugs tore in his back. It froze me just as certainly as the child had.

That freeze gave the rest of them the chance they needed. They surrounded me, gliding out of the woods like they were on rollers. Dozens of them. Dozens and dozens of them. I reached for the controls, trying to set the mecha back on its automated path to the shaman. My finger never made it.

There was a blinding headache. It grew and grew, like a supernova. I didn't know how it could hurt more. It hurt more.

It is possible to mindrape an immortal, I discovered, if you don't care about the immortal's mind when it's all over.

PART 4: TURN BACK, TURN BACK

Dad handed me the delicate hydraulic piston, still warm from the printer.

"You know where this goes, right?" He was sweating in the June heat. Keeping all of Comerica Park air conditioned, even with the dome, was impossible, especially during one of those amazingly wet midwestern heat-waves.

"I know, Dad," I said. "I can fix this thing in my sleep, you know."

He smiled at me, then switched to a mock frown. "Well, I *used* to think that, but given your recent treatment of one of my prize machines–" He gestured at the remains of the big mecha, blasted open in the Battle for Detroit.

"Oh, Dad!" I said. "What did you *want* me to do? Let

them raid us? You know, I took down *eight* of them. Single-handedly."

The flea bounced me, landing on my shoulders and leaping away. I staggered and would have dropped the piston, had Dad not caught me. "You had some help," he said.

He gave me a hug. "It's OK, you know. You were brave and amazing. I love you."

"I love you, too," I said. It was awkward saying it, but it felt good.

"Good," he said. "Now, back to work, you! I'm not paying you to stand around."

"You're paying me?"

"When was the last time you paid rent? You're getting it in trade."

The Carousel sat in the middle of the field, where second base had been. We'd dug it in, sitting it flush to the ground, the way it was supposed to be. It looked great, but it made reaching the maintenance areas a bit of a pain, so we'd winched out the entire Jimmy's Bedroom assembly and put it on the turf next to the Carousel.

Poor Jimmy. One of his arms hung to one side, jerking spastically when I powered him up. I unbuttoned his shirt, fumbling with the unfamiliar fasteners, and undressed him. The arm hydraulics were not easy to get at. Man, screws sucked. I tossed them in the air as I got them free, letting Ike and Mike fight to snatch them out of the sky.

"Aren't you afraid you'll lose one?"

I looked up from my work. Lacey looked prettier than ever, wearing a sleeveless shirt and a pair of shorts that showed off her hips, which had really changed shape in the past couple months, all for the better.

"Jeez," I said. "Don't sneak up on me like that, OK?"

She gave me a playful shove and I shoved her back and then she snuck me a kiss. I broke it off.

"Not in front of my Dad," I said, pleading.

"Your Dad adores me–don't you, Harv?"

I turned around and there he was, wiping his hands on his many-pocketed work-shorts, then tugging his shirt out of his belt-loop and pulling it on. "You'll do," he said.

I set down the piston carefully.

It sank a few inches below the surface. I tried to pretend it hadn't happened.

Pepe flew over us, then swooped in for a landing. His aim was off, though. He swooped right at my chest. Right *through* my chest.

"Dammit," I said.

"It's OK," Lacey said. "They'll fix it. Let's go for a walk."

"I can't," I said. "I just can't do it. If the spacial stuff isn't working, I can't believe it."

"Debugging is a process. We'll file a bug against it. They'll have it fixed soon enough."

"Look," I said. "If the platform is so buggy that it can't even keep track of collisions, how do we know it's running *us* accurately?"

"Of course it's not running us accurately," she said. "Otherwise, you'd still hate my guts, your Dad would still be dead–" Dad nodded "–and you'd be like 400 years old. Can't you just be happy for once?"

"You keep telling me that things will get better–"

"So forget about a great big, beautiful tomorrow, Jimmy," Dad said. "Maybe they'll never debug it. But tell me that now isn't the best time of your life."

I tried to argue. I couldn't. Whether that was because there was a bug in me, or because he was right, I couldn't say.

A GLIMPSE OF THE MARVELLOUS STRUCTURE (AND THE THREAT IT ENTAILS)

Sean Williams

Born in the dry, flat lands of South Australia, Sean Williams is the author of 70 short stories, five collections, and 30 novels aimed at adult, young adult, and child readers. Multiple winner of both Ditmar and Aurealis awards for science fiction, fantasy and horror, and Philip K Dick Award nominee for his 2007 space opera Saturn Returns, *he also works in the Doctor Who and Star Wars universes, resulting in several good stories to tell at parties.*

2010 sees the publication of Castle of the Zombies *and* Planet of the Cyborgs, *the first two instalments of a science fiction adventure series for kids, and the sequel to* Star Wars: The Force Unleashed, *the the first computer game tie-in novel to debut at #1 on the* New York Times *hardback bestseller list.* Troubletwisters, *a series co-written with Garth Nix, commences in 2011.*

Former winner and now a judge of the international Writers of the Future Contest," Sean takes an active role in writing-related organizations – he is the current Overseas Regional Director of SFWA – and enjoys the odd teaching stint, such as Clarion South. He still lives in Australia, where he received an MA in Creative Writing from Adelaide University in 2005 and is currently a PhD candidate at the same institution, not solely so he can one day call himself "Doctor".

It is difficult to measure the time since my last communication. Too much has passed, I fear, for the suspicion of my demise not to have become a certainty in some minds. Suspend all judgement, Master Catterson, on that score and any other, until I have conveyed the full import of recent events to you.

As suspected, the citizens of Gevira have uncovered something wondrous beneath the veneer of their civilisation—wondrous and at the same time utterly strange and deadly. Here is my account of it, sent a second time in full now I know my previous missives have gone unread. I leave to you, as always, the divination of the will of the Guild.

<FIRST ACCOUNT>

Security Officer Gluis alerted the shift supervisor of his discovery at 1900 hours. I arrived at 1910. Both Gluis and Supervisor Nemke were in attendance, but no other security officers beyond a small detail preserving the scene from the public.

(As Guild regulations demand, I have attached audiovisual recordings of the events should you need to verify my abbreviated transcript.)

"I've called topside." Nemke indicated the unsealed container that Gluis had pulled out of the habitat walls. "They're sending an investigator immediately. Before they come, Donaldan, I want you to tell me what you see. Step aside, Rudi, and let him look."

Gluis backed away with a contemptuous look solely for my benefit. It irked me that Supervisor Nemke insisted on using our first names, but I swallowed my irritation and complied. As the greenest of Nemke's security detail, I allowed her to educate me only so far as it complied with my goals. You know, Master Catterson, that I consider you my only teacher. That day's lesson, however, was one I am unlikely to forget.

The container was a standard-issue one-meter cube that slid on low-friction runners from its recess and opened by rolling its flexible top panel along runners down the front of the container, revealing a catalogue number stenciled in black. A quick search of inventory determined that it was supposed to contain scrubbers for the masks used on the main face. Someone–Gluis, I presumed at the time, and have no reason to doubt now–had swept aside the scrubbers to reveal something much more sinister.

The body was curled in a foetal position, with its thighs against its chest and arms tightly folded around its legs. The head had been tipped back to reveal its face. Slight features; a delicacy of ears, nose and jaw; brown hair longer than a man's; full lips, slightly parted–all suggested, correctly, that the corpse was that of a woman. An attractive one too, I thought, allowing myself the observation in case it related to the woman's demise and subsequent concealment. Deep frown lines suggested recent unhappiness, not yet smoothed away by death. More scrubbers had been pushed away to reveal her clothing, a khaki fieldsuit of crisply synthetic material. There were no bulges in the pockets, and no obvious sign of injury.

Forensic technology on Gevira lags significantly behind ours, but I could tell that the corpse had been scanned by Gluis and Nemke, and that neither officer had teased the cause of death from other intimate details. It didn't appear to be murder; that much was clear. The body's organs had ceased functioning by an act of will. Euthanasia is socially acceptable on Gevira, but that fact prompted more questions than it answered. Why had this woman chosen such an option and then hidden her body in a container where it might never be found? Why was I called out in the middle of the night to witness its examination? Why summon a topsider, furthermore, to investigate what must surely have been a case of no great importance?

The seven habitats on this level are kept uniformly cool in order to prevent thermal leakage into the bedrock outside. So close to the planet's South Pole, the mine cannot afford any slippage due to melting permafrost. Touching the corpse's smooth forehead, I found it be precisely at room temperature. The corpse's memory dump was protected by security algorithms I could not penetrate.

"Well? What do you think?"

"She's dead, Supervisor Nemke," I said with practised nonchalance. "Have you IDed her?"

"That's where it gets interesting." Nemke looked up as footsteps sounded in the corridor behind us. "Here's our colleague now. Donaldan, I'd like you to meet Investigator Cotton."

I turned to see a slight woman approaching with her hand extended, but it was not her hand that made me recoil. Her face took me so completely off-guard that I stumbled backwards a step, caught my boot on the corner of the container, and fell gracelessly onto my backside.

Officer Gluis uttered a restrained but clearly audible guffaw.

"Hello, E. C.," said Supervisor Nemke, taking the woman's hand and shaking it firmly. "You'll have to excuse young Donaldan, here. He's new. I've taken the opportunity to introduce him to the realities of our work."

"Of course. How better?" Her manner was guarded but not hostile. I felt a feather-light touch on my faked credentials. She was searching my details as smoothly as any Guild operative. Donaldan Shea Lough: security officer in the mines of Gevira, of no interest to anyone.

"You pronounce that . . . Lou? Luff?"

"Low," I answered, regaining my feet, embarrassed and furious at myself.

"My name is Cotton. E. C. Cotton. Would you care to show me the body?"

I did so, able to take my eyes off her face only while presenting her with the container's morbid contents. Glancing between them, I confirmed my initial impression.

They were the same. E. C. Cotton and the woman in the container were identical. One wasn't the clone of the other, however; the match was far too precise to allow for either possibility. Neither was the corpse a manufactured doppelganger of the living version, since even my brief scan proved that the body had once been perfectly vital. The only remaining possibility was impossible–logically, sensibly, patently–but fitted with rumours I had previously regarded as being too strange to be true.

While I stared at her, reassessing all my former opinions, Cotton knelt down to repeat the examination I had performed. She came to the same conclusion.

"Without a doubt, it's me," she said. "No sign of foul play. Have you hacked into the dump?"

"I thought we'd leave that to you, E. C. It's your property, after all."

"Fair enough."

She leaned over the corpse and pressed two fingers to the bone behind its right ear. I was close enough to feel the warmth of her living body but found no opportunity to eavesdrop on the data transaction. She, like the corpse, was protected.

"It's empty," she said. "The memory has been erased."

"Completely?" Supervisor Nemke looked disappointed.

"I'm afraid so." Cotton stepped back, wiped her hand on the thigh of her fieldsuit, and glanced at me. "You look like you've seen a ghost, newbie. Don't worry about it. Things like this happen all the time down here."

That she could be so nonchalant about it was perhaps the strangest thing of all. "Why is that, precisely?"

"We'd all like to know the answer to that question. You'll forget you asked, one day."

Not me, I swore–and I renew that pledge to you now, Master Catterson, never to become like those who live in this place, inured to all that is fearsome or fantastic. No matter how many conundrums we encounter, the insoluble is not something to be shrugged off lightly or, worse, turned into a joke.

Gluis, smirking, wandered off to talk to the perimeter detail.

"We're analyzing the surveillance records of this area," Nemke said as though this were a perfectly ordinary murder scene. "Someone must've placed the body here. We'll find out who it was and–"

"What, track them in the mines?"

"We'll do our best, E. C."

"I won't hold my breath. In the meantime, you have my authority to dispose of the body as you see fit. Autopsy it, recycle it, donate it to science–I don't care. I have no use for it, and no next of kin."

The perimeter detail snickered at something Gluis said, and I studiously ignored them. E. C. Cotton interested me more. There was something decidedly odd about her, something beyond the fact that she was simultaneously alive and dead, like some kind of Schrödinger experiment.

Her own body lay before her, tangling her timeline in ways that boggled the mind and subtly unravelled her insouciance. Confronted with the dire certainty of her death, her self-control was predictably less than perfect. Instead of fear or grief, however, I sensed excitement. Anticipation. Challenge.

"I want you to know I'm sorry," Supervisor Nemke was saying in a sober voice.

Cotton didn't shrug aside the hand Nemke had placed on her upper arm. "Thank you. I'm glad you called me here. If I'd never known–"

A cry of alarm cut her off. Our heads turned. The security detail had bunched as one around a fallen figure. Red blood splashed between outstretched fingers. The sight was shocking, even at a fatal crime scene. Cries for help drew people from all directions.

Nemke pushed into the huddle. I followed, almost slipping in a crimson pool that spread fast as I approached. Cotton was beside me, her face ashen.

The body at our feet was bruised and burst like an overripe fruit. His features were barely recognizable as male. I averted my eyes, keen both to isolate the cause of his death and to hide my revulsion,. What had killed him was not immediately apparent. If it struck again–

"Good god," Nemke said. She had bent down and wiped the gore from the dead man's name badge, revealing his identity.

Rudi Gluis.

I felt as though I had been punched in the gut. Just a second ago, Gluis had been within meters of me, mocking me, and now he was dead, killed by persons or forces unknown. The universe rarely dispenses such immediate and well-deserved justice, so I was forced to look elsewhere for an explanation.

The thought formed in my mind the very moment someone put it into words.

"The Director."

Others took up the rumour, passing it from mouth to ear like a curse.

My heart beat even more rapidly, if that was possible. At long last I had witnessed the work of the mine's most deadly inhabitant.

The list of anomalies attributed to the Geviran mines grows longer every day of my infiltration. To the staffing irregularities, the outrageous energy imbalance, the curious mineral flows, and the problems with keeping any coherent kind of calendar, we can now add a corpse whose very existence ties time in a Gordian knot.

Of them all, however, the Director is of the most immediate import to those who live here, reminding all of their fragile position between toil and terrible fate.

I have already collated the rumours circulating regarding its activities, many of them borne out by records purloined from the security mainframe. The pertinent points, as they returned to me at that moment, are that the Director appears rarely in the upper levels of the mine, but does so with increasing frequency as one proceeds deeper. It comes invisibly, leaving no physical record of its existence. It strikes between image frames like a ghost, killing or kidnapping its victims with chilling ease—as it killed Gluis, while his comrades laughed at my expense. The Director's victims share no obvious connections or traits. The bodies of those taken have never been found. Its weapons and methodologies are unknown and perhaps unknowable. Its very presence is anathema to reason—yet it stays, and humanity lives alongside it, willing to accept its toll in exchange for the riches the mines bring.

The Gevirans know as little about the Director's origins as the Guild. If it is otherwise, they are careful to keep such knowledge from me. That lack of knowledge only makes their fear far greater. Panic is concealed beneath a veil of civilization, but the slightest twitch sets it free. One has only to see the wildness in their eyes each time the Director strikes to know how delicate the pretence is. Even I, a stranger to their world and set apart from their troubles, was briefly swept up in the moment. It could have taken any of us, I thought. It could have taken me.

Nemke woke the entire sector and called in reinforcements from outside. E. C. Cotton's cryptic corpse was forgotten along with the woman herself during the post mortem examination of Gluis's wounds, and in that time she slipped our attention. We were all shaken, even I who had liked Gluis not at all and been strongly disliked in return. I am abashed to admit, Master Catterson, that more than an hour passed before I thought to ask after Cotton's whereabouts.

"I let her go," Nemke said.

"You did what?"

"Why wouldn't I? I know her; we all know her. She worked here for a period, before you arrived. Looking for someone, I think, but didn't find him, so she moved on."

I could barely conceal my dismay. The Director had struck for the first time in my presence just moments after E. C. Cotton arrived. Was it too much to speculate that the two things were connected? That she was the key to this confluence of mysteries was a possibility I could not ignore.

"Where did she go?"

"Topside. She had that look they all get, when they've been searching down deep–"

"I mean just now. Did she go back up?"

"I presume so. It's none of our business what she does. People handle things like this differently. Some go off the rails, but she seemed–Donaldan, where are you going? We need you here!"

I had turned my back on her and was pushing through the secure perimeter. Her cries fell behind me. I ignored, too, her subsequent requests to return to duty. Let her think I was running out of weakness, or perhaps fear, using Cotton as an excuse to flee from the Director's handiwork. I knew otherwise.

First I called at security HQ, where I uploaded Cotton's personnel records into my memory dump. Even at a quick glance, they seemed inauthentic. Her full name, true or otherwise, was listed as Emmaline Celeste Cotton, and details were sketchy prior to her arrival on this level. She was 34 years old, the same approximate age as her corpse–a fact that only exacerbated the puzzle. If the body was genuine–as it appeared to be–and some twist in time had delivered it to her in advance of her actual demise, why was she unconcerned about the small amount of time remaining to her? The haste with which she had hurried off struck me as at odds with human nature–unless the body had already told her everything she needed to know, and set her off on errands unknown.

I downloaded the audiovisual record of the body's placement, intending to analyze this later, since surely the means of its arrival in our jurisdiction would provide a clue. Once I had that data, I traced Cotton's movements through the mine to determine where she had got to. Hoping against hope that she had not already reached the surface, I followed her recorded image along its path through this habitat to the next. She was heading for the elevators in sector eight.

By then I was on the move too, not stopping to fabricate an explanation for the staff at HQ. If they wondered why I was disobeying Supervisor Nemke's orders, they said nothing. These were bridges, I decided, that I could mend on my return, for at that moment, my orders were clear: to follow the mystery for the glory of the Great Ship and the Guild. It would be a lie of omission not to add that being shamed by my pratfall in front of my erstwhile colleagues was also an incentive.

E. C. Cotton had already left the elevator cluster by the time I arrived. With utmost haste, I determined which shaft she had taken. To my surprise, she had not gone up at all, but down–down the sole shaft connecting the upper levels to the lower. Wherever she was heading, it wasn't back to the surface.

I commandeered the next carriage from a gaggle of young miners heading coreward to pursue their fortunes. It was imperative that I be able to think without their distracting babble. As the carriage disengaged from the habitats, I felt a clear sense of vertigo, even though the floor beneath my feet was absolutely steady. My first visit to the lower levels wasn't supposed to be like this. I hoped that the rumours I have been gathering for you, Master Catterson, would prepare me for what lay ahead.

The drop lasted several minutes. In that time, I reviewed the audiovisual record. The container had not been in position as recently as a day earlier, so I jumped forward in increments of one hour to a point where it was extant, and then scrolled back. People came and went, going about the business of the mine. Some of them I recognized; others wore full-body fieldsuits with semi-opaque pressure masks covering their faces. It was one such who placed the container for Officer Gluis to discover 13 hours later, so I knew my hope of an easy answer was ill-conceived.

The captured image was of a slender male displaying no identification, physical or electronic. His fieldsuit was different to the ones worn by miners on that level, but not so different as to attract attention. Moving calmly into view from the camera's left, he slid the container into position and made certain it was secure, then walked just as casually out of the frame. As he disappeared, I caught a faint profile of his face through the semi-transparent mask. It was barely a glimpse, but something about it struck me as familiar. I cannot say what, exactly, and I analyze the records now with increasing perplexity. There is barely a hint of cheek and nothing more than an outline of a nose. I wonder if I am reaching at something that does not exist. How could I know the face of this mysterious man? What are the odds against such a happenstance? Nevertheless, I present the blurry image to you, Master, in the hope that you will decipher what I cannot.

The carriage moved beneath me, the first sensation I had registered during the journey. A short time later, the doors opened. I stepped out into a very different space. Instead of cramped, dimly-lit corridors and an ever-present tang of recycled air, this level was bright to my eyes. I squinted for a moment, noting white walls, vaulted ceilings, and gleaming observation blisters set into the floor, smelling people instead of industry, and taking stock of those nearby as best I could. There were miners, officials in unfamiliar blue uniforms, and even a child walking hand-in-hand with an adult. (A child! I could barely believe my eyes. What madman would bring an infant into a mine?) Standing not four meters from me, gazing down through one of the bulging blisters, was the woman I sought.

Emmaline Celeste Cotton looked up as I approached, and said, "I wasn't expecting you."

I had no answer for her, not immediately. My attention was caught by the downward view through the blister. It showed an endless sea of lava upon which bobbed islands of semi-molten stone. Green flames licked and danced like djinns, dodged by graceful flitter-craft and ignored by sturdier extraction platforms. The habitat in which I stood hung not 100 meters above the hellish ocean, but the floor was hardly warm, and the ambient temperature perfectly comfortable. Were the environmental controls to fail, I had no doubt that we would be burned to ash in a second.

No one but Cotton and I so much as glanced through the blisters. To them, I supposed, the view was commonplace. The human mind learns to accept all manner of wonder, if it is presented every day. The same goes for horror, as the miners' coexistence with the Director proves beyond doubt.

With some effort, I brought my attention to the matter at hand. "You were expecting *someone*."

She nodded. Her eyes were light brown, I noted for the first time, and they hid a calculating mind. "Why are you here, Donaldan Lough?"

"You left a crime scene, your own body–"

"The truth, now. You're not like the others. Why are you the only one to come after me, and not them?"

You will comprehend, Master, the care with which I chose my next words.

"None of the others seem to give a damn. You saw them. To Gluis, your body was nothing but a joke to frighten newbies–and look what happened to him. Nemke's well-meaning but a plodder. No one's asking the questions that need to be answered."

"So you're curious."

"I am curious," I said, "to know why you are going down rather than up, to your death rather than away from it."

She examined me as closely as I was examining her. What she saw helped her come to a decision. Although I was not privy to her reasoning, I believe I conveyed only muddled trustworthiness, and that was sufficient.

"I'm not going any further down," she said. "I'm going sideways."

"To where? There's only one entrance to the mines."

"Look behind you, Donnie Boy."

I did as she instructed, half-anticipating that she would strike me or attempt to flee the moment my back was turned. She did neither.

Set into the wall behind me I saw the entrance to the elevator shaft down which I had just descended. The gaggle of miners I had disenfranchised emerged from it at that moment, casting me dark looks but finding the observation blisters entirely more interesting. What I had not noticed–distracted in a similar fashion–was a second entrance next to the first, identical in design but with no matching counterpart on the level above.

I crossed to it in a dozen easy strides. (It occurred to me later that I had felt lighter on this level, but that is only to be expected so much closer to the center of the planet.) The door did not open for me, despite my security credentials, and displayed no information regarding its destination.

"Where does this lead?" I confronted Cotton right there, in front of the closed sliding doors. "Tell me."

"I already did. Sideways." She raised an empty hand. "If you like, I'll show you."

I tripped over the thought that she wanted to take my hand, as a lover might. Then I realized that she wished only to communicate via the receptors in her skin, the same receptors by which she had accessed her corpse's memory dump.

I tightened my firewalls and raised my hand in return.

The moment our fingers touched, three strings of alphanumeric symbols appeared in my mind.

> rmei68q9ve42izms7tj
> 5ek38eoqwjup40dwgg5
> TRELAYNE

They meant nothing to me.

"To get through that door," she said, "you need access codes. I had one, but it was cancelled nine weeks ago. I've been stuck here ever since."

The implication was simple enough to follow: these 19-digit strings were examples of the codes she needed. "Where did you get these from?"

"My body," she said, with a defiant smile. "The dump was erased, but only because I wiped it clean."

"You lied, then. Why?"

"Isn't a better question for the moment: why *two* access codes?"

"That's why you expected someone to meet you here, but didn't know who."

"Exactly. But you're not Trelayne," she said, "unless you too have a secret."

I withdrew my hand, keeping my expression carefully neutral. "Trelayne is a person?"

"A very important person, Don. The most important person in the mines. Some say he's a thousand years old and lives in a fortress at the center of everything. Others say he's just a legend, and he never existed at all. Either way, remember those questions you had? Find Trelayne and you'll have your answers."

"He's the person you're looking for," I said, remembering

with a flash of inspiration what Supervisor Nemke had said about her unsuccessful search.

"Yes." Her stare was a challenge. "And now I have two access codes to set me on my way again. Are you coming with me or not?"

It was not an easy decision, Master Catterson. If I rejected her offer, I could return to my post beneath Supervisor Nemke and resume my patient exploration of Gevira's mysteries, aided by her slow but considerate attempts to educate me in the ways of the mines.

Or I could travel with Cotton to a whole new section of the mine–the existence of which I had never suspected just one level up–and pursue the man she said could tell me everything I had ever wanted to know. The opportunity promised untold revelations. It hinted at mysteries we had barely suspected. How could I decline her offer?

I did not. For the Great Ship and the Guild, I resolved to keep following the mystery wherever it led, no matter how many bridges I left burning behind me.

Cotton entered the access codes electronically. The panels slide open, allowing us entry into a carriage identical to the one I had just left. They shut behind us, and with no sensation of motion at all we were underway.

My interrogation of her began almost immediately.

"The view back there," I said. "That doesn't look like any mine I've ever seen before."

"What do you think is going on here, exactly?"

I told her what I had learned during my covert surveillance: that the deeper levels harness the resources of Gevira's lower mantle and core, using the temperature differential between it and the Polar Regions to power the enterprize. That is the official story, anyway. You and I know this to be only partly true, Master, but I did not comprehend until that moment that she knew as well.

"Yeah, it's bullshit," she said. "The mine is a net energy exporter degrees of magnitude higher than even an optimistic estimate. And the elements it extracts from the mantle don't display the expected isotopic proportions. Core-mining can't possibly be the whole story."

I asked her for her theory, but she didn't answer.

"Perhaps twists in causality are a side-effect," I prompted her, thinking of her abandoned corpse.

"Of what? The kind of concentrated mass-energy you'd need to create a loop in time would suck Gevira into a black hole. I haven't stumbled over any of those lately. Have you?"

"It's impossible to define the characteristics of a technology we know nothing about."

"True."

"Particularly if that technology is of alien origin."

"ROTH? Here?"

I asked her to define the term.

"Races Other Than Human, Don. Where have you been living?"

I was tempted to say: far from here. But the urge to put her in her place was controllable.

"The possibility of an alien artifact cannot be ignored," I said, frostily. "I believe that the Director is protecting it."

"There's something odd going on, that's for sure, but I don't think that little green men on Gevira are the answer. Most people assume there's a secret society running things behind the scenes. Those they like, they take. Those they don't like, they kill. Occam would find that more acceptable."

Her superior attitude was a constant irritation, but no secret is safe with a braggart. It emerges of its own accord, eventually. I decided to suffer in exchange for the information she promised.

"Have you ever heard of Terminus?" she asked.

For the second time that day, I experienced vertigo. "No."

"The Structure?"

"No."

"There's a lot you don't know, Donaldan Lough. Stick with me. I'll do my best to keep you out of trouble."

"What kind of trouble are you anticipating?"

"How should I know?" Her façade cracked. "The only thing I'm sure of is that when this knot in time unwinds, I'm going to be dead."

"We must all die, one way or another."

"And curiosity kills the cat. I'd be careful if I were you, Donnie Boy. This is my problem. You don't want to be tied to me when I go down."

"You didn't seem to consider that much of a problem before."

"Yeah, well, maybe it's just sinking in. Maybe I'm starting to feel the full weight of my mortality." Her chest rose and fell. "You ask too many questions. Do you know that?"

The floor jolted beneath us, signalling our arrival at a new section of the mine. Cotton took up a position in front of the door. I stood to her right, expecting to see a habitat very much like the one in which I lived. There was no reason to believe otherwise.

The doors slid open, revealing armed guards, two militaristic checkpoints, and a queue of miners in unfamiliar fieldsuits waiting to be processed. Low rectangular windows in the checkpoint barriers offered a glimpse of the what lay beyond them, but it was not easy to examine those vistas at a casual glance, not from my position. The air stank of intimidation and fear, putting my nerves on edge. My right hand flexed, aching for the grip of a Guild blaster.

"Let me do the talking," said Cotton, leading the way out of the elevator. "You should be okay; you have Geviran ID. But around here it never pays to be–"

A bark of anger cut her off in mid-sentence. Heads turned, including ours, towards a sudden disturbance near the checkpoints. My first thought was that someone had attempted to force their way through the blockade, but a spreading ripple of alarm and shock told me that something more serious was afoot. Anger became distress. The sideways shuffling of people waiting in line took on an urgent Brownian motion while some tried to get closer to the source of the problem and others tried just as insistently to get away. Individual voices rose up out of a growing hubbub. Two familiar words stood out more clearly than any others.

The Director.

"Stay back," Cotton said, pressing me against the doors behind me. They had closed. Three more entrances stood to our right, also shut. She inched us towards them. "Don't do anything until I tell you."

I let her take charge of the situation. We were significantly outnumbered, and I had no choice but to place my faith in her greater knowledge of the situation. Not until the guards noticed us, the latest arrivals, and raised their weapons to target us did I begin to be seriously concerned.

Cotton presented her ID and shouted something. I don't know what. The words are lost in the growing chaos captured in memory dump. Her protestations didn't have the intended effect.

A ring of armed soldiers pressed towards us, pushing bystanders out of the way. What did they think we had done? Killed or kidnapped a bystander ourselves and stuck around to witness the effect?

I understood their terror, though. One of their own had been struck down by the Director. Explanations were required. A superstitious need for answers and scapegoats had to be addressed.

I tensed, readying myself to fight. We were unarmed and had nowhere to run. If we were lucky, I remember thinking, we might only end up in a cell. If we were unlucky . . .

Behind us, one of the entrances slid open. Cotton grabbed my upper arm so tightly it hurt and pulled me inside. I had no sensible reason to resist.

The doors closed barely in time. Pounding fists echoed from the far side for a second, then were gone.

Cotton's breathing was loud but I suspect mine was louder.

"That could've gone better," she said, letting go of my arm and flicking her dark fringe out of her eyes.

"Was that the kind of trouble you were expecting?

"No. I've never seen the Director so active." The look in her eyes told me that I had correctly surmised the reason behind our rapid retreat. "And no, I don't know where we're going. Somewhere safe, I hope."

"Safe from the Director or from goons like them?"

"Both." Then she laughed. "The stupid thing is, they were never going to shoot me. I was killed by my own choice, not by a bullet."

"That fact offers me little comfort, Cotton."

"Call me E. C."

I avoided this attempt at intimacy by taking the opportunity to review the AV data stored in my memory dump. You have that data, Master Catterson. You will witness as I did the tense situation prevalent in that level of the mine. Why it should be so, I have not yet learned. Perhaps that level contains conditions hostile to human life, or minerals–even ruins!–considered valuable by the Geviran government. Perhaps this level is the source of the mine's paradoxical profligacy. For now, it remains unfathomed. The images in my memory dump–of brilliant sparks spraying in an arc against an entirely metal backdrop–offer no illumination at all.

With that inglorious beginning, our circuitous odyssey through the mines commenced. I will not burden you with torturous details of our headlong flight, Master, and neither will I attempt to convey the horror of it: the tense anticipation for the doors to open, the growing certainty that the

Director would strike wherever we appeared, and the terrible fear that the codes would stop working, thereby rendering us unable to flee from such near-misses.

After hastily eluding the armed forces of the Militaristic Zone (as I have come to think of it), Cotton and I escaped to another level of the mine an unknown distance from our starting point. It was to all appearances a gentler place than the last, one bedecked with vines and plants and smelling sweetly of fresh oxygen. I had time enough to take in the vistas offered by its elegant observation deck before tragedy struck a third time that day. A woman screamed a man's name not ten meters from where I stood, prompting bedlam all around us. The man was dead, killed by the Director. An influx of bystanders could do nothing to save him or to relieve the horror of the woman who had witnessed the attack. I imagined the body, bloodied and battered as Gluis's had been, and was glad we had been no closer.

Cotton decreed that we should move again.

"Keep your eyes on me," she said as she used our access codes to open another door.

"Why?"

"The Director can only take someone while they're not being observed."

"Do you think we're its targets?"

"Who else, Don? Three attacks in as many hours. We're the only common denominators."

I could accept her reasoning, but for one flaw. "You're not afraid of bullets, but you run from the Director. Why is that?"

"Time's in knots. I'm not ruling out anything I can't see."

That was a fair point. Given the awesome subtlety of its art, who was to say the Director could not reach into her mind and trigger the chemical cascade that would leave her dead? That fate was no more suicide than a bullet, but it could look the same.

The "Greenhouse" Zone was followed by another, chosen

at random from the five routes available to us. Cotton was relying on fate to guide her, or else she possessed a means of navigating the unfolding mines that I have not guessed.

Barely had the doors opened when cries alerted us once more to the presence of our deadly traveling companion.

I did as instructed and kept Cotton within plain sight. She, I am pleased to note, did the same for me. We stayed barely long enough to taste the air and capture several seconds of data, revealing that this level was a very different place to any I had visited before or since, with long-limbed servomechanisms passing a greenish material of unknown constitution endlessly between them. I dubbed it the Jade Zone.

There followed the Dark, the Underwater, and the Antiquated Zones, all visited only briefly, all distinct in a variety of ways. It is quite impossible to capture the variety I glimpsed at each of our destinations. All I can do is attach the images I recorded for you and my fellow Guildsmen to pore over. I am certain that you will reach the same conclusion as I.

We know from our own history that human civilization has existed on Gevira for approximately 300 years. It is a homogenous culture founded on egalitarian principles different to ours, but not inimically so. The Great Ships of the Guild have been trading with Gevira for at least half of its colonized history, but until now we have had no suspicion of the wealth and diversity lying beneath its surface. A veritable maze of mine shafts and levels exist here–and perhaps existed here long before humanity arrived in force to claim the planet. Could aliens have built these spaces, these wonderful contrivances, and then abandoned them? In the light of recent events, I do believe that is possible. How else could such a subterranean labyrinth ever have been built–and populated–with no one noticing? And no wonder its population is so much larger than the official figures recorded on the surface! The miners might have been breeding down here for generations, creating their own odd pockets of society, disconnected from worlds above, perhaps even from each other.

The Superior Zone. The Electric Zone. The Loud Zone. I was soon hard-stretched to find adjectives. Across these transits we might have covered hundreds, even thousands of kilometers, in any number of directions. There was no way of telling one point within the planet from the next. I am just one Guildsman, alone in this enucleate enigma and finding myself increasingly at a loss.

We came at last to a level empty of all life, apart from our own. I feared for a moment that the Director had snatched everyone away a bare instant before the doors opened, but that was soon revealed to be unfounded: this level has been abandoned for some time, judging by the staleness of the air. When we stepped out the only entrance on that level, we were greeted by flat echoes off unadorned walls. Our feet kicked up dust with every step. Shadowy windows revealed nothing of the level beyond this dim entrance hall, which was vaulted and gloomy like a tomb. There was power–piped in, I presume, along the shaft we had followed–but little else.

"I do not know this place," Cotton said, visibly sagging with exhaustion but not yet relief. That we were alone meant that the Director could attack no one else but us.

We did nothing for some time, standing together in the silent hall, watching each other and waiting for the Director to strike. If it tried to take both of us at once, would our combined perceptions offer any protection at all? We could only wait and hope. I don't know if Cotton prayed. Me, I offered my faith up to the Great Ship and the parent world far away, in the hope that my life would not be so meaninglessly squandered.

Nothing happened. The eye of the Director has passed over us, it seems. Perhaps it is toying with us. Perhaps it enjoyed watching us run far and wide, and has temporarily retracted its malevolent claw just as we steeled ourselves in resignation for its deathly touch.

How many people have died or been taken in our wake is impossible to know. Dozens, probably. If Cotton's theory is correct, we are responsible for every innocent lost this day. There is comfort in the thought that we ourselves have survived, but it is bitterly cold.

Resigned, temporarily, to running no more, Cotton and I have agreed to rest in this lifeless space. I volunteered to keep watch while she, exhausted, sleeps. She has no way of knowing if I will be there when she wakes. I could run away, or be snatched by the Director during her slumber. The latter is entirely possible, by the strange illogic of this world, but sleep she must. In the last day, she has traveled from topside to view her own corpse, fled with a stranger through far-flung sections of the mine, and found herself in this desolate, empty hall. In its relative calm we will both seek what ease there is to find.

For my own part, I have taken the opportunity to prepare this account. Master Catterson, I urge you to consider carefully everything I have revealed to you, and to respond forthwith. It has been too long since I last took direct counsel from you, and I fear that I have become lost in more ways than one. Here I am, led far off my chosen course by a guide who may not be completely reliable, and whom I must avoid trusting any more than sense dictates.

You have my data, Master Catterson. Study it and advise me how best to proceed.

I await your orders with some anxiety, in fear of wandering forever.

(There ends, Master Catterson, my first account since leaving the post you assigned me. I have altered not a word, trusting in my first impressions and the conveyance thereof—and in your open-mindedness too, for what is to come necessarily colors what came before. A new light is about to shine, one that will provide a second, more pertinent interpretation of everything I have shared with you thus far.)

<SECOND ACCOUNT>

While Cotton slept, I explored as much of this Dead Zone as I dared, monitoring with all my senses for sudden drops in pressure, radiation spikes, biological interference, and any other potentially lethal signs. Without knowing what had caused the evacuation of its miners, the care I took was unparalleled. It would not do to escape the Director only to fall in some pointless accident. Until Cotton was either dead or somehow spared her unavoidable fate, I was bound to pursue the mystery and the answers she promised.

The shape of the empty habitat was a tube, spiralling like a strand of DNA on its side through the planet's subduction zones. I surmised from an examination of its inert engines that ferriferous minerals had been mined here a decade or so earlier. The crusted furnaces were cold, abandoned rather than chopped up and returned to the surface. I walked along corridors and through barracks that retained not the slightest trace of their former inhabitants. There were neither bodies nor physical effects. It was as though such traces had been erased along with their existence.

I thought yearningly of my cell in the Great Ship. The memory of the closeness of my fellow Guildsmen succors me in these echoing spaces. How alien this place is to us! How strange that people choose to live here, deep underground, where the furthest one can see is measured in meters. No wonder even the topsiders don't understand the miners, let alone we who come from spaces surface dwellers in turn could barely grasp. They are mad, all of them–and the madness of the mines, I am coming to believe, is extremely contagious.

Ultimately I decided that the level had simply been mined out. Its tidy emptiness spoke of an orderly withdrawal, not a rout. There were, however, several instances of graffiti left by the last of the miners and by those like Cotton and I, who had stumbled across the level by chance. Perhaps it was one of these latter wanderers who wrote in vulgar tone of the Director's parentage. Perhaps one of the miners scrawled the message of love and longing to an absent partner that I found in an empty bedroom. I could not decide who had been responsible for the endless series of bullseyes encircling a boardroom, where the level's manager might have pondered the difficult decision to leave.

While reading one of the strangest pieces–an ode in charcoal to stars apparently glimpsed in the deepest levels of the mine–a metaphor, surely–I heard the sound of a door hissing open.

My heart jumped into my throat. Fearing that Cotton had woken and taken the opportunity to abandon her clueless companion, I retraced my steps at full-tilt to the entrance hall.

I arrived to find Cotton lying on her side with her fieldsuit sealed right up to her throat, exactly as I had left her, with an unknown man looking down at her sleeping form. It must have been he who had entered via the sliding portal that stood open behind him. His footsteps were distinct in the dust, larger than either of ours and spaced well apart.

I skidded to a halt in the dust opposite him. His gaze shifted to me, with something of Cotton in its cool regard. I was momentarily nonplussed at both his presence and size. He wore a sturdy black fieldsuit and carried a pack, and displayed no ID.

"You're with her, I presume," he said.

"I am. Who are you and what are you doing here?"

"I'm with Terminus. Aren't you?"

At the sound of our voices, Cotton stirred. Her eyes flickered open. She stared blankly up at us until the scales fell away. The retrograde trajectory of her recollection was played out nakedly across her face. The abandoned level; the Director; her own corpse. I understood that part of her had thought she might never awake from that slumber.

Both of us went to offer her a hand, and she took the largest, that of the new arrival.

"Huw Kindred," she said. "What are you doing here?"

"I was going to ask you the same question, Emma." He set her on her feet and brushed dust gently from her cheek. "The Director carved a trail right across the Structure. I never thought to find you at its end."

"That's not the half of it."

"I bet. Want to tell me what's going on?"

"Later. Got any food? I've been running on internals for a week."

"Sure." Kindred shrugged off his pack and reached inside. My stomach grumbled as he handed Cotton a silver packet. Our eyes briefly met. His were ocean blue.

"Who's this guy?" Kindred asked. "I mentioned Terminus and he looked as blank as a fish."

"Donaldan Lough," she said around a mouthful of the concentrate he had given her. "He's a Geviran."

"Never thought I'd see you running with a native. How'd that come about?"

She frowned as though struggling to recollect a dream: her wiped memory dump; the codes; our hurried flight. I wondered if it always took her this long to wake up. "It's a long story. Later."

I temporarily put aside my curiosity regarding the mysterious Terminus, just as I let them accept the mistaken assumption about my origins. Kindred seemed to swallow it easily enough. We shook hands. Still wary of this stranger in our midst, I responded to his offer of food with a simple negative. He nodded and re-sealed the pack.

"How long's it been, Emma? The last time I saw you was in Margelise, I think, almost a year ago."

"Just a month for me." Sudden fright struck her. "You're not safe, Huw. We're marked. The Director is following us, and it'll take you if you stay around."

He shrugged. "I've been here–how long? Minutes now and nothing's happened. I'll take my chances if you'll keep your eyes on me. Okay?"

Kindred looked to us for agreement, and I nodded automatically. Whoever he was, Cotton knew and trusted him. For my part, I was coming to view him as a possible source of information about the wider expanses of the mine. Thus far, Cotton had been reticent on almost every point I wished to explore.

"We shouldn't stay here, though," said Kindred. "I'm not the only one following that trail."

"Not sideways," she said, looking haunted and harried at the thought of going. "I'm not putting anyone else at risk by heading somewhere populated. There's just the one door. I'm sure we'd get a fine reception back the way we came."

"Deeper, then. There might be another exit. At the very worst, we can hide in the lower levels until the fuss dies down."

He put his suggestion to her in easy tones, as though considering a walk through a hydropark.

She took a deep shuddering breath, and looked down at her feet.

"Yes," she said. "You're right."

"I found an elevator cluster not far from here," I informed them. "If the shafts are clear, we should be able to get them working."

"Are you going to come with us, Don?" she said, looking at me with her cool brown eyes. "You don't have to, you know. You can step away and go home any time you want."

If only it was that easy, I thought. Home was further away than she could possibly imagine.

Follow the mystery.

"Let's go, then," she said. "It's just us, Huw. We didn't bring anything. If Don and I had known how far we were going, we would've packed, eh?"

I could not help but echo her smile. "Lunch, at least."

She tossed me the remains of her concentrate bar, and this time, gratefully, I accepted.

I led them through the empty corridors to where I had found several inert freight carriages, thick with dust and cobwebs. Spiders are rare in the mines but not unknown. Many forms of life have crept down from the surface, and most have evolved resistance to the usual forms of pest control. In this abandoned level, nature was claiming a new home. As well as webs, I had seen a dead cockroach, a line of ants, and several patches of mould. In a century, I fantasized, it might be completely overgrown.

Kindred proved a dab hand at reviving old equipment. Whether rousing inactive chips or goading static programs into action, he worked calmly and coolly, issuing instructions to either Cotton or myself, whoever happened to be nearest when need arose. The three of us soon had a sizeable chunk of the abandoned level functioning again. Lights blazed; air stirred; electrons flowed.

The mouth of one of the giant freight elevators opened with a cadaverous sigh. Cotton and I stepped inside. Kindred followed a moment later, after instructing the machines to resume their dormancy the moment we were safely at the bottom. He also swept the floor clean of footprints behind us. The trail would end there, in that cold and empty ruin.

"Does this place have a name?" Cotton asked him as the elevator shuddered and began to descend.

"Samagrinig," he said.

"Never heard of it. I recognized Iesia and Baskaba as we passed through, but we were running blind most of the way. There wasn't time to consult the charts."

The names meant nothing to me, but I didn't interrupt

the conversation to interrogate them. I hoped to learn simply by letting them talk.

"Word reached me in Panaion," Kindred said. "I was in the middle of something, but I couldn't resist. The trail was close, and still warm. Hot, even. Most people were running from it, but you know that's not my way."

"Huw's notorious," Cotton said to me with prideful tones. "We don't have tornados down here, obviously, but he'd be chasing them if we did. It's a miracle he hasn't been sucked up yet."

He shrugged off her concern. "I'm in no more danger than anyone else. Less, probably. Statistically speaking, the chances of the Director striking twice in one place are minimal. Once satiated, it moves on. You're more likely to be hit anywhere other than where the ground is still smoking."

"Don here thinks it's protecting the mine's alien origins."

"He might be right."

"He might be wrong, too."

"We're all wrong until proven otherwise." Kindred granted me a conspiratorial wink.

"Any word of Trelayne?" she asked him.

"Still obsessed, I see."

"Now more than ever."

"Well, as it happens," he said, "I was on Panaion for just that very reason. But come on, kid. You haven't told me what you're doing here yet."

"It's all connected, Huw. One thing leads to the other."

With a groan and a shudder, the elevator ground to a halt. Kindred stood at the fore of the carriage, waiting for the heavy metal doors to divide, but Cotton and I hadn't forgotten the lessons we'd learned during our headlong flight. We waited well back until we were sure what lay beyond.

The opening doors revealed nothing but blackness. Kindred produced a torch from his pack and snapped it on. Stepping out of the pool of light spilling from the carriage, he blazed the way for us, pacing out a rectangular narthex more than ten meters square, lined with blocky, functional control panels. All were inactive until he prodded them into life.

I stepped out with Cotton and breathed deeply of thick, dry air. A distant subsonic rumble through the floor and walls made itself felt in my bones. Not until Kindred once again brought the machines to life did I realize its source.

First came lights, flickering like tiny eyes all across the control boards, then a whir as two panels on opposite walls slid up into the ceiling, revealing windows to the mine-face beyond. Floodlights flared somewhere above us, shining powerfully into a hellish landscape, one where heavy gases roiled and tore at exposed rock. I stepped back, reminded of footage I had seen of worlds in the grip of a runaway greenhouse effect. Subjected to crushing pressure, powerful acids, and soaring temperatures, the surfaces of such planets are flatly inhospitable to human life. Somehow, in the belly of Gevira, such a place existed–and thus I perceived why this level had been abandoned. Something must have gone wrong, I told myself. An industrial accident must have created this vile cocktail, or else a misguided exploratory probe had found a pocket of primordial fumes, preserved in a toxic bubble since the world's creation. Rather than clean it up, the manager of the level had ordered it contained and the facility abandoned. Given the extensive reach of the Geviran excavations, there had undoubtedly been greener pastures elsewhere.

So I told myself as I stared out into that foul, turbulent soup. Half-visible through the murk, frozen in attitudes of abandonment, giant diggers crouched over great rents in the rock, waiting for the command to resume their labor. Despite their Brobdignagian size, I was amazed they hadn't corroded away to nothing–as my own certainties were to corrode in due course.

But I am leaping ahead of myself–something that becomes harder to avoid, the deeper one gets in the mines. By this point in our journey, I had no idea how deep I actually was. My heaviness had changed several times during the previous day, so much so that I had begun to ignore what every member of the Guild knows instinctively from birth: one's mass, and the ability to determine from apparent fluctuations in weight the strength of a gravitational field.

A door led from the narthex into the level's maze of airlocks and workstations, but the three of us made no immediate move to explore further. The tortured view had captured us, and the rumbling of the wind challenged us to speak only that which was most profound. It came as no surprise, then, when Cotton broke the silence to tell Kindred of her fate.

"I'm going to die, Huw. That's where all this starts and ends."

Kindred turned to face her, worry openly displayed on his face. "How do you know that?"

"I saw my own corpse. Don showed it to me. There were two access codes in its memory dump."

"That's why he's along for the ride, then." His ready sympathy was for me, now. "I thought you two were–"

"No," she said, before I too could disabuse him of the notion. "But he's important, I think. Everything is. It has to be. Otherwise I wouldn't be here. I'd be hiding under a bunk somewhere, keeping my head down. Or in a rundown dive, drinking myself to death."

"That would be in character."

"Don't joke with me, Huw. This is serious."

"Of course it is. I'm sorry."

"You need to know something," she said. "You both do. About the body."

"It's a fake?" I asked, startled by the way hope suddenly leapt at the thought.

"No, Don. It's real. But it's not random; it's not the kind of thing the mine throws up sometimes, for no reason at all. It's a message."

Kindred's mighty brows bunched into a frown. "From whom?"

"From me."

He folded his arms and shook his head. "Don't joke with *me*, Emma. Not about this."

"I'm serious, Huw. If you let me explain–"

"No. I don't want to hear it."

"I do," said I. "We may not understand it, but I think she's telling the truth."

She wasn't the only one. I could see that mortality was hanging heavily on her, but the excitement I had seen earlier was also present. The certainty of her death was not entirely a millstone.

She smiled with a mixture of gratitude and grief. "It takes a newbie to cut through the crap, sometimes. Forget the mines, Huw: we tie *ourselves* in knots, and then we have no idea how to untangle them. That's us, Huw, and that's me, and that's how it's always going to end. We live by the sword. We know what's coming."

The light was brightest in her corner of the control room. A halo seemed to surround her form, drawing the eye irresistibly to her. Even Kindred couldn't look away forever.

"Tell me," he said, his voice surprisingly soft from such a large frame.

"I've been chasing Trelayne and his answers half my life," she said. "I've followed clues from one side of the mine to the other. It's consumed my every thought as long as I've known you. Like the freehold miners, few of my seams pay out. Fool's gold and quartz are all I ever seem to find. But I know the mother lode is out there somewhere, and there are only two ways I'm ever going to stop looking for Trelayne and his answers. One is if the search kills me first. The other is if it doesn't.

"The moment I saw my body, I knew it had finally come down to one or the other. When I checked the memory dump, I knew exactly which one."

I thought I saw Kindred wince, but his face was too deep in shadow to be sure of it.

I simply stared at her in amazement. Two access codes and a name: that was all it took to send her hell-bent through the mines, trusting in the Möbius strip of time to lead her along the path her future self had already followed–the future self who for some presently unknown reason had sent her own body back to herself, both as a clue and in order to complete the loop.

"My own corpse," she said, "is proof that I've found–that I *will* find–the mother load. Trelayne, answers, everything. After so many dead ends and disappointments, it takes a clue like that to convince me, and I'll follow it without question, wherever it takes me. I die, but I die complete. That's why I'm here. That's why–" She stopped and pressed the back of her wrist to her mouth. She swallowed twice, then dropped her hand, continued: "That's why, Huw, I need you to tell me everything you learned on Panaion."

"No." Kindred shook his head. "Don't ask me to do that."

"I have to, and you will tell me."

"No!" He paced one circuit around the control room, glaring at her as he passed.

"In a sense, you've already done it."

"Never."

One slab-like fist punched at the switches he had brought to life. The door leading from the narthex deeper into the level hissed open. Stale air rolled over us all, but that wasn't enough to prevent Kindred stalking off into the darkness, away from Cotton and her demands.

"Huw!"

He ignored her. His bear-like shoulders were bunched and tight. The doors slid shut behind him, and Cotton sagged.

I thought that I should offer her something, but I knew not what. Reassurance? Space? I was unwillingly embroiled in their shared history, when all I desired were answers.

Looking back on it now, on her entreaty and Kindred's brooding frustration, I suppose she felt the same.

"I'm sorry," she said.

"It's okay."

"We had–Huw and I had one of those things that is never really alive but never really dies either."

"You don't need to explain."

"I guess I did warn you," she said, "about getting tangled up in this."

"You did, and I'm still here." I essayed a weak smile. "So are you, if that gives you any reason to be hopeful."

She returned the smile. "Of what?"

"I'm not sure."

The only sound for a long time was the howling of the acrid wind.

Seeking to occupy my mind with more than just idle introspection, I followed an instinct. If Cotton's bizarre story about sending her own body back as a message were true, it wasn't *entirely* true. She hadn't mentioned an accomplice, and I knew she had at least one. Calling up the image of the man who had placed her body in its final resting place, I studied it with fresh eyes. Again the hint of familiarity in that cheekbone and nose. Comparing the figure against Kindred's, however, proved fruitless. Not only was Kindred's face an entirely different structure, but his physical form was considerably larger. There was no possible way the two could be said to match. Thus I dismissed that theory, plausible though it had initially seemed.

I had other threads to follow. Restless and chilled, I began to pace around the control room as Kindred had done.

"Tell me about Terminus," I said.

She looked up with red eyes, caught momentarily off-guard. "About what?"

"You know what, Cotton. You mentioned it moments before we were almost shot, and your friend brought it up twice. He asked me if I was *with* Terminus. Should I feel left out of something?"

"No," she said, leaning her hip against one of the control panels, folding her arms and crossing her legs. She couldn't have looked more defensive if she tried. "Terminus is an organization–an affiliation might be better–that stretches right across the mines. People don't join so much as become absorbed into it. If you ask enough questions, maybe even answer a few, and if you survive long enough, you'll eventually find yourself hooked up to it."

"So Kindred is part of Terminus," I said, "and so are you."

"Yes–but don't look at me like that. I'm not a spy, skulking and thieving from your friends back home. I was just passing through, looking for answers. Trelayne's trail had gone cold. It helps, sometimes, to flail about at random."

"Who do you report to?"

"No one. That is, no boss or anyone like that. I talk to other agents when the opportunity arises; there are channels for passing information back and forth; sometimes, although very rarely, we'll leak something to the public, if we think it's in their best interest."

"So if you knew what the Director was, you wouldn't keep it a secret."

"I don't see why we would. Terminus exists to find out who built the mines and how they managed it–a living architect would be the Holy Grail for most of us–but making the mines safer for everyone is the most important thing of all. I'd trade a proper map for that, at the moment."

"Are you suggesting that the mines haven't been completely charted yet?"

"It's a big job."

"But you've been at it for hundreds of years. Gevira must be riddled through like Emmental cheese!"

She laughed. "Donaldan Lough, you are *such* a newb. Where do you think we are right now? Not Gevira, surely."

"Where else would we be?"

"You heard Huw. We're on Samagrinig, and that could be halfway across the universe from where we started."

"Very funny."

"I'm serious. What do you think that is outside the windows?"

I ceased my pacing, a familiar sense of anger and humiliation swelling like cancer in my breast. This new mockery revealed her to be no better than Officer Gluis, a fact made all the worse by our joint endurance of the previous day's crises. The very moment one of her compatriots joined us, thus forming a bloc–if a fractious one–against my minority of one, she expelled me from her confidence and would throw my lot, no doubt, among the mine's other newbies.

Is that how she saw me, I wondered–as fodder for the Geviran mines, as mere sport for the Director?

"Don't play me for a fool, Cotton. I'm not the naïf you take me to be."

"I'm not taking you for anything. I'm just telling you the way it is."

"That we've traveled from one world to another by–by elevator? Next you'll propose that the Director is an invisible white rabbit or that we should ask directions from the Queen of Hearts!"

"What the hell are you talking about?" Her anger was rapidly becoming the equal of mine. "You said no one was asking the questions that need to be answered. Well, maybe it's because, like you, they don't like answers. The first thing everyone in Terminus does is the math. It tells you that the mine contains enough people to fill a dozen planets. The mine exports sufficient energy to light up a solar system. The mass of every mineral extracted comes to several Jovian worlds. Where do you think all that comes from? From a tiny backwater world like Gevira? You can say that the numbers are lying, but deep down you'll know that it's really you, lying to yourself, and the sooner you accept it, the happier and crazier you'll be."

"Like you?"

"Damn straight like me. Do you have a better solution?"

We stood nose to nose, yelling at each other. My fury

was so great that the cover I had carefully maintained seemed an irrelevant thing beside the impulse to prove to this woman that there was more to the world than the mines and her obsession. Far across the gulfs of space glittering civilizations reached, connected by the Great Ship Fleets and the Guild to which I myself belonged. It has taken millennia to establish and unimaginable efforts to maintain. My ache to impress upon her the impossibility of a network such as the one she described–in which those empty gulfs could be crossed in a matter of moments, with no more effort than the pushing of a button–could not be measured.

Somehow I subsumed that impulse. I thought of you, Master Catterson, and the ranks of Guildsmen depending on my steadfastness. I would not betray my vows solely to impress a madwoman, no matter what revelations she promised. Such a promise was tainted, anyway, if this proposition was a taste of that to come.

"The only solution I have," I said in level tones, "is to retrace our steps and return to the surface. Once we're out of the mines, we and the people around us will be safe from the Director. We'll have time to examine your theory with clinical dispassion and see where it leads us. We won't need to cower like criminals in the dark, lending credence to propositions we would never entertain in the clear daylight. What do you say?"

"I can't leave here until I find Trelayne," she said firmly. "He has all the answers I need."

"What if he turns out to be nothing but a rumour? You'll have wasted your final hours chasing the ghost of hope."

"It's no more a ghost than I am. Look at me. You've seen my corpse. I've told you what it means. How much more proof do I need?"

"That aliens learned how to connect worlds by tissue paper and a bit of pluck? A lot more proof than your word on it, I'm afraid."

"What about Huw and all of Terminus? What about the

evidence of your senses?" She turned away with palms pressed to her forehead as though containing a migraine. "Oh, Don, you can't possibly be so ignorant about *everything*!"

"Indeed he can't, Emma," said Huw Kindred from behind me. "Don't say any more. I think he's heard quite enough."

I turned to find Kindred standing in the entrance we had come through with a compact firearm in his hand. He must have looped around through the empty level and returned to the elevator cluster via a corridor we had not noticed. That, however, was the least of my present concerns. The firearm was pointed directly at me. It looked tiny, like a toy, but I was convinced of its lethality.

"What is the meaning of this?" I spluttered.

"Just step away from her, flyboy, and don't make any sudden moves. That's it. Put your hands above your head. Now, do you want to tell her where you're from or shall I?"

It's no exaggeration to say that every muscle in my body went rigid.

"Have you gone completely insane, Huw?" Cotton went to put herself between us, but Kindred's hefty forearm pushed her back.

"I was thinking, Emma," he said, "about what you told me. Your corpse, the deal you made with yourself, the information you want from me. I had just about decided to give in to you, when it came to me. None of this is real. It's a fake, like this guy suggested." The gun shifted to indicate me, then returned once more to target the center of my chest. "Only he's the one behind it. It's a trick, Emma, and you fell for it."

My thoughts moved at lightning speed. I was ready for either fight or flight the very moment an opportunity presented itself.

"It's not a trick," I said.

"Shut up."

"Are you going to tell *me* to shut up too, Huw?" Cotton stared up at him with a pained look on her face. "I can tell the difference. He's not lying. Why would he? What's he got to gain?"

"Everything," said Kindred, eying me with intense animosity along the gun's sights. "He's a spacer."

Her gaze darted to me, then back to Kindred. "What?"

"Ask yourself, Emma. Why *does* he seem so ignorant? He's not just a newbie; he's after everything we've learned about the mines for bosses elsewhere. That's why he's hitched up with you. He wants answers and he doesn't care how he gets them. You and your obsession would have given him everything he wanted, if I hadn't come along to stop you."

"No," she said. The blue sky of her certainty was beginning to cloud over with doubt. "I'm not that gullible."

"Really? Remember that time you tunneled a mile into a volcano just because someone had told you Trelayne had left a memory dump there? You almost died, and for what?"

"Nothing, but this is different."

"Sure it is. Not satisfied with all the stars, the spacers want what we've got too." His lips tightened and I braced myself for the gun to fire. "What flag do you fly under, star man? Whose picture do you salute each morning?"

I would never tell him. "You've made a mistake, Kindred. I'm not who you think I am."

"Don't," he snarled. "You're all the same. You and your fucking empires. You can't keep your noses out of the Structure. You're vermin."

That struck a nerve. "And what are you? This place–whatever it is–it's amazing, but you no more than occupy it. You're squatters, that's all. Humanity has become rats in the walls."

"The Director, Huw," Cotton persisted, defending my lie without knowing it. "It chased us. How could he fake that?"

"Coincidence. Or some spacer trick."

"Now you sound paranoid."

"Do I?"

They were shouting at each other now. "It's my decision, Huw. Put the gun down–"

"You're crazy to trust this astronaut!"

"–put the gun down and tell me what I need to know."

"I'm not going to let you kill yourself!"

They were as distracted as they were ever going to get. Turning sideways to present a smaller target, I moved suddenly to my left. Kindred's gun arm went to follow me but collided with Cotton, putting his aim off. He fired anyway, and the discharge was deafeningly loud. I ducked automatically, unharmed, and ran.

Ran through the door he had come through, heading not for the exit–the doors would take too long to open–but for the route I suspected he had followed. He had left the portal ajar, and I threw myself headlong into the darkness on the other side. Two shots followed me, but Kindred's aim was poor. I was fast and desperate where he was big and conflicted. My lead was the only advantage I had. I was determined to keep it as long as I could.

My eyes adjusted to the darkness, picking out faint edges in infrared and the flaming patches where Kindred had walked. I stuck to those footprints to throw him off even though it slowed me down. Two sharp turns put walls between me and the door, so when his voice boomed out at me at least I knew I wouldn't be shot in the back.

"Come here, sky boy. You can't hide forever!"

No, I answered to myself, but I can loop around to the control room and hope to get out the exit before either of you catch up.

"Don't run, Don." Cotton's voice from further away, and falling behind. "It looks bad if you won't even try to explain."

"What's to explain, Emma? He's a rocket jockey, and he's not getting his hands on the mines."

Kindred was hard on my heels. Switching back to visible light, I saw torchlight dancing at the periphery of my vision.

I realised then that I had made a mistake. Kindred wasn't relying on infra-red, so my heat-signature was irrelevant. Putting on a burst of speed, I managed to gain an extra second or two, dodging and weaving down corridors and rooms that had not seen human life for a decade or more. My internal compass–still working even if my gravity-sense was addled–told me that I had looped almost completely around and was already returning to the control room. I had to act soon or hand myself over to Kindred.

A T-junction loomed out of the darkness. His footsteps went left, so I ducked right and pressed myself flat against the wall, suppressing every audible breath. My heart pounded in time with his approach. The thudding of his feet sounded as loud as thunder.

My slavish pursuit of his path had lulled him into believing that I would turn left. Timing my move for the moment he reached the junction, I struck up and out with my left elbow. The blow carried my entire weight plus his considerable momentum, and struck him hard between the eyes. His head snapped back while the rest of his body kept moving. Loosened from his fingers, the torch continued forward into the wall. Darkness descended with a smash.

All was momentarily a confusion of limbs and senses. The glare of the torch had blinded me to the entire spectrum of frequencies and the impact jarred my body, making me feel as though I'd been hit by a pile-driver. I staggered away, nursing my shoulder and blinking in confusion. Behind me, I could hear Kindred struggling to cling to consciousness, which in itself was amazing. His skull must have been made of rock! Then he fell silent, either giving up the fight or becoming alert enough to realize that the sound was giving away his location. I was still seeing stars, but I turned and readied myself to do battle with him in the way I had been trained.

Something moved in the air. Something impossible to define and completely without sound, but I knew beyond certainty that it had come and gone. I blinked and tuned my ears to their highest sensitivity. Nothing apart from my heartbeat and shallow breathing. Kindred was making no noise at all. I felt forward with my left foot, seeking his inert body. Nothing. My left hand patted the wall on that side through a blur of musculoskeletal pain. There was the intersection. My feet crunched on broken glass: the torch. Here, then, was where Kindred must have fallen.

He wasn't there. He wasn't anywhere. My eyes cleared and the glowing pool of warmth where he had briefly lain became visible, but no more than that. Kindred had vanished into thin air, as though he had never existed.

A sequence of terrible logic unspooled in my mind.

In the dark, for a moment, silent and unseen by my dazzled eyes, no one had been observing him.

In that moment, the Director had struck.

I took a deep, sobbing breath and backed away from the volume of space he had occupied, as though distance alone would spare me the same fate.

A glowing shape appeared behind me–humanoid, burning hot. I spun, moaning in fear and raised my hands in an impotent gesture. All my training counted for naught in that moment. I am ashamed to say, Master Catterson, that I was completely unmanned.

"Huw? Huw, is that you?"

It was Cotton, of course. My horror had been so great that I didn't hear the footsteps approaching and failed to recognize her silhouette. My fear had magnified that glowing shape until it seemed monstrously large.

"He's gone," I forced out.

She rushed forward, eyes seeing me standing over the pool of heat where Kindred had fallen. "No." Her mind performed the kind of mathematics she had urged me to perform, earlier. "No!" Not realizing yet that I had only witnessed Kindred's demise, not killed him myself, and seeing me reaching for her in turn, she assumed the worst and lashed out.

I cannot say, Master Catterson, what my precise intentions were, in that dark hour. I can only say that I was taken by surprise, and so Cotton succeeded where Kindred had failed. The blow caught me in the left temple. Stars flared again, and I dropped to my knees. The last things I experienced before blackness engulfed me were Cotton's glowing shape looming over me, and the raw, anguished sound of her scream.

I woke an hour later on my right side in the control room with my wrists and ankles securely tied. I ached all over, and my mouth was desperately dry, but for the moment I was glad that Cotton had not slit my throat and left me for dead. She must have dragged me there herself, over some considerable time. I am small, like all my brothers in the Guild, but not light.

Her voice came from somewhere behind me.

"It's true, isn't it?"

I wrenched myself to a sitting position and twisted on my buttocks to face her. She was crouched in a corner with Kindred's pistol on her lap. Its size was a better match for her petite hands. That it wasn't yet pointed at me I took to be another good sign.

The question, though, was not.

"Is what true?"

She rolled her eyes. "That you're a spacer–astronaut, sky boy, rocket jockey, whatever."

"We were all spacers once, Cotton."

"Just give me a straight answer." Tears eased freely from eyes as though from a surfeit of grief. She wasn't weeping, but I perceived that she had been. "Under the circumstances, I think you owe me that."

"If you'll be straight with me in return," I said, "regarding the mines."

"You must be kidding."

"Put yourself in my shoes. If you were about to be shot, wouldn't you want to know the truth?"

The muscles of her jaw clenched. Her mouth twisted into an ugly line.

"All right," she said. "You go first."

I took a moment to compose my thoughts. The reasoning behind my offer was simple. Whatever she told me, I could transmit that information to you, Master Catterson. The broadcast would only take a second and be undetectable to her, so at least my death at her hands would not be for nothing.

But breaking my vows did not come easily. My heart quailed at the very thought of telling the truth, no matter the circumstances.

"The Guild of the Great Ships," I began, slowly at first. "That's who I work for. And yes, I was sent here to investigate the mines. But if you think about it, I haven't really lied to you. I just asked questions. You assumed on your own that I was a newbie, along with everyone else."

"Stop," she said. "Stop talking now."

The gun was in her hand and I was close enough that even her shaky aim couldn't miss. But I didn't obey.

"I was born in orbit above a world called Alfvén IV. It shines like a diamond at its poles, but the temperate regions are green, so green it hurts your eyes to look at it. My name was given to me by my hub-mothers, who raised me until I turned five and commenced training to be a Guildsman. I was one of 20 new recruits. We all looked alike. That we were clones was never hidden from us, not from the moment of our births. I was proud to be like my brothers, and we never mixed each other up. I knew we were all different on the inside. We all dreamed the same thing, in our own ways: of boarding one of the Great Ships and voyaging to the stars ourselves. That was our destiny. There we would find our true home."

Her tears dried up, but my words did not. I told her everything, Master Catterson: of my graduation to full service and my first missions with the Guild; of promotion through the ranks and individual training in your capable hands; of the gradual accumulation of data concerning Gevira and the mission to ascertain the facts behind them; of being specifically chosen by you to infiltrate the mine and relay what I found there. I told her (as I tell you now) that I felt safe revealing so much to her because I knew that in the short time remaining to her she was unlikely to pursue the matter with what higher authorities existed in the mines. Let the spacers visit and explore, I told her. What harm can come of it? We are scientists, not conquerors. It is the very nature of the mines to make people curious. Perhaps we can find answers that others before us have not.

Last of all, I admitted that I would feel duty bound to communicate any discovery concerning new means of traversing interstellar space. If the shape of the mine was as she said, why should it be hoarded and not shared by all? What possible reason would stay my lips, were I to survive beyond the next ten minutes?

"How confident do you feel on that score?" she asked.

"I'm afraid I can't read your thoughts." I struggled to find a comfortable position on the hard, cold floor. My left side still ached from my collision with Kindred, and my temple throbbed with a bloody heat. Keeping both arms behind my back was proving increasingly painful. "Would you care to share them with me?"

She avoided meeting my gaze directly. "Well, I was telling the truth about the mines, which puts us in a bit of a bind. I don't want to shoot you in cold blood, but I'm not convinced I shouldn't."

"Do you think Kindred would have?"

That made her look at me again.

"It's possible," she said, "although I think he was angrier at me than you."

"I think so too. I'm sure he wasn't going to tell you about Trelayne."

"Say we're no worse off and I really will shoot you now."

"As you wish. Do I need to point out that while I might have been a fake–"

"My body was definitely real. That had occurred to me, Donnie Boy–or whatever your name is."

"It's as you know it. I swear."

She stared at me for a long while, and I was content with that. I wanted her attending to me as the person in whose company she had run from Gevira, not building up the courage to shoot someone she had redefined as an enemy combatant.

"If I let you go," she said, "are you going to follow me to Trelayne?"

"No," I promised her, "but I will come with you if you ask me to."

She bowed her head, and I wondered if it was because she was weeping again. Her shoulders shook, and although she made no easily distinguished sound, it did appear to me that she was in distress.

When she looked up, however, I saw that it was in fact silent laughter that gripped her.

"You've got a fucking nerve," she said. But she did come over and release my hands and feet from their bindings, so I felt I had no grounds on which to argue that particular point.

The first thing I did upon my release was assuage my thirst with water provisioned from Kindred's pack. Fortunately, he had left it behind before barreling off in pursuit of me. Cotton has charge of it–if I want something, I have to ask–but by tacit agreement it seems that we won't be parting in Samagrinig, as she now calls this level, so his abandoned resources are fair game. Unless she changes her mind, I will be going at least as far Panaion, the place Kindred went to pursue his mysterious lead. From there, the map is blank.

Therefore, Master Catterson, the second thing I have done is prepare this account for you. Cotton says that we are far from Gevira, not without conviction, and if that is true then my earlier reasoning is tragically flawed. If the mines truly are scattered across numerous far-flung worlds, this document might never reach you. My mission should be to return to a point where the relays to the Great Ship will pick up my packets and convey them to you.

I am, however, yet to be wholly convinced. I need evidence before committing myself solely to that belief. For all I know, Terminus is a counter-insurgency group designed to seed misinformation in the minds of those seeking the truth. Until I have proof that I am not the one being misled, I will operate on the assumption that nothing has changed, and the relay drones on Gevira will detect any transmission I dispatch and pass it on to you.

I send these words to you, therefore, in the hope that a reply will be swift on their heels. Your advice is sorely needed, Master Catterson, by this Guildsman far out of his depth.

(Thus concludes my second transmission since meeting the Terminus agent E. C. Cotton. Everything that follows is taken from notes compiled during our subsequent expedition and transcripts of pertinent conversations.)

<THIRD ACCOUNT: AIDE-MÉMOIRES>

Kindred secreted his charts and other data in memory wire woven into his pack's hardy fabric. Cotton knew where to look and how to access the data thanks to her familiarity with him and his methods. I am building up a picture of him as a rugged idealist, an academic born into the body of a giant. For all his violent outrage, aimed at me and spacers in general, I am certain that he was no trained fighter. I am reassured, therefore, that Terminus is not necessarily a paramilitary group devoted to defending the mines from incursion.

The chart reveals that 17 levels lie between us and Panaion. (I refuse to refer to them as "planets." Levels or zones they will remain until I can be convinced otherwise. The truth of the mines, if such it is, must take time to sink in.) Cotton pores over the complicated map for an hour, seeking a shorter route. Her tension grows as the futility of the exercise becomes increasingly certain. Seventeen is the minimum, so seventeen it must be.

The knowledge weighs heavily on me too. Seventeen times will the Director strike before we reach our destination—and who knows what will happen there, when we attempt to stay?

But there is no turning back. My mission, until I am told otherwise, is to follow the mystery, and if Trelayne truly has the answers I seek, then there is no other clear course open to me.

The pool of heat where Kindred fell must have long dissipated into the ambient chill, but it burns in my mind still, like a ghost. I fear it will haunt me forever.

We are both exhausted, physically and emotionally. When we set out, we switch off the lights behind us and return the control room to its endless slumber.

The freight elevator seems to take forever. During our ascent, Cotton begins to explain her perception of the mine's topology, sketching crudely with her toe on the dusty floor as she does so.

"It helps to think of it in terms of horizontal and vertical, even though the topology is obviously much more complicated than that.

"There are two different sorts of shafts, too: those that move ordinarily through space, and those that cut through it. The ordinary sorts are no different to those in any mine, connecting faces drilled horizontally out of the earth. All the shafts leading down from the surface of Gevira are this sort."

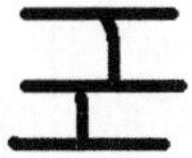

"We call the second sort transcendents because they cut through multidimensional space. Either end of the shaft can be literally anywhere–on the other side of the same planet, or on the other side of the universe. It's hard to tell, because it takes so long to connect the dots by conventional means.

"You probably haven't realized it, but we've been using transcendents ever since we left Gevira. Every time you use an access code, that's how you're travelling."

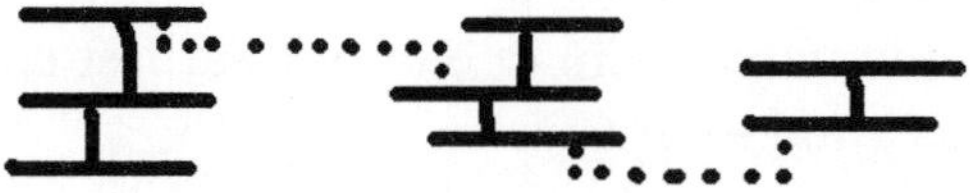

"Now, transcendents are usually charted horizontally because it makes sense to think of them that way. But they can move vertically too. A vertical sequence of ordinary and transcendent shafts is called a stack."

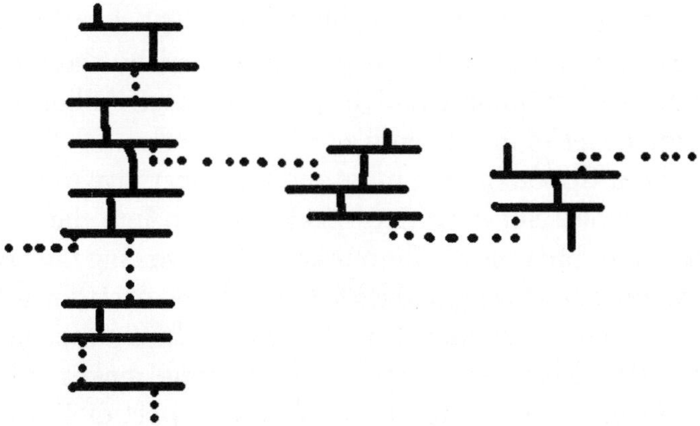

"Calling them stacks is more than just a convention. To each there's a top–always a planetary surface like the one on Gevira, a different planet for each stack–and there's also a bottom. The bottoms are–well, they're much harder to describe. But what you get is always the same, broadly speaking."

I press her to elaborate, but she insists that seeing is the only way to believe it.

The freight elevator chooses this moment to arrive, and she scrubs out the sketch with the sole of her shoe.

My mind is left in a tangle of horizontals and verticals, shafts and stacks, ordinaries and transcendents. Could any of this be true? That she seems wholly convinced of it is no proof at all. My feelings on the matter remain sharply divided.

When I ask her how big the mine is, she is similarly evasive.

"We call it the Structure," she concludes as we summon the carriage to take us elsewhere.

I recognize the name from one of our earliest conversations. It seems as good as any.

Our first port of call is the last we traversed on the way to the level called Samagrinig. The Director has already killed there in our wake, and we brace ourselves for a repeat when we emerge from the transcendent shaft.

None occurs. We stand blinking in the light of this vibrant space, surrounded by people untouched by the menace of our very existence, and I am momentarily filled with the urge never to move again.

But Cotton has the map, and the imperative to continue is irresistible. Not daring to speak, we step into the next shaft and wait breathlessly for our arrival. By voicing the hope that the curse has been lifted we fear bringing it back down upon us again. That is patently absurd, of course, but cannot be helped.

The dashing of that unvoiced hope makes us feel all the worse. As we step into the second port of 17, cries and alarms break out almost immediately. A woman has been killed, crushed with inexplicable force by something unseen even as she nestled in her lover's arms. He was spared.

Cotton and I exchange guilty looks. Can any knowledge be worth this?

To that question, we both know the answer.

Hurriedly, she uses the access codes to summon the next carriage.

Cotton recites the names as we travel from one to the next.

. . . *Emkemi, Idris, Taftefiah* . . .

With each transfer, the list grows one name shorter. Soon we know the last dozen off by heart, but the recitation continues. It is a mantra composed of meaningless syllables that expunge from our minds all other consideration.

. . . *Chanoch, Tantemy, Dynamis* . . .

We are no longer thinking creatures. We are electrons caught in a wire, moons tidally locked in a shared orbit, entangled particles without self-determination or morality. We have no care for anything beyond that list of names for, temporarily, that is all that exists for us.

. . . *Itmon, Sarha-Olam, Yeshaya* . . .

The human race becomes an abstract concept in which all distinctions are blurred. Spacers, miners, Terminus agents, individuals–all are meaningless. What are one or two deaths on such a large canvass? How can we be blamed for the screams and panic? We are just dots on a line, dots moving slowly from one abstract to another.

. . . *Panaion.*

<THIRD ACCOUNT: FRAGMENT>

Writing this account from what seems a place of sanctuary, at least for the time being, I look back on our arrival with no small amount of chagrin. This is the level where Huw Kindred had come seeking information on Trelayne. (Cotton is pursuing that information while I compose this portion of my account and prepare myself for what lies ahead.) It seemed unreasonable to expect that we would find what we needed immediately, so the two of us were prepared for a slaughter on a grand scale before we could move on.

On that score we were to be relieved, but not after a moment's panic on seeing an entrance hall filled with hundreds of people. Conveyances in their dozens whirred along maglev tracks and even through the air above us. The hall was huge, nearly 50 meters high. A reverberating hum filled the space, created spontaneously by so many people speaking at once.

So great was the throng that the Director's first and only act was not noticed for some minutes. The absence of one solitary person among so many came to light only when his luggage was found unattended in a niche, from which a nearby stall-owner reported seeing him enter but not exit. Security guards were called but no tumult erupted. The scene was investigated, the luggage impounded, and that was the sum of it.

Cotton and I waited five minutes for the Director to strike again. When no one else was afflicted by a visitation from the mine's deadly apparition, it dawned on us that the threat had passed.

"Could it be so easy solved?" I asked as we moved away from the elevator cluster from which we had emerged and blended into the crowd.

"Things rarely are," she said, "but I'll take this one if it's going."

The moment I had stepped from the carriage I knew that the stack called Panaion was different from the others we had visited. That impression was confirmed as we explored its buttressed halls and vine-covered thoroughfares. Tens of thousands of people live here in quarters that seem palatial by Geviran standards. (I say "Geviran" now, master, simply out of convenience. My null hypothesis remains that we are ensconced within that planetary body and have never left it.) Its air is rich with the exhalations of life and industry, both of which thrive under a moderate gravity allowing considerable feats of engineering and endurance. Citizens wave from terraces to passers-by far below. Hawkers call and chant in a melange of languages and pidgins. Musicians play. There are children in abundance, and schools to educate them in both science and the arts, as practised by those who live in the mines.

Cotton and I walked wide-eyed for an hour, seeking the residence Huw Kindred had occupied while in Panaion. The rooms had already been let out, for which I was secretly glad, but we found others nearby. Cotton paid with Kindred's credit, and a shadow passed over her delicate features. When the transaction was concluded, she locked herself in her suite and left me to my own devices. It never seemed to cross her mind that I might wander away and never come back.

I did wander, aimlessly and in unrelieved amazement at the size of the habitat. It truly was an underground city, and any actual mining that took place was kept at a distant remove. I imagined generations of miners and their contraptions hollowing out this vast space, then leaving it to their descendants to inherit and make into anything they desired. The machines dug for riches while a more gentle life blossomed in their wake.

When I returned to the rooms, Cotton was waiting for me.

"From here on, it's guesswork," she said. "Huw is–was–a creature of habit. He'll have left dumps for himself and other Terminus agents to find. But they won't be lying around in the open. I've been poring over the maps of Panaion, looking for the kind of places that would appeal to him. I've found three. The information we need could be in any of them, or none of them."

"All right," I said. "Let's find out."

"No," she said, putting a hand on my chest. "I'm doing this alone. You've got somewhere else to be."

I braced myself for an argument. To have come this far, to have risked so much, and to be turned away was unacceptable.

"I mean *down*, space boy," she quickly corrected me. "You need to see the bottom for yourself or else you'll never accept anything Trelayne says about the Structure. I've given up on you taking me at my word."

Whatever she thinks is waiting in the lower levels of the Panaion stack, I could only agree to undertake this side-mission. To refuse would sound like closed-mindedness, or even cowardice, and if I did indeed learn more about the nature of the mines along the way, all the better.

Cotton divided Kindred's supply of concentrates in two and shrugged the pack back onto her shoulders.

"Just don't stay down there too long," she warned me before we took our leave of each other. "It might be months before you come back here–or you might return before we arrived, which would be really messy."

She meant it as a joke, but I didn't laugh.

We parted without shaking hands or embracing. I watched her blend into the crowds of Panaion with only a mild apprehension. She had Kindred's charts in the pack, so if she failed to return I would be set adrift.

I reassured myself that I could always ascend to the top of the stack and–if *my* theory was correct–simply travel across country to the entrance I had originally used. Or scouts from the Great Ship could be summoned and return me to you, Master Catterson. It unnerved me slightly that her wild speculations were infectious enough to rouse my anxiety on this score, but I suppressed all negative emotions and returned to my quarters to plan my exploration of Panaion. The truth will out. Of that I am completely certain.

I leave in an hour.

<THIRD ACCOUNT: AIDE-MÉMOIRES>

Panaion possesses eleven levels. Our rooms are in the sixth. I have created this partial map from interviewing those queuing alongside me for a carriage leading to the seventh level. Their testimonies conflict, and not one of them has visited the deepest level. I am informed that an access code is needed, as though it were a horizontal transcendent. I can only hope that the one Cotton provided me will work.

- minerals
- machinery and maintenance
- habitat
- minerals
- hydrocarbons (?)
- habitat (our rooms)
- minerals
- gas extraction
- diamonds (?)
- fusion
- (bottom–unknown)

Every miner I ask denies knowing the name "Gevira," except for one who referred to it as a backwater he had passed through some years back. I did not feel compelled to disavow him of that notion.

At last I am properly underway. The seventh level proves to be little different to anything I have seen before, only on a larger scale. The air is thick with particulate matter–the dust and microscopic debris inevitably produced as after-effect of mineral extraction–and many of the miners wear filtration masks to preserve their lungs. Distant pounding speaks to massive earthworks underway no great distance from here. Occasionally the earth literally moves beneath my feet.

The eighth level is cleaner, and home to a particular breed of miner. More chemist than engineer, they wear white field-suits that cover them from head to foot, rendering their sex unknown. I stand out among them, and feel that I am being stared at.

Before proceeding to the next level, I am compulsorily required to change my own clothing. The outfit I am given is preposterously thick and as heavy as lead. No one questions my decision to proceed, but I am given no encouragement to do so, either. There is a hardness to the silence of those around me. They do not answer my questions. All I receive are terse instructions sufficient to prepare me for my ongoing descent. Why these men and women have rejected conversation is unknown to me.

With trepidation, I confess, I step into the elevator shaft and continue downward.

The ninth level creaks like an aging sea-vessel. Its corridors are dark and cramped, and sparsely populated. No one greets me on my arrival. Only after stumbling around for some minutes do I find anyone at all: a dull-eyed technician who takes me without a word to what passes for an observation deck. There is nothing visible through the smoke-blackened porthole, and I soon desist peering through it. My guide has gone. I am left alone in the groaning habitat. The thick, sterile air is difficult breathe, and gravity seems impossibly to have increased, making my heavy suit even more burdensome. I resolve to leave, and set about searching for the next shaft.

The bottoms are, Cotton told me, *well, they're much harder to describe.*

At last I begin to understand why. I also understand the reticence of the miners who occupy these deep, inhuman spaces. Language cannot convey what our senses seem to be showing us. I say "seem" because I have yet to fully verify these impressions. The few facts at my disposal do suggest certain interpretations, but it would be irresponsible of me to offer them, colored in any way by the stranger theories that have occurred to me. Like Cotton's, they are almost too wild to be borne.

The eighth level processes and purifies noble gases in quantities unheard of in any terrestrial mine. Of this I am certain. The Guild only manages such productivity by grazing the turbulent atmosphere of a gas giant. They *could* be extracted terrestrially, theoretically, but then . . .

Diamonds are among the anomalous minerals exported en masse by the mines. They can be mined from hard rock via declines and stopes, but I saw nothing like that on the ninth level. Only now, as I stand in awe amid the plasma channels of the tenth level, does it occur to me that diamonds can also be found in the hearts of brown dwarfs.

Again, the Panaion stack *could* be a statistical fluke, except . . .

The tenth and penultimate level, if my eyes are to be believed, extracts energy from the convection of superheated gases in the belly of a small star.

Words have failed me. All I have is raw data to convey the wonders to be found in these mysterious mines. Images and such will have to suffice.

If this is the tenth level, what lies at the very bottom of the stack? What is that Cotton so adamantly insisted I should see? What phenomenon is replicated from stack to stack, in principle if not in detail?

My access codes work.

I descend to the final level alone, as I have traveled these last two legs. Previously, I have been accompanied by miners heading down for shifts or on their own personal excursions. Some chattered about mundane things; others stood in silence, wrapped in their thoughts and avoiding others' eyes. The Director has not struck since my arrival in Panaion, but I see the fear of it in their eyes. The deeper you go, the closer death stands to everyone. That was the wisdom whispered on Gevira–which I once dismissed as superstition–and it is writ large down here. Humans are transient. Perhaps humanity is transient too. Whoever–whatever–built these mind-bending spaces, the shock and awe of it defeats individual thought.

The eleventh level–the bottom of the Panaion stack–is a transparent dome just five meters wide fixed to the surface of an angular, rocky body, most likely an asteroid, tumbling with dizzying rapidity in the gulfs of space. I stand in that bubble of air and look up, fighting tears and vertigo, not knowing until this moment just how much I have missed the stars. These are no metaphor; they are as real I am. And I am a creature of the void, not the subterranean depths. I was born and raised to take stock of infinity. The minutiae of the mines almost made me forget it.

Despite this, I can only take so much of asteroid's incessant rotation. Closing my eyes, I call up blurry snapshots of the starscape and seek to identify my location. None of the constellations match those around Gevira. My stomach sinks, and I broaden my search. There is a band of stars in one section of the sky, perhaps a glimpse of a galactic band. I focus my search on that stellar artifact and seek a match in the Guild's extensive archives.

There is none. This sky is more than just anomalous for its position–purportedly–at the base of a mine. It is unknown to the Guild of the Great Ships.

I remember the ode to stars that I glimpsed in Samagrinig, where Huw Kindred died. That is what every stack has in common. A different sky. A different view of the universe.

I gaze one more time from my alien perspective–alone apart from a small, automated instrument package, scanning and blinking busily to itself–and then I retreat to the transcendent shaft that brought me here. My quest now leads me in entirely the opposite direction.

It takes me two full days to reach the top of the Panaion stack, and once there little more than a minute to ascertain that the stars visible from the planet's surface don't match those at the bottom of the mine.

I call for the Great Ship, but there is no answer.

My grand tour of the mines of Panaion has left me more bereft than ever–exactly the effect Cotton intended, I assume.

"You've just come out, right?"

The question takes me by surprise. I am being addressed by a grizzled old man leaning against the railing separating the mines from the wider world, cupping a fragrant cigarette in his right hand. My reply takes some time to formulate. It feels like weeks since last I spoke in conversation to anyone.

"Yes," I say. "There's a girl–we're looking for someone."

He nods and I feel as though I have uttered something completely unsurprising. "You know it's a one-way trip. If you go back down, I mean. You only get one chance to come out."

"I don't believe that," I say.

He shrugs and draws on his cigarette. "It's your decision not to."

I feel an irrational urge to argue with him. "How could it be possible? I didn't see the Director checking my ticket as I came out."

"How could any of this be possible?" His cool blue eyes hold me pinned, like a butterfly. "You've seen it. You've got that look they all have when they come up from the deep. The sooner you stop asking questions, the longer you'll last. Trust me." He broke into a cracked smile. "That's if you're still going down."

"I am." Cotton could be waiting for me even now, and Trelayne holds at least the possibility of answers to the questions I must keep asking. "It's my duty."

"Well, then." He flicks ash away from him and turns his attention back to the night sky.

"Goodbye."

He didn't answer, rudely, I thought. I understand only as I enter the mine's uppermost elevator complex–heading back to fusion arcs and air masquerading as fresh–that I intended that farewell for the stars, and he knew it better than I.

Cotton isn't in her rooms when I return to the sixth level. She has left no note. I have no choice but to wait for her, using Kindred's credit to buy food and a change of clothes. My old fieldsuit was left behind in the deeper levels, and the standard fare with which I have been issued is growing uncomfortable. I buy something sturdier, darker in color, almost black. It suits my mood.

I compose three draft accounts but erase them all. What is the point if they will not be received? I am cut off from the Guild for the first time in my life. I am completely alone.

I dream of stars spinning and galaxies tied in knots. My fellow Guildsmen walk past me with no recognition in their faces. I try to call their names, but my voice is stilled. I hear only the moaning of acid wind, and the creaking of bulkheads stressed almost to breaking-point by surging, lava tides.

In the middle of the seventh night she comes to me, letting herself into my quarters with a key I didn't know she possessed. She says nothing, and I am too sleep-befuddled to stop her getting into bed with me. I am lying on my side, curled like a child, and she fits herself to my curves and angles. She does nothing more than that, at first, and I lie in the silence with my heart pounding, thinking about what this means. I decide that I understand her. I know what her silence means.

Her quest was successful. She knows the way to Trelayne.

I cannot speak for her, but I know I will not return to sleep this night. Answers and death await us. As with all the mysteries of the mines, words are inadequate.

We wake and dress in the morning. She does take her time at it, as I once suspected she might. When we talk, the subject is confined to our disparate adventures, not the events of last night. It was something that simply occurred, neither premeditated nor particularly profound, between two people who have no one else to turn to. On Gevira she said that she has no next of kin, and in the hard light of this morning, I believe her.

"There's a place Huw spoke of in his memory dump," she says over a breakfast of concentrates and water. "It's a legend. I've heard of it before, but I never connected it to Trelayne. Someone did, another agent, and it looks like Huw found a location. There's a chart, anyway. It leads to a place called Naar: a small stack with one entrance. He was planning to go there, once he found a way."

"What's so special about this place?"

"It's protected by the Director," she says. "Anyone who goes there is killed."

"And that's where we're going?"

"Yes, but you don't have to–"

"I do. I am."

We eat in silence for a minute. I think about death-sentences and wonder if I might be signing my own by not turning back. What price a cure for curiosity?

"You were gone ten days," I say. "A map's all you've got to show for it?"

"Ten days for you. By my calendar, I was been gone around 40 hours." She smiles at my discomfort. "How was your trip to the bottom?"

"Informative."

"I bet."

More silence.

"I've been thinking," she says, "about the Director. The way it follows us. It struck when we met in Gevira, then again every place we went, including Samagrinig, when Huw turned up. When we doubled back, though, it didn't strike somewhere we'd already been. It wasn't until we came to a new stack that it killed again.

"Note also that it strikes just once, when we arrive, and then it goes away. That's what happened here in Panaion. We also know that it *will* strike, even if we can hold it off for a while. Again, Huw is proof that."

"That's true," I tell her.

"But here's the thing. When it killed Huw on Samagrinig, it could have taken you or me instead. None of us were looking at each other. We were completely unobserved. But it wasn't us. It was Huw. What's so special about us that we were spared?"

That question I can't answer, but I have another one for her with more immediate ramifications.

"Do you think we can walk into Naar and out again without being killed?

"I do," she says, and she stares at me as though daring me to argue.

I won't. There's no point. We are fishing for facts and theories in an information vacuum. Her guess is at least as good as any I could come up with.

A few seconds is all it takes to break camp. We came here with nothing but Kindred's pack, and with just as little we leave. I've grown no attachment to Panaion and the tiny corner of it I occupied for a week, yet our brief constitutional to the central elevator cluster fills me with a heaviness I cannot dispel.

At the cluster, a delegation awaits us.

"Hello, E. C.," says a man with a face like squeezed putty and eyes as sharp as needles. "We've been waiting for you to show up again."

A panicky look passes across Cotton's features. "What do you want?"

"To see you on your way." His potent gaze shifts to me. "Osred Guyonnet," he said, proffering his hand. "And you must be Donaldan Luff."

"That's 'Lough'," I say, ignoring his hand until I know the reason for Cotton's sudden nervousness.

"There's no need to be antagonistic," he says, retracting his hand and addressing Cotton once more. "I only want to help."

Around us, the cluster hall is slowly emptying as men in light-armored fieldsuits usher commuters and their companions towards the exits.

"We don't need your help," Cotton says.

"Oh, I'm not helping *you*. My concern is for the people you'll kill if you go stumbling across the Structure as you plan to." His face angles forward. "You do know about them, don't you?"

"Yes," said Cotton. "But this is important. You can't–"

He waves away her protest. "We're not going to stop you, E. C. Don't worry about that. We just ask that you tell us where you're going so we can clear the way ahead of you."

"That's sounds reasonable," I say when Cotton doesn't immediately respond.

She turns to me. "Osred is a Terminus agent," she says. "He's obviously seen the trail we left behind us and connected us to the cause. Anyone with a sharp eye and a bit of persistence could have done it."

Guyonnet bows his head at the damnably faint praise.

"It's not his job to direct traffic," she adds.

"This is true," he acknowledges, "but at the same time I like to think there's more to being with Terminus than exploring and taking notes. Saving lives, for instance."

"What happened to looking for spacers?" Cotton asks, and my heart trips between one beat and the next.

He smiles. "One thing at a time, E. C. I can't be in two places at once."

"Unfortunately for me, you chose this one."

Cotton casts me a cautionary glance, and I know that my secret is safe with her. The relief I feel is profound but tempered by the knowledge that others exist like Kindred who would murder me in a second if my true identity became known.

"I know we've had our differences in the past, E. C.–"

"Stop playing the saint," Cotton tells Guyonnet. "You just want what I know. If the Director is following us, what I know must be important, right?"

"One could be forgiven for supposing that."

The hall is empty now. I have no doubt that Guyonnet and his agents could prevent us leaving any number of ways. Apart from Kindred's miniscule pistol we are unarmed, and even the most capable Guildsman would be unlikely to prevail in a six-to-one fight.

Cotton sags and offers her hand. "All right, Guyonnet. But I want your word you will actually clear the way for us.

You're not going to take what I give you and then disappear. Okay?"

"You have my word."

She and Guyonnet press palms. The data takes a split-second to transfer and not much longer to verify.

"All right." Guyonnet whistles and his agents converge around us. People begin to rush back into the space. "Have a safe trip. See you at the end of it."

"Be careful," I tell him, thinking of what might lie in wait for him in Naar.

"Don't worry about me, Mister Lough," he tells me as the doors close between us. "Think only of yourself."

With that, he and his agents are on their way to Naar, where Trelayne might be hiding and legends speak of death for any who set foot there.

I don't know how much credit to lend to folklore in a place like this. I just know that Guyonnet will either be dead or not when we arrive–and I am unsure which possibility I like the least.

"We'll give them a minute," Cotton said, "just in case he plans to do the right thing for once."

She fidgets and paces as the seconds count down. She doesn't speak, but I know what she's thinking. It's a race now, a competition, and she may already have lost. Death is not much of a second prize under these circumstances.

My reserves of sympathy are not inexhaustible, however. The trip is going to be a long one, cooped up with that much restless anxiety. I let her needlessly expend her energy and save mine for finding a way to endure.

Our first destination is abandoned. We are the only things moving in the entire space. Although I was expecting it–or at least hoping for it–I am perturbed nonetheless. Guyonnet's word holds; our travel is guilt-free, inasmuch as we can tell (the Director might still be striking, after all; we are simply not aware of it); but I begin to feel as though we are refugees fleeing through a vast, abandoned subway.

Was this, I wonder, what it was like for the first humans to explore the Structure's endless, evacuated depths?

After a dozen silent processions from one shaft to the next, the emptiness becomes unbearable.

This time, Cotton is the one who breaks the silence.

"You'd never know it to look at me, but I come from an agrarian community. A small one, too. My mother was a genetic engineer and my father was an artist. They never agreed about anything, but it didn't seem to matter. Yes, Merraton was a Structure world, but that's not what this is about. Let me finish, and then you can pump me for information."

I bow my head, ashamed. She is right. This moment isn't about the Structure or the knowledge we seek. It is all about her. Life is flashing before her eyes: her birth, childhood, adolescence, and adulthood; her upbringing, education, vocation, and career; her hopes, dreams, nightmares, and failures. It is about her death, too, for we both believe that this is imminent.

She talks, and I do not interrupt. Neither do I record the details for my accounts. I will remember without notes and decide later what I will do with this knowledge. Should I consider it data regarding a Structure inhabitant that might prove valuable in future analysis, or something that should be left to fade along with the rest of her?

I know that even by asking that question I am admitting that my objectivity is compromised. If I cared for advancement, I would remove that detail from my account. But I was born a Guildsman, and I have a duty to disclose everything to my master. If the Structure has corrupted me, then that must be known by my fellows on the Great Ship.

Cotton talks on, and I consider for the first time what I will do when she is gone. Until now I have assumed that I will return either to undercover work or to my former life on the Great Ship. I suspect now that it is too late to walk away unscathed. The Structure's claws are long and thin, and not always as visible in effect as its most malevolent actor, the Director. I may be a dead man walking and not know yet it.

But then I think of the man who delivers Cotton's body to its ignominious interment–the haunting familiarity of his half-glimpsed profile–and I wonder. That man is definitely not Huw Kindred. He has the look of a Guild clone.

I know the answer now, and I believe that Cotton has known from the beginning.

I'd be careful if I were you, she told me. *You don't want to be tied to me when I go down.*

The words were meaningless to me then, and their utterance changed nothing. It was already too late.

Time's twisted skein has entangled us both.

Guyonnet's arrangement sees us all the way to Uvaya, where we will take the last transcendent shaft to Naar, purported home of the mysterious Trelayne. The entrance is the most secure we have encountered to date, with checkpoints and guard posts, and warning signs in multiple languages. The guards have all been dismissed, however, and none of the automated security systems impede our progress. We come to the doors, input our access codes, and step into the carriage.

"This is it," she says. Her restless energy has crystallized. She is almost glowing with anticipation.

The floor jolts beneath us. I feel the momentary giddiness that always afflicts me during transcendent transfers.

The doors open, and we step through them to our fates.

The Director does not strike us. We are as unafflicted in Naar as anywhere else. But of Guyonnet and his agents there is no sign. No sign at all. Not a single drop of blood; not a scuff mark on the floor. They have disappeared into the air–which thrums with tension, as though an invisible wire as large as a planet has been strained to breaking point.

Our footsteps echo across the flat, empty expanse of Naar's reception area. There are no windows, no obvious doors, and no signs.

"Hello?" Cotton calls. "Trelayne?"

The sound of her voice falls flatly back to silence.

"Let's check the walls," I say, and we conduct a thorough search.

There are three sliding panels hidden almost seamlessly, one in the center of each empty wall. We try the one opposite the shaft through which we entered.

It glides smoothly open, revealing an expanse so large my eyes struggle to comprehend it. We are standing on a balcony overlooking a hollowed-out world. Scarring on the interior testifies to the massive earthworks that have occurred here in the past. Spherical light sources, like small, white suns, cast multiple shadows, and hum with barely suppressed energy.

We retreat and take the door to our right. There we find a chamber identical to the one we left, and just as empty.

The third door takes us along a corridor to a closed door. It doesn't open as we approach, or to our touch. Cotton knocks loudly, three times.

We both jump as it hisses open, revealing a gray-haired man in a loose-fitting uniform with a sheet of plastic paper in one hand. He looks at us in surprise and annoyance through bright green eyes.

"Trelayne?" Cotton asks him.

"Yes, I'm Royce Trelayne," he says. "What took you so long?"

"Sorry about the mess. I've been here a month and it's taken me that long to unpack. What do you mean, you're not from the expedition? I ordered a re-supply a week ago and nothing's come yet.

"No, I've not seen anyone else today–or any other day, for that matter. Honeyman and his idiots must still be sorting out the supply lines. I tried telling him that automation is the way to go, but he wouldn't listen. The crew needs to be kept busy, he said. Morale doesn't fix itself on its own, you know. Well, I do know that, and I dislike being patronized as much as anyone. Bad enough that he's wasting resources and valuable time playing tin soldiers; worse that I'm going starve down here if he doesn't get his act together soon.

"Honeyman? Oh, I should probably call him 'the Professor General.' He's chief engineer and leader of the First Expeditionary Mission to Surya, where we found the mine entrance. You say you didn't come from there? Well, I suppose I'm not terribly surprised. We though we were blazing new territory, burrowing like Carnarvon and Howard into alien tombs, and what did we get? Mines not tombs, signs of human habitation long before our arrival–and a curse as well, most likely. Makes you think, eh?

"See this thing here. It's a clock, one of several thousand I've scattered through the mines, along with the instrument packs you might have seen at the bottom of the stacks. An army of soldiers would have taken years to make and distribute these things, but my drones accomplished the feat in a matter of a fortnight. The data's been rolling in for a week. Packets cross the transcendent shafts every time a carriage moves from one end to the other. The packets find their own way through the Structure and recombine here, via that thick cable leading into the wall over there. Isn't it obvious that I could never have accomplished so much on my own? Even with an army, as I said, it'd take forever. Best to leave the machines to it so I can do all the hard work of contemplation. That's what humans are best at, you know. Good at thinking; not so good at doing. There's a block somewhere, an execution failure. Everything we create is flawed, somehow. We thrive despite our ineptitude because the universe despises perfection.

"That more than anything convinces me that the Structure is not alien. Look at it! A sprawling insanity that seems from one angle like a clutch of high-rises connected by walkways, and from another a–well, like nothing we've ever built before. The kind of thing our armies might build if we left them to it. In would go our flawed designs, and out would come this madness. *Reductio ad absurdum,* except in the opposite direction, whatever that is in Latin. Extrapolation beyond all reason. All we do now is ask what its original purpose might have been.

"Yes, I'm sure that's one of the many answers you've come seeking from me, and I've thoughts on the matter, of course. The mines do provide valuable resources for the worlds at the top of each stack; there's no denying that, although it seems a small ambition for something so grand. I wonder if it is a device of some kind–an antenna, perhaps, transmitting vibrations through the temporal ether; or a generator, similar to wires connecting far-flung points of differing electrical potential. It could be a kind of cosmic glue, or conceivably even a weapon. I'm no closer to knowing the Structure's intended purpose, and I'm the first to attempt a systematic study of it. See where it's got me?

"Immortal, my arse. That's just an error of parallax.

"Let me show you one thing I've learned. This is an analysis of the clock data I've collected from the bottoms of all the stacks. It's crazy, isn't it? I can barely look at it sometimes. It gives me bad dreams. Clocks ticking slow; clocks ticking fast–clocks going backwards, even. What does it all boil down to?

"My theory is that the transcendent shafts connect, not just different locations in the spacetime we come from, but locations in different space-times–universes, continuums, branes, whatever you want to call them. The Structure is the web tying all these different points together. The critical thing is that at some, perhaps all, of these locations, the arrow of time points in a different direction. Not just reverse, but left-right or up-down, or directions we can barely guess at. These different arrows of time exert a drag on the Structure as a whole, twisting and stretching the stacks so that there's no universal time in the web at all any more. It's all tangled and warped.

"Why? I don't know. Maybe it was an accident. Maybe it's part of a grand design we can only guess at. Either way, that's how I can have been here a month, yet you think I've been here forever.

"And you–you tell me you're tangled in a loop of some kind. That sounds perfectly possible, maybe even likely, given the mess around us. Why ever not? There's nothing acausal about such loops, nothing acausal at all. They can be navigated–indeed they *must* be navigated, one way or another. The ravages of information entropy haven't gobbled you up, so I take that as a proof of concept.

"What this means for the people who live here is a different question. Perhaps it's nothing especially profound. We go about our lives as we always do, not really noticing any more than is necessary to ensure our day-to-day existence. Perhaps the finest ramification is one that Honeyman and I experienced. We're among the first wave of explorers to leave Earth, which beyond doubt lacks the capacity to build something like this–but despite this very important fact, humans have somehow beaten us here. If time moved linearly in the Structure, it would have been empty. It wouldn't even have existed for us to find! Yet everyone who comes to the Structure finds people here ahead of them. Where did they come from? Our future, I suppose. And in their past, they found the same thing. No one got here first. It's always been inhabited. It always will be. There is no end to it, in time as well as in space. It just continues being. That's why 'Terminus' is a terrible name for this organization you talk about. If there's no beginning to the mine, there won't be an end either.

"You know as well as I do that there's no such thing as a free lunch. Such loops and twists come at a cost to the Structure. It's not infinitely elastic; it can only stretch so far. It must release tension in small ways or else it would've snapped long ago. You might have seen something like this in your travels. Timelines truncated, perhaps, or strange sheer effects, particularly near those most afflicted by temporal back-flips.

"Does that ring any bells?

"I see. 'The Director,' eh? I suppose to someone without access to my data it might look like an intelligent being at work in the mine. And we–we flawed, we brilliant, we imaginatively blind–we persist in seeing the universe through our human-shaped glasses. We perceive an invisible hand where there is none at all. It's just the tangled fabric of cause and effect in the Structure adjusting itself, sealing off complicated ends, healing.

"And that other legend you related about me–my fortress of death, which killed the others you say preceded you here. I surmise now that it's nothing more than another presentation of this same phenomenon. My clocks connect me to many, many conflicting arrows of time, gathered by harmless, unconscious machines and reported to me here, where I observe them. It's like being surrounded by archers. I have been, unknowingly, caught in a vortex of twisted causality. While I remain connected to the clocks, I myself am safe, but anyone who gets too close will be erased from the Structure's sum state. Instantly and without reprieve.

"That is a grim realization for someone such as I, who never intended harm to anyone.

"You? Well, if I had to guess I would say that you are protected by virtue of the fact that you are midway through causal loops of your own. You can't be erased from the Structure here and now because you have actions to perform elsewhere and elsewhen. Your certain fate protects you, even while it guarantees your eventual death.

"And yes, you are most probably a danger to those around you. Perhaps a single loop could be tolerated, but two crossing loops . . . ? Bound to be inimical to the grand design, whatever that is.

"You seem downhearted, and I assure you that I both sympathize and apologize. My friends, I am speculating wildly. There hasn't been time enough to conduct systematic experiments–or so I have been telling myself these past weeks. Were Honeyman here, he would remind me of the important of the scientific method before coming to any firm conclusions. Physicists like me are plagued by engineers like him. No answers come from idle speculation, just more questions. Of those we have plenty enough already.

"Remember that my theories are open for disproof to one and all. I could be nothing but a mad old hermit obsessed with clocks whose word you'd do best to ignore. Forget my delusions; go back to your lives and enjoy them while you can. You have been successful where so many others have failed, coming this far! And you've shown me a thing or two that I'd managed to miss, that's for sure.

"Honeyman has been silent for an age, or so it seems me. I have missed my old friend, you know. Perhaps it really has been an age. It would be a terrible thing if the arrows of time twisted unfavourably and claimed him before I could tell him all about the execution failure we discovered together–marvellous and terrifying, and exactly the sort of thing he would build if given his head . . ."

<THIRD ACCOUNT: CONCLUSION>

We left Trelayne staring contemplatively at the thick bunch of cables connecting his workstation to the clocks scattered all across the Structure.

Cotton didn't speak, for all that I tried to engage her. She had barely said a word through the last half of our interrogation of Trelayne. I had been the one asking questions, guiding the old man through his rambling mix of recollections and speculations. She had withdrawn into herself, and I resisted the impulse to remonstrate with her that this was the culmination of her life's work. She had said herself that it would complete her, and therefore her disengagement seemed counterproductive.

A moment's thought would have revealed to me what was going through her mind. But I had my own problems to work through–first and foremost how to convey to you, Master Catterson, all that we had learned. Weapon, accident, or trap? The nature of the mine was no closer to my understanding, even having met Trelayne and listened to all he said.

Of more immediate importance was the revelation that our time-loops were the sole things protecting us from the Structure's causality-repairing censorship. Once my loop was closed, by putting Cotton in place in Gevira for my former self to examine, what was to stop my being wiped out of existence? Nothing. Cotton, by killing herself and expecting me to finish the job, was effectively killing me too.

That I was distracted at the crucial junction is regrettable but I hope forgivable.

I do not dare believe that events would have unfolded any other way than as they did, as they were always going to, in the end.

When we arrived at Uvaya, a sole Terminus agent was waiting for us.

"Finish it," he said, removing his pressure mask and tossing it to me.

I caught the mask automatically, struck by how much

like a Guildsman this man looked–except for his eyes, which had the far-horizons look of someone who had spent too long deep in the mines.

I had expected Osred Guyonnet.

Instead, he was me.

I felt the Structure flex around me, and I wondered how many timelines were being truncated as we stood in each other's presence. Who was paying the cost of this strange encounter? Who must have died in order that we might meet?

It was over in a second. Without another word, he turned and walked away. A transcendent shaft opened its portals for him. He stepped inside and was gone.

Cotton gasped and folded awkwardly to the floor.

I was at her side, all thoughts of my self and this strange new development forgotten.

"Cotton, what's wrong?"

Her pupils were pinpricks and her skin had turned a deathly shade of gray. There was no strength in her hands as they reached for me.

I knew the answer to my question even as I pleaded with her to respond. She must have started the process in the shaft for it to be so advanced now.

"E. C., talk to me!"

"Always going to end here, Donnie Boy."

"Don't listen to him. He doesn't know what he's talking about.' "

"He wasn't talking to me. We got the answers–"

I leaned in close, barely able to hear her.

"–got the answers we deserved. Tell everyone. You know–I–"

Her last words emerged as little more than a sigh.

"–can't live–we can't–"

I cradled her in my arms as the metabolic cascade ran its course. It ruined her mind first, then spread through her nervous system. Her organs succumbed one by one, with lungs and heart failing last of all. I held her tightly, relishing her body's warmth while it lasted.

The first time I touched her she had been cold, and I knew the last time would be the same, but I did not want to remember her that way.

When the last electrical activity had died away in her brain stem, I laid her flat on the ground, closed her brown eyes, and went about finding a way to transport her to Gevira.

I have reached the conclusion of my account, but not the end of my life. Although that I have a future I am now certain, how long that future will last I cannot know in detail. It may be hours, or months. Years, even. At least I know that despair will not immediately claim me, as it claimed Emmaline Celeste Cotton.

An hour ago, I put her body where it will be discovered by Security Officer Gluis just minutes before his own death. In theory, I suppose, I could have refused to see it through. I remain a creature of free will, despite this cocoon of causality in which I find myself. But the moment I learned the true nature of the mines, I knew I would return to Gevira. I had to get in touch with you, Master Catterson. I am the vanguard of an invasion, as Huw Kindred said, and if I don't make the results of my observation known someone else is sure to follow. Some other Guildsman will devise similar theories to mine, never knowing just how inadequate his imagination will be.

I have parcelled up my notes–all except Cotton's precious life story–in the hope of sparing my predecessor both his misconceptions and my fate.

I understand now that that glimpse of my future self–and the surety that I was caught in another loop even before the first closed–is both my insurance and my curse. I cannot die on Gevira when I have a role to play elsewhere, no matter how small. This is my very human attempt to survive the machine of nature, and humanity's greatest folly. "Execution failure" indeed.

Knots in time bind as well as protect. What would happen if I tried to leave the mines before fulfilling the future ahead of me? What damage could I wreak on spacetime and those around me, upon the Great Ship, upon the Guild, and upon you–teacher, master, and confessor these last few days?

The old man who addressed me on the surface of Panaion was absolutely right when he said that my return to the mines was bound to be a one-way trip.

To him I also spoke of duty, as I have to you, Master Catterson, and to Cotton. I am coming to believe that her final instruction to me is the highest–perhaps the only–form of duty I could consider following now.

"Tell everyone."

Take this transmission as a warning, if you will. Do not be blinded by the mines' wonders to the threat it entails. While the potential it offers for the Guild's expansion appears limitless, at what cost would it come? I have seen it kill many whose lives were devoted to understanding its nature–not just E. C. Cotton, but Huw Kindred and Osred Guyonnet as well. How can we strangers to its halls hope to fare any better?

Although the mines were not designed as a trap, that is what they have undoubtedly become. Any incursion is doomed to failure. Send no more Guildsmen to suffer as I have suffered, through ignorance and pig-headedness, however deservingly.

My bridges are all burned now, but to be condemned to spend the rest of my days here is perhaps not the worst fate imaginable for a man such as I–even if I may wander its labyrinthine halls forever, extolling the truth and being ignored for it. I write this in the hope that the temporal tides have not already flung me up on some future shore, one in which you have abandoned hope of ever hearing from me again. If the suspicion of my demise has become a certainty in some minds, Master Catterson, I ask you to suspend all judgement on that score, if no other.

As you suspected, the citizens of Gevira uncovered something utterly strange and deadly beneath the veneer of their civilisation. Thus ends my account of it. I leave to you the divination of the will of the Guild, and the way forward for the people I once called my own.

ALONE

Robert Reed

Robert Reed was born in Omaha, Nebraska in 1956. He has a Bachelor of Science in Biology from the Nebraska Wesleyan University, and has worked as a lab technician. He became a full-time writer in 1987, the same year he won the L. Ron Hubbard Writers of the Future Contest, and has published eleven novels, including The Leeshore, The Hormone Jungle, *and far future science fiction novels* Marrow *and* The Well of Stars. *An extraordinarily prolific writer, Reed has published over 180 short stories, mostly in* F&SF *and* Asimov's, *which have been nominated for the Hugo, James Tiptree Jr. Memorial, Locus, Nebula, Seiun, Theodore Sturgeon Memorial, and World Fantasy awards, and have been collected in* The Dragons of Springplace *and* The Cuckoo's Boys. *His novella "A Billion Eves" won the Hugo Award last year. Nebraska's only SF writer, Reed lives in Lincoln with his wife and daughter, and is an ardent long-distance runner.*

More than a decade ago Reed launched a continuing series of stories that featured one of the great godlike machines in modern science fiction, the Jupiter-sized 'Great Ship,' which was found abandoned in space, salvaged by humans, and sent on a grand tour of the galaxy. In "Alone," Reed returns to the Great Ship and looks at an unlikely seeming passenger who has been onboard for far longer than seems possible.

1

The hull was gray and smooth, gray and empty, and in every direction it fell away gradually, vanishing where the cold black of the sky pretended to touch what was real. What was real was the Great Ship. Nothing else enjoyed substance or true value. Nothing else in Creation could be felt, much less understood. The Ship was a sphere of perfect hyperfiber, world-sized and enduring, while the sky was only a boundless vacuum punctuated with lost stars and the occasional swirls of distant galaxies. Radio whispers could be heard, too distorted and far too faint to resolve, and neutrino rains fell from above and rose from below, and there were ripples of gravity and furious nuclei generated by distant catastrophes–inconsequential powers washing across the unyielding, eternal hull.

Do not trust the sky, the walker understood. The sky wished only to tell lies. And perhaps worse, the sky could distract the senses and mind from what genuinely mattered. The walker's only purpose was to slowly, carefully move across the Ship's hull, and if something of interest were discovered, a cautious investigation would commence. But only if it was harmless could the mystery be approached and studied in detail. Instinct guided the walker, and for as long as it could remember, the guiding instinct was fear. Fierce, unnamed hazards were lurking. The walker could not see or define its enemies, but they were near, waiting for weakness. Waiting for sloth or inattentiveness. Regardless how curious it was or how fascinating some object might be, the walker scrupulously avoided anything that moved or spoke, or any device that glowed with unusual heat, and even the tiniest example of organic life was something to be avoided, without fail.

Solitude was its natural way.

Alone, the ancient fear would diminish to a bearable ache, and something like happiness was possible.

Walking, walking. That was the purpose of existence. Select a worthy line, perhaps using one of the scarce stars as a navigational tool. Follow that line until something new was discovered, and regardless whether the object was studied or circumvented, the walker would then pick a fresh direction—a random direction—and maintain that new line with the same tenacity.

There was no need to eat, no requirement for drink or sleep. Its life force was a minor, unsolvable mystery. The pace was patient, every moment feeling long and busy. But if nothing of note occurred, nothing needed to be recalled. After a century of uninterrupted routine, the walker compressed that blissful sameness into a single impression that was squeezed flush against every other vacuous memory—the recollections of a soul that felt ageless but was still very close to empty.

Eyes shrank and new eyes grew, changing talents. With that powerful, piercing vision, the walker watched ahead and beside and behind. Nothing was missed. And sometimes for no obvious reason it would stop, compelled suddenly to lower several eyes, staring into a random portion of the hull. From the grayness, microscopic details emerged. Fresh radiation tracks still unhealed; faint scars being gradually erased by quantum bonds fighting to repair themselves. Each observation revealed quite a lot about the hyperfiber, and the lessons never changed. The hull was a wonder. Fashioned from an extremely strong and lasting material—a silvery-gray substance refined during a lost age by some powerful species, perhaps, or perhaps a league of vanished gods. They were the masters who must have imagined and built the Ship, and presumably the same wondrous hands had sent their prize racing through the vacuum. A good, glorious purpose must be at work here; but except for the relentless perfection of the Great Ship, nothing remained of their intentions, their goals, or even an obvious destination.

When the walker kneeled, the hull's beauty was revealed.

And then it would stand again and resume its slow travels, feeling blessed to move free upon this magnificent face.

2

There was no purpose but to wander the perfection forever: That was an assumption made early and embraced as a faith. But as the centuries passed, oddities and little mysteries gradually grew more numerous. Every decade brought a few more crushed steel boxes and empty diamond buckets than the decade before, and there were lumps of mangled aerogel, and later, the occasional shard of some lesser form of hyperfiber. As time passed, the walker began to come across dead machines and pieces of machinery and tools too massive or far too ordinary to be carried any farther once they had failed. These objects were considerably younger than the Ship. Who abandoned them was a looming mystery, but one that would not be solved soon. The walker had no intention of approaching these others. And in those rare times when they approached it–always by mistake, always unaware of its presence–it would flatten itself against the hull and make itself vanish.

Invisibility was a critical talent. But invisibility meant that it had to abandon most of its senses. Even as they strode across its smooth back, these interlopers were reduced to a vibration with each footfall and a weak tangle of magnetic and electrical fields.

Days later and safe again, the walker would rise up carefully and move on.

Another millennium passed without serious incident. It was easy to believe that the Great Ship would never change, and nothing would ever be truly new; and holding that belief close, the walker followed one new line. No buckets or diamond chisels were waiting to change its direction. As it strode on, the stars and sky-whispers silently warned that it was finally passing into unknown territory. But this did happen on occasion. Perfection meant sameness, and the walker could imagine nothing new. Then what seemed to be a flat-topped mountain began to rise over the coming horizon. Puzzled, it made note of the sharp gray line hovering just above the hull. More years of steady marching caused the grayness to lift higher, just slightly. Perhaps a mountain of trash had been set there. Perhaps a single enormous bucket upended. Various explanations offered themselves; none satisfied. But the event was so surprising, enormous and unwelcome, and the novelty so great, that the walker stopped as soon as it was sure that something was indeed there, and without taking one step, it waited for three years and a little longer, adapting its eyes constantly, absorbing a view that refused to change.

Finally, curiosity defeated every caution, and altering its direction, the walker steered straight toward what still made no sense.

At a pace that required little energy, it pressed ahead in half-meter strides. Decades passed before it finally accepted what was obvious: That while the Ship was undoubtedly perfect, it was by no measure perfectly smooth and eternally round. Rising from the hull was not one gigantic tower, but several. The nearest tower was blackish-gray and too vast to measure from a single perspective. Occasionally a small light appeared on the summit, or several tiny flecks of light danced beside its enormous bulk, and there were sudden spikes in dense, narrow radio noise that tasted like a language. Various explanations occurred to the walker. From where these possibilities came, it could not say. Maybe they arose from the instincts responsible for its persistent fears. But like never before, it was curious. It started to move once again, slowly and tirelessly pushing closer, and that was when it noticed how one of the more distant towers had begun to tip, looking as if it was ready to collapse on its side. And shortly after that remarkable change in posture, the tower suddenly let loose a deep rumble, followed by a scorching, sky-piercing fire.

But of course: These were the Ship's engines. No other explanation was necessary, and in another moment, the walker absorbed its new knowledge, a fresh set of beliefs gathering happily around the Ship's continued perfection. Fusion boosted by antimatter threw a column of radiant blue-white plasmas into the blackness, scorching the vacuum. This was a vision worth admiration. Here was power beyond anything that the walker had ever conceived of. But soon the engine fell back into sleep, and after thorough reflection, it decided to choose another random direction, and another, selecting them until it was steering away from the gigantic rocket nozzles.

If objects this vast had missed its scrutiny, what else was hiding beyond the horizon?

Walk, walk, walk.

But its pace began to slow even more. Flying vessels and many busy machines were suddenly common near the engines, and some kind of animal was building cities of bubbled glass. An invasion was underway. There were regions of intense activity and considerable radio noise, and each hazard had to be avoided, or if the situation demanded, crossed without revealing its presence.

Ages passed before the engines vanished beyond the horizon. A bright red star became the walker's beacon, its guide, and it followed that rich light until the ancient sun sickened and went nova, flinging portions of its flawed skin out into the cooling, dying vacuum.

Younger stars appeared, climbing from the horizon as the walker pressed forward. A second sky was always hiding behind the hyperfiber body. The walker felt the play of gravity and then the hard twisting, the Ship leaving the line that had been followed without interruption for untold billions of years. After that, the sky was changed. The vacuum was not nearly so empty, or quite as chilled, and even a patient entity with nothing to do but count points of light could not estimate just how many stars were rising into its spellbound gaze.

A galaxy was approaching. One great plate of three hundred billion suns and trillions of worlds was about to intersect with a vessel that had wandered across the universe, every previous nudge and great reaches of nothingness leading to this place and this rich, perfect moment.

And here the walker stood, on the brink of something entirely new.

There was a line upon the hull that perhaps no one else could have noticed. Not just with their eyes and the sketchy knowledge available, no. But the walker recognized the boundary where the hull that it knew surrendered to another. Suddenly the thick perfect hyperfiber was replaced with a thicker but considerably more weathered version of faultless self. Even in the emptiest reaches of the universe, ice and dust and other nameless detritus wandered in the dark. These tiny worlds would crash down on the Ship's hull, always at a substantial fraction of light-speed, and not even the best hyperfiber could shrug aside that kind of withering power. Stepping onto the Ship's leading face, the walker immediately noticed gouges and debris fields and then the little craters that were eventually obscured by still larger craters–holes reaching deep into the hard resilient hull. Most of the wounds were ancient, although hyperfiber hid its age well. All but the largest craters were unimportant to the Ship's structure, their cumulative damage barely diminishing its abiding strength. But some of the wounds showed signs of repair and reconditioning. The walker discovered one wide lake of liquid hyperfiber, the patch still curing when it arrived on the smooth shoreline. Kneeling down, it looked deep into the still-reflective surface. For the first time in memory, there was another waiting to be seen. But the entity felt little interest in its own appearance. What mattered was the inescapable fact that someone–some agent or benevolent hand–was striving to repair what billions of years of abuse had achieved. A constructive force was at work upon the Ship. A healing force, seemingly. Enthralled, the walker looked at the young lake and the reflected Milky Way, measuring the patch's dimensions. Then it examined the half-cured skin, first with fresh eyes and then with a few respectful touches. A fine grade of hyperfiber was being used, almost equal to the original hull. Which implied that caretakers were striving to do what was good and make certain that their goodness would endure.

The endless wandering continued.

Eventually the galaxy was overhead, majestic but still inconsequential. The suns and invisible worlds were little more than warm dust flung across the emptiness, and still all that mattered was the Ship, dense and rich beyond all measure. Walk, and walk. And walk. And then it found itself on the edge of another crater–the largest scar yet on the hull–and for the first time ever, it followed a curving line, the crater's frozen lip defining its path.

Bodies and machines were working deep inside the ancient gouge.

From unseen perches, it watched the activity, studying methods and guessing reasons when it could not understand. The vacuum crackled with radio noise. The sense of words began to emerge, and because the skill might prove useful, the walker committed to memory what it understood of the new language. Hundreds of animals worked inside the crater–humans they called themselves, dressed inside human-shaped machines. And accompanying them were tens of thousands of pure machines, while on the lip stood a complex of prefabricated factories and fusion reactors and more humans and more robots dedicated to no purpose but repairing one minuscule portion of the Ship's forward face.

As it kneeled there, unseen, a bit of cosmic dirt fell with a brilliant flash of light, leaving a tiny crater inside the giant one.

The danger was evident, but there were blessings too. The walker slipped across a narrow track lain on the unbroken hull, presumably leading from some far place to the crater's edge. The track was a superconductive rail that allowed heavy tanks to be dragged here, each tank filled with uncured, still liquid hyperfiber. From another hiding place, the walker watched as a long train of tanks arrived and subsequently drained before being set on a parallel track and sent away. Before the third was empty, it understood enough to appreciate just how difficult this work was. Liquid hyperfiber was fickle, eager to form lasting bonds but susceptible to flaws and catastrophic embellishments. Down in the crater, a brigade of artisans was struggling to repair the damage–a tiny pock on the vast bow of the Ship–and their deed, epic as well as tiny, was ringing testament to the astonishing gifts of those who had first built the Great Ship.

All but one of the empty tanks was sent home. The exception was damaged in a collision and then pushed aside, abandoned. Curious about that silver tank, the walker approached and then paused, crept closer and paused again, making certain that no traps were waiting, no eyes watching. Then it slipped near enough to touch the crumbled body. That innate talent for mechanical affairs was awakened again. Using thought and imaginary tools, it rebuilt the empty vessel. Presumably those repairs were waiting for a more convenient time. Unless the humans meant to leave their equipment behind, which was not an unthinkable prospect, judging by the trash already scattered about this increasingly crowded landscape.

One end of the tank was cracked open, the interior exposed. In slow, nearly invisible steps, the walker slipped inside. The cylinder was slightly less than a kilometer in length. Ignoring every danger, the walker passed through the ugly fissure, and once inside, it balanced on a surface designed to feel to slick to every possible limb. Yet it managed to hold its place, retaining its pose, peering into the darkness until it was sure that it was alone, and then it let light seep out of its own body, filling the long volume with a soft cobalt-blue glow.

Everywhere it looked, it saw itself looking back.

Reflected on the round wall were distorted images of what might be a machine, or perhaps was something else. Whatever it was, the walker had no choice but stare at itself. This was indeed a trap, it realized, but instead of a secret door slamming shut, the mechanism worked by forcing an entity to gaze upon its own shape and its nature, perhaps for the first time.

What it beheld was not unlovely.

But how did it know beauty? What aesthetic standard was it employing? And why carry such a skill among its instincts and talents?

A long time passed before the walker could free itself from the trap. But even after it climbed back onto the open hull, escape proved difficult. It slinked away for a good distance and then stopped, and then it walked farther before turning back again. Where did this obligation come from, this need to stare at an empty, ruined tank? Why care about a soulless object that would never function again? How could that piece of ruin bother it so? And why, even after walking far enough to hide both the tank and the crater beyond the horizon . . . why did its mind insist on returning again and again to an object that others had casually and unnecessarily cast aside?

3

It walked. It counted steps. It had reached two million four hundred thousand and nine steps when humans suddenly appeared in their swift cars. The invaders settled within a hundred meters of the walker. With a storm of radio talk and the help of robots, they quickly erected a single unblinking eye and pointed it straight above. The walker hid where it happened to be, filling a tiny crater. Unnoticed, it lay motionless as the new telescope was built and tested and linked to the growing warning system. And then the humans left, but the walker remained inside its safe hole, sprouting an array of increasingly powerful eyes.

The sky might be untrustworthy, but there was beauty to the lie. The Great Ship was plunging into a galaxy that was increasingly brilliant and complex and dangerous. More grit and chunks of wayward ice slammed against the hull, and the bombardment would only strengthen as the Ship sliced into the thick curling limb of suns. But the humans were answering the dangers with increasingly powerful weapons. Telescopes watched for hazards. Then bolts of coherent light melted the incoming ices. Ballistic rounds pulverized asteroids. Sculpted EM fields slowed the tiniest fragments and shepherded them aside. There was splendor to that awful fight. Flashes and sparkles constantly surprised the lidless eyes. Ionized plasmas generated squawks and whistles reaching across the spectrum. An accidental music grew louder, urgent and carefree. No defensive system was unbreakable. Death threatened everything foolish enough to walk upon the bow. Each moment might be its last. But the scene deserved fascination and wonder. It stared upwards, and it grew antennae and listened, and its mind began to believe that this violent magic had a rhythm, an elegant inescapable logic, and that whatever note and whichever color came next could have been foreseen.

That was when the voice began.

At least that was the moment when the walker finally took notice of the soft, soft whispers.

These mutterings were not part of the sky. Intuition told the walker that much. Perhaps the voice rose from the hull, or maybe it came from the chill vacuum. But what mattered more than its origin was the quiet swift terror that defined its presence–an inarticulate, nearly inaudible murmur that came when it was unexpected and vanished before any response could be offered.

Following the first 11 incidents, the walker remained silently anxious.

But the 12th whisper was too much. With a radio mouth formed for the occasion, and using the human language that it had learned over the last centuries, the walker called out, "What are you? What do you want?" And when nothing replied, it added, "Do not bother me. Leave me alone."

By chance or by kindness, the request was honored.

The walker rose and again wandered across the bow. But after witnessing several jarring impacts, it returned to the stern, ready to accept the safety afforded by the Ship's enormous bulk. Yet there were even more humans than before, and they brought endless traffic on what had been delicious, seemingly infinite emptiness. Following a twisting, secretive line, the walker journeyed to the nearest engine, and with some delight, it touched the mountainous nozzle at its base. But machines were everywhere, investigating and repairing, and the human chatter was busy and endless, jabbering about subjects and names and places and times that made no sense at all.

Where the bow and stern joined, starships were landing. The walker tracked them by their bright little rockets. Hunkering behind piles of trash, it watched the slow taxis and quicker streakships drop onto the hull, and then enormous doors would pull open, and the visitors would vanish. The walker had never seen a spaceport, never even imagined such a thing was possible. Once again, the Great Ship was far more than it pretended to be. Creeping even closer, it estimated the size of the incoming vessels. Considering how many passengers might be tucked inside each little ship, it was easy to understand why the hull had grown crowded. The human animals were falling from the sky, coming here for the honor of living inside their bubble cities on the hull of this lost, unknowable relic.

Finally, in slow patient stages, the walker crept to the edge of a vast door, and with a single glance, its foolishness was revealed. The Great Ship was more than its armored hull. What the entity had assumed to be hyperfiber to the core was otherwise. Inside the spaceport, it saw a vast column of air and light and warm wet bodies moving by every means and for no discernable purpose. Everything the port was swift and busy and devoid of any clear purpose. Humans were just one species among a multitude, and beneath the hull, the Ship was pierced with tunnels and doorways and hatches and diamond-windows, and that was just what the briefest look provided before it flattened out and slowly, cautiously crawled away.

The Ship was hollow.

And judging by the evidence, it was inhabited by millions and maybe billions of organic entities.

These unwanted revelations left it shaken. Months were required to sneak away from the port. Unseen, it returned to the bow face and the beautiful sky, accepting the dangers for the illusion of solitude. But the ancient craters were being swiftly erased now. The Ship's lasers were pummeling most of the cometary debris that dared pass nearby, and the repair crews were swift and efficient now. The pitted, cracked terrain was vanishing beneath smooth perfection. The new hyperfiber proved fresh and strong, affording few hiding places even for a wanderer who could hide nearly anywhere. By necessity, every motion was slow. Was studied. But even then, a nearby robot would notice a presence, and maybe EM hands would reach out, trying to touch what couldn't be seen; and by reflex, the walker stopped living and stopped thinking, hiding away inside itself as it pretended to be nothing but another patch lost among the billions.

Eventually it came upon a freshly made crater, too small to bring humans immediately but large enough to let it walk down inside the wounded hull.

A brief sharp ridge stood in its way–the relic of chaotic,

billion-degree plasmas. After five hours of careful study, the walker slowly crossed the ridge. Humans never came alone to these places, and there was no sign of any machine. But standing on the ridgeline, urgency took hold. Something here was wrong. And what was wrong felt close. The walker began to lower itself, trying to vanish. But then a strong voice said, "There you are."

It hunkered down quickly.

Then with amusement, someone said, "I see you."

The voice–the mysterious and uninvited phenomena–was always quieter than this. It has always been a whisper, and far less comprehensible. Perhaps the young crater helped shape its words. Perhaps the bowl with its sharp refrozen hyperfiber lip lent strength and focus.

In myriad ways, the walker began to melt into the knife-like ridge.

Yet the voice only grew louder–a radio squawk wrapped around the human language. With some pleasure, she said, "You cannot hide from me."

"Leave me be," the walker answered.

"But you're the one disturbing me, stranger."

"And I have told you," the walker insisted. "Before, I told you that I wish to be alone. I must be alone. Don't pester me with your noise."

"Oh," the voice replied. "You believe we've met. Don't you?"

Curiosity joined the fear. A new eye lifted just a little ways, scanning the closest few meters.

"But I've never spoken to you," the voice continued. "You've made a mistake. I don't know whose voice you've been hearing, but I'm rather certain that it wasn't mine."

"Who are you?" the walker asked.

"My name is Wune."

"Where are you?"

"Find the blue-white star on the horizon," she said.

It complied, asking, "Are you that star?"

"No, no." Wune could do nothing but laugh for a few moments. "Look below it. Do you see me?"

Except for a few crevices and delicate wrinkles, the crater floor was flat. Standing at the far end was a tiny figure clad in hyperfiber. An arm lifted now. What might have been a hand waved slowly, the gesture purely human.

"My name is Wune," the stranger repeated.

"Are you human?" the entity whispered nervously.

"I'm a Remora," said Wune. Then she asked, "What exactly are you, my friend? Since I don't seem to recognize your nature."

"My nature is a mystery," it agreed.

"Do you have a name?"

"I am," it began. Then it hesitated, considering this wholly original question. And with sudden conviction, it said, "Alone." It rose up from the ridge, proclaiming, "My name is Alone."

4

"Come closer, Alone."

It did nothing.

"I won't hurt you," Wune promised, the arm beckoning again. "We should study each at a neighborly distance. Don't you agree?"

"We are close enough," the walker warned, nearly two kilometers of vacuum and blasted hyperfiber separating them.

The Remora considered her response. Then with an amiably tone, she agreed, "This is better than being invisible to one another. I'll grant you that."

For a long while, neither spoke.

Then Wune asked, "How good are those eyes? What do you see of me?"

Alone stared only at the stranger, each new eye focused on the lifesuit made of hyperfiber and the thick diamond faceplate and what lay beyond. Alone had seen enough humans to understand their construction, their traditions. But what was human about this face was misplaced. The eyes were beneath the mouth and tilted on their sides. The creature's flesh was slick and cold in appearance, and it was vivid purple. The long hair on the scalp was white with a hint of blue, rather like the brightest stars, and that white hair began to lift and fall, twirl and straighten, as if an invisible hand was playing with it.

"I don't know your species," Alone confessed.

"But I think you do," Wune corrected. "I'm a human animal, and a Remora too."

"You are different from the others."

"What others?" she inquired.

"The few that I have seen."

"You spied on us inside the big crater. Didn't you?" The mouth smiled, exposing matching rows of perfect human teeth. "Oh yes, you were noticed. I know that you strolled up to that busted tank and climbed inside before walking away again."

"You saw me?"

"Not then, but later," she explained. "A security AI was riding the tank. It was set at minimal power, barely alive. Which probably kept you from noticing it. We didn't learn about you until weeks later, when we stripped the tank for salvage and the AI woke up."

Shame took hold. How could it have been so careless?

"I know five other occasions when you were noticed," Wune continued. "There have probably been more incidents. I try to hear everything, but that's never possible. Is it?" Then she described each sighting, identifying the place and time when these moments of incompetence occurred.

"I wasn't aware that I was seen," it stated.

Ignorance made its failures feel even worse.

"You were barely seen," Wune corrected. "A ghost, a phantom. Not real enough to be taken seriously."

"You mentioned a spaceport," it said.

"I did."

"Where is this port?"

Wune pointed with authority, offering a precise distance.

"I don't remember being there," Alone admitted.

"Maybe we made a mistake," she allowed.

"But I did visit a different port." With care, it sifted through its memories. "I might have troubles with my memory," it confessed.

"Why do you think that?"

"Because I know so little about myself," confessed the walker.

"That is sad," Wune said. "I'm sorry for you."

"Why?"

"Life is the past," she stated. "The present moment is too narrow to slice and will be lost with the next instant. And the future is nothing but empty conjecture. Where you have been is what matters. What you have done is what counts for and against you on the tallies."

The walker concentrated on those unexpected words.

"I have a telescope with me," Wune said. "I used it when I first saw you. But I'm trying to be polite. If you don't mind, may I study you now?"

"If you wish," it said uneasily.

The Remora warned, "This might take some time, friend." Then with both gloved hands, she held a long tube to her face.

Alone waited.

An hour later, Wune asked, "Are you a machine?"

"I don't know. Perhaps I am."

"Or do you carry an organic component inside that body?"

"Each answer is possible, I think."

Wune lowered the telescope. "I'm a little of both," she allowed. "I like to believe that I'm more organic than mechanical, but the two facets happily live inside me."

Alone said nothing.

The Remora laughed softly, admitting, "This is fun."

Was it?

To her new friend, she explained, "Thousands of years ago, humans learned how to never grow old. No disease, and no easy way to kill us." The hands were encased in hyperfiber gloves. One of those fingers tapped hard against her diamond faceplate. "My mind? It's a bioceramic machine. Which makes it tough and quick to heal and full of redundancies. My memories are safe inside the artificial neurons. Whenever I want, I can remember yesterday. Or I can pull my head back five centuries and one yesterday. My life is an enormous, deeply personal epic that I am free to enjoy whenever I wish."

"I am different than you," Alone conceded.

Wune asked, "Do you sleep?"

"Never."

"Yet you never feel mentally tired?" The purple face nodded, and she said, "Right now, I'm envious."

Envy was a new word.

"I'm trying to tell you something," she said. "This old Remora lady has been awake for a very long time, and she needs to sleep for a little while. Is that all right? Do whatever you want while my eyes are closed. If you need, walk away from me. Vanish completely." Then she smiled, adding, "Or you might take a step or two in my direction. If you feel the urge, that is."

Then Wune shut her misplaced eyes.

During the next hour, Alone crept ahead a little more three meters.

As soon as she woke, Wune noticed. "Good. Very good."

"Are you rested now?"

"Hardly. But I'll push through the misery." Her laugh had a different tone. "What's your earliest, oldest memory? Tell me."

"Walking."

"Walking where?"

"Crossing the Ship's hull."

"Who brought you to the Ship?"

"I have always been here."

She considered those words. "Or you could have been built here," she suggested. "Assembled from a kit, perhaps. You don't remember a crowd of engineers sticking their hands inside you?"

"I remember no one." Then again, with confidence, Alone claimed, "I have never been anywhere but on the Great Ship."

"If that was true," Wune began. Then she fell silent.

Alone asked, "What if that is so?"

"I can't even guess at all of the ramifications," she admitted. Then after a few minutes of silence, she said, "Ask something of me. Please."

"Why are you here, Wune?"

"Because I'm a Remora," she offered. "Remoras are humans who got pushed up on the hull to do important, dangerous work. There are reasons for this. Good causes, and bad justifications. Everything that you see here . . . well, the hull is not intended to be a prison. The captains claim that it isn't. But now and again, it feels like an awful prison."

Then she hesitated, thinking carefully before saying, "I don't think that was your question. Was it?"

"Like me, you are alone," it pointed out. "Most of the humans, Remoras and engineers and the captains . . . these humans usually gather in large groups, and they act pleased to be that way . . ."

With a serious tone, she said, "I'm rather different, it seems."

Alone waited.

"The hull is constantly washed with radiation, particularly out here on the leading face." She gestured at the galaxy. "My flesh is immortal. I can endure almost any abuse. But these wild nuclei crash through my cells, wreaking terrible damage. My repair mechanisms are always awake, always busy. I have armies of tiny workers marching inside me, trying to lift my flesh back to robust health. But when I'm alone, and when I focus on my body's functions, I can influence my regenerating flesh. In some ways, with just willpower, I can direct my own evolution."

That seemed to explain the odd, not quite human face.

"I'm out here teaching myself these tricks," Wune admitted. "The hull is no prison. To me, it is a church. A temple. A rare opportunity for the tiniest soul to unleash potentials that her old epic life never revealed to her."

"I understand each of your words," said Alone.

"But?"

"I cannot decipher what you mean."

"Of course you can't." Wune laughed. "Listen. My entire creed boils down to this: If I can write with my flesh, then I can write upon my soul."

"Your 'soul'?"

"My mind. My essence. Whatever it is that the universe sees when it looks hard at peculiar little Wune."

"Your soul," the walker said once again.

Wune spoke for a long while, trying to explain her young faith. Then her voice turned raw and sloppy, and after drinking broth produced by her recyke system, she slept again. The legs of her lifesuit were locked in place. Nearly five hours passed with her standing upright, unaware of her surroundings. When she woke again, barely 20 meters of vacuum and hard radiation separated them.

She didn't act surprised. With a quieter, more intimate voice, she asked, "What fuels you? Is there some kind of reactor inside you? Or do you steal your power from us somehow?"

"I don't remember stealing."

"Ah, the thief's standard reply." She chuckled. "Let's assume you're a machine. You have to be alien-built. I've never seen or even heard rumors about any device like you. Not from the human shops, I haven't." After a long stare, she asked, "Are you male?"

"I don't know."

"I'm going to call you male. Does that offend you?"

"No."

"Then perhaps you are." She wanted to come closer. One boot lifted, seemingly of its own volition, and then she forced herself to set it back down on the hull. "You claim not to know your own purpose. Your job, your nature. All questions without answer."

"I am a mystery to myself."

"Which is an enormous gift, isn't it? By that, I mean that if you don't know what to do with your life, then you're free to do anything you wish." Her face was changing color, the purple skin giving way to streaks of gold. And during her sleep, her eyes had grown rounder and deeply blue. "You don't seem dangerous. And you do require solitude. I can accept all of that. But as time passes, I think you'll discover that it's harder to escape notice out here on the hull. The surface area is enormous, yes. But where will you hide? I promise, I won't chase after you. And I can keep my people respectful of your privacy. At least I hope I can. But the Great Ship is cursed with quite a few captains, and they don't approve of mysteries. And we can't count all the adventurers who are coming here now, racing up from countless worlds. Maybe you don't realize this, but our captains have decided to take us on a tour of the galaxy. Humans and aliens are invited, for a fat price, and some of them will hear the rumors about you. Some of these passengers will come up on the hull, armed with sensors and their lousy judgment."

Alone listened carefully.

"My reasons are selfish," Wune admitted. "I don't want these tourists under my boots. And since you can't hide forever in plain sight, we need to find you a new home."

Horrified, he asked, "Where can I go?"

"Almost anywhere," Wune assured. "The Great Ship is

ridiculously big. It might take hundreds of thousands of years just to fill up its empty places. The caverns, the little tunnels. The nameless seas and canyons and all the dead-end holes."

"But how can I find those places?"

"I know ways. I'll help you."

Terror and hope lay balanced on the walker's soul.

With those changeless human teeth, Wune smiled. "I believe you," she offered. "You say you know nothing about your nature, your talents. And I think you mean that."

"I do."

"Look at the chest of my suit, will you? Stare into the flat hyperfiber. Yes, here. Do you see your own reflection?"

His body had changed during these last few minutes. Alone had felt the new arms sprouting, the design of his legs adjusting, and without willing it to happen, he had acquired a face. It was a striking and familiar face, the purple flesh shot with gossamer threads of gold.

"I almost wish I could do that," Wune confessed. "Reinvent myself as easily as you seem to do."

He could think of no worthy response.

"Do you know what a chameleon is?"

Alone said, "No."

"You," she said. "Without question, you are the most natural, perfect chameleon that I have ever had the pleasure to meet."

5

Simply and clearly, Wune explained how a solitary wanderer might secretly slip inside the Ship. Then as she grew drowsy again, the Remora wished her chameleon friend rich luck and endless patience. "I hope you find whatever you are hunting," she concluded. "And that you avoid whatever it is that you might be fleeing."

Alone offered thankful words, but he had no intention of accepting advice. Once Wune was asleep, he picked a fresh direction and walked away. For several centuries, he wandered the increasingly smooth hull, watching as the galaxy–majestic and warm and bright–rose slowly to meet the Great Ship. Now and again, he was forced to hide in the open. Practice improved his techniques, but he couldn't shake the sense that the Remoras were still watching him, despite his tricks and endless caution. He certainly eavesdropped on them, and whenever Wune's name was mentioned, he listened closely. Never again did her voice find him. But others spoke of the woman with admiration and love. Wune had visited this bubble city or that repair station. She had talked to her people about the honor of serving the Great Ship and the strength that came from mastering the evolution of your own mortal body. Then she was dead, killed by a shard of ice that slipped past every laser. Alone absorbed the unexpected news. He didn't understand his emotions, but he hid where he happened to be standing and for a full year did nothing. Wune was the only creature with whom he had ever spoken, and he was deeply shocked, and then he was quite sad, but what wore hardest was the keen pleasure he discovered when he realized that she was dead but he was still alive.

Eventually he wandered back to Ship's trailing face, slipping past the bubble cities and into realm of giant engines. Standing before one of the towering nozzles, Alone recalled Wune promising small, unmonitored hatches. Careless technicians often left them unsecured. With a gentle touch, Alone tried to lift the first hatch, and then he tried to shove it inwards. But it was locked. Then he worked his way along the base of the nozzle, testing another 50 hatches before deciding that he was mistaken. Or perhaps the technicians had learned to do their work properly. But having little else to do, he invested the next 20 months toying with every hatch and tiny doorway that he came across, his persistence rewarded when what passed for his hand suddenly dislodged a narrow doorway.

Darkness waited, and with it, the palpable sense of great distance.

He crawled down, slowly at first, and then the sides of the nearly vertical tunnel pulled away from his grip.

Falling was floating. There was no atmosphere, no resistance to his gathering momentum. Fearing that someone would notice, he left the darkness intact. Soon he was plunging at a fantastic rate, and that's when he remembered Wune cautioning, "These vents and access tubes run straight down, sometimes for hundreds of kilometers."

His tube dropped 60 kilometers before making a sharp turn.

The impact came without warning. One moment, he was mildly concerned about prospects that he couldn't measure, and the next moment saw discomfort and flashes of senseless light as his neural net absorbed the abuse. But he never lost consciousness, and he soon felt his shattered pieces flowing together, making healing motions that continued without pause for three hours.

A familiar voice found him then.

Lying in the dark, unable to move, something quiet came very close and then said, "The cold," before falling silent again.

He didn't try to speak.

Then after a long while, the voice said, "For so long, cold."

"What is cold?" Alone whispered.

"And dark," said the voice.

"Who are you?" he asked.

The voice said, "Listen."

Alone remained silent, straining to hear any sound, no matter how soft or fleeting. But nothing else was offered. Silence lay upon silence, chilled and black, and he spent the next long while trying to decipher which language was used.

No human tongue, clearly. Yet those few words were as transparent and simple as anything he had heard before.

Once healed, he seeped light.

The engine's interior was complex and redundant, and most of its facilities were scarcely used. Except for the occasional crackling whisper, radio talk never reached him. He could wander again. Happy, he discovered a series of nameless places where the slightest frosting of dust lay over every surface, that dust never disturbed. Billions of years of benign neglect promised seclusion. No one would find him in this vastness, and if nothing else happened in his life, all would be well.

Centuries passed.

Technicians and their machines traveled through these places, but always bound for other, more important locations.

Hiding was easy inside the catacombs.

The Ship gave warning when the overhead engine was about to be fired. Great valves were opened and closed, vibrations traveling along the sleeping tubes. A deeper chill could be felt as lakes of liquid hydrogen were prepared for fusion. Alone always found three sites where he could quickly find shelter. His planning worked well, and he saw no reason to change what was flawless. And then one day, everything changed. Alone was sitting inside a minor conduit, happily basking in a pool of golden light leaking from his inexplicable body. He was thinking about nothing of consequence. And then that perfect instant was in the past. There was a deep rumble and the ominous feel of dense fluids on the move, and before he could react, he was picked up and carried along by a hot viscous and irresistible liquid. Not hydrogen, and not water either. It was some species of oil dirtied up with odd metals and peculiar structures. He was trapped inside juices and passion, life and more life, and he responded with a desperate scream.

Tendrils touched him, trying to bury inside him.

He panicked, kicked and spun hard. Then he pulled his body into the first disguise that occurred to him.

Electric voices jabbered.

A language was found, and what surrounded him said in the human tongue, "It is a Remora."

"Down here?"

"Tastes wrong," a third voice complained.

"Not hyperfiber, this shell isn't," said a fourth.

No voice spoke twice. This oily body contained a multitude of independent, deeply communal entities.

"The face is," said another.

"Look at the face." Another.

"You hear us, Remora?"

"I do," Alone allowed.

"Are you lost?"

He knew the word, but its precise meaning had always evaded him. So with as much authority as possible, he said, "I am not lost. No."

In an alien language, the multitude debated what to do next.

Then a final voice announced, "Whatever you are, we will leave you now in a safe place. For this favor, you will pay us with your praise and thanks. Do this and win our respect. Otherwise, we will speak badly of you, today and for the eternity to come."

He was spat into a new tunnel–a brief broad hole capped with a massive door and filled with magnetic filters, meshed filters, and a set of powerful grasping limbs. The limbs gathered him up. He immediately transformed his body, struggling to slide free. But his captors tied themselves into an enormous knot, their grip trying to crush him. Alone felt helpless. He panicked. Wild with terror, fresh talents were unleashed, and he discovered that when he did nothing except consciously gather up his energies, he could eventually let loose a burst of coherent light–an ultraviolet flash that jumped from his skin, scorching the smothering limbs–and he tumbled back onto the mesh floor.

A second set of limbs emerged, proving stronger, more careful.

Alone adapted his methods. A longer rest produced an invisible but intense magnetic pulse. The mechanical arms flinched and died, and then he changed his shape and flowed out from between them. The chamber walls and overhead door were high-grade hyperfiber. With brief bursts of light, he attacked the door's narrow seams. He attacked the floor. Security AIs made no attempt to hide their presence, calmly studying the ongoing struggle. Then a pair of technicians stepped through an auxiliary door–humans wearing armored lifesuits, complete with helmets that offered some protection to their tough, fearful minds.

The man asked the woman, "What is that thing?"

"I don't damn well know."

"You think it's the Remoras' ghost?"

"Who cares?" he decided. "Call the boss, let her decide."

The humans retreated. Fresh arms were generated, slow and massive but designed just moments ago to capture this peculiar prize. Alone was herded into a corner and grabbed up, and an oxygen wind blew into the chamber, bringing a caustic mist of aerosols designed to weaken any normal machine. Through the dense air and across the radio spectrum, the humans spoke to him. "We don't know if you can understand us," they admitted. "But please, try to remain still. Pretend to be calm. We don't want you hurt, we want you to feel safe, but if you insist on fighting, mistakes are going to be made."

Alone struggled.

Then something was with him–a close, familiar presence–and the voice said, "The animals."

Alone stopped fighting.

"They have us," said the voice.

He listened to the air, to the empty static.

But whatever spoke to him was already gone, and that's when a low whistling noise began to leak out of the prisoner—a steady sad moaning that stopped only when the ranking engineer arrived.

6

"I think you do understand me."

He stared at the woman. Except for a plain white garment, she wore nothing. No armor, no helmet.

"My name is Aasleen."

Aasleen's face and open hands were the color of starless space. She was speaking into the air and into an invisible microphone, her radio words finding him an instant before their mirroring sound.

The woman said, "Alone."

He wasn't struggling. Doing nothing, he felt his power growing quickly, and he wondered what he might accomplish if held this pose for a long time.

"That's your name, isn't it? Alone?"

He had never embraced any name and saw no reason to do so now.

With her nearly black eyes, Aasleen studied her prisoner. And as she stood before him, coded threads of EM noise pushed into her head. Buried in her organic flesh were tiny machines, each speaking with its own urgent, complex voice. She listened to those voices, and she watched him. Then she said one secret word, silencing the chatter, and that's when she approached, walking forward slowly until he couldn't endure her presence anymore.

He made himself invisible.

She stopped moving toward him, but she didn't retreat either, speaking quietly to the smear of nothing defined by the giant clinging limbs.

"Twisting ambient light," she said. "I know that trick. Metamaterials and a lot of energy. You do it quite well, but it's nothing new."

Alone remained transparent.

"And I understand how you can alter your shape and color so easily. You're liquid, of course. You only pretend to be solid." She paused for a moment, smiling. "I once had a pet octopus. He had an augmented brain. To make me laugh, he used to pull himself into the most amazing shapes."

Alone let his body to become visible again.

"Step away," he pleaded.

Aasleen stared at him for another moment. Then she backed off slowly, saying nothing until she had doubled the distance between them.

"Do you know what puzzleboys are?" she asked.

He didn't answer.

"Puzzleboys build these wonderful, very beautiful machines–hard cores clothed with liquid exteriors. Their devices are durable and inventive. Their best machines are designed to survive for ages while crossing deep space." Aasleen paused, perhaps hoping for a reaction. When she grew tired of the quiet, she explained, "Puzzleboys were like a lot of sentient species. They wanted the Great Ship for themselves. Thousands of worlds sent intergalactic missions, but my species won the race. I rode out here on one of the earliest starships. Among my happiest days is that morning when I first stood on the Ship's battered hull, gazing down at the Milky Way."

He said, "Yes."

"You know the view?"

"Yes."

She smiled, teeth showing. "A couple thousand years ago, as we were bringing the Great Ship into the galaxy, puzzleboys started singing their lies. They claimed they'd sent a quick stealthy mission up here. The laws of salvage are ancient–far older than my baby species. Machines can't claim so much as a lump of ice for their builders. But the aliens claimed that they'd shoved one of their own citizen's minds into a suitable probe. Like all good lies, their story has dates and convincing details. It's easy to conclude that their one brave explorer might have actually reached the Great Ship first. If he had done that, then this prize would be theirs. At least according to these old laws. The only trouble with the story is that the mission never arrived. I know I never saw any sign of squatters. Which is why we've made a point of insulting that entire species, and that's why the legal machinery of this cranky old galaxy has convincingly backed our claim of ownership."

Quietly, he said, "Puzzleboys."

"That's a human name. A translation, and like most approximations, inadequate."

With a burst of radio, the species' name was offered in its native language.

"Do you recognize it?" asked Aasleen.

He admitted, "I don't, no."

"All right." She nodded. A thin smile broke and then vanished again. "Let's have some fun. Try to imagine that somebody we know, some familiar civilization, dreamed you up and send you to the Great Ship. Maybe they borrowed puzzleboy technologies. Maybe you've sprung from a different engineering history. Right now, I'm looking at a lot of data. But despite everything I see, I can't pick one answer over the others. Which is why this so interesting. And fun."

Alone said nothing.

She laughed briefly, softly. "That leaves me with a tangle of questions. For instance, do you know what scares me about you?"

He took a moment before asking, "What scares you?"

"Your power supply."

"Why?"

Aasleen didn't seem to hear the question. "And I'm not

the only person sick with worry," she admitted. She closed one of her eyes and opened it again abruptly. "Miocene," she said, and sighed. "Miocene is an important captain. And you're considered a large enough problem that right now, that captain is sitting inside a hyperfiber bunker three kilometers behind me. Three kilometers is probably far enough. If the worst happens, that is. But of course nothing is going to go bad now. As I explained to Miocene and the other captains, you seem to have survived quite nicely and without mishap, possible for many thousand years. What are the odds that your guts are going to fail today, in my face?"

He considered his nature.

"Do you have any idea what's inside you?"

"No," he admitted.

"A single speck of degenerated matter. Possibly a miniature black hole, although you're more likely a quark assemblage of one or another sort." She sighed and shrugged, adding, "Regardless of your engine design, it is novel. It's possible, yes, and I have a few colleagues who have done quite a lot of work proving that this kind of system might be used safely. But to see something like you in action, and to realize that you've existed for who-knows-how-long, and apparently without demanding any significant repair . . .

"Alone," she said, "I am a very good engineer. One of the best I've ever met, regardless of the species. And I just can't believe in you. Honestly, it's impossible for me to accept that you are real."

"Then release me," he begged.

She laughed.

He watched her face, her nervous fingers.

"In essence," she continued, "you are a lucid entity carrying a tiny quasar inside your stomach. A quasar smaller than an atom and enclosed within a magnetic envelope, but massive and exceptionally dense."

"Quasar," he repeated.

"Matter, any matter, can be thrown inside you, and if only a fraction of the resulting energy is captured, you will generate shocking amounts of power."

He considered her explanation. Then with a quiet tone, he mentioned, "I have seen the Ship's engines firing."

"Have you?"

"Next to them, I am nothing."

"That's true enough. In fact, I've got a few machines sitting near us that can outstrip your capacities, and by a wide margin. But as Submaster Miocene has reminded me, if your magnetic envelope is breached, and if your stomach can digest just your own body mass, the resulting fireworks will probably obliterate several cubic kilometers of the Ship, and who knows how many innocent souls."

Alone believed her. But then he remembered that good lies have believable details and he didn't feel as certain.

Aasleen smiled in a sad fashion. "Of course I don't know exactly what would happen, if your stomach got loose. Maybe it has safety mechanisms that I can't see. Or maybe its fire would reach out and grab my body, and everything else in this room would be consumed, as well as Miocene . . . and with that, the Great Ship would be short one engine, and the survivors would have an enormous hole in the hull, spewing poisons and nuclear fire."

"I won't fail," he promised.

She nodded. "I think that's an accurate statement. I know I want to believe that both of us are perfectly safe."

"I won't hurt the Ship."

"All right. But why do you feel certain?"

He said, "Because I am."

Aasleen closed her eyes, once again concentrating on the machines inside her head.

"Please," said Alone. "Let me go free."

"I can't."

He changed his shape.

Aasleen's eyes opened. "I know that story about you and

Wune. My guess? That you'd take on my appearance like you did hers."

But he hadn't. He had no limbs now, no face. To the eye, he looked like a ball of hyperfiber with giant rockets on one hemisphere, thick armor on the other. Using a hidden mouth, he promised, "I won't do any harm. I shall not hurt anyone and I will never injure the Ship."

"You just want to left by yourself," she said.

"Nothing else."

"But why?"

He had no response.

"Which leads us to another area of deep concern," she continued. "A machine built by unknown hands is discovered wandering inside another machine built by unknown hands. But there seems to be two mysteries, there might be only one. Do you understand what I mean?"

He said, "No."

"Two machines, but only one builder."

He didn't react.

She shook her head. "We don't know how old the Great Ship is. Not precisely, but we have informed guesses. And no matter how well engineered you appear to be, I don't think you're several billion years old."

He remained silent.

Aasleen took one step closer. "There's the third terror involving you: A captain's nightmare. Maybe you are the puzzleboys' machine. Or you're somebody else's representative. Either way, if you arrived here on the Ship before any human did, and if there's a lost soul inside whatever passes for your mind . . . well, then it's possible that a different species might legally claim possession over the wealth and impossibilities that the Great Ship offers. And at that point, no matter how sweet your engineering is, your fate is out my hands . . ."

Her voice trailed away.

She took a tiny step forward.

"I have no idea," he said. "I don't know what I am. I know nothing."

The tiny machines inside Aasleen were speaking rapidly again.

"I'm watching your mind," she confessed. "But I'm not at all familiar with its neural network. It's a sloppy design, or it's revolutionary. I don't know enough to offer an opinion."

"I wish to leave now," he said.

"In the universe, there are two kinds of unlikely," Aasleen warned. "The Great Ship is one type–never attempted or even imagined, but achievable, provided someone has time and the muscle to make it real. And then there's the implausible that you imagine will come true, and one day your worst fears turn real. If the Great Ship belongs to someone else, then my species has to surrender our claim. And even though I believe that I am good and charitable soul, I don't want that to happen. Facing that prospect, I would fight to keep that from occurring, in fact."

Alone did nothing, gathering his strength.

"And even if you are safe as rain," she said, "I don't relish the idea of you wandering wherever you like. Not on my ship. Certainly not until we can find the answers to all these puzzles."

Without warning, Alone lost his shape, turning into a hot broth that tried to flow around the grasping arms.

The arms seemed to expect his trick, quickly creating one deep bowl that held him in place.

"I promise," said Aasleen. "You'll be somewhere safe. We will keep you comfortable. And as much as possible, you'll be left alone. Not even Miocene wants to torment you. And that's why a special chamber is being prepared–"

A new talent emerged.

The liquid body suddenly compressed itself, collapsing into a tiny dense and radiant drop hotter than any sun. And as the bowl-shaped limbs struggled to keep hold of this fleck of fire, Alone stole a portion of their mass, turning it into energy, shaping a ball of white-hot plasma.

And with that, he shrank into an even tinier, hotter bit of existence.

Aasleen turned and ran.

The arms were pierced. Not even the hyperfiber floor could resist his descent. He struck and sank out of sight, and when he was beneath the floor, hyperfiber turned into a bed of pale pink granite, and much as a ship passed between the stars, he was slicing quickly through what felt much like nothing.

7

Creating a narrow hole, Alone fell.

The hole was lined with compressed, distorted magma that flowed and bubbled and soon hardened above him. But despite the minuscule trail, his enemies would follow. He felt certain. Alone had value in their eyes, or he was dangerous, or they simply could not approve of his continued existence. Whatever their reasons, Aasleen and the captains would go to considerable trouble to chase him. But the Great Ship was full of holes and tunnels, and it occurred to him that his enemies would simply gather below him, waiting inside the next chamber.

To fool these hunters, Alone let his body balloon outwards, one final burst of blazing heat leaking out before his descent was finished.

Fifteen kilometers beneath Aasleen, the machine built a new chamber. It was a tiny realm, the spherical wall glowing red as the residual heat bled away, and he lay silent in the middle for long minutes before sprouting delicate fingers, pushing their tips into the cooling magma. Falling from above were vibrations–bright hard jarrings marking the closing and sealing of every hatch and orifice and superfluous valve. Then something massive and quite slow passed directly beneath him. But the subtle noises were never regular, never simple, creating distortions and echoes as the waves broke around empty spaces deep within the cold rock. Swim in one downward angle, and a large chamber would be waiting. Another easy line promised a more distant but far more extensive cavern. But what caught Alone's interest was a line that might be an illusion, a flaw in the rock, perhaps, or it might be a tunnel leading nowhere. But that target was close. Alone pulled his body into a new shape. Looking like the worms common to a hundred billion worlds, he began slithering and shoving his way forward.

He missed his goal by 80 meters.

But instinct or a wordless voice urged him to pause and think again. What was wrong? An urge told him what to do, and he obeyed, following a new line until he was not only certain that he was lost but that the Great Ship was solid to its core, and his fate was to wander this cramped darkness until Time's end.

Suddenly the rock beneath him turned to cultured diamond.

With the worm's white-hot head, he pushed through the gemstone. The Great Ship was laced with countless tiny tunnels, and this was among the most obscure, barely mapped examples. He glowed brightly for a long moment, new eyes probing in both directions before one was chosen. Then inside a space too small for a human child to stand, he began to run—sprouting limbs as necessary, pushing off the floor and the sides and that low slick diamond ceiling. With every junction and tributary hole, he picked for no reason. Eventually he was hundreds of kilometers from his beginning point, random choice his guide until the moment when he realized that he was beginning to wander back toward his starting point. Then Alone decided to pause, listening to the diamond and the rock beyond. The next turn led to a dead end, and he backed out of that hole and hunkered down, and with a soft private voice asked, "What now?"

"Down," the familiar voice coaxed.

Nothing else was offered. No other instruction was needed. He burned a fresh hole into the diamond floor, and after plunging three kilometers, his fierce little body exploded out into a volume of frigid air that stretched farther than the light of his body could reach.

Alarmed, he made himself black as space.

He fell, and a floor of water and carbon dioxide ice slapped him when he struck bottom.

The cavern was five kilometers in diameter, bubble-shaped and filled with ancient ice and a whisper of oxygen gas. Except for the dimpled footprints of one robot surveyor, there was no trace of visitors. No human had ever stepped inside this place. But as a precaution, Alone erased his tracks, and where his warmth had distorted the ice, he made delicate repairs.

A walker's existence gave way to the sessile life. He moved only to investigate his new home. Every sealed hatch leading out into the Ship was studied, and he prepared three secret exits that wouldn't appear on the captains' maps. Sameness made for simple memories. The next 17,000 years were crossed without interruption. Life was routine, and life was silent and unremarkable, and the old sense of fear subsided into a slight paranoia that left each sliver of Time sweet for being pleasantly, unashamedly boring.

Doing nothing was natural.

For long delicious spans, the entity sat motionless, allowing his heat to gradually melt the ice. Then he would cool himself and his surroundings would freeze again, and he would pretend to be the old ice. With determination and a wealth of patience, he imagined billions of years passing while nothing happened, nothing in this tiny realm experiencing any significant change. Sometimes he sprouted a single enormous eye, and from another part of his frigid body he emitted a thin rain of photons that struck the black basalt ceiling and the icy hills around him, and with that eye designed for this single function, he would slowly and thoroughly study what never changed, and with his mind he would try to imagine the Ship that he could not see.

"Speak to me," he might beg.

Then he would wait, wishing for a reply, tolerant enough to withstand a year and sometimes two years of inviting silence.

"Speak," he would prompt again.

Silence.

Then he might offer a soft lie. "I can hear you anyway," he would claim. "Just past my hearing, you are. Just out of my reach, out of my view."

But if the strange voice was genuine, then its maker was proving itself more stubborn even than him.

Seventeen millennia and 37 years passed, and then with a thunderous thud, a hatch on one wall burst inward. Unsealed for the first time, the open door let in a screaming wind and a brigade of machines–enormous swift and fearless assemblages of muscle and narrow talents that knew their purpose and had only so much time to work.

Alone was terrified, and he was enthralled. Imagining that he could escape at will, he retreated to the chamber's center. But then the other hatches exploded inwards, including a big opening at the apex of the ceiling. Machines began to burrow into the ice and string lights, and then they carved the black walls and built a second, lower ceiling. And all the while, they were leaking enough raw heat that the ancient glacier began to melt, transformed into fizzy water and gas.

Alone huddled inside the rotting shards of the ice.

Each of his emergency exists were either blocked or too close to active machines. The chamber floor was quality hyperfiber, difficult to pierce without creating a spectacle. Alone pretended to belong to the floor. For the next awful week, he did nothing but remain still. Then the ice had melted and the first wave of machinery vanished, replaced by different devices that worked rapidly in smaller ways, but with the same tenacious purpose.

Mimicking one common machine, he drifted to the new lake's surface.

A shoreline was being constructed from cultured wood and young purple corals and farm-raised shellfish, everything laid across a bed of glassy stone filled with artificial fossils–ancestors to the chamber's new residents. Humans stood beside the aliens, the species speaking through interpretive AIs. The aliens wore broad purple shells, and they were happiest when their gills lay in the newly conditioned water. The humans wore uniforms of various styles, different colors. One uniform had the bright reflective quality of a mirror, and the woman inside it was saying, "Beautiful, yes." Then she knelt down and sucked up a mouthful of the salted, acidic water. Spitting with vigor, she said, "And a good taste too, is it?"

The aliens swirled their many feet and the fibrous gills, stirring up their lake. Then their chittering answers were turned into the words, "We are skeptical."

"To your specifications," said the woman. "I pledge."

The aliens spoke of rare elements that needed to be increased or abolished. Proportions were critical. Perfection was the only satisfactory solution.

"It shall be done," the captain promised.

The aliens claimed to be satisfied. Confident of success, they slithered into the deeper water, plainly enjoying their new abode.

The captain looked across the lake, spying one machine that was plainly doing nothing.

With a commanding tone, she said, "This is Washen. We've got a balky conditioner sitting in the middle. Do you see it?"

Quietly, Alone eased beneath the surface, changing his shape, merging with the glassy sediment. His disguise was good enough to escape the notice of watching humans and machines. As he waited, he gathered enough power to make a sudden explosive escape. But then the artificial day faded, a bright busy night taking hold, complete with the illusion of scattered stars and a pale red moon; and it was an easy trick to assume the form one shelled alien, mimicking its motions and chattering tongue, casually slipping out through the public entrance into a side tunnel that led to a multitude of new places, all empty.

8

Twenty centuries of steady exploration, and still the cavern had no end. Its wandering passageways were dry and often cramped, unlit and deeply chilled. The granite and hyperfiber were quite sterile. Humans and aliens didn't wish to live in places like this. Machine species set up a few homes, but their communities were tiny and easily avoided. Once more, the habit of walking returned to his life. To help track his own motions as well as the passage of time, Alone would count his strides until he reached some lovely prime number, and then he would mark the nearest stone with slashes and dots that only he could interpret–apparently random marks that would warn him in another thousand years that not only had he had passed this way before, but he had been moving from this tunnel into that chamber, and if at all possible, he should avoid repeating that old route.

The voice found him more often now, but it was quieter and even harder to comprehend. Sometimes a whisper emerged from some slight hole or side passage–like a neighbor calling to a neighbor from some enormous distance. But more often the voice was directly behind him, and it didn't so much speak as offer up emotions, raw and unwelcome. The sadness that it gladly shared was deep and very old, but that black mood was preferable to the sharp, sick fear that sometimes took hold of Alone. One dose of panic was enough to make his next hundred days unbearable. Something was horribly wrong, the voice insisted. Alone couldn't define the terror, much less the reasons, but he didn't have any choice but believe what he felt. He had his solitude; there was no cause to be scared. No captains or engineers chased after him. Occasionally he slipped into some deep corner of the cavern, and for several months he would hide away, waiting for whatever might pass by. But nothing showed itself, and whatever the voice was, it was wrong. Mistaken. Alone was perfectly safe inside this private, perfect catacomb, and he welcomed no opinion that said otherwise.

One day, walking an unexplored passageway, he happened upon a vertical shaft. Normally he might have avoided the place. A human had been here first, leaving behind tastes of skin and bacteria and human oils. Leaking a faint glow, Alone spied the machine abandoned by this anonymous explorer: A winch perched on the edge of the deep shaft, anchored by determined spikes. The sapphire rope was broken. The drum was almost empty, but the winch continued to turn–an achingly slow motion that for some reason fascinated the first soul to stand here in a very long while.

After several days of study, Alone touched the drum, and that slight friction was enough to kill what power remained inside the superconductive battery. How long had it been here, spinning without purpose? And what was inside the hole, waiting at the other end of the broken blue thread?

Alone snapped two handles from the winch and uncoiled the remaining sapphire rope, tying one handle to one end. Then he dropped the handle into the dark shaft. Two hundred meters, and there was no bottom. Then he tied the rope's other end to the winch and climbed down. The shaft turned to hyperfiber, slick and vertical, and then its sides pulled away. When Alone couldn't reach easily from one side to the other, he let go, falling and making his body brighter as he fell, watching the dangling handle fly past. Then feeling no one but himself, he lit the entire chamber with his golden fire.

A human shape lay upon the flat floor.

Alone turned black and cold again, and he dropped hard and repaired his body and then carefully crept close to the motionless figure.

For three days, nothing changed.

Then he brightened, just slightly, straddling the figure. The human male hadn't moved in decades, perhaps longer. There was enough thread on the winch to put him down here, but it must have broken unexpectedly. The hyperfiber floor showed blood where the man struck the first time, hard enough to shatter his tough bones and shred his muscles. But humans can recover from most injuries. This stranger would have healed and soon stood up again, and probably by a variety of means, he had worked to save himself.

Most of the Ship's passengers carried machines allowing them to speak with distant friends. Why didn't this man beg for help? Perhaps that machinery failed, or this hole was too deep and isolated, or maybe he simply came to this empty place without the usual implements.

Reasons were easy, answers unknowable.

Whatever happened, the man had lived inside this hole for some months and perhaps several years. He had brought food and water, but not enough of either to last long. The cold that Alone found pleasant would have stolen away the body's precious heat, and the man starved while his flesh lost its moisture, reaching a point where it could invent no way to function. Yet the man never died. With his last strength, he stripped himself of his clothes and made a simple bed, his pack serving as his pillow, and then he lain on his back with his eyes aimed at the unreachable opening, his face turning leathery and cold and blind.

The eyes remained open but dry as stone. They might not have changed for centuries, and nobody had ever found this man, and perhaps no one had noticed his absence.

Alone considered the implications of each option.

Eventually and with considerable caution, he opened the pack and thoroughly inventoried its contents. What was plainly useful he studied in detail, particularly the sophisticated map of this cavern system. Then he carefully returned each item to where it belonged and laid the pack beneath the unaware head. That frozen, wasted body weighed almost nothing. A good hard shake might turn the dried muscle to dust. Yet he was careful not to disturb anything more than absolutely necessary, and without a sound, he retreated. The lower length of sapphire lay nearby, coiled into a neat pile. He tied one end to the second handle, and despite the distance and darkness, he managed a perfect toss on his first attempt, the two handles colliding and then wrapping together, and he climbed past the rough knot, pulling it loose and letting the lower rope fall away before he continued his climb out from the hole.

More centuries passed; little if anything changed. But there were a few episodes–intuitive moments when the bright gray fear took hold, when some nagging instinct claimed that he was being sloppy, that he was being pursued. Three times, Alone found marks resembling his own but obviously drawn by another hand. And there was one worrisome incident when he slipped aside and waited only 13 days before a solitary figure followed him down the long tunnel. The biped was towering and massive, covered with bright scales and angry spikes, and the low ceiling forced him to walk bent over inside the passageway, both hands carrying an elaborate machine that resembled a second head.

Mechanical eyes and a long probing nostril studied the rock where Alone had stepped, teasing out subtle cues. With a hunter's intensity, the creature slowly moved to a place where the second head noticed that the trail had vanished, and the machine whispered a warning, and the harum-scarum turned in time to see an amorphous shape sprout long limbs, and without sound, silently race away.

After that, Alone adapted his legs and gait, changing his stride, hopefully becoming less predictable. But he refused to abandon the cavern. His home was far too large to be searched easily or in secret, and he had nearly walked every passageway, every room—a hard-acquired knowledge that he would have to surrender if he journeyed anywhere else.

Most encounters came through chance, fleeting and harmless. As the millennia passed, human numbers had swollen, but other species plainly outnumbered the Ship's lawful owners. Aliens wore every imaginable body, and there were always new species waiting to surprise. One glimpse in the dark or some long study at a safe distance didn't make an expert, but Alone had adequate experience to gain several rugged little epiphanies: Life must be relentless, and it had to be astonishingly imaginative. Every living world seemed unique, and those oceans of living flesh were able to thrive on every sort of unlikely food and bitter breath. The beasts that came slipping through his home drank water, salty or clear, acidic or alkaline, or their drinks were chilled and laced with ammonia, or they wore insulated suits and downed pitchers of frigid methane, or they sucked on peroxides, on odd oils, while quite a few drank nothing whatsoever. Yet despite that staggering range of form and function, every creature was curious, peering into some black hole, sometimes slipping fingers and antennae into places never touched before—if not hunting for invisible, legendary entities, then at least seeking the simple, precious novelty of Being First.

On occasion, Alone watched visitors coupling. One eager pair of humans fell onto a mat of glowing aerogel, naked and busy, and standing just a few meters away, immersed in darkness, Alone observed as they bent themselves into a series of increasingly difficult poses, grunting occasionally before finally shouting with wild voices that echoed off the distant ceiling. Then their violence was finished, and the woman said to the man, "Is that all there is?" and her lover called her a harsh affectionate name, and she laughed, and he laughed, and after drinking the brown alcohol from a treasured bottle, the performance began again.

More centuries and thousands of kilometers were slowly, carefully traversed. And then came one peculiar second where he heard what sounded like a multitude passing through the cavern's largest entrance. The presence of many was felt; he smelled their collective breath. They might whisper respectfully and try to move like ghosts, but there were too many feet and mouths, too many reasons to praise the solitude and beg their neighbors to be silent. Alarmed, he approached the newcomers and then followed them, and from a sober distance he watched as they assembled at the center of the cavern's largest chamber. A quick count found 20,000 bodies and a staggering variety of species, and after an invisible signal was given, they began to talk in one shared voice. He heard rhythmic chanting, the sloppily performed songs. Normally he would have fled any spectacle, but the strangers were singing about the Great Ship, begging for its blessings and its wisdom. And hope upon hope, the Ship's voice.

Using every trick, Alone approached unseen.

The celebration was joyous, and it was senseless. But he felt the urgency and earnest passion. At least a hundred alien species were represented. But the lighting was minimal, and hovering at the edges, it was impossible to observe the full crowd, much less comprehend more than a fraction of what was being said.

"We thank the Ship," he heard.

Then from someplace close, one enormous voice chanted, "For the home and safety You give to us, we thank You!"

"You are a mystery," the nearest souls declared.

Alone hovered at the edge of the crowd, unnoticed but near enough to touch the backs and feel the leaked heat of bodies.

A hill of smooth basalt stood on the cavern floor, and perched on the summit was a human male crying out, "For so long and for so far, You have journeyed. We cannot measure the loneliness You endured in Your wanderings. But in thanks for Your shelter, we give You our companionship. For Your speed, we give You purpose. After the countless years of being empty and dead, we have made You into a vibrant, thriving creature! At long last, the Great Ship lives! And we hear Your thanks, yes! In our dreams, and between our little words, we hear You!"

Precisely when Alone turned to flee, he couldn't say.

He was at a loss to understand which word triggered the wash of emotion, even as he was rushing away from the room and its densely packed bodies . . . even as a few of the less devoted worshippers heard what might be a moan and turned in time to notice the faint but unmistakable glow, red as a dying ember, racing off on legs growing longer by the stride.

9

Ten thousand and forty-eight years after first discovering the hole, Alone returned. The winch remained fixed in place, but someone else had visited, and possibly more than once. Boot prints showed in the dust. He could smell and taste signs of a second human. But nobody had stood upon this ground for a very long while, and when he went below, he found the body exactly where he had left it–only more dried, more wasted. More helpless, if that was possible.

Once again, Alone emptied the pack of its belongings, but this time he tenaciously studied the design and contents of even the most prosaic, seemingly useless item. He taught himself to read. He mastered the old, once-treasured machines that had thoroughly recorded one life. The mummified man had a long, cumbersome name, but he answered easiest to Harper. Eyes pushed against the digital readers, Alone marveled at scenes brought by Harper from the distant earth. Here were glimpses of strange brightly lit lives, the toothy faces of a family, and a sequence of lovers. But each of those individuals were left behind when Harper sold every possession, surrendering his home and safety for a ticket to ride the Great Ship—embarking on a glorious voyage to circumnavigate the Milky Way.

Between the man's arrival at Port Alpha and this subsequent disaster, barely 50 years passed. Which was no time at all. What's more, Harper had filled his days with a single-minded hunt for the Ship's ancient builders. Infused with a maniacal hunger, the human not only presumed that some grand and purposeful force had built the derelict starship, but the same force was still onboard, hiding in an odd corner or unmapped chamber, biding its time while waiting for that brave, earnest explorer that would discover its lair.

Harper intended to be that very famous man.

Alone studied every aspect of the lost life. There were gaps in the records, particularly near the end. But he wasn't familiar enough with human ways to appreciate that another hand might have blanked files and entire days, erasing its presence from the story. What mattered was digesting the full nature of this alien beast, learning Harper's manners and looks and duplicating his high, thin voice. Then Alone refilled the pack. But this time, he left the hole with the lost man's possessions carried under what looked like a human arm.

At the top of the hole, he transformed his face, his body.

There were many ways to be alone. The next weeks were spent duplicating the voice and gestures on the digitals. Then he abandoned the safety of the cavern. The local time was night, as he had planned. Obeying customs learned only yesterday, Alone summoned a cap-car that silently carried him halfway around the Ship. He paid for the service with funds pulled from an account that hadn't been touched for thousands of years. The modest apartment hadn't seen this face for as long, but its AI said, "Welcome." The master's sudden reappearance didn't cause suspicion or curiosity. Entering a home that he didn't know, Alone spent the next ten days and nights studying the lost man. Then his apartment announced, "You have a visitor, sir."

Baffled, he asked, "Who?"

"It is Mr. Jan."

"Who is Mr. Jan?"

"I have no experience with the gentleman. But he claims to be your very good friend."

Alone considered the implications.

"What shall I tell him, sir?"

"That I have no friends," he replied.

"Very well."

The matter seemed finished. But 53 minutes later, the apartment warned, "Mr. Jan is still waiting at your door, sir."

"Why?"

"Apparently he wishes to speak with you."

"But I'm not his friend," Alone repeated.

"And I told him as much. But the man is quite upset about some matter, and he refuses to leave until he shares words with you."

"Let him into the front hall."

A narrow, nervous human crept inside the apartment. Mr. Jan had a familiar scent, and judging by the intricacy of the braids, he was quite proud of his thick red hair. The hallway was 30 meters long, which wasn't long enough. The two figures stared at one another from opposite ends, and when Mr. Jan took a small step forward, the other soul said, "No. Come no closer, please."

"I understand," the guest whispered. "Sure."

"What do you want with me?"

What did Mr. Jan want? The possibilities were too numerous or too vast for easy explanations. He gazed down at his pale hands, as if asking their opinion. Then quietly and very sadly, he said, "I'm sorry."

"Sorry?"

"Yes I am."

Alone felt sick to be this near a stranger. But his voice remained calm, under control. "For what are you apologizing?"

Mr. Jan straightened his back, surprised by those words, and on reflection, angered by them too. "I'm apologizing for everything, of course! I'm sorry for the entire mess!"

Alone waited, his new face unchanged.

"But these things weren't just my fault," the visitor insisted. "You used me, Harper. And I know you made fun of me. We were supposed to have a business relationship, a partnership. I heard quite a few promises about money, but did you give me even half of what I'd earned?"

"What did I give you?"

"None of it. Don't you remember?"

"Then I must have cheated you," Alone observed.

"'Cheat' doesn't do it justice," Mr. Jan insisted.

Alone wasn't certain what word to offer next.

"Look," said Mr. Jan. "What I did . . . I was just trying to scare you. Taking you that deep, down where your nexuses couldn't reach anybody. And then cutting the sapphire before you went down into that room. It looks bad, if you look at things that way. But it was meant to be a warning. Nothing else."

"You were trying to scare me," Alone guessed.

"Don't you remember? I spelled out all of my reasons afterwards." Mr. Jan looked at the granite floor and then the matching ceiling. With a stiff, self-absorbed voice, he said, "You heard me calling down to you. I know you heard, because you answered me. I told you that I was going to let you sit there and commune with the Great Ship until you promised to give me everything that I was owed."

"I remember," Alone lied.

"Money and respect. That's what I wanted, that's what I deserve. And that's why I did what I did." The walls were only partly tiled. Like the rest of the tiny apartment, the hallway was far from finished. Mr. Jan leaned against the shifting quasicrystals, beginning to cry. "All you needed to do . . . I mean this . . . was to say a few words to me. You could have just told me another lie. I never wanted to leave you down there. I'm not cruel like that. If you'd made any promises, anything at all, I'd have pulled you right out of there. Yes, I would have saved you in an instant."

The voice faded.

"I should have done that," Alone agreed. "Lying would have been right."

"Well, I don't know if that's quite true." The weeping man looked at his nemesis–a ghost that had stalked him for eons. "But listen, Harper. You have no respect for anyone but you. Yelling those insults up at me. Yes, you hurt me. Words like that . . . they last forever. They're cutting me still, those awful things that you said to me."

"I was wrong," Alone agreed.

Mr. Jan looked at him. He took three steps forward, and when the other figure didn't complain, he admitted, "I came back to the hole. You don't realize that, but I did. I went there to check on you. After you fell into the coma, I used a little lift-bug to reach your body." A trembling hand tugged at the braided hair. "I meant to bring you out, but I got scared. It looks bad, what happened, and I didn't want trouble. So I scrubbed away every trace of me, from your field recorders and in here too. Then I convinced your apartment that I never existed and that you were always coming home tomorrow. In case anybody became curious about your whereabouts."

"People can be curious," Alone agreed.

Mr. Jan smiled grimly. Then he wiped at his eyes, adding, "I was always your best friend."

Alone said nothing.

"You know, when you suddenly vanished, nobody noticed. Oh, they might ask me about you. Since they knew we were close. For several years, they'd wonder if I'd heard any noise from Crazy Harper and where you might have gone."

"'Crazy Harper'?"

"That's what some of them called you. I never did."

Alone made no remark.

For a long while, Mr. Jan concentrated on his mind, searching for courage to say, "I'm a little curious. How did you finally climb out of that hole?"

"There is a story," Alone admitted. "But I don't wish to tell it."

Mr. Jan nodded, lips mashed together. Then he asked, "Does anyone know the story? About us, I mean."

Silence.

Mr. Jan wrapped his arms around his chest and squeezed. "Not that you're in terrible shape now. I mean, it's not as if I murdered anybody." He paused, dwelling for a moment on possibilities. Then he pointed out, "You lost time. I know, it was quite a lot of time. But here you are, aren't you? And everything is back where it belongs."

"I've told no one about my years."

With a deep sigh, Mr. Jan said, "Good."

"No one knows anything. Except for you, of course."

The human nodded. He tried to laugh, but his voice collapsed into soft sobs. "I won't tell, if you don't."

"I don't know what I would say."

Wiping at his wet face, Mr. Jan quietly asked, "What can I do? Please. Tell me how to make this up to you."

Alone said nothing.

"I was wrong. I've done something criminal, and I'll admit that much, yes. And you should deliver the punishment. That's the right solution. Not the captains, but you." The smile was weak, desperate. "I promise. I'll do whatever you tell me to do."

Alone had no idea to say, but then a memory took hold. He thought to smile, nodding knowingly. Then with quiet authority, Alone explained, "You will leave me. Leave here and climb to the Ship's hull. Since you're a criminal, you need to be where criminals belong. Live under the stars and help keep the hull in good repair." Alone took a small step forward, adding, "The work is vital. The Great Ship must remain strong. There is no greater task."

Mr. Jan straightened his back. "What?" He didn't seem to understand. "You want me to work with the Remoras? Is that your punishment?"

"No," said Alone. "I wish you to become a Remora."

"But why would I?"

"Because if you do otherwise," Alone replied, "other people, including the captains, will hear what you did to your good friend, Crazy Harper."

The demand was preposterous. Mr. Jan shook his head and laughed for a full minute before his frightened, slippery mind fell back to the most urgent question. "How did you get out of that hole?"

Alone didn't answer.

"Somebody helped you. Didn't they?"

"The Great Ship helped me."

"The Ship?"

"Yes."

"The Ship pulled you out from that hole?"

"Yes."

Mr. Jan looked at the sober face, waiting for any hint of a lie. But nothing in the expression gave hope, and he collapsed to the stone floor. "I just don't believe you," he sobbed.

But he did believe.

"The Ship needs you to walk on the hull," Alone explained. "It told me exactly that. Until you are pure again, you must live with the followers of Wune."

"For how long?"

"As long as is necessary."

"I don't know what that means."

Alone hesitated. Then quite suddenly he was laughing, admitting, "I'm sorry, Mr. Jan. I don't know either. Even with me, it seems, the Great Ship refuses to explain much about anything."

10

Harper must have been a difficult, solitary man. No one seemed to have missed his face or companionship, and his sudden return caused barely a ripple of interest. Word spread that somebody was again living inside his apartment, and the apartment's AI dutifully reported communications with acquaintances from the far flung past. But the greetings were infrequent and delivered without urgency. Maintaining his privacy proved remarkably easy. For 20 busy years, Alone remained inside those small, barely furnished rooms. And the apartment never asked where its only tenant had been or why he had been detained, much less why this new Harper never needed to eat or drink or sleep. The machine's minimal intelligence had been damaged by Mr. Jan. Alone spent a month dismantling and mapping his companion's mental functions, and all that while he wondered if he was the same, his mind incomplete, mangled by clumsy, forgotten hands.

Harper had painted himself as an important explorer and an exceptionally brave thinker. Inside his pack, he had carried dated records about mysterious occurrences inside the Great Ship. But there were larger files at home, each one possessed by one broad topic and a set of tireless goals. In the man's long absence, those files had grown exponentially. Alone uncovered countless stories about ghosts and monsters and odd lost aliens. Over thousands of years, one thin rumor of a Builder being seen by the first scout team had become a mass of rumors and third-hand testimonies, plus a few more compelling lies, and several blatant fakes that had been discounted but never quite set aside.

Believe just a fraction of those accounts, and it would be

difficult not to accept that the Great Ship was full of ancient, inscrutable aliens–wise souls born when the Earth was just so many uncountable atoms cooking inside a thousand scattered suns.

Each resident species had its preferred Builder.

Humanoids like to imagine ancient humanoids; cetaceans pictured enormous whales; machine intelligences demanded orderly, nonaqueous entities. But fashions shifted easily and in confusing directions, dictating the key elements to the most recent fables. Each century seemed to have its favorite phantom, its most popular unmapped cavern, or one mysterious phenomenon that was fascinating yet never rose to a point where physical evidence could be found. But even a stubborn lack of evidence was evidence. Harper had reasoned that the Builders had to be secretive and powerful organisms, and of course no slippery wise and important creature would leave any trace of its passing. Skin flakes and odd tools were never found in the deep caves, much less a genuine body, because if hard evidence did exist, then the quarry wouldn't be the true Builders. Would they?

One file focused on the Remora's ghost.

On Alone.

He had discovered references about himself in Harper's field recorder. But in his absence, new sightings and endless conjecture made for years of unblinking study. Alone absorbing every word, every murky image, fascinated by the mystery that he had walked through. According to most accounts, he was more real than the Whispers that haunted a mothballed spaceport. But people like Harper generally preferred the Clackers who supposedly swam inside the Ship's fuel tanks, and the Demon-whiffs that were made of pure dark matter. Tens of thousands of years after the event, Alone watched the recording of him standing inside the empty hyperfiber tank–a swirl of cobalt light that could mean anything, or nothing–and he began to wonder if perhaps he wasn't quite real back then. Only recently, after all of the steps and missteps, had he acquired that rare and remarkable capacity to stand apart from Nothingness.

For every portion of the hull where he was seen, Remoras and other crewmembers and passengers had spotted at least ten more examples of the ghost wandering beneath the stars.

What if there was more than one Alone wandering loose?

He didn't know what to believe. After he abandoned the hull, those sightings fell to the level of occasional, and no Remora pretended to have spotted Wune's mysterious friend. In no file was there mention of Aasleen and the nightmare inside one of the Ship's engines. Which meant that the captains and crew were good at keeping secrets, and what else did they know? A related file focused on shape-shifting machines currently lurking in the dark corners and deepest wastes. Alone's cavern held a prominent but far from dominating place. Other realms seemed to be haunted by his kind. Dozens of sprawling, empty locations were named. But the only cavern to capture Alone's imagination was named Bottom-E. Again and again, he found sketchy accounts of tourists wandering down an empty passageway, and when they glanced over their shoulder, a smear of dim light was silently racing out of view.

Bottom-E was an even larger cavern than Alone's old home. And if nothing else, it would provide the perfect next home.

But what if another entity like him already lived there?

After two decades of study and consideration, Alone made one difficult choice. He identified the humans who had tried to contact Harper on his return. Most were small figures, many with criminal records and embarrassing public files. But despite those same limitations, one man had all the qualifications to give aid to an acquaintance that he hadn't seen for ages.

With Harper's face and voice, Alone sent a polite and brief request.

Eighteen days passed before any reply was offered. The recorded digital showed a smiling man who began with an apology. "I was off. Wandering in The Way of Old. It's an ammonia-hydroxide ocean. On a small scale, but it's still a hundred cubic kilometers of murk and life, and that's why I couldn't get back to you, Harper."

The man was named Perri.

"So you're interested in Bottom-E," the message continued. "I can't promise much in the way of help. I haven't seen more than one tenth of one percent of the place. But there is one enormous room that's worth the long walk. Its floor is hyperfiber, and a fine grade at that. And the ceiling is kilometers overhead and inhabited by the LoYo. They're machines, not sentient as individuals but colonial in nature. A few thousand of their city-nests hang free from the rafters, and that's one of the reasons for going down there."

The grinning man continued. "The LoYo give that big room a soft, delicious glow. I've got good eyes, but even after a week in that, I couldn't see far. The immediate floor and what felt like a distant, unreachable horizon. Once, maybe twice, I saw a light in the distance. I can't say what the light was. But you know me, Harper. Don't expect ghost stories. Usually the truth is a lot more interesting than what we think we want to see . . .

"Anyway, what I like best about Bottom-E, and that huge room in particular . . . what makes the trip genuinely memorable . . . is that when you walk on that smooth hyperfiber, and there's nothing above you but the faint far off glow of what could be distant galaxies . . . well, it's easy to believe that this is exactly how it would have felt and looked just a couple billion years ago, if you were strolling by yourself, walking across the hull of the Great Ship.

"Understand, Harper? Imagine yourself out between the galaxies, crossing the middle of nothing.

"I think that's an experience worth doing," Perri said.

Then with a big wink, he added, "By the way. I know

you keep to yourself. But if you feel willing, you're more than welcome to visit my home. For a meal, let's say. For conversation, if nothing else. I don't think you ever met my wife. Well, I'll warn you. Quee Lee likes people even more than I do, if you can believe that."

Perri paused, staring at his unseen audience.

"You were gone a very long time," he mentioned. "Jan claimed you were off chasing Clackers, and that's what the official report decides too. Lost in the fuel tanks somewhere. But I didn't hear any recent news about bodies being fished out of the liquid hydrogen, which makes me wonder if our mutual friend was telling another one of his fables.

"Anyway, good to hear from you again, Harper. And welcome back to the living!"

11

As promised, Bottom-E held one enormous room, and except for the occasional smudge of cold light on the high arching ceiling, the room was delightfully dark. Each step on the slick floor teased out memories. That lost and now beloved childhood returned to him, and Alone wasn't just content, but he was confident that the next step would bring happiness, and the one after, and the one after that.

More than 1200 square kilometers of hyperfiber demanded his careful study. Unlike the hull, there was an atmosphere, but the air was oxygen-starved and nearly as cold as space. Like before, Alone's habit was to follow a random line until an oddity caught his attention. Then he would stop and study what another visitor had left behind–a fossilized meal or frozen bodily waste, usually–and then he would attack another random line until a new feature caught his senses, or until a wall of rough feldspar defined the limits of this illusion.

For almost two years, he walked quietly, seeing no one else.

The LoYo were tiny and weakly lit, and there was no sign that they noticed him, much less understood what he was.

Perri's mysterious glow failed to appear. But Alone soon convinced himself that he'd never hoped the story would prove real. One step was followed by the next, and then he would pause and turn and step again, defining a new line, and then without warning, there was a sliver of time when that simple cherished pattern failed him. He suddenly caught sight of a thin but genuine reddish light that his big eyes swallowed and studied, examining the glow photon by photon, instinct racing ahead of his intelligence, assuring him that this new light was identical to the glow he leaked when he was examining a fossilized pile of alien feces.

On his longest, quietest legs, Alone ran.

Then the voice returned. Decades had passed since the last time Alone felt its presence, yet it was suddenly with him, uttering the concept, "No," wrapped inside a wild, infectious panic.

His first impulse was to stop and ask, "What do you want?"

But the red glow was closer now, and Alone's voice, even rendered as a breathless whisper, might be noticed. If that other entity heard him, it could become afraid, vanishing by some secret means. The moment was too important to accept that risk. The end of a long solitude might be here, if only Alone was brave enough to press on. That's what he had decided long ago, imagining this unlikely moment. He would accept almost any danger to make contact with another like him. But only now, caught up in the excitement, did Alone realize how much this mattered to him. He was excited, yes. Thrilled and spellbound. Every flavor of bravery made him crazy, and he refused to answer the voice or even pay attention when it came closer and grew even louder, warning him, "Do not." Telling him, "No. They want, but they will not understand. Do not."

The light was still visible, but it had grown weaker.

The intervening distance had grown.

The other Alone must have noticed something wrong. A footfall, a murmur. Perhaps his brother heard the voice too, and the wild, unapologetic fear had taken possession of him. Whatever the reason, the light was beginning to fade away, losing him by diving inside a little tunnel, abandoning this room and possibly Bottom-E because of one irresistible terror.

Alone had to stop his brother.

But how?

He quit running.

The voice that had never identified itself–the conscience that perhaps was too ancient, too maimed and run down, to even lend itself a name–now said to him, "Go away. This is the wrong course. Go!"

Alone would not listen.

Standing on that barren plain, he made himself grow tiny and exceptionally bright, washing away the darkness. In an instant, the enormous chamber was filled with a sharp white light that reached the walls and rose to the ceiling before vanishing in the next instant.

Then he was dark again, drained but not quite exhausted.

With the last of his reserves, Alone spun a fresh mouth, and in a language that he had never heard before–never suspected that he was carrying inside himself–he screamed into the newly minted darkness, "I am here!"

Suddenly a dozen machines emerged from their hiding places, plunging from the ceiling or racing from blinds inside the towering rock walls.

Alone tried to vanish.

But the machines were converging on him.

Then he grew large again, managing legs. But the power expended by his desperate flash and careless shout was too much, and too many seconds were needed before he would be able to offer them any kind of chase. After thousands of years, the door of a trap was closing over him, and in the end there wouldn't even be the pleasure of a hard chase fought to the dramatic end.

12

Since their last meeting, the two organisms had walked separate lines–tightrope existences inspired by chance and ambition, deep purpose and the freedom of no clear purpose. An observer on a high perch, watching their respective lives, might have reasonably concluded that the two souls would never meet again. There was no cause for the lines to cross. The odd machine was quiet and modest, successfully avoiding discovery in the emptiest reaches of the Ship, while the engineer was busy maintaining the giant engines, and later, she was responsible for a slow-blooming career as a new captain. The remote observer would have been at a loss to contrive any situation that would place them together, much less in this unlikely terrain. Embarrassed, Aasleen confessed that she had had no good idea where Alone might have been and not been over these last tens of thousands of years. For decades, for entire centuries, she didn't waste time pondering the device that she once cornered and then let get away. Not that she was at peace with her failure. She was proud of her competence and didn't appreciate evidence to the contrary. Somewhere onboard the Great Ship was a barely contained speck of highly compressed matter, and should that speck ever break containment, then the next several seconds would become violent and famous, and for some souls, exceptionally sad.

This was a problem that gnawed, when Aasleen allowed it to. But as an engineer, she handed her official worries to the Submaster Miocene, and as a novice captain, she had never once been approached with any duty that had even the most glancing relationship to that old problem.

She told her story now, assuming that her prisoner would both understand what he heard and feel interested in this curious, quirky business.

Then several centuries ago, Aasleen and another captain met by chance and fell into friendly conversation. It was that other captain who mentioned a newly discovered machine-building species. Washen had a talent for aliens, Aasleen explained. Better than most humans, her colleague could decipher the attitudes and instincts of organisms that made no sense to a pragmatic, by-the-number soul like her. But the aliens, dubbed the Bakers, had been superior engineers. That's why Washen mentioned them in the first place. She explained their rare genius for building inventive and persistent devices, and millions of years after their rise and fall and subsequent extinction, their machines were still scattered across the galaxy.

"Bakers is our name for them," Aasleen cautioned. "It shouldn't mean anything to you."

Alone was floating above the cavern floor, encased in a sequence of cages, plasmas and overlapping magnetic fields creating a prison that was nearly invisible and seemingly unbreakable. Drifting in the middle of the smallest cage, he was in a vacuum, nothing but his own body to absorb into an engine that everybody else seemed to fear. With a flickering radio voice, he agreed. "I don't know the Bakers."

"How about this?" Aasleen asked.

Another sound, intense and brief, washed across him. He listened carefully, and then he politely asked to hear it again. "I don't know the name," he confessed. "But the words make sense to me."

"I'm not surprised," Aasleen allowed.

Alone waited.

"We know what you are," she promised.

His response, honest and tinged with emotion, was to tell his captor, "I already know what I am. My history barely matters."

"All right," Aasleen allowed. "Do I stop talking? Should I keep my explanations to myself?"

He considered the possibility. But machines and teams of engineers were working hard, obviously preparing to do some large job. As long as the woman in the mirrored uniform was speaking, nothing evil would be done to him. So finally, with no doubt in the voice, he said, "Tell me about these Bakers."

"They built you."

"Perhaps so," he allowed.

"Seven hundred million years ago," Aasleen added. Then a bright smile broke open, and she added, "Which means that you are the second oldest machine that I have ever known."

The Great Ship being the oldest.

Quietly, with a voice not quite accustomed to lecturing, she explained, "The Bakers were never natural travelers. We don't know a lot about them, and most of our facts come through tertiary sources. But as far as we can determine, that species didn't send even one emissary out into the galaxy. Instead of traveling, they built wondrous durable drones and littered an entire arm of the galaxy with them. Their machines were complicated and adaptable, and they were purposefully limited in what they knew about themselves. You see, the Bakers didn't want to surrender anything about themselves, certainly not to strangers. They were isolated and happy to be that way. But they were also curious, in a fashion, and they could imagine dangerous neighbors wanting to do them harm. That's why they built what looks to me like an elaborate empty bottle–a bottle designed to suck up ideas and emotions and history and intellectual talents from whatever species happens to come along. And when necessary, those machines could acquire the shape and voice of the locals too."

Nothing about the story could be refuted. Alone accepted what he heard, but he refused to accept that any of it mattered.

Aasleen continued, explaining, "The Bakers lasted for ten or twelve million years, and then their world's ecosystem collapsed. They lived at the far end of our galaxy, as humans calculate these measures. The only reason we've learned anything about them is that one of our newest resident species have collected quite a few of these old bottles. In partial payment for their ongoing voyage, they've shared everything they know about the Bakers. It's not the kind of knowledge that I chase down for myself. But Washen knew that I'd be interested in dead engineers. And she mentioned just enough that I recognized what was being described, and I interrupted to tell her that I knew where another bottle was, and this one was still working.

"'Where is it?' she asked.

"I told her, 'Wandering inside the Great Ship, he is, and he answers to the very appropriate name of Alone."

The captain paused, smiling without appearing happy.

Alone watched the workers. An elaborate needle was being erected on the cavern floor, aiming straight up at him.

"We approached Miocene with our news," Aasleen continued. "I know Washen was disappointed. But I was given the job of finding you again, and if possible, corralling you. Washen helped me profile your nature. Your powers. I decided to lure you in with the promise of another machine like you, and that's why I turned Bottom-E into a halfway famous abode for a glowing shape-shifting soul. If something went ugly-wrong down here, then at least the damage could be contained."

"What about the LoYo?" Alone asked.

"They've been moved to other quarters. The lights above are hiding sensors, and I designed them myself, and they didn't help at all. Until that light show, we couldn't be certain that you were anywhere near this place."

The needle was quickly growing longer, reaching for the cage's outermost wall.

"What will you do now?" Alone asked.

"Strip away your engine, first. And then we'll secure it and you." Aasleen tried to describe the process, offering several incomprehensible terms to bolster her expertise. But she seemed uneasy when she said, "Then we'll isolate your neural net and see what it is and how it works."

"You are talking about my mind," Alone complained.

"A mind that lives beside a powerful, unexploded bomb," the captain added. "The Bakers didn't design you to survive for this long. My best guess is that you pushed yourself outside the Milky Way, and in that emptiness, nothing went wrong. You drifted. You waited. I suppose you slept, in a fashion. And then you happened upon the Great Ship, before or after we arrived. You could have been here long before us, but of course the Bakers are lost, and you weren't what I would consider sentient."

"But I am now," he said, his voice small and furious.

Aasleen paused.

Without apparent effort, the needle began to pass through the wall of the first impenetrable cage.

"You are going to kill me," he insisted.

The human was not entirely happy with these events. It showed in her posture, her face. But she was under orders, and she was confident enough in her skills to say, "I don't think anything bad will happen. A great deal of research and preparation has been done, and we have an excellent team working on you. Afterwards, I think you'll prefer having all of your memories pulled loose and set inside safer surroundings."

With a sudden thrust, the needle pierced the other cages, and before it stopped rising, its bright plasmatic tip was touching his center.

Damage was being done.

Quietly but fiercely, he begged Aasleen, "Stop."

One of the nearby machines began to wail, the tone ominous and quickening. Aasleen looked at the data for a moment, and then too late, she lifted one of her hands, shouting, "Stop it now. We've got the alignment wrong!"

The captain and every engineer vanished.

They were projections, Alone realized. The real humans were tucked inside some safe room, protected from the coming onslaught by distance and thick reaches of enduring hyperfiber.

He was injured and dying. But the damage was specific and still quite narrow, and the faltering mind lay exposed like never before. And that was when the Voice that had always been speaking to him and to every soul that stood upon or inside the deep ancient hull could be heard.

"I am the Ship," the Voice declared.

"Listen!"

13

In a place that was not one place, but instead was everywhere, Those-Who-Rule received unwelcome news. There was trouble in Creation, and there was sudden talk of grand failures. A portion of the everywhere was in rebellion. How could this be? Who would be so foolish? Those-Who-Rule were outraged by what they saw as pure treachery. Punishment was essential, and the best punishment had to be delivered instantly, before the rebellion could stretch beyond even Their powerful reach. A ship was aimed and set loose, burrowing its way through the newborn universe. When it reached its target, that ship would deliver a sentence worse than any death. Nonexistence was its weapon—oblivion to All—and with that one talent, plus an insatiable hunger for success, the ship dove on and on until it had passed out of sight.

But then the revenge lay in the past. A moment later,

upon reflection, Those-Who-Rule questioned the wisdom of their initial decision. Total slaughter seemed harsh, no matter how justified. In a brief discussion that wasted time on blaming one another, these agents of power decided to dispatch a second ship–another vessel full of talents and desires and grand, unborn possibilities.

If the second ship caught the first ship–somewhere out into that mayhem of newborn plasmas and raw, impossible energies–disaster would be averted. Life and existence and death and life born again would remain intact. But the universe was growing rapidly, exploding outwards until two adjacent points might discover themselves separated by a billion light-years.

The chase would be very difficult.

And yet, the second ship's goal could be no more urgent.

Through the fires of Creation, one ship chased the other, and nothing else mattered, and nothing else done by mortals or immortals could compare to the race that would grant the universe permission to live out its day.

Alone listened to the insistent relentless piercing voice. And then he felt his center leaking, threatening to explode. That was when he interrupted, finally asking, "And which ship are you?"

The Voice hesitated.

"But you can't be the first ship," Alone realized. "If you were carrying this nonexistence . . . then you wouldn't know about the second ship chasing after you, trying to stop your work . . ."

In a mutter, the Voice said, "Yes."

"You must be the second Ship," he said. "What other choice is there?"

"But a third choice exists," the Voice assured.

"No," said Alone.

Then in terror, he said, "Yes."

"I am," the Great Ship said.

"Both," Alone blurted. "You're that first ship bringing

Nothingness, and you're the second ship after it has reached its target."

"Yes."

"But you can't stop the mission, can you?"

"I have tried and cannot, and I will try and nothing will change," the Great Ship declared. Sad, yet not sad.

"You're both ships, both pilots."

"We are."

"Working for opposite ends."

"Yes."

"And the humans are happily, foolishly riding you through their galaxy."

"Doom everywhere, and every moment ending us."

Alone felt weak, and an instant later, stronger than ever. As his energies flickered, he said, "Tell them. Why can't you explain this to them?"

"Why won't they hear me?"

"I hear you."

"Yes."

"I could tell them for you."

"If you had survived, you would explain. Yes."

"But."

"It is too late."

Alone said nothing.

The Great Ship continued to talk, repeating that same tale of revenge and the chase, of nonexistence and the faint promise of salvation.

But Alone had stopped listening. He heard nothing more. With just the eye of his mind, he was gazing back across tens of thousand of years, remembering every step, marveling how small his life appeared when set against the light of far suns and the deep abyss of Time.

HOT ROCK

Greg Egan

*Greg Egan (*www.gregegan.net*) published his first story in 1983, and followed it with more than 50 short stories and seven novels. During the early 1990s Egan published a body of short fiction—mostly hard science fiction focused on mathematical and quantum ontological themes—that established him as one of the most important writers working in science fiction. His work has won the Hugo, John W Campbell Memorial, Locus, Aurealis, Ditmar, and Seiun awards. His latest books are a new novel,* Zendegi, *and a new collection,* Oceanic.

Having written very little during the first half of the decade, Egan has returned to science fiction recently with a handful of excellent stories, arguably the best of which is this rich, strange story that follows.

1

Azar turned away from her assembled friends and family and walked through the departure gate. She tried to keep her gaze fixed straight ahead, but then she paused and looked over her shoulder, as if there might yet be a chance for one more parting gesture. It was too late; there was nobody in sight. She had left her well-wishers far behind.

She managed a nervous laugh at the sheer seamlessness of the transition; she hadn't registered so much as a shift in the light. The corridor around her appeared unchanged, its walls bearing the same abstract blue-and-gold mosaics as the one she had entered, but when she walked to the far end and turned to the right, she found herself in a glass-walled observation deck, looking out into the rich blackness of space.

Doorway to the stars was the style of travel she had chosen, just one among dozens of decorative scenarios she might have wrapped around the raw, imperceptible act itself. There was no doorway; stepping through the departure gate had merely been a gesture of consent, the signal she had chosen to initiate her journey. In mid-stride, her mind had been copied from the processor that sat within her birth flesh, encoded into gamma rays, and transmitted across 1,500 light years. In a subjective instant, she had been transported from her home world of Hanuz into this scape, which mimicked a capacious habitat orbiting the planet Tallulah. She really was orbiting Tallulah, but the habitat, and the body she perceived as her own flesh, were illusory. The machine she now inhabited was scarcely larger than a grain of rice.

Azar pressed her palms to her eyes and composed herself. If she turned around and marched back through the gate it would take her home with no questions asked, but 3,000 years would have passed since her departure. That price had been paid, and no second thoughts, no hasty retreat, could reverse it. All she could do now was try to make it worthwhile.

The observation deck was unlit, but a gentle glow from the floor tracked her footsteps as she crossed to the far side and looked down on Tallulah. The scape's illusory gravity almost made her feel that she was on solid ground, gazing eastwards on a cloudless night from some mountain eyrie at a rising moon: a new moon, its gray disk lit only by starlight. But she knew that however long she waited, dawn would not come creeping across the limb of this disk; no crescent, no sliver of light would appear. Tallulah had no sun; it had been an orphan for at least a billion years, drifting untethered through the galaxy. Yet distant astronomers had surmised–and the instruments here and now confirmed–that its surface was awash with running water. In the cold of interstellar space even its atmosphere should have been frozen down to a sludge of solid nitrogen and carbon dioxide, but instead its long night was alive with balmy breezes wafting over starlit seas.

"Salaam! You must be Azar!" A tall, smiling woman strode across the deck, stretching out her arms. "I'm Shelma." They embraced briefly, just as Azar would have done when meeting someone for the first time back on Hanuz. This was no more a coincidence than Shelma's human appearance and common phonetic name: for the sake of mutual intelligibility, the scape was translating every sight, every word, every gesture that passed between them.

Shelma turned to face the blank gray disk, and her eyes lit up with pleasure. "It's beautiful!" she exclaimed.

Azar felt slightly foolish that she'd been so slow to take a proper look herself. Tallulah's surface would be emitting a far-infrared glow, but its atmosphere was virtually opaque at that frequency, so the easiest way to see any detail would be to increase her sensitivity to the usual visible spectrum. She willed the change–and the scape obliged, just as if her eyes were real.

The ocean sparkled in the starlight. Two broad continents shared the hemisphere below. Long mountain ranges, vast bare plains, and expanses of mysterious vegetation colored the shadowless land.

"It is lovely," she said. Every world had its own peculiar beauty, though, and Azar would not have sacrificed 3,000 years just to gaze upon even the most ravishing landscape.

When Tallulah had first shown up in telescopic surveys, long before Azar's birth, people had soon realized that the best chance to visit it would come when it passed fortuitously close to an imaginary line joining the distant systems of Hanuz and Bahar. If the two worlds cooperated by launching probes that arrived simultaneously, the two spacecraft could brake against each other, sparing both of them the massive amounts of fuel needed to decelerate.

Accordingly, Mologhat 1 and 2 were sent on their way, launched in time to meet at Tallulah and merge in an intricate electromagnetic embrace. But then the news had reached Hanuz that Bahar would not be leaving the mission in the hands of insentient robots: a traveler would follow the Bahari probe, to wake inside the unified Mologhat Station and supervise the exploration of the orphan world.

No native-born traveler had left Hanuz for millennia, and Azar's people were not so crippled with pride that the absence of a representative of their own would have been intolerable. The software they had already sent with Mologhat 1 was perfectly capable of protecting their interests in the mission; they might have simply left the Bahari to their alien ways without lessening their own enjoyment of whatever discoveries followed. And yet, a ripple had spread across the planet, a shocked whisper: *One of us could go, could be there, could live through it all in person.*

"A billion years in deep space," Shelma marveled, "and not an iceberg in sight."

"It's hard to believe," Azar replied. The endless night on Tallulah rivaled the height of summer on Hanuz. When a planet was stripped of its sun, the decay of long-lived radioisotopes could eke out enough warmth over billions of years to keep its core molten–but even with abundant greenhouse gases to trap the heat, that could not account for Tallulah's surface temperature. However warm its heart, its skin should have felt the chill by now.

Mologhat had been orbiting Tallulah for three years before their arrival, and Azar now ingested the results of its observations. No obviously artificial structures were visible on the surface, but a faint stream of neutrinos was radiating out from deep in the planet's crust. The spectrum of the neutrinos did not correspond to the decay of any known radioisotopes, natural or otherwise; nor did it match the signatures of fission or fusion. Someone had worked hard to keep this orphan warm, but it was far from clear how they had done it–and impossible to say whether or not they were still around.

"What do you think?" Azar asked Shelma. "Is there anyone home?"

"People have been beaming signals at Tallulah for 30,000 years," Shelma said, "and never raised a peep. So they're either dead, or resolute hermits."

"If they want to be left in peace, we have no right to disturb them." Azar hoped that this declaration was redundant, but she wanted the ground rules absolutely clear.

"Of course," Shelma agreed. "But if they insist on playing dead to perfection, all they'll get are the rights of the dead. Which, while not negligible, are somewhat diminished."

Once a civilization became extinct–not merely mutating into something new, but leaving no sentient heirs whatsoever–it was widely accepted that its history devolved into a common legacy that anyone was entitled to investigate. If sovereignty really had ceased to be an issue, Tallulah was certainly worth exploring. Tens of thousands of orphan planets had been found in the past, but only a few dozen had shown signs of habitation, and those worlds had yielded nothing but sad ruins buried beneath the permafrost. In the age of the Amalgam–the meta-civilization that now ringed the galaxy–the extinction of an entire world was unthinkable; if a catastrophe could not be averted, people who already had a robust digital form could be evacuated in seconds, and even those who had chosen purely biological modes could be scanned in a matter of days at the most.

The people of Tallulah, it seemed, had been halfway in between. When some cosmic mishap tossed them from their stellar hearth they had been unwilling or unable to evacuate, but they had not stood by and watched the air around them fall to the ground like snow. Whether trapped by their fate or just stubbornly resolved to ride it out, they had found a way to survive it. If they had since succumbed to some other tragedy, or merely surrendered to the passage of time, Azar saw no disrespect in digging up their secrets. Their achievements had endured for a billion years; they deserved recognition and understanding.

2

Mologhat's orbit was a discreet 100,000 kilometers from Tallulah, but it had dispatched a swarm of microprobes into smaller, faster orbits of various inclinations, providing complete coverage of the surface. If there had been any lingering suspicion that the heating of the crust might have been due to some freakish natural process, the details put that idea to rest: not only was the temperature modulated by latitude, diminishing toward the planet's rotational poles, the records showed that it cycled over a period of about three months, creating imitation seasons. These nostalgic echoes of a long-lost circumstellar orbit were so clear that Azar was surprised they'd put the heat source in the ground at all, rather than launching an artificial sun.

"Not only would that have given them light from above," she suggested to Shelma as they strolled through Mologhat's library, "they could have kept the old diurnal rhythm too." Heat conduction from deep in the crust would have washed out any cycle as short as a typical planetary day.

Shelma said, "It's a lot of extra work to make a microsun efficient–to keep it from pouring energy out into space."

"That's true."

"And perhaps they were insecure as well," Shelma added, sliding out an image from the stack beside her that showed an animated model of Tallulah's weather patterns. "They were already on the verge of losing one sun. They might have preferred to keep their energy source buried, rather than risk being parted from this one too."

"Yeah. Still, it's interesting that they tweaked the biosphere for such a radical shift–ground heat replacing sunlight–but kept the seasons."

Shelma smiled. “Days, seasons, you’ve got to have something. People go mad without change.” Both she and Azar had chosen to retain sleep cycles, their software following the dictates of their ancestral phenotypes. But Azar knew that the Baharis’ ancestors were nocturnal; what Azar perceived as the station’s night would be day to Shelma, and vice versa.

Azar pulled out a map of vegetation density. Using synthetic aperture methods, the microprobes had resolved details on Tallulah’s surface down to about a tenth of a meter, and even at that coarse resolution they had identified thousands of different kinds of plants. Spectroscopy could not untangle the detailed biochemistry from orbit, but the biosphere was clearly carbon-based/anaerobic, with the plants synthesizing carbohydrates but releasing no free oxygen.

Shelma spread her arms to take in the whole collection of data around them. “Everything here is open to interpretation. We’re going to need to make landfall to get any further.”

“I agree.” Azar was nervous, but relieved by the verdict. She was glad she hadn’t traveled this far just to find that Tallulah was clearly occupied by hermits, and there was nothing left to do but abandon them to their solitude.

“The question, then,” Shelma said, “is how we want to do it.” She began reeling off options. They could sprinkle a few nanotech spores on the surface, then sit back and wait for the army of robot insects they built to scour the planet. Or they could leave Mologhat and travel to the surface themselves, in various ways. Of course they could always combine the two, delegating most of the exploration while still being in the thick of it.

Azar had studied all of these methods before her departure, but Shelma sounded too blasé to be merely reciting theoretical knowledge. “You’ve done this kind of thing before, haven’t you?”

“Dozens of times.” Shelma hesitated. “This is your first time out-of-system?”

"Yes." That wasn't a lucky guess; everyone knew about the dearth of travelers from Hanuz. "It's hard for us," Azar explained. "Leaving everyone we know for hundreds of years. You don't mind doing that?"

"My ancestors were solitary for part of their life cycle," Shelma said, "and sociable for the rest. Now we're flexible: we can switch between those modes at will. What I don't understand is why you don't just travel in packs, if that would make things easier."

Azar laughed. "I know some people do that, but our social networks are so tangled that it's hard to find a truly self-contained group–least of all a group where everyone can agree on a single destination. And if they do, they're more likely to emigrate than to take a trip and come home again."

"I see."

"Anyway, forget about Hanuz. We need to make some decisions." Azar wasn't going to sit around on Mologhat while robots had all the fun, but there were practical limits on how far she could go just to get some dirt beneath her fingernails. If she had her own standard body reconstructed down on the surface, tweaked to survive the local conditions, she'd spend all her time foraging for food. Mologhat had only a few micrograms of its original antimatter store left; the few hundred megajoules that would generate were enough for its own modest needs, but pilfering any of it to power a 60-kilogram behemoth would be insane; she could burn up the whole lot in a month. If Tallulah had had a reasonable abundance of deuterium she could have powered her body with D-D fusion, but the isotope was rare here.

"What if we build a high-capacity processor into one of the explorer insects?" Azar suggested. "Then we download into that. We get to see the world firsthand and make some real-time decisions, but we don't waste energy or leave a big footprint." If Tallulah turned out to be inhabited after all, the difference between being perceived as friend or enemy might easily hang on something as simple as the amount of local resources they'd used, or how physically intrusive their presence had been.

Shelma thought it over. "That sounds like as good a choice as any."

3

Azar persisted with her doorway metaphor, and walked through an "airlock" from Mologhat Station into the robot insect as if the two were docked together. Amused by the conceit, Shelma followed behind her, but she couldn't resist a mild rebuke. "The poor balloon doesn't even rate a mention?"

Azar shuddered. "Please, heights make me dizzy." Only gamma rays had the bandwidth to transmit their software in a reasonable amount of time, but gamma rays couldn't penetrate far through a planetary atmosphere. So the nanotech on Tallulah's surface had built a small hydrogen balloon, which had risen high enough into the stratosphere to receive their transmission and transcribe the data into a densely encoded molecular memory, before deflating and descending.

The scape Azar had constructed inside the insect resembled the kind of transparent-domed flight deck found in sightseeing aircraft back on Hanuz. Shelma would be perceiving some very different furnishings, but at least the two of them shared the same view of the jungle beyond the windshield; Shelma's vision had always stretched into the far infrared, and now Azar had chosen to match her.

The insect was perched on a broad, flat leaf, one of dozens of papery structures sprouting from a slender trunk. The leaf's veins glowed with the heat of warm sap, and a hot mist wafted up from the blotchy hexagonal pores that dotted the surface. When Azar looked up into the sky, the stars were barely visible through the fog.

Scout mites had already crawled up and down this plant

and begun deciphering its strange biochemistry. Sap that was cooled and concentrated by evaporation in the leaves was pumped down to the roots, where it was diluted in chambers of fresh water. The increase in entropy that the dilution entailed allowed enzymes in the sap to drive an endothermic reaction, absorbing heat from the ground while synthesizing sugars from dissolved carbon dioxide.

The plant's heritable replicator was a carbohydrate polymer known as C3, which had been found on many other worlds. Once they'd built up a database of sequences from a sufficient number of species, they could start trying to construct an evolutionary tree, as well as looking for signs of technological tinkering.

Azar took hold of a joystick and flew their host across to another plant, a small bush adorned with twigs that sprouted leaves like radial cooling fins. They landed on a twig while the scout mites burrowed and sampled.

"There's not much sap in this one," Shelma noted. "The leaves just look like mats of fiber." There were no pores here, no steamy exudations.

Azar watched a display of the scouts' discoveries. There were long, fibrous structures running all the way from the leaves to the tips of the roots, and they were packed with interlocking polymers. In some fibers the polymers were rich in mobile electrons; in others they had positive "holes," electron deficits that could shuffle along the molecule's backbone from site to site.

"Thermoelectric diffusion?" she guessed. The electrons and holes would conduct heat from the ground up into the leaves, and in doing so they'd set up an electric potential, which in turn could be used to drive chemical reactions.

As the details came through, they confirmed her suspicion. The plant was a living thermocouple, with the heat-pumped currents in the polymers shuffling electrons to and from the enzymes that synthesized carbohydrates.

The thermocouple bush had no easily digestible nutrients above ground, so Azar flew back to the entropy tree and thrust the insect's proboscis into a vein, drawing out a tankful of sugary sap. There was no free atmospheric oxygen to help metabolize the sugars, but like the plant itself, their robot could make use of nitrate ions in the sap as an oxidizing agent, reducing them to ammonia in the process. Scout mites were still hunting for the organisms responsible for creating the nitrates in the first place.

Shelma said, "So where are the insects? Where are the animals?" So far, they'd seen nothing moving in the jungle.

"Maybe the Ground Heaters didn't have time to tweak any animals for the new conditions," Azar suggested. "If they were about to get ejected from their solar system, their priorities would have been a new form of energy, and a primary food source that could exploit it. The old animals just died out, and nobody had the heart to try to create new ones."

"Maybe," Shelma conceded. "But wouldn't your first response to the prospect of losing your sun be to build a few domed arks: sealed habitats with artificial heat and light that preserved the original ambient conditions, and as much of the original biosphere as possible?"

Azar said, "And then you'd slowly begin modifying the species from the arks to live off the new energy source. Still, they might have started with the plants but got no further."

The scout mites collected more C3 sequences, and as the numbers reached the point where comparisons became meaningful it grew increasingly clear that these genomes were natural, not engineered. Even the genes responsible for building the gloriously technomimetic thermocouple fibers had the same messy, incrementalist, patchwork character of all the others.

Stranger still, the genetic analysis pointed to a common ancestor for all these plants just two hundred million years ago, long after Tallulah had been orphaned.

As Azar reviewed descriptions of other C3 worlds, pulling the data down from Mologhat's library, she realized that in a couple of hours the station would set below the horizon. The time lag for her queries was already ponderous, and re-routing everything around Tallulah through the limited-bandwidth microprobes would only make that worse.

"We should clone the station's library," she suggested to Shelma. The library was far bigger than their personal software, and there was no room for it in their present insect host, but they could at least bring it down into the stratosphere, making the data far more accessible than it was from Mologhat's distant orbit.

Shelma agreed. They set the nanotech to work fitting out the balloon for a new flight, then continued exploring the jungle.

As in many communities of plants there was competition for access to the sky, but here it was all about shedding heat rather than catching sunlight. The healthiest plants had their roots deep in the ground and their leaves exposed to the darkness of space. To be caught in too warm a cranny, sentenced to uniform tepidity, was fatal. The only exceptions to that rule were parasites: vampiric vines that stretched over trunks, branches and leaves, their barbed rootlets anchoring them to their victims and drawing out nutritious sap.

As they moved through the jungle, the new sequence data that came in from the scouts only shored up their original conclusions: the life they were seeing was entirely natural, and this branch of it was relatively young.

"Suppose," Shelma ventured, "that the Ground Heaters didn't need to engineer anything to live this way."

"You mean there were species that exploited thermal gradients all along?" Azar frowned. "How do you evolve to use *that* as your energy source? A single cell can never do it alone; you need to be a certain minimum size to access a useful temperature difference."

"I'm not saying that the very first lifeforms used it," Shelma replied. "They might have relied on chemosynthesis, extracting energy from volcanic gases or mineral-rich geysers."

"Right." That was how Azar's own ancestral lineage had begun, back on Earth; photosynthesis had come much later. "So they grew to a certain size using chemosynthesis, then found they could switch to thermal effects. But this is all before the Ground Heaters have even evolved, so what's keeping the surface rocks so hot?"

Shelma pondered this. "Tidal heating? What if Tallulah was orbiting close to a cool red dwarf, or even a brown dwarf. With such weak sunlight, tidal heating might have been a far more potent energy source than photosynthesis."

"But it can't last," Azar protested. "Eventually the planet would end up tidally locked." The energy used to stretch and squeeze the rock, heating it up by internal friction, would ultimately be extracted from Tallulah's spin, slowing its rotation until its day matched its year and one hemisphere faced forever sunwards.

"Eventually, yes. But what if the Ground Heaters evolved before that happened? They would have been facing a slow, predictable decline in their energy source over millennia. So instead of responding frantically to a sudden catastrophe, they could have spent centuries perfecting a replacement."

"And the ejection from their star came much later, but by then there was nothing they needed to do. They'd already made themselves independent." Azar laughed, delighted. The artificial seasons and the variation in heat with latitude would still make sense: tidal heating would have been strongest at the equator, and at higher latitudes it would have been affected by seasonal changes in the angle between the planet's axis and the direction of the tidal force.

What this elegant hypothesis didn't explain was why the plants here were so young. Nor did it shed any light on exactly what the Ground Heaters had done to achieve their independence.

The data-collecting balloon was in place again. Before Mologhat vanished below the horizon, Azar instructed the station to send down a copy of its library.

As she was checking the interface with the cloned library, a message arrived from the microprobes. Thousands of kilometers away, something had exploded on the ocean floor and hurled a few billion tons of water skywards.

Azar turned to Shelma, still watching the satellite vision with her mind's eye. "What's happening? Some glitch with the heat source?" For a system that had survived for a billion years, this hiccup packed a mighty punch: the eruption was already high above the atmosphere, steam turning to ice like a cometary impact in reverse.

Shelma looked nervous. "Mologhat saw no vulcanism anywhere on the planet, in the last three years. Do you think we've annoyed someone?"

"If we have, why are we still alive? It's not the ground beneath our feet that's exploded." The balloon clearly wasn't the target, nor were any of the microprobes–and though the water missile was heading roughly in Mologhat's direction, it wouldn't reach anywhere near that far. But when Azar tried to contact the station, the microprobes replied that it was not responding.

Shelma said, "Don't jump to any conclusions. Mologhat might have imposed a communications blackout; if it thought it was under fire it would shift orbits and try not to do anything to give its position away."

Azar felt sick. "You think the gamma ray transmission was mistaken for some kind of attack?" Nothing had happened when she and Shelma had arrived the same way, but that burst had been considerably shorter, and it had come down almost vertically. The second beam had come from close to the horizon, giving it a longer path through the upper atmosphere–which would have made it more noticeable, and easier to trace back to its source.

Within minutes, the microprobes had reported six more eruptions, from underwater sites scattered around the planet. It made no sense to Azar; these gigatons of water were rising into orbits about a thousand kilometers up, but if they were meant as weapons, who were they aimed at? The microprobes were much lower down, and Mologhat was a hundred times further away. A direct hit with a solid iceberg could have done a lot of damage to any intruder, but these glistening snowballs weren't even holding together; Tallulah was just shrouding itself with a tenuous halo of tiny ice crystals.

"This isn't warfare!" she declared. "They don't think they're under attack. They saw the gamma rays, and thought: *antimatter.* They're afraid they're drifting into a cloud of antimatter. The ice is to tell them if there's any more around."

Shelma considered this. "I think you're right. They picked up a flash of annihilation radiation, and jumped to the conclusion that it was a natural source."

Never mind that there was no natural source of bulk antimatter anywhere in the galaxy; if you'd spent a billion years in space without encountering another civilization, perhaps a small cloud of antihydrogen seemed like a far less extravagant hypothesis than alien visitors using proton-antiproton gamma rays for communications.

"So they still don't even know we're here?" Azar wondered. "All those radio messages came to nothing. What do we have to do to get noticed–tattoo the binary digits for pi across the stratosphere?"

Shelma said, "I wouldn't advise that. But it's not even clear to me that there's anyone home; this might just be a non-sentient device that's outlived the people it's meant to be protecting."

The water missiles had stopped; the absence of any answering flash of radiation must have made it clear that if there was antimatter around, it was far too thinly spread to pose any kind of hazard.

Azar tried calling Mologhat again, but it was still not responding. "They must have hit it," she said. "Whatever they thought it was, they must have launched something small and fast, and knocked it out before the ice storm even started." She felt numb. *So much for the doorway to the stars.*

Shelma touched her arm reassuringly. "It might yet reply–but even if it's gone, we're not stranded."

"No?" The microprobes had nowhere near enough power for interstellar transmissions, or even the raw materials to build the kind of hardware they'd need. And the data-ferrying balloon couldn't send them anywhere; their return path to Mologhat would have involved a gamma-ray mirror on the balloon, modulating and reflecting radiation coming down from the station itself.

Azar slumped into her seat. *How had she ever imagined she could do this? Travel 1,500 light years as if it was nothing?* There was no magic gate leading home, just fourteen quadrillion kilometers of vacuum.

Shelma said, "We have plenty of resources down here."

Azar rubbed her eyes and tried to concentrate. "That's true." Given time, the nanotech could build them almost anything–and they didn't even have to reach all the way back to Hanuz or Bahar; they just had to connect to the Amalgam's network. Still, the nearest node was 700 light years away; getting a signal that far was a daunting prospect. "Can we do this from the ground?"

"Well . . . we could build a radio dish a few hundred kilometers across," Shelma replied, deadpan. "Factoring in suitable error correction for the signal-to-noise ratio, it might only take two or three centuries to complete the transmission."

Azar got the message. "OK: better to build a rail gun and launch a transmitter into orbit. But even if we can power a rail gun, how do we power the transmitter? We don't have any antimatter. There's virtually no deuterium here; are we going to try to build a hydrogen-boron fusion reactor?" The most efficient way to produce gamma rays was from antimatter–that would certainly make for the lightest power source to loft into orbit–but trying to create even a few micrograms of antihydrogen with nothing but *plant carbohydrates* as the energy source made Shelma's giant radio dish sound like a good idea. Whatever was guarding Tallulah might be a tad obtuse, but it was difficult to imagine a particle accelerator powered by industrial-scale deforestation slipping under the radar.

"What's the point of this transmission anyway?" she said bitterly. "To arrive home empty handed, with no news worth hearing? If it comes to that, I'd rather let my backup wake."

"So would I," Shelma said, "but I think you're missing something."

"Yeah?"

"The news worth hearing," she said, "and the energy source we need in order to send it, are the very same thing. Whatever's keeping this planet warm is just a few kilometers beneath our feet. If we can reach it, study it, understand it and harness it, we'll have both the means to get home, and the reason."

4

A few kilometers beneath our feet was an encouraging way of putting it; from where they stood the actual distance was 27,000 meters. The nanotech built some robot moles, powered by long thermoelectric tails, and sent them on their way. They would reach the heat source in about 200 days.

The oceanic crust was much thinner in places. Azar did some calculations. It wasn't clear what kind of food there'd be in the water, but she thought it was worth finding out. Shelma agreed, and they set out for the coast.

The insect made good time, averaging about 30 kilometers an hour, but when they reached the edge of the jungle food became more sparse and the scattered plants less nutritious. Flying across the flat, monotonously glowing savannah, Azar ached for sunrise to come and banish the interminable night. But she fought down the pang of homesickness and tried to find the beauty in this upside-down world.

Other explorer insects were already fanning out from a dozen sites where the spores had landed, building up a picture of the continent's geochemistry. A tentative analysis of the data suggested that the surface had only been above sea level for about a quarter of a billion years.

"Before that, there might have been no dry land at all," Shelma suggested. "That would explain why the ecosystem here is so young."

"So where did all the water go?" Azar wondered. "Unless their antimatter detectors have a lot of false alarms." Even the modest amount that they'd seen thrown skywards would mostly rain back down again.

"A collision?" Shelma frowned and withdrew the suggestion. "No, the odds would be very low out here, to hit something big enough." The current estimate of Tallulah's galactic orbit suggested that it hadn't even crossed another system's Oort cloud in the last billion years.

They reached the shoreline. Waves lapped gently on a lifeless beach; the infrared glow of the placid ocean made Azar think of liquid metal, but if she'd been wearing her body this water would have made a luxurious warm bath.

In the waves they found only single-celled creatures, living off a very thin soup of organic debris. They flew out a kilometer and took another sample, sending scout mites a few hundred meters down. The soup was thicker here; with a little tweaking, the insect would be able to make use of it.

There was a trench some 600 kilometers off the coast, where the mysterious neutrino source was just 9,000 meters below the ocean floor. They set out across the waves, stopping every couple of hours to dive and feed.

Each time they plunged into the water, Azar noticed Shelma tensing. She wondered about the propriety of commenting on this; if she'd been looking at Shelma's true self-image–a Bahari body with five limbs and five tails, like the rear end of a cat caught in a kaleidoscope–she would not have been able to distinguish tranquility from terror. Still, it was not as if the scape was reading Shelma's mind; it was merely translating information that she had chosen to make public.

As they approached the trench, Azar finally spoke. "You don't have to do this if you don't want to." The trench was 3,000 meters deep; if Shelma had retained a primal fear of drowning, Azar had no wish to see her suffer. "We can split the processor, and you can stay up here."

Shelma shook her head, a little puzzled by this offer. "No, I'll go with you. But first I want to bring in as much of the library as we can fit."

"Oh." Azar understood now; this was nothing to do with how Baharis felt about getting their fur wet. Once they were underwater they'd lose radio contact with everything, including the balloon-borne library.

Shelma began communing with the library, trying to choose a selection of its contents that would fit inside the insect without leaving them ill-equipped in the face of some crucial problem or opportunity. "I don't want to meet the Ground Heaters and then find we can't even make sense of their language!"

"If they're so smart," Azar replied, "let them make sense of ours." Then again, if they'd spent a billion years living alone on the ocean floor, it would probably be unwise to expect too much of their communications skills.

Hanuz had sent no travelers out into the galaxy for 100,000 years, and that had been long enough. Though Tallulah had been an enticing destination, Azar had left home less for the sake of the orphan's secrets than for the sake of breaking the curse. As the window for joining Mologhat had approached, she'd thought: *If we don't do this now, it will only grow harder.* And she'd finally stopped waiting for someone else to volunteer.

Shelma announced that she'd completed her selection, then she changed her mind and dived back into the interface. Azar thought of her great-great-granddaughter, Shirin, struggling to pack for an overnight trip. Shirin would be ancient when Azar returned; she'd have left all her toy animals behind.

"This is it now," Shelma declared. "We're prepared for anything." Her avatar wasn't quite hyperventilating, but Azar could imagine her letting a breeze of random skills and factoids play through her mind, soaking her tissues with the oxygen of information before the conduit slammed shut.

"I could always give myself amnesia, if you want a little more room," Azar suggested. Shelma actually looked tempted for a moment, before smiling thinly at the joke.

Azar took the joystick and the insect dived beneath the waves.

Their infrared vision wasn't quite useless here; if they tuned to a wavelength a little shorter than the peak thermal emissions around them, they could see the shadows that nearby objects cast against the glow of the warmer water below. Augmented with the strobe flashes of sonar, the vague shadows became fluttering vertical ribbons, drifting in the current but maintaining their orientation. Azar sent in the scout mites, who found the ribbons to be packed with tiny buoyancy chambers that exchanged gases in a complex cycle, eking a few microwatts out of the temperature gradient. The ribbon-weed's C3 sequence made it a close cousin of the land plants; in fact, it had probably changed very little from the ancestor whose other offspring had invaded the continents.

Five hundred meters down, they saw the first animals: small, segmented worms about a millimeter long, feeding off the ribbon-weed. The scout mites grabbed a few cells from the worms' skin for analysis. As Azar watched the data coming through, she felt a sense of disorientation to rival anything since she'd stepped on to Mologhat. The worms had no C3 in their cells; they were no more related to the weed they were munching on than she was to Shelma. Their replicator was P2, a polypeptide. What's more, their genome had been the subject of some blatantly artificial modifications, probably less than a million years ago.

"Introduced?" Shelma suggested.

"They must be," Azar replied. Colonists from a P2 world

must have come to Tallulah, bringing a few species from their home planet and tweaking them in order to survive here. It was a curious strategy; almost all interstellar travelers were digital in transit, not biological, and even if–like the founders of Hanuz–they had a fetish for recreating their original biochemistry upon arrival, such travelers tended to colonize sterile worlds. But then, nobody traveled to an orphan world for the sake of its real estate value. "It looks as if someone else came treasure-hunting long before we did."

"Apparently," Shelma concurred. "But if Tallulah is such old news, why isn't the heating process known halfway around the galaxy by now?"

As they descended further the ribbon-weed grew larger, the soup of microbes thicker, and the P2 creatures more numerous and diverse. There were shrimp-like animals straining microbes from the water, floating gas bladders with poisonous tentacles, and sinuous, muscular fish of every size, feeding on each other, the ribbon-weed and the shrimp.

A vast forest came into sonar range, rising up from the ocean floor. Azar had already been impressed by the size of the free-floating ribbon-weed, but its anchored cousins were giants, 50 or 60 meters high. With convection currents in the water sweeping heat away more efficiently than air, the temperature gradient was far less steep here than on land, but the water also made it easier for taller structures to support themselves. The scout mites counted 80 species of animals in the forest's upper reaches alone; some were P2, but there were C3 species as well, the first such animals the mites had found. And some were N3, with their genome encoded in nucleic acid.

"This place really has been popular," Shelma observed dryly. "It's enough to bring out the biograffitist in anyone. You sprinkle some N2 microbes in the water; I'll add the C1." N2 was DNA, Azar's ancestral replicator.

The N3 species, like the P2, had been engineered, but the best estimates put the date of intervention much earlier, between two and three hundred million years ago. Azar checked their local copy of the library; there was no previous archaeological evidence for an interstellar civilization with N3 ancestry in that epoch–and this was not one of the databases Shelma had trimmed. How could a civilization reach such a difficult target as Tallulah, but leave no trace anywhere else?

As they descended slowly into the forest, the insect announced a discovery that had nothing to do with Tallulah's polyglot biology. The robot's mass spectrometer was constantly analyzing samples from the water around them, and it had just stumbled across an extraordinary find. The object in question had a mass of 40.635 atomic units; this far-from-integral figure might have made sense as an average for a sample containing a mixture of calcium-40 and its heavier isotopes–but it wasn't an average, it was the mass of a single ion. Stranger still, when stripped of all its electrons the thing had a charge, not of 20 or so, but *210.* This was double the charge of any known stable nucleus, and ten times greater than its atomic weight implied.

"Who ordered *that*?" Azar quipped. Shelma didn't even smile; the depleted library wasn't up to providing the scape with the context for a proper translation.

"It's femtotech," Shelma declared.

Azar hesitated, then agreed. It was a staggering notion, but what else could it be? A new fundamental particle . . . with a charge of 210? Femtotech–the engineering of matter on the scale of atomic nuclei–was still a primitive art within the Amalgam; there had been some ingenious creations but they all had to do their job quickly, before they blew apart in a few trillionths of a second. The insect's find had endured for at least 300 seconds, and counting.

"How do you create a femtomachine with a binding energy equal to 90 percent of its mass?" she wondered. The most stable nuclei, nickel and iron, weighed about one percent less than the sum of their parts, thanks to the potential energy associated with the strong nuclear force. But increasing that effect by a factor of *90* was almost unimaginable.

The insect measured the ion's magnetic moment. The result was orders of magnitude higher than that which a nucleus of atomic number 210 would be expected to possess if it was sitting quietly in its ground state; to generate such a strong magnetic field, it would need to be spinning at relativistic speeds. This only made the overall picture even stranger: the kinetic energy from this rotation should have added substantially to the ion's total mass, rendering the actual 40-something value even more bizarre. The one thing that made a warped kind of sense was the failure of the ion to tear itself apart from centrifugal force. How could it explode, when the fragments would need to possess ten times more energy than the whole?

Azar said, "I take it this is ash from the heating process?"

Shelma managed a dazed smile. "If it's not, it certainly should be. *Ninety percent mass-to-energy conversion.* No wonder it's still going strong after a billion years!"

Tallulah's crust was generating heat at a rate of about two petawatts, stabilizing the planet's temperature by replacing the energy that leaked out of the greenhouse blanket. At 90 percent mass conversion, that would consume less than 800 tons of fuel each year, so in principle the process could continue for about ten-to-the-eighteenth years: a billion times longer than it had been running so far. Unlike fission or fusion, even if the starting point for the femtotech process had to be one particular kind of nucleus, it really didn't matter how rare it was in nature, since the energy required to synthesize it from anything else would be trivial in comparison. If each ton of the Ground Heaters' "gold" burned so fiercely that it could power the transmutation of a hundred tons of nickel or iron into yet more fuel, then Tallulah's bonfire would easily outlive the stars.

Technology like this could transform the Amalgam.

Antimatter had never been more than a wonderfully compact storage device, costing as much energy to make as it released. The most exquisitely efficient fusion systems extracted about *half a percent* of their fuel's mass as usable energy. There were some unwieldy tricks with black holes that could do better, but they weren't very practical, let alone portable. If everyone could harness the Ground Heaters' femtotech, it would be like a magic wand that could turn nine parts in ten of *anything* into energy, leaving nothing behind but this strange spinning ash.

Azar said, "This is a lot to conclude from one weird ion. Are we sure it's not an instrument error?"

Before the insect touched the ocean floor it picked a second speck of ash out of the water. Azar had the nanotech rebuild the relevant instruments from scratch and repeat the analysis. There had been no error; all the properties were the same.

5

The nanotech built more moles and sent them down into the rock, but even here where the crust was thinner, Azar knew she would have to be patient.

"Sixty days?" she lamented, pacing the flight deck. She didn't expect to be able to unravel the nucleon-by-nucleon details of the femtotech in a hurry, but if they could obtain a sample of the deep crust and observe the way its composition was changing as energy was released, that would at least confirm that their overall picture of the Ground Heaters' process was correct.

Until they had some of this white-hot rock to play with, the practicalities of harnessing the femtotech remained obscure, but Azar's sense of anxiety at their isolation had almost vanished. To be stranded for nothing, with little to be gained if they managed to return, had been a dismal prospect, but now that the stakes were so high the situation was exhilarating. *Prometheus, eat your heart out.*

While they waited for the moles to hit pay dirt they continued to explore the ribbon forest, building up a catalog of the three kinds of life that Tallulah's mysterious fire sustained. Perhaps unsurprisingly, the P2 animals–the newest–were by far the most numerous, having been engineered to be able to digest everything that had come before them. To the older N3s, and the even rarer C3s, the P2s were unpalatable–though not indestructible; the scouts witnessed cases of N3 fish killing off their P2 rivals, even though they were useless as food. What's more, a few of the C3 creatures were able to feed on N3 flesh; evolution had finally granted them a belated revenge on the first wave of invaders. In another hundred million years, who knew who would be eating whom?

When they first came across the colony of P2 "lizards," Azar thought that they were charming animals. Spread across a dozen square kilometers of the forest floor, their network of burrows was entwined with the giant ribbon-weeds' roots, which they tapped for food.

The lizards had two eight-clawed limbs that they used for digging and grasping objects; all their motive force came from their powerful tails. They sensed the world around them with a mixture of IR vision and sonar. Glands in their cheeks excreted complex molecular cocktails, which they squirted at each other almost constantly. Olfactory signaling within a colony of social animals was nothing surprising; the shock came when the scout mites caught some of them squirting the chemicals at inanimate objects in certain chambers within their burrows–and the inanimate objects squirted back replies. On closer examination, the devices turned out to be sophisticated chemical transceivers, linked by a fiber optic network.

"So these are our predecessors," Shelma said. "They came all the way to Tallulah, in the middle of nowhere, to solve the mystery of its warmth. But they must have found the femtotech long ago, so why are they still here? Why not take the treasure home? Why not spread it across the galaxy?"

"Why leave a world that will keep you warm for a million times longer than any star?" Azar replied.

"Why not build a hundred more worlds just like it?" Shelma countered.

"Let's ask them."

The scouts set to work sampling the chemical signals that comprised the lizards' language, and trying to correlate them with elements in the environment and the creatures' behavior. It was an impertinent level of eavesdropping, but they had to bootstrap communications somehow, and with no culture or biology in common they couldn't simply march up to the lizards and start playing charades. Ideally the scouts would have included children as their subjects, in order to share in any lessons they received, but in the entire colony of 50,000 there were currently no young at all–which suggested that the lizards had cut back their fertility to stabilize the population, while living more or less as long as they wished.

Fiber optic trunk lines connected the colony to others around the planet, and all the data traffic passing through appeared to conform to a single language. If there were any intelligent N3 creatures still around, either they weren't plugged into the same network, or there'd been a radical assimilation of cultures in one direction or the other.

Fed by the forest and served by their own rudimentary nanotech, the lizards seemed to pass the time socializing. The chemical transceivers granted them access to libraries, but most of the content being summoned appeared very similar to their habitual person-to-person exchanges, suggesting that it was closer to narrative history or fiction than anything more specialized and technical. Then again, even the most naturalistic dialogues might have encoded subtle themes that remained elusive at this stage of the analysis.

The lizards had no apparent social hierarchies, and as hermaphrodites they exhibited no sexual dimorphism, but the scouts identified one curious form of division. Many of the lizards identified themselves as belonging to one of three groups, which were named for the actions of spiraling inward, spiraling outward, and, the clear majority, following a circle. Since this was not a description of anyone's actual swimming style, it had to be a metaphor, but for what? The scouts had failed to observe anything tangible that correlated with this classification.

After 30 days Shelma declared, "It's time to introduce ourselves."

"Are you sure?" Azar was impatient for answers, but it seemed as if the scouts could easily spend another month piecing together further subtleties of the lizards' language.

"We've reached the point where we can greet them politely and explain who we are," Shelma said. "The way to get more reliable language acquisition now is through dialogue."

Shelma instructed the nanotech to build two facsimile lizard bodies. These robots would be obvious caricatures, functional but not such perfect imitations that the lizards could mistake them for fellow colonists.

The insect communicated with the robot lizards by line-of-sight laser pulses with a range of just a few meters. Azar and Shelma kept their software on the insect's processor and operated the lizards by telepresence, monitoring the robots' points of view without becoming fully immersed in their sensoria or giving up the feeling of being located on the insect's flight deck.

With her lizard body swimming toward the edge of the colony, weaving its way between the ribbon-weeds, Azar was overwhelmed with happiness. She was more than just a traveler now; she was about to become an ambassador to a hitherto unknown culture. And however physically isolated she was at this moment, she did not feel cut off from her roots in Hanuz. In her mind's eye, she could almost see the faces of the people she hoped to regale with her adventures.

A lizard approached, seemingly unafraid. The puff of

chemicals it squirted through the water was barely visible, but Azar heard the translation loud and clear. "Who are you?"

"We come in peace from another world," Azar announced proudly. The lizards had not been seen discussing astronomy, but they did have a word for the planet as a whole, and a general inflection for "not this thing, but another of its kind".

The lizard turned and fled.

On the flight deck, Azar turned to Shelma. "What did I do wrong?" She'd half-expected her claim to be greeted with skepticism–their robot bodies were well within reach of the lizards' own technology, after all–but perhaps the gamma rays that had triggered the ice halo had served as an ominous calling card.

"Nothing," Shelma assured her. "Summoning other witnesses is a common response." Shelma had no prior experience of first contact, but the library confirmed her claim.

Azar said, "What if they've forgotten that there *are* other worlds? They've been here for a million years. They might not even remember their own history."

Shelma was not persuaded. "There's too much technology around; even if they fell into a dark age at some point, they would have reconstructed everything by now." The lizards' nanotech maintained their health; it could easily have sequenced all the plants and animals around them, just as the Amalgam nanotech had done. Still, without the right context–without libraries of replicator sequences from a thousand other worlds–would they know how to interpret the data?

Azar saw bodies darting through the fronds. The first lizard had returned, with ten, twelve, fourteen friends. She could never have distinguished one from the other unaided, so she invoked software to track their features and assign phonetic names to them all.

Shelma said, "Please accept our good wishes. We come in peace from another world."

Omar, the first lizard they'd met, replied, "How can that be? It's not time."

His companion Lisa added, "You're not taking Tallulah from us. We'll never accept that."

Suddenly all 14 lizards were speaking at once. Azar's robot's senses had no problem following their words; the chemical emissions were tagged with individual markers, so there was no chance of confusing one lizard's words for another's. Azar had the audio translation untangled into separate streams.

Some of the lizards were expressing surprise and skepticism, not at the notion of visitors from another world, but at the timing of their arrival. Others seemed to think that she and Shelma were the vanguard of an army of colonists who had come to seize Tallulah, and they defiantly expressed their intention to resist.

Shelma said, "We're not colonists, we're merely explorers. We saw Tallulah and became curious."

"Where is your own world?" a lizard dubbed Caleb demanded.

"My companion and I come from different worlds," Shelma explained. "Both more than a thousand light-years away." The software would translate this into the local measure of distance, but with no units suitable for astronomical scales the number attached would be awfully large.

The lizards broke into a fresh cacophony. Such a journey was inconceivable.

Omar said, "Please come with us."

The crowd pressed around them from all sides, urging them forward. Shelma said privately, "Just go where they ask, don't resist."

The lizards seemed unaware of the tiny insect hovering between the larger robots; certainly its laser flashes were outside their visible spectrum. "You think they're *taking us prisoner*?" Azar said. It was hard to decide which was more bizarre: the fact that someone might wish to do this, or the fact that they believed it could be done.

"More or less," Shelma replied. "But at this point I'd rather cooperate than escape. If we can clear up a few misunderstandings, everything should be fine."

Azar let the pack of lizards guide her through the ribbon-weeds, then down into a burrow. Watching events through the flight deck's dome made her feel much less claustrophobic than the impression she got from her jostled robot's senses, but when the narrowing tunnels and the ever tighter crush meant the insect risked becoming conspicuous, they had it crawl inside Shelma's body. The line of sight between the two larger robots came and went, so Azar put her own lizard on autopilot, meekly complying with the flow of the crowd, and changed the insect's flight deck scape to show her an external view rather than the innards of its host.

They were taken to a small, bare chamber with a single entrance. After six of the lizards piled in with them, there was little room to spare.

Omar resumed the interrogation, his skepticism undiminished. "Your star must be very dim," he declared. "We believed that we had many more years."

Azar thought she was beginning to understand. Tallulah would not come close to another star for a very long time; the lizards had somehow fixed on that event as the most likely occasion for visitors.

"Our stars are very bright, but very distant," she insisted. "Why do you doubt that? Didn't your own ancestors travel far to reach this world?"

Omar said, "Their journey took half a year."

Half a year? Perhaps the real story had degenerated into myth, retold with cozy, domesticated numbers to replace the terrifying reality of interstellar distances.

"At the speed of light?" asked Shelma.

The chamber erupted with expressions of mirth and derision. "Only light travels at the speed of light," Lisa explained.

The scouts had found no evidence of the lizards digitizing themselves. Had they lost that technology, or had they never possessed it? Could their ancestors really have crossed the light years as flesh?

"So how far would they have traveled," Azar asked, "in that half-year?"

"Perhaps a billion kilometers," Omar replied.

Azar said nothing, but the claim was absurd; a billion kilometers was the size of a small planetary system. The lizards had spent too long dozing away the centuries at the bottom of this warm ocean; not only had they forgotten their own history, they had forgotten the true scale of the universe around them.

Shelma persisted. "When we follow the path of Tallulah back in time, it doesn't come that close to the path of any star for a billion years. Have you been here for a billion years?"

Omar said, "How can you know Tallulah's path? How long have you been watching us?"

"Thirty thousand years," Shelma replied. "Not me personally, but people I trust."

Mirth again. Why was this claim so laughable?

"Thirty thousand years?" Omar said. "Why did you imagine that would tell you the whole story?"

Shelma was bewildered now. "We've tracked your position and your speed," she said. "We know the motion of the stars. What else is there to account for?" Tallulah's galactic orbit was sparsely populated; chaos would eventually make retrodiction impossible, but the confidence levels over a billion years were still quite tight.

"Eight times since we arrived on Tallulah," Omar explained, "this world has changed course. Eight times, the heat rose from the ground to bring our path closer to our destination."

6

An argument broke out among the lizards; they withdrew from the discussion and left the chamber, leaving their guests with only two taciturn sentries. The insect probably could have slipped past these guards, or even burrowed its way back to the surface if necessary, but Shelma insisted that it was better to try to keep the dialogue open, and on consideration Azar agreed.

"So our orphan is a tourist," Shelma mused. "It steered its way right into the lizards' home system, and now it's heading for a new destination. But did the Ground Heaters arrange that, or did the N3 colonists bolt on the engines later?"

"Maybe that's where the water went," Azar suggested. The eruptions they'd seen earlier would have no long term effect on the planet's motion, but a hotter jet that reached escape velocity would do the trick.

Shelma said, "Water would be a strange choice of propellant. Photonic jets would be more efficient."

"If it was the N3ers doing it," Azar said, "maybe they didn't have fine enough control over the femtotech."

"Maybe. But the N3ers left no biological presence on the land, so they must have been ocean dwellers. Would ocean dwellers throw so much water into space that they lost 30 percent of their real estate?"

"Good point," Azar conceded. "But why does *anyone* steer a whole planet from system to system? If it was the Ground Heaters, surely they could have made smaller, faster spacecraft using the femtotech."

Shelma threw up her hands. "Let's go back to the beginning. The Ground Heaters grew up with tidal heating. When that started running down, they got lucky; they managed to devise a spectacularly good replacement. So what would they do next?"

"Some cultures would have sent out nanotech spores," Azar said, "followed by a wave of digitized travelers. But we know they didn't do that, or the femtotech would still be around somewhere else."

"They didn't found colonies, but they still ended up traveling." Shelma laughed. "I was going to say that it must have been a deliberate choice–that they could have resisted any natural ejection from their system if they'd really wanted to–but maybe they only had fusion power then. That would explain why's there's no deuterium around: they used it all up while they were developing the femtotech."

"But either way," Azar said, "once they were free of their star and able to steer themselves, they decided to make the best of it. To see a few sights along the way. And where do you go, if you grew up around a dwarf star? You take a tour of other dwarf stars–"

"Until you find one with an inhabited planet," Shelma said, "where they're facing the same problems you faced."

"And then what?" Azar frowned. "I can't believe the N3ers conquered the Ground Heaters!"

"No," Shelma agreed. "And why would they need to? Why wouldn't the Ground Heaters simply share the femtotech, to help out their fellow thermophiles? If they weren't feeling generous and sociable, why visit an inhabited world at all? If they'd simply been looking for territory there would have been plenty of sterile worlds for them to choose from."

Azar said, "Maybe the Ground Heaters died out before they reached the N3 world. They'd programmed some billion-year spree for Tallulah into the femtotech, but they lost heart along the way. The ghost ship came into the N3 system, and the locals couldn't believe their luck: an empty planet, habitable for ten-to-the-eighteenth years, right on their doorstep! But they couldn't park it, they couldn't steer it, they had to go along for the ride. And a quarter of a billion years later, the same thing happened to the lizards."

Shelma thought for a while. "That almost makes sense, but I can't quite believe that neither of these free-riders had any interest in turning the femtotech into a propulsion system and founding a few colonies elsewhere."

"Maybe they did. Maybe we've missed them. Tallulah went unnoticed for a very long time."

"We're missing something," Shelma said. "But perhaps our hosts will be able to enlighten us."

Hours passed with no more contact from the lizards. The sentries were changed, but the replacements were equally determined not to engage with them.

Azar paced the flight deck. "They must be trying to work out if we're telling the truth or not. Checking to see if Tallulah's brought them close to a very faint brown dwarf–a port of call that they failed to anticipate."

"You'd think they'd have good enough telescopes to be sure," Shelma said irritably. "Given what's at stake."

"Maybe they got complacent. I mean, if you do a thorough sweep of the sky and get a very clear verdict that there's nothing to worry about for the next 100,000 years, how motivated are you to keep repeating the search?"

"Ideally, it would all be automated," Shelma replied. "Motivation wouldn't come into it."

"Well, we might not have landed on the best of all possible worlds after all."

The lights on the flight deck were starting to soften. Ever since she'd arrived on Mologhat, Azar had been sticking scrupulously to her usual diurnal rhythm; to sleep was part of her identity. But she was too anxious now, and she willed the urge away. Her sense of self would just have to stretch to encompass an exception when she was captive to confused, paranoid lizards.

The sentries were changed again. Azar recognized them as two of the crowd who'd first appeared in the forest; her software had dubbed them Jake and Tilly, but they hadn't said much then, and she didn't bother trying to speak to them now. Let the telescopes confirm her and Shelma's honesty, and then they could all finally engage in a civilized discussion.

Jake said, "Come with us. Quickly. We don't have much time." He swam a short way toward his prisoners, then darted back toward the chamber's entrance.

Azar was dumbfounded.

"Come with you where?" Shelma asked.

"Out of here," Tilly said. "We think the Circlers are planning to kill you."

Azar glanced at Shelma. The insect could probably defend itself against most of the lizards' technology, but it was not indestructible. They'd left backups in the jungle before setting out for the coast, but those snapshots of their minds were missing all the crucial discoveries they'd made since. In any case, even if they survived here, what kind of dialogue could they have with people who wanted them dead?

Shelma addressed her privately. "So do we leave the bodies as decoys?"

Azar was unsure. The insect on its own would face technical problems communicating with the lizards–it was too small to stock the raw materials for more than a few minutes' speech–and she also found something comforting about the way it was now hidden inside a larger target.

"What if we split the difference?" she suggested. Her lizard body had enough redundancy in its engineering to allow its nanotech to make two bodies from the same materials; she instructed it to divide into a mimic of Shelma's, along with a somewhat less sturdy copy of its original form. Then she loaded both with non-sentient software that could easily pass a half-baked Turing test from their would-be executioners.

Tilly remained guarding the fake prisoners, and they followed Jake through the tunnels, leaving by a different route than they'd come. They did not travel unobserved, but the few lizards Azar glimpsed at intersections merely watched them pass in silence; presumably they belonged to Jake's faction, and were standing lookout in aid of their escape.

On the surface the ribbon-weeds carved the forest floor into a kind of maze, and while it was possible to cheat and squeeze your way between the edges of the fronds that didn't quite touch, it certainly was faster if you knew the maze so well that you didn't have to.

After a while, Jake halted and gestured urgently at a stubby, bulbous plant in the undergrowth. Since leaving the chamber he hadn't spoken at all; words decayed quickly in the water, to the point of losing their meaning, but the residue would still be easy to track. When Shelma did nothing he ducked down, tore a bulb from the plant, and stuffed it into his mouth. Shelma took the hint and did the same. The scouts hadn't come across this plant before, but the robot's nanotech quickly analyzed the bulb's contents. There were few conventional nutrients in it, but it was packed with organic azides, nitrogen-rich compounds with an extremely high energy density. The plant was C3, but its genome suggested that the lizards had modified it to produce this edible rocket fuel, and despite its modest appearance its roots probably ran deeper into the ground than the ribbon-weeds rose up into the ocean. The nanotech didn't take long to devise a pathway to metabolize the azides safely–which was lucky, because Jake was already powering ahead at five times his previous swimming speed.

As their robot body struggled to catch up with him, Shelma said, "Now I know why they don't bother with vehicles." Azar had once tweaked her own flesh to enable her to run non-stop across a continent–purely for the physical joy of it–but it seemed that with the right dietary supplement, anyone on Tallulah could moonlight as a high-performance submarine.

As they sped through the forest, the thermal/sonar images of the ribbon-weeds on either side of them blurred together like the walls of some long, twisted canyon. "If 'the Circlers' really want to kill us," Azar said, "I hope that doesn't mean all of them." References to that cryptic self-description had been present even in distant traffic coming through the fibers; the group was certainly not confined to one colony.

Shelma said, "I'm sure this is all just a misunderstanding. They think this is the end of the line for them–that Tallulah's come within reach of another dying world, and we're its inhabitants, intent on taking over."

"You think they have a guilty precedent in mind?" Azar suggested. "Maybe that's what happened with them and the N3ers."

"Maybe. But I think it's more likely that the N3ers were long gone, and that's part of the shock. The lizards weren't expecting to be around to meet their own replacements, either."

Azar said, "So how do we convince them that there is no threat, if they refuse to believe the evidence of their own telescopes?"

"Good question. How faint is the faintest dwarf star, and how far would they be willing to believe we've come?"

The forest gave way to a dense carpet of smaller plants, but Jake still knew how to find the fuel bulbs among them. This time when they stopped, he risked talking. "I think you're safe for now," he declared. "But we should keep moving. I have friends who'll shelter us, but they're still a few hundred kilometers away."

"We don't want to put anyone's life in danger," Azar said, borrowing Shelma's lizard body but inflecting the words with the identity tag she'd used when she'd had her own.

"You won't," Jake assured her. "The three philosophies have been at peace for millennia; we're not going to start killing each other now."

"The three philosophies?" Shelma asked.

"Circlers, Spiral In, Spiral Out."

"We've heard those phrases, but we don't know what they mean."

Jake flexed his body like an athlete limbering up for a sprint. "If you want to keep talking, swim close beside me and synch your tail with mine." As he started moving, Shelma followed his advice. The layer of water trapped between them let them communicate without their words being lost in the flow.

"The Circlers," Jake said, "are resolved to stay. To stay on Tallulah, and to stay as they are. They accept that we didn't build this world ourselves, that it came to us as a gift, but to the Circlers that's not the point. The Builders are gone, and now Tallulah belongs to us."

Azar said, "So they're ready to fight off any intruders?"

"They're willing," Jake replied, "but I wouldn't call them ready. They weren't expecting you. Nobody was."

"We really don't want this place as our home," Shelma said. "We have worlds of our own, powered by sunlight. You believe that, don't you?"

Jake considered the question. "I suppose it's possible for life to evolve that way, around the right kind of star. Some experts claim the radiation would be fatal, but I believe there could be a narrow habitable zone. To travel more than a thousand light years, though . . ."

Shelma explained about Mologhat 1 and 2, meeting and canceling their momentum against each other. About the digital forms she and Azar had taken, crossing the light years as gamma rays in a subjective instant.

Jake said, "Now you're trying to tell me that Spiral In is really the same as Spiral Out."

"Spiral Out is about travel?" Azar said. "The idea that you should leave Tallulah and look for a new home?"

"Yes. Spiral Out is my own philosophy."

Azar tried to frame her next question as politely as possible, and hoped the translator would be able to honor her intent. "Then if you don't mind me asking, why are you still here?"

"Travel isn't easy," Jake declared. "We've been waiting for Tallulah to bring us close to an empty world that we could claim as our own. But the last time that happened–before I was born–our numbers were small and our technology was untested. The opportunity was lost."

Shelma said, "So what's Spiral In?"

"They aim to take the form you claim to have taken. To become pure information. But not for travel: to stay on this world. To join with this world."

It was an odd way of putting it, but Azar thought she caught his meaning. In almost every culture with the means to go digital, there was a subculture who advocated a kind of implosion: a retreat into a universe of scapes divorced from physical reality.

"To join with this world?" Shelma pressed him.

"With the heat. With the hoops. With the Builders themselves." Jake emitted a token of mirth that Azar heard as curt laughter. "Some Spiral In people believe that there are ten thousand cultures under the ground."

The ocean floor passed beneath them in a blur.

"Hoops?" Azar said.

"You haven't seen the hoops yet?" Jake replied. "When the rock turns to heat, what's left are the hoops."

"The ash," Shelma said privately. "He's talking about the ash!"

"We've seen them," Azar said. "But we're not quite sure what they are."

Jake fell silent for a while, then he said, "How much do you know about relativity?" The translator marked the final word with a cautionary footnote: the scouts hadn't heard it in use before, so the meaning was being inferred purely from its etymology.

"I understand the basics." Azar had studied relativity as

a child, but without the full library to call on she would be unwise to claim to be an expert.

"Imagine," Jake said, "a hoop made of something extraordinarily strong, spinning at close to the speed of light. From the hoop's point of view, it's under enormous tension. But from the point of view of a bystander watching it spin, it's moving so rapidly that some of that tension manifests itself as a decrease in its energy."

Azar was familiar with the principle, though she was more used to thinking of the opposite effect. When you considered a gas under pressure, that pressure was due to the momentum of molecules moving from place to place. But if you were moving rapidly relative to the gas–or vice versa–then some fraction of that *momentum in motion* looked to you instead like *energy standing still.* The shift in perspective transformed pressure into energy.

Tension was simply negative pressure, so for a moving object under tension the effect changed sign: the total energy would be decreased. The quantities involved would normally be immeasurably small, though. Azar said, "Are you telling us that these hoops are under so much tension that their energy drops to *ten percent of their rest mass*?"

"Yes."

"Despite the kinetic energy of rotation? Despite the energy that goes into stretching the hoop?"

"Yes," Jake replied. "The effect of the tension outweighs both of those increases."

Shelma passed some calculations privately to Azar, then addressed Jake. "I think there's a problem with your theory. If you take a hoop and spin it ever faster, the only way its energy will begin to decrease is if the speed of sound in the hoop exceeds the speed of light."

Azar checked the calculations; Shelma was right. The total energy of the hoop depended on the precise relationship between the elasticity of the hoop material and the tension it was under. But so, too, did the speed of sound in the material. Linking the two equations showed that the total energy couldn't fall in response to an increase in tension without the speed of sound becoming greater than lightspeed–which was relativity's way of telling you that no material with the necessary properties could exist.

Jake was unfazed. "We've known that result for a long time. It doesn't change the facts."

"What are you claiming?" Shelma asked incredulously. "That the speed of sound *does* exceed the speed of light?"

"Of course not," Jake said. "I agree that you can't construct a motionless hoop and then simply spin it up to a velocity so great that its energy begins to fall. But hoops that are already rotating can change their composition–spitting out particles and transforming into a new material that can only exist under tension. So you have to approach the final state through an intermediate structure: a high-energy, low-tension hoop that decays into a high-tension, low-energy hoop, with the energy difference going into the particles that are emitted in the decay process."

Shelma considered this. "All right, I think I see what you're getting at. But can you explain the details of this intermediate structure, and exactly how it can be synthesized?"

"The details?" Jake said. "We've been on Tallulah for a million years. What makes you think that we've untangled all the details?"

7

They reached an isolated burrow, far from any colony. Jake went in first, then emerged with two friends, whom Azar's software named Juhi and Rahul.

Juhi said, "Jake tells us you came from the world of a bright star. Is that true?"

Shelma replied, "Absolutely."

"So your real body is not like this at all?"

Shelma sketched her ancestral, five-fold symmetric shape in the sand. Juhi said something that the translator couldn't parse.

They entered the burrow and swam together to the deepest chamber, a much larger space than the prison they'd escaped from. It contained a transceiver and some other equipment that Azar didn't recognize–and in the circumstances it seemed both discourteous and unwise to send the scouts to sniff it out.

Rahul said, "Our friends in Jute"–the colony they'd left–"tell us that the Circlers still think they're holding you. They're hoping to find out more about the invasion plans."

Invasion plans was a phrase Azar associated with ancient history and broad comedy. The zombie software she'd left in the bodies would keep reciting the truth to the bitter end, but now she almost wished she'd programmed some kind of parody of a confession.

Shelma said, "We're grateful for your help. We didn't come here to cause trouble, but before we even knew that Tallulah was inhabited we lost the means to depart." She explained Mologhat's fate.

Jake said, "I thought that was no coincidence. The Old Passengers' machines have blasted specks of dust before, but when you appeared so soon afterward I knew it wasn't down to chance."

The N3ers? "The Old Passengers lived here after the Builders?" Azar said.

"Yes," Juhi replied. "A few of their animals are still around. They built thousands of machines that aim to protect Tallulah, but some of them are a bit trigger happy."

"So your ancestors met the Old Passengers?" Shelma asked.

"Hardly!" Rahul sounded as amused as Azar would have been by the same query in relation to trilobites or dinosaurs. "At least, not above ground. For all we know, some of the

Old Passengers might still be alive, deep in the rock. But if they are, they're not very communicative."

Azar said, "What exactly is going on in the crust, besides the heating process? How do the hoops connect to the Spiral In philosophy?"

Juhi said, "Once you give up your flesh and become information, don't you look for the fastest way to process that information?"

"Not always," Azar replied. "In our culture most of us compromise–to stay connected to each other, and to the physical world."

"In our culture," Rahul said, "there is no one coming and going over thousands of light years. There are only your biological cousins–and to Spiral In, if your cousins don't follow you down, that's their loss."

Shelma said, "So the hoops can be used for information processing?"

"Some of them," Jake replied. "The ones you've seen up in the water, probably not. But in the ground there are a billion different varieties."

"*A billion?*" Shelma turned to Azar so they could exchange stunned expressions–or at least so Shelma could hallucinate a version of Azar curling her five tails in the appropriate manner.

"Maybe more," Jake said. "The truth is, nobody above ground really knows. But we do know that some of them can be used as computing elements. Every time Spiral In becomes serious, they study the hoops, learn how to use them . . . then disappear into the ground."

Azar was beginning to realize that she hadn't really thought through the implications of the Ground Heaters' process; even the ash it left behind opened up avenues that the Amalgam had only dreamed of. Amalgam femtocomputers were blazingly fast while they lasted, but they decayed as rapidly as the most unstable nuclei. You then had to rebuild them from scratch, making the whole process a waste of time for all but a handful of specialized applications. If you could build complex structures on a nuclear scale that were permanently stabilized–by virtue of possessing far less energy than their individual parts–then that changed the rules of the game completely. A femtocomputer that didn't blow itself apart, that kept on computing non-stop, would run at least six orders of magnitude faster than its atomic counterparts.

She said, "So Spiral In use the hoops to retreat into virtual reality. But why don't you use the heating process yourself, just for the energy? If you want to escape from Tallulah, why not take this process and run?"

Rahul gestured at one of the machines in the corner of the chamber, a clunky, unprepossessing structure with a dozen cables snaking out of it. "There's a sample of deep rock in there. Do you know how much power it's generating? Less than a microwatt."

Azar stared at the machine. Her intuition balked at Rahul's claim, but on reflection it was entirely plausible. In bulk, buried beneath an insulating blanket of rock several kilometers thick, the miraculous fuel would be white hot, but up here in the water a small piece would barely be warmer than its surroundings. Its power to keep the whole planet from freezing came from its sheer quantity, and its spectacular efficiency was tuned for endurance, not a fast burn.

She said, "So in its normal state the process runs slowly. But this isn't like some radioisotope with a half-life that can't be changed."

"No," Rahul said, "it's worse than that. If you take a sample of ore containing a radioisotope, you can concentrate the active ingredient. If we purify deep rock–if we remove some of the ordinary minerals it contains in the hope of producing a denser power source–the process down-regulates automatically, maintaining the same output for a given total mass. It knows what you're doing, and it cheats you out of any gain."

"Ah." Azar was torn between empathy for the lizards' frustration and admiration for the Ground Heaters' ingenuity. It seemed the femtotech had been designed with very strong measures to protect against accidents and weaponization.

Shelma said, "But in all the time you've been studying it, surely you've made some progress? You say Spiral In have learned to use the hoops as computing devices; that must give you some insight into the whole process."

"Using the hoops isn't the same as controlling their creation," Juhi said. "It's like . . . building a computer out of fish bones, compared to engineering the biology of a fish. Spiral In learn enough to embed their minds in the rock in the simplest possible way. From that starting point, perhaps they migrate to more refined modes. Who knows? They've never come back to tell us."

"If Spiral In can migrate into the rock," Azar said, "why are so many of them still here, above ground?"

"After each migration the philosophy dies out," Juhi replied, "but every few generations it becomes popular again. It starts out as an abstract stance–an idea about what we ought to do, eventually, sometime before we find ourselves confronting the Next Passengers–but then it reaches a critical mass, with enough people taking it seriously for the practicalities to be rediscovered. Then everyone who was serious goes underground . . . and everyone who was just spouting empty rhetoric defects to a different philosophy. We're at a point in the cycle right now where there's a lot of rhetoric, but not much else."

Azar was too polite to suggest that Spiral Out seemed to be in much the same state themselves, but in their case there was nothing cyclic about it.

Shelma turned her robot's gaze from lizard to lizard, as if searching for a crack in their pessimistic consensus. "It must be possible to harness this process," she said. "To adjust it, to manipulate it. A single nuclear reaction has its rate fixed by physical laws, but this is a *system*–a flexible, programmable network of nuclear machines. If someone built this system for their own purpose–with details that they chose for themselves, that weren't forced upon them by the underlying physics–then it can be *rebuilt.* You should be able to reverse-engineer the whole thing, and put it together again any way you like."

Jake said, "Someone built the deep rock, that's true. And if we were willing to choose the same path as the Builders, perhaps we could match their feat. But though the Builders set Tallulah in motion, in the end their philosophy was Spiral In. To make deep rock, the Builders *became* deep rock.

"I don't believe it can be done any other way. To understand it well enough to change it, we would have to become it. And then we would have changed ourselves so much that we would no longer want the very thing that we set out to achieve."

8

As the discussion wound its way back and forth between Tallulah's uncertain history and the competing visions of its future, Azar seized upon one piece of good news that Rahul let slip almost in passing. The lizards couldn't re-create the femtotech from scratch, or even ramp it up into a useful form of propulsion, but they did believe that there was a very good chance that they'd be able to *graft it.* Given an empty world on which to experiment, they hoped that introducing samples of the deep rock into the crust would cause the femtotech to replicate, spreading through the native rock and ultimately creating a second Tallulah.

That was a wonderful prospect, but they'd already missed at least one opportunity. Some 200,000 years before, Tallulah had passed through an uninhabited system, but Spiral Out had been at a low ebb and hadn't even managed to launch exploratory probes. Since then they'd simply been hanging around waiting for their next chance. The Ground Heaters had given them an extraordinary gift, rescuing them from their dying planet, but between the culture of dependency that gift had created, the constant temptations of Spiraling In, and the stress of not knowing whether the next world they encountered would turn out to be the home of the Next Passengers, they had ended up paralyzed.

"You should join the Amalgam," Azar said, "and use their network to migrate. The kind of world you're looking for is not in high demand; a frozen planet tidally locked to a faint brown dwarf is of no interest to most space-faring cultures."

"And it's no use to us either," Jake replied, "unless we can enliven it. We can't send the deep rock through your network, can we?"

"No, but if you spent a century or two manufacturing antimatter from geothermal energy, you could build an engine to carry samples of rock at a significant fraction of lightspeed. And even if for some reason you didn't have enough spare power to do that, I guarantee that you could find a partner in the Amalgam who'd trade you a few tons of antimatter for some deep rock samples of their own. And I mean a few tons on arrival at Tallulah, not a few tons when it left home!"

Juhi said, "We need to be careful. It's one thing to hand Tallulah over to the Next Passengers, as the Builders intended, but we don't want a million strangers flocking here just to mine the planet."

"Nobody's going to do that," Shelma assured her. "If deep rock has any value at all in the Amalgam, it will come from the ability to graft it, or the ability to reverse-engineer it. In either case, a few kilograms would be enough."

Rahul said, "Whether we choose to join the Amalgam or not, you need antimatter for your own journey, don't you?"

"A few micrograms would come in handy," Shelma admitted.

The transceiver sprayed out a chemical ringtone and Rahul replied with a command for it to speak. Azar found the conversation that followed cryptic–and she suspected that parts of it were literally in code–but when it was over Rahul announced, "Someone spotted you in the forest with Jake. The Circlers have destroyed your puppets, but they know more or less what happened now. I think we need to move from here."

Azar was dismayed. "Can't you talk to them? Explain the situation? None of our plans should be any threat to them." The Amalgam would happily leave the Circlers in peace, sending no travelers and no further explorers, but the Spiral Out faction were entitled to emigrate, and to trade a few small pieces of Tallulah's exotic legacy with the wider galaxy.

Rahul said, "They're convinced that you're the New Passengers, and that the fight to retain Tallulah has begun. In the past they've viewed Spiral Out as timid fatalists, but now that we've come to your aid we're something worse. We're traitors."

On the flight deck Shelma muttered a string of obscenities. "We're not going to spark a civil war," she told the lizards. "We'll surrender ourselves. It doesn't matter if they destroy us; we'll make backups."

Jake said, "But they understand now that you can do that. You could surrender a thousand machines to them–or one pair of living creatures, and call them your true form–but it won't be enough to convince them that they've put an end to your plans."

Azar wanted to contest this bleak verdict, but from what she'd seen of the Circlers firsthand it rang true. Whatever the original intention of Tallulah's creators, it had sounded like a beautiful story: a chariot traveling between faint, forgotten stars, rescuing the inhabitants of dying worlds, offering them a safe, warm home for a few million years so they could build up their strength then fly from the nest–or, if they wished, dive into its depths, into a femtoscale mansion of a quadrillion rooms. In a way, she admired the Circlers for their determination to tear up the script, to scream at their long-vanished benefactors that they would make their own decisions and not just meekly come along for the ride. But the irony was that they were so intent on rebelling against the Builders that they seemed blind to anything that didn't conform to their own version of the scenario. It was chiseled in stone that one day they would fight the New Passengers for Tallulah, and they had spent so long rehearsing this play that you couldn't even tap them on the shoulder and suggest a different ending without being dragged into the plot and cast as the villain.

Shelma had their mock-lizard body destroy itself, and found a dim but agile P2 fish for the insect to parasitize and modify. A talking fish would attract suspicion, but with some help from the library they managed to engineer speech glands for it that created rapidly decaying words; if they swam up close to a chosen confidante they could emit some short-range chemical whispers with little chance of being overheard. Unfortunately, the lizards' own medical nanotech wasn't flexible enough to do the same for them, and Jake and the others recoiled from a friendly offer to let the aliens tweak their speech organs.

Shelma said privately, "This is going to get messy."

"So how do we fix it?" Azar replied.

"I wish I knew."

They agreed on a place and time to rendezvous, then Jake, Rahul and Juhi scattered.

Shelma said, "I think we should go back to the surface for a while."

They took the fish as high as it could go, then left it parked and rode the insect alone for the last few hundred meters. When they broke the water, Azar found herself almost weeping with relief. She was still as far from home as ever, but just a glimpse of the stars after so long without them made her feel that she was back in the right universe again.

Neither the balloon nor the orbiting microprobes had experienced any form of aggression, or noticed anything else unusual. It seemed that the Circlers, for all their paranoia, had been too complacent to create a world bristling with sensors and weapons while Tallulah's next stop was still so far from sight.

Shelma said, "We should bring the balloon down on the ground somewhere and replicate the library a few times. I think we're already carrying everything vital, but if our backups have to take over from us we want to be sure that they're not disadvantaged." Their backups in the jungle were already receiving incremental memory updates, by radio via the microprobes.

Azar agreed, and they sent the instructions. She paced the flight deck, rubbing her eyes. She had given up the need for sleep, but there was still something irredeemably strange about the feeling of unpunctuated consciousness stretching back into the distance.

"I screwed up," Shelma said. "I rushed to make contact. We didn't even know what the factions' names meant."

"And I let you do it," Azar replied. "We're both at fault. But I don't believe the situation's irretrievable. The Circlers have killed some alien zombies, but according to Jake the philosophies have been at peace for millennia; it could still be a step too far for them to start harming each other."

"How do we defuse their anxiety," Shelma said, "when there's no invading army for them to defeat? Do we offer them the microprobes as sitting ducks? I doubt that they could hit targets that small, and even if they could they'd just assume that there were 10,000 more."

Azar looked up at the stars again, and tried to see them

as a hostile, threatening sight. "They need some theater. They need some catharsis." Clearly Shelma thought the same way too, but then neither of them were exactly experts in the lizards' psychology. "And we need to talk to Jake again."

"What do you have in mind?"

"The microprobes are too small, and Mologhat is already gone. So maybe we should think about launching a bigger target."

Only Juhi turned up at the rendezvous point in a remote stretch of ribbon-weed forest. "Jake and Rahul are safe," she said, "but they're too far away at the moment."

"What's been happening?" Azar asked her.

"We've been in contact with most of Spiral Out, and they've made a decision. They want to send a delegation with you to the closest world in the Amalgam, to make contact with this culture and report back on the possibilities for trade and migration."

Azar was encouraged; at least Spiral Out had proved willing to break from its preconceptions.

"We're prepared to start manufacturing antimatter," Juhi continued. "But we should compare notes on the process first; if you have a more efficient method we should adopt that."

Shelma said, "What kind of power sources do you have access to?" The everyday lizard culture they'd seen was based on plant thermoelectrics.

"There are some deep-bore geothermal turbines that are used for specialized research projects," Juhi replied. "Obviously we can't tap the whole output, but we should be able to siphon some off discreetly."

"What if you just built your own turbine?" Azar said. "Would the Circlers do anything to stop you?"

"Right now," Juhi said, "I don't think it would be wise to find out."

Azar turned that statement over in her mind. If people were about to begin clandestine antimatter production, what would happen to them if they were caught?

"We've had an idea," she said, "but I don't know if it will make sense to you. The Circlers believe we've come from a nearby planet, from a star too dim to see. What if we built a spacecraft that might have made a short journey like that . . . and then let the Circlers shoot it down?"

Juhi said, "How are you going to power this spacecraft?"

"The azide bulbs you eat when you travel; enough of them could actually get a small craft into low orbit. The Circlers accept that we're digitized, so they don't expect the invasion force to be a fleet of thousand-ton arks."

"It's an interesting idea," Juhi said, "but the hardest part would be contriving their success in destroying the craft. Since your arrival they've been dredging up plans for weapons that our ancestors constructed for the last close approach, 200,000 years ago. But nobody's sure now that they still understand those designs."

Shelma said, "What about surveillance? Are they already monitoring what's happening in near space?"

"Yes. You can be sure of that."

"Then the problem," Shelma said, "is that they'd see us taking off. It would better to convince them that something new is coming in from deep space."

Juhi paused, the front of her body twitching from side to side, a motion that Azar now recognized as a sign of anxiety. "I don't see how we can do that. But let me take this to the others."

Shelma had the insect's nanotech construct a sample of a solid-state antimatter factory, and passed it to Juhi for the lizards to copy. It was the Amalgam's most efficient design, but nothing could get around the fact that it would still need thousands of times more power than any ordinary burrow consumed.

After parting from Juhi they stayed away from Jute and

the other colonies, but the scout mites had placed intercepts on some of the intercolony trunk fibers long ago. The lizards had no infrastructure in place for quantum encryption, and their standard communication codes were easily cracked; clearly this wasn't a culture with an entrenched history of bitter enmities and closely held secrets. It was a culture polarized by sudden panic, and Azar clung to the hope that cooler heads would soon prevail.

The tapped conversations were discouraging, though. The idea of Spiral Out as traitors was spreading throughout the Circlers, many of whom were urging each other to keep a close watch on their treacherous neighbors and erstwhile friends. The claim that the alien visitors were benign explorers with no territorial ambitions was largely discounted; two previous examples of Tallulah being colonized were, apparently, sufficient to render other motives unlikely. Azar began to wonder if the best course would be to lie low for a century or two and simply wait for the non-arrival of the trumpeted invasion force to leave the prophets of doom looking like fools.

Rahul met them for the next rendezvous. "Jake's disappeared," he said. "I think he's been imprisoned, but nobody will admit to holding him."

Azar was speechless. For all the bad news she'd heard from the taps, she'd never believed it would come to this.

"We can send machines to hunt for him," Shelma said.

"If you can, please," Rahul replied. "But they will have moved him to another colony, so I don't know exactly where you should start."

Azar came her to senses. She instructed the scouts that were already hovering near the fish; they would spread out and replicate, following the fiber trunk lines from colony to colony, spawning search parties as they went.

"We have an idea to placate the Circlers," Rahul said. "To give them the triumph they think they need."

"Go on," Shelma urged him.

"We can't get a craft into deep space, unseen," he said. "And even if we could, I doubt the Circlers could hit it. But the Old Passengers' machines are still working very well after all this time–as you know, to your cost. If they were seen to repel the would-be New Passengers, I think the Circlers would treat that victory as their own."

Shelma said, "But how do we get the target up there? And how do we guarantee that the machines strike it?"

"We cheat," Rahul said. "We hack into the Old Passengers' network, and make it respond with as much sound and fury as possible to something that isn't really there."

Azar said, "Do you know how to do that?"

"Not quite," Rahul admitted. "This is where we need your help."

The lizards had mapped parts of the Old Passengers' network long ago. It was bioengineered from native C3 plants, and used a modified form of the conductive polymers that Azar had first seen in the thermocouple bush. There were sensors of various kinds scattered across the continents, processing hubs on land and in the water, and dozens of geothermal cannons on the ocean floor.

Every thousand years or so someone had tried tapping into the network, but the protocols had always eluded them. There had been talk of trying to decommission the whole eccentric, unpredictable system, but the contrary view–that the Old Passengers had known what they were doing, and always had the interests of Tallulah at heart–had prevailed. Certainly the system had been benign enough to allow the lizards themselves to cross from their home world unmolested, and if the cannons sometimes spat steam and ice at phantoms that was a small price to pay.

Armed with Rahul's map, Azar and Shelma returned to the surface and sent instructions to the other explorer insects, which had now reached every continent. As the insects tapped into the network, the microprobes monitored the flashes of Cerenkov radiation that incoming cosmic rays created in the upper atmosphere. Whatever else might elicit a response from the system, radiation was a proven irritant.

As they waited for the data to accumulate, Azar couldn't stop thinking about Jake. What would his captors do? *Torture him?* While the lizards had engineered senescence away, and pumped their bodies full of medical nanotech that could combat the subtlest toxins and parasites, a simple metal blade could still be as painful, or as fatal, as it would have been for their earliest ancestors.

In three days, the insects had cracked the protocol: they knew how the Old Passengers' network represented the atmospheric flashes, and how the data was cross-checked and confirmed. Though the system was moderately robust against errors, if the lizards' anecdotes meant anything it was prone to the occasional false positive, and it certainly hadn't been designed with resistance to tampering as a high priority. Azar was beginning to suspect that the Old Passengers had never actually contemplated an invasion; all of their concerns had revolved around natural hazards.

Would the Circlers understand as much, and know that they were being had? Or would they seize upon the evidence as vindication of their fantasies?

They dived to meet Rahul again, and Shelma told him that the network was now in their hands.

"Make it happen," he said. "Shoot down the invaders."

Azar communed with the scout mites. There was still no news of Jake.

9

The insect glided in a gentle helix a few meters above the ocean, but Azar locked the flight deck scape to the stars, banishing the perceived rotation. She fixed her gaze on the horizon and waited.

Data was being fed into the Old Passengers' network,

painting an elaborate mirage: a cloud of antihydrogen heading straight for Tallulah, three million kilometers away and closing fast. Interstellar gas and dust colliding with the cloud was creating highly energetic gamma rays; in turn, these gamma rays were striking nitrogen molecules in Tallulah's stratosphere and generating particle-antiparticle pairs. None of this exotic radiation would be getting close to the ground, so the whole hallucination was being played out in terms of flashes of light from high in the atmosphere.

Shelma said, "Given their proclivities, you'd think they would have put satellites in orbit: gamma-ray telescopes at least."

"Maybe they did," Azar replied, "but the orbits were destabilized when Tallulah entered the lizards' system. Or maybe they were just corroded away." A quarter of a billion years was a long time; deep rock in the satellites might have provided a constant trickle of power, and nanotech could have carried out repairs, but if they lost material to abrasive dust or cosmic ray ablation, however slowly, nothing could have kept them intact forever.

"There she blows!" Shelma cried out happily; with the full library now accessible to the scape, the translations Azar heard of her speech were much more evocative. In infrared, the distant column of superheated steam glowed like an electric arc, rising out of the ocean and stretching into the sky. The ascending tip grew dim and faded into the distance, but when Azar added an overlay with visible frequencies amplified she could see the end of the icy spear glistening in the starlight as it hurtled into space.

This time there was no planet-shrouding halo needed to flush out the danger; the target was all too clear. The microprobes were tracking the ice missiles, and would feed their interaction with the imaginary antimatter cloud into the models that were generating the hoax atmospheric light show for the network, ensuring that all the data continued to reflect a consistent scenario. Of course, if the Circlers also happened to be looking for atmospheric flashes they would see no such thing, but that shouldn't matter, since they had no way of knowing exactly what the Old Passengers' defenses thought they were firing at.

Azar said, "If someone had told me that I'd be faking a battle for Tallulah between an extinct species and an imaginary invader, I would never have walked through that gate."

"Oh, this is nothing," Shelma scoffed. "One day I'll tell you about the time–"

A message from the microprobes half a world away cut off the boast in mid-sentence. Something was emerging from the middle of a continent on the other side of the planet, and it wasn't a fountain of steam. A narrow beam of gamma rays was rising up from the ground, just millimeters thick but energetic enough to have wrapped itself in a radiant cylinder of plasma as it punched its way out of the atmosphere.

Azar let out an anguished moan. "What have we done now?" Her skin crawled as one alarming possibility crossed her mind: someone could be messing with the microprobes, feeding them a vision of non-existent radiation. But that was just paranoid; who would gain anything from hoaxing the hoaxer? Perhaps the insects had screwed up their analysis of the Old Passengers' protocols and inadvertently injected a second phantom target into the data–one that had elicited a far harsher response.

For several long seconds Shelma was frozen, either in shock or in contemplation. Then she declared, "It's a photonic jet. *We've triggered an unscheduled course correction.*"

"What?"

"The steam jet is exceeding escape velocity, which means it's pushing Tallulah off course, very slightly. So the Builders, the Ground Heaters, are compensating."

Azar wasn't sure yet what she believed, but she hoped the Circlers reached the same conclusion as Shelma; they'd have no reason, then, to question their interpretation of the steam jet as a defensive measure. The photonic jet was just a technical detail, an anti-recoil device for Tallulah's big guns. In any case, the Old Passengers' network seemed to know that such a response was only to be expected; it wasn't treating it as yet another interstellar hazard that needed to be dispelled by its own separate fire hose.

But assuming it wasn't a counter-hoax, this beam of radiation was infinitely more substantial than the non-existent hazard that *was* being pummeled. "There are now real gamma rays blasting through the atmosphere," Azar said. "Hitting nuclei, undergoing pair production. *The photonic jet will be surrounded by antimatter.*"

Shelma said, "I believe you're right."

They instructed the closest insects to fly up near the beam and investigate. The central cylinder of plasma was rich in antiprotons, and though they weren't lasting long before annihilating, the annihilation gamma rays themselves were in turn striking nitrogen nuclei and creating more proton-antiproton pairs, giving rise to a long cascade before the energy was converted into heat, or escaped into space at the top of the beam.

Nanotech in the insects took just minutes to construct the necessary magnetic harvesters, which plucked the slowest antiprotons from the relatively cool margins of the plasma. There were only a few dozen insects in range, and they could only sip from a small part of the beam, but the bounty here dwarfed the travelers' needs. The task that might have taken their Spiral Out accomplices months of furtive, dangerous work would now be complete in less than an hour.

Azar felt an intense surge of relief. The Amalgam was almost within reach now, and no one else would need to put themselves at risk to make the journey possible.

Shelma said, "I think I know where the water went."

"Yeah?"

"When Tallulah came into the Old Passengers' system, the Ground Heaters were nowhere in sight; they were either dead or they'd gone femto. So the Old Passengers had no one to negotiate with, no one to learn from, no one to spell out the rules. They'd simply found this luxurious abandoned lifeboat, and they wanted to take control. But it takes a long time to evacuate a planet physically, building and launching thousands of spacecraft; it's possible that there were still millions of people who wanted to make the crossing even as Tallulah was going out of range of their ships."

"So they built the geothermal cannons," Azar said, "to try to bring it back in range. They were so desperate to let the stragglers come on board that they were willing to pump half the ocean into the sky."

"To no avail. The ghosts of the Ground Heaters–or some insentient navigation system–fought them every step of the way. The femtotech couldn't shut off the cannons; even if it switched off the heating process locally, the rocks would have stayed hot for thousands of years. But the photonic jets it already used for steering could easily compensate for the momentum of the steam." Shelma hesitated, then added, "That could also explain why the Old Passengers ended up allergic to antimatter. An ordinary course change would have taken Tallulah clear of any debris from its own jets, but after a series of long, complicated tussles, there might have been clouds of antimatter lying around that really were worth sweeping aside."

Azar said, "What drives me crazy is that if the deep rock can be grafted, it was all for nothing. The Old Passengers could have brought a sample back to their own world and solved all their problems without anyone leaving."

"That was probably the Ground Heaters' original plan," Shelma said. "To travel the galaxy handing out deep rock, to reheat dying worlds. But to the Old Passengers, *grafting rock* would probably have sounded as ridiculous as trying to reignite a dead star with a spoonful of lukewarm helium. By the time they understood the first thing about the femtotech it would have been too late."

Azar watched the column of luminous steam, still

rushing into the sky. "Now we've thrown away a few more gigatons of water, just to deceive the lizards."

Shelma said, "If you want it to sound slightly less tawdry when you tell your great-great-grandchildren, I recommend the version where we were doing it for the antimatter all along."

"I don't mind lying if it saves people's lives," Azar replied, "but I'd like to return to Hanuz with some prospect that we're not leaving behind a civil war."

"Yeah. We need to find out how far this charade has gone in cleaning up our mess." Shelma inhaled deeply. "Let's dive."

At the rendezvous point, Rahul explained that the Circlers were still debating the significance of the steam jet. The ice halo had been written off as a false alarm until Azar and Shelma had introduced themselves, but this time nobody doubted that such an intense, sustained effort from the Old Passengers' machines had something to do with encroaching aliens.

When Azar told him that they'd now harvested enough antimatter to make a transmission, Rahul confessed that the photonic jet hadn't taken him entirely by surprise. "Some people have always believed that the Old Passengers fought against the Builders to control Tallulah's path. That's been enough to keep the Circlers from trying to do the same thing themselves; they take it as given that they can't steer the world, and their only choice is to fight to defend it."

Shelma said, "Why not trade to defend it? Why not offer any would-be invaders a few kilograms of deep rock grafts?"

"Because grafting is unproven," Rahul replied. "We've done a thousand experiments with different minerals at various temperatures and pressures, and it *looks* as if there's a balance we can exploit between the hoop system's ability to spread and the safety mechanism that stops it running amok . . . but the only real proof will come when we try it on a completely new world. Until then, what is there to trade? A handful of warm pebbles that might turn your planet into a fireball, or might do nothing at all."

As they spoke, a wave of scout mites swam inside the camouflage fish and docked with the insect. They had found Jake; he was being held in an isolated burrow, almost 3,000 kilometers away.

Azar gave Rahul the position. He said, "We have no one close. Do you know how many Circlers are guarding him?"

"Our machines saw 20."

"Then I don't know how to help him," Rahul confessed. "When he broke you out it was easier, everything was still in a state of confusion. Half the people around you had no declared allegiance; Jake and Tilly were not known as Spiral Out before, it was your presence that forced them to take sides. But all twenty people with Jake now will be resolute Circlers, committed to that philosophy for centuries."

Shelma said, "The invasion has been repelled! What would the Circlers have to gain now by harming him?"

"It would set an example for future collaborators."

They swam together to the closest intercept point on the trunk line; the scouts were piggy-backing their own data onto the fiber, using methods too subtle for the lizards to detect. Azar and Shelma watched through the scouts' senses, and passed on the Circlers' chemical conversation to Rahul. Jake was in one chamber, along with four guards; in a nearby chamber the other Circlers had gathered to discuss the latest news and plan their next move.

Shelma spoke to Azar privately. "I've got the nanotech primed to go in and digitize him, if it comes to that. But if we wait for them to kill him it might be too late; if they mutilate the body or use corrosive chemicals we won't have time to capture him properly."

Jake hadn't given them explicit consent to do anything, but Azar swallowed her objections. According to Juhi he had wanted to be part of a delegation to the Amalgam, and if he turned out to be displeased about being snatched into the infosphere without warning, they could always write him back into ordinary flesh once they'd smuggled his software to safety. The real danger here was jumping in too soon or too late. Too soon and they risked re-igniting tensions with an unmistakable alien intervention. Too late and Jake would be dead.

Among the Circlers in the other chamber were two that Azar recognized from their first encounter: Omar and Lisa. Most of the talk here so far had been petty squabbling, but now the subject turned to Jake.

"We should release him," Omar insisted. "The fleet has been destroyed or turned back; it doesn't matter what he does now."

"Spiral Out need to know what happens to traitors," Lisa replied. "He set New Passengers free among us. He put everyone in danger."

Another Circler, Silas, said, "You saw their technology; they could have escaped anyway. Whatever Spiral Out do, we're never going to be sure that we're safe, that we're alone. That's the reality now, and we need to find a way to live with it."

Half a dozen other Circlers responded to this angrily, swimming around the chamber in tight, anxious loops. "We need to kill him," Judah declared. "We need to draw a clear boundary between the right of Spiral Out to make their plans to leave Tallulah, and our right to live here safely and defend our own world."

Omar said, "If we kill him we'll start another war. Do you know how many people died in the last one?"

"Better a million die than we lose the whole world to the New Passengers," Lisa replied.

"Better *nobody dies*," Omar retorted, "and we spend our efforts on something that can help us all. We've been living like fools. We don't deserve to feel safe, and killing our own people won't change that. We don't even know with certainty where the closest world really lies! And we have no idea what kind of life there might be around the bright stars; I doubt that the aliens were telling us the truth, but none of us really know what's possible."

"We've been caught sleeping," Judah conceded. "That much is our fault. But what do you suggest we do about it?"

Omar said, "We need to work together with Spiral Out to explore the nearest worlds, before any more of their inhabitants reach us themselves. If we send out small robots to gather information, the results can serve everyone: defenders of Tallulah, and those who want to leave."

Lisa was scornful. "After this, you're going to trust Spiral Out as our allies?"

"Jake freed two aliens that you were threatening to kill," Omar replied. "They had done us no harm, and we don't even know for sure that they were lying. Because of that, we should slaughter all of Spiral Out? Or treat them all as our enemies? If everything that's happened wakes them from their sleep the way it should wake us, we can benefit from each other's efforts."

Azar looked to Rahul for a reading of the situation, but he was motionless, his posture offering no verdict. Jake's fate could go either way.

After 40 minutes of discussion with no clear consensus, Omar said, "I'm releasing him." He paused for a few seconds, then left the chamber. Lisa squirted wordless, dissatisfied noise, but nobody moved to stop him.

Omar entered the chamber where Jake was being held and spoke with the Circlers who were standing guard.

"I don't agree," said Tarek. "You've come alone to demand this. Who else is with you?"

Omar and Tarek went together to the other Circlers. Omar said, "I repeat, I'm releasing Jake. If anyone here wants a war, I will be an enemy of the warmongers, so you'd better kill me now."

Judah said, "No one's going to kill you." He swam with Omar to Jake's chamber and spoke with the remaining guards. Then all five of them departed, leaving Jake alone.

Jake circled the chamber nervously a few times, then headed out of the burrow. Azar sent a swarm of scouts after him, but they had no data channel back to the fiber, and Jake was soon out of sight.

Almost an hour later, a message came through from the scouts; Jake had reached a nearby colony where the scouts could tap into the fiber again. Azar told Rahul their location.

Rahul said, "He's safe, he's with friends. It's over for now."

Azar sat on the flight deck weeping, hiding her tears even from Shelma.

10

Launched from a rail gun on Tallulah's highest mountain, Mologhat 3 spent six seconds plowing through the atmosphere before attaining the freedom of space. Its heat shield glowed brightly as it ascended, but if the Old Passengers' machines noticed it they found no reason to molest this speck of light as it headed out of harm's way. When it reached an altitude of 1,000 kilometers it fired its own tiny photonic jet, but the radiation was horizontal and highly directional; nothing on Tallulah had a hope of detecting it.

Jake, Tilly, Rahul, Juhi and a fifth delegate, Santo, swam across the flooded observation deck, looking down on their world for the first time. Azar swam among them, but not as a lizard in anyone's eyes. Her words would come to them as familiar chemicals, but they could cope with the sight of her as she really was.

As Azar gazed upon Tallulah, she dared to feel hope. There would be no war, no pogrom, but there was still a daunting task ahead for the millions of Spiral Out who remained. They would need to prepare the Circlers for the truth: for the eventual return of this secret delegation, for trade with the Amalgam, for a galaxy that was not what they'd imagined at all. For a future that didn't follow their script.

Jake said, "Do you think we'll ever meet Shelma again?"

Azar shrugged; he wouldn't recognize the gesture immediately, but he'd soon learn. "She once told me that she could choose for herself between solitude and a connection with her people. If she wants to come back, she'll make those connections as strong as she can."

"No one's ever returned before," Jake said.

"Did Spiral In ever really want to?"

When the moles finally hit pay dirt beneath the ocean floor, their mass spectrometers had detected more than a hundred billion variants of the hoop, and that was only counting the stable forms. The deep rock was more complex than most living systems; no doubt much of that complexity was fixed by the needs of the heating process, but there was still room for countless variations along the way–and room for a new passenger hitching a ride on the hoops as they turned iron and nickel into heat.

If you had to become deep rock in order to understand it, Shelma had decided, she would become it, and then come back. She'd drag the secrets of the hoops out of the underworld and into the starlight.

"What if you can't?" Azar had asked her. "What if you lose your way?"

"There's room in there for a whole universe," Shelma had replied. "If I'm tempted into staying, don't think of me as dead. Just think of me as an explorer who lived a good life to its end."

Jake said, "Tell me more about your world. Tell me about Hanuz."

"There's no need," Azar replied. She gestured at the departure gate. "If you're ready, I'll show it to you."

"Just like that?" Jake twitched anxiously.

"It's fourteen quadrillion kilometers," she said. "You won't be back for 3,000 years. You can change your mind and stay, or you can gather your friends and swim it with me. But I'm leaving now. I need to see my family. I need to go home."